In the Shadow
of the Glacier

In the Shadow
of the Glacier

Vicki Delany

Poisoned Pen Press

Library of Congress Catalog Card Number: 2007924786

ISBN: 978-1-59058-448-4 Hardcover

Poisoned Pen Press
6962 E. First Ave., Ste. 103
Scottsdale, AZ 85251
www.poisonedpenpress.com
info@poisonedpenpress.com

Printed in the United States of America

To the C&F Friday gang:
Mary O'Brien, Helen Brown, and Jan Toms.
Your loving enthusiasm has made me strong.

Acknowledgments

The town of Trafalgar in British Columbia has no existence outside of my imagination, and places, people and events set there are entirely fictional (with the notable exception of BC/DC who drop in from their real lives to perform in Trafalgar). However, if you're looking for a piece of paradise on Earth, you couldn't do much better than to visit Nelson B.C.

I'd like to express my sincere thanks to Brita Wood and Detective Paul Burkart of the Nelson City Police for answering my many, many questions with patience and a sense of fun while giving me valuable insight into the workings of a small Canadian police department, and to Alex Delany, who provided information on paramedic and firefighting procedures. Any errors are entirely mine. Thanks are also due to Alex for the idea; to Gail Cargo, Julia Vryheid, and Karen Wold for reading the manuscript, providing much-appreciated suggestions, and pointing out glaring errors; to Tomas and Jim, Don and Wendy, and Rose, for letting me play with their names; and to Barbara Peters, Robert Rosenwald, and the dedicated staff at Poisoned Pen for believing in me. Thanks also to Cheryl Freedman and Rick Blechta for the incredible job they do for all of us at Crime Writers of Canada, and to CWC for being such a supportive community.

Many times I've been struggling late at night to come up with the right line, and stopped for a few minutes of Warfish to clear my head—thanks to everyone who's played Warfish with me.

Chapter One

People were of two minds about Reginald ("Call me Reg") Montgomery. They either hated him or thought he was the best thing to happen to this town in years. He never spoke when a shout would do, and never shouted when a bellow would do even better. Slighter men had been heard to complain that a slap on the back from Reg could send them head first across the room. And as for the women, most of them had learned to take a step backward, out of hugging range, at Reg's approach. His suits were too loud, his face red and dotted with beads of sweat regardless of the temperature, and his handshake too strong.

But he made a point of shopping at the local stores, rather than the Wal-Mart in Nelson, eating out regularly, usually at family-owned restaurants, and tipping well. Ellie, his wife, had her hair done at Maggie's Salon on Front Street, bought her clothes from Joanie's Ladies Wear and contributed generously, in time as well as money, to the hospital and the seniors center.

Reg and Ellie had only been in town for a few months, but in that time he had managed to make a few friends and a good number of enemies.

And, apparently, one person who hated him enough to kill him.

Constable Molly Smith had eaten curried tofu for supper. In retrospect that was a mistake: spicy bile rose into her throat and she swallowed heavily, trying to keep the food in her stomach, where it belonged.

She had seen plenty of traffic injuries, including fatalities. After the first few times, she'd learned to control her stomach and let her mind throw up a shield behind which she could hide from some of the ugliness that was the human body exposed to violent, unexpected death. But she'd never seen anyone who appeared to have been killed by another human being, and for some reason that made it harder for her protective armor to settle into place.

Reg Montgomery lay in the alley; urine stained his beige slacks and blood and brains stained the pavement. He was lying on his back, facing the long twilight of a gentle summer's evening. Smith turned away and fingered the radio at her shoulder.

"Go ahead, Officer."

She pressed her hand to her chest, and took a single, deep breath. "I'm…" The word came out as a frightened squeal, and she coughed once to clear her throat. "Smith here. I'm in the alley behind Alphonse's Bakery on Front Street. That's just west of Elm. I have a Code 5, suspicious circumstances, and need assistance."

"Someone will be there shortly, Constable Smith."

A small animal rustled in the green garbage bags behind the convenience store beside the bakery. She rested her hand on the butt of the Glock at her side and cast the light from her flashlight around the bags. Her nerve endings tingled. If a rat ran out of the shadows, she'd scream. But the garbage fell still.

The scent of the day's baking lingered around the edges of the alley, blending with the odors of garlic, caramelized onions, and cooking spices from the restaurant on the other side of the bakery. Lights were on in the kitchen, the blinds only partly drawn, and Smith could see the cooks working—a flurry of barely controlled chaos. It was coming up to nine o'clock, on a Thursday night in the middle of tourist season. Feuilles de Menthe, the popular French restaurant, would be in full service frenzy.

The kitchen windows were open and the clatter of crockery, shouted orders, and bursts of laughter poured from the restaurant along with light and the smell of good food cooking. The rest of the alley was quiet.

Smith realized that she was gripping her gun, and forced her fingers to relax. She wiped her palms on the seat of her trousers and told herself she had nothing to fear. If the person responsible for Montgomery's death had been lingering in the alley, he'd have jumped her before she radioed for help.

She looked up. It was a two-story building, bakery on the street, probably an apartment above. The upper windows were closed, curtains drawn. If he'd fallen, if it had been an accident, he wouldn't have closed the window behind him. Suicide? No one wanting to kill himself would try a two-story drop, would he? More likely to end up with a broken leg than dead. At a quick glance Smith could see nothing that might have been used as a weapon, and she knew better than to start poking around before the detectives and scene-of-the crime officers arrived.

It had to be murder. There hadn't been a murder in Trafalgar since she'd joined the police. The average annual murder rate of Trafalgar, British Columbia, was zero.

She stuffed her hands in her pockets to keep them from touching anything, and dropped to her haunches to take a good look at the remains of Reginald Montgomery. She'd seen him around town, glad-handing everyone in sight—you'd have thought he was running for mayor. He'd made a point of being friendly with the entire Trafalgar City Police. She'd heard that he was angling for a place on the police board when an opening next came up. In life, Montgomery hadn't been an attractive man: a belly that made him look nine months pregnant, thin, badly cut grey hair, a bulbous nose that testified to copious quantities of liquor. In death, now that he was no longer trying his hail-fellow-well-met routine, his face had taken on a repose that almost suited him.

Proud of herself for keeping her stomach contents in place, Smith dared not look too closely at the seepage from the man's skull: just close enough to see that the blood was still wet, glistening in the poor light from the back of the restaurant.

She started at the blast of a siren, straightened up, and pulled her hands out of her pockets. Headlights flooded the alley; heavy doors slammed. Paramedics unloaded their stretcher and pushed it toward her. A bulky figure passed in front of the ambulance lights.

"Smith," Chief Constable Paul Keller said, "what have you got here?" His clothes smelled, as always, as if they'd been hanging in a tobacco barn when it caught fire.

"It's Reginald Montgomery, sir. Of Grizzly Resort?" Her voice squeaked as it always did when she was nervous.

"I was having dinner with my wife and daughter when the dispatcher called. Said you told her suspicious circumstances?"

Oh, God. Let it be so. If I've dragged the CC away from his dinner en famille *because Montgomery tripped over his shoelace I'll be finished.*

"Looks that way, sir," she said.

"Definitely dead," one of the paramedics said, "visible grey matter."

The Chief Constable stepped forward to have a closer look.

The investigating detectives wouldn't be short of suspects. There were two camps in Trafalgar—everyone in town over the age of two either belonged to the group that hated Reg Montgomery, or the one that loved him.

Smith pushed aside the thought that her mother could be counted prominently among the haters and tried to look as if she knew what she should be doing now.

Chapter Two

Not long before Constable Molly Smith walked down Elm Street heading for the alley, Rosemary Fitzgerald flipped the sign on the shop window to "closed" with a happy sigh. It had been a good day. A long day, but a good one. She owned a small store on Front Street, between Mid-Kootenay Adventure Vacations and Wolf River Bookstore. The perfect location for her business: making homemade foods suitable to take camping. She also sold a wide selection of packaged and freeze-dried meals and ready-to-eat trail snacks. She and her husband, Ben, had often talked, while sitting around a campfire, or paddling across a lake, about the day when they'd pack their corporate cube-farm jobs in and move to a wilderness town. They'd vacationed in the interior of British Columbia ten years ago, and Ben announced that he'd found his own heaven on earth. But Ben had died, only a year later, struck down by a heart attack working late at the desk he hated. Rosemary continued to dream their dream, and last year she'd retired with a small pension and moved to Trafalgar. She loved her shop, loved being her own boss, and scarcely had time to miss her children back in Toronto.

Rosemary grabbed her backpack, checked that the oven was off, turned down the lights, and let herself into the alley. She locked the back door and turned to get her bike.

The blue bike lock lay on the ground. Rosemary stared at it. Where was her bike? The blue-grey mountain bike had cost more than she wanted to spend, but the town was situated at the bottom of a mountain, so she needed a good, sturdy bike.

She looked around. The stores along the same stretch of Front Street as hers were closed, shadows deep in the darkening alley. A couple of cars drove by on Elm Street; to the west light spilled from the restaurant Feuilles de Menthe. Leaves of Mint. The scent of garlic and roasting meats drifted toward her. Two shapes stood under the light at the back of the restaurant. Rosemary started toward them, intending to ask if they'd seen her bike, perhaps noticed anyone suspicious hanging around. She soon saw that they were arguing; voices were raised and the fat one was punching his fist into his other hand.

She retreated and let herself back into her shop. The comfortable closeness, the scent of the day's cooking, the shine of the countertops, the neatness of the cans and packaged goods stacked on the shelves, even her pride in owning her own business, had diminished in the few minutes Rosemary'd been in the alley.

Her car was at home. She didn't want to waste money on a cab, but it was too far to walk. And tonight, for the first time since she'd driven over the big black bridge across the wide Upper Kootenay River, Rosemary Fitzgerald didn't feel safe in Trafalgar.

"I think," John Winters said to the woman across the table, "that if I had to live my life again, I'd meet you in kindergarten so I wouldn't waste all those years without knowing you."

The woman laughed and tilted her glass to watch the swirl of red wine move across the sides of the bowl. "You do go on, John." She leaned back to allow the waiter to slide a plate in front of her. "Thank you."

Winters scarcely noticed as his own plate was placed on the table. His dinner companion was a highly sought-after model. Men's heads had turned as they entered the restaurant. Men's heads always turned when she walked into a room.

She slipped a plump oyster between her pink lips and chewed with delicate bites of white teeth. They were in the dining room of one of the best resorts in the British Columbia Interior, a place well out of the budget of a Sergeant in the Trafalgar City Police. But Winters was determined to make this a very special evening. Wasn't that why credit cards had been invented? He cast a silent prayer to the god of banking that his card wouldn't have reached its limit. He'd bought the diamond necklace just this morning, so the charge shouldn't have been placed on his card yet. He was planning to present her with the gift over dessert, and it would spoil the mood if a sneering waiter rejected the card.

The words slipped out. "You are so beautiful."

"Oh, John, how you do go on." She looked at him through sea-green eyes over the rim of her glass.

He was the luckiest man in the world. While most of his colleagues sat at home with their dumpy *hausfrau* wives, he was dining in one of the best restaurants in the area with a woman who was regularly photographed for women's magazines. If his credit card could take the load of this dinner, he'd be scoring tonight.

The waiter cleared the appetizer dishes. He was young, blond, buff, handsome, yet he almost melted under the force of the smile from John's date.

Their main courses arrived. She'd chosen the poached wild salmon; he'd wanted the filet mignon but at forty bucks a pop it was too much, so he settled for a T-bone. Potatoes and vegetables cost extra; the cash register in his brain clicked up the numbers. Why couldn't he stop thinking about how much this meal was costing? He looked into the woman's deep décolletage. That took his mind off the price of the meal. "Shall I order another bottle of wine?"

"I'm game if you are," she said. She winked.

Winters' arm shot up to summon the waiter. At the same moment his jacket rang.

"Oh, no," he said.

"John," she said. "Not tonight."

He pulled the phone out of his jacket pocket and pointed to the empty bottle of wine in the cooler as the attentive waiter slid up to their table.

"Winters."

The woman across the table threw sea-green daggers at him.

He put the phone back without daring a glance at her. "If you want dessert," he mumbled, picking at mashed potatoes running with yellow butter, "we should have time. I told them I've been drinking so they're sending someone to pick me up."

"John…"

"Oh, by the way, I bought this." He fumbled in his pocket for the small blue box, and handed it across the table.

She took it in perfectly manicured fingers.

"It's for you," he said.

She gave him a soft smile. A smile full of love, yet tinged with disappointment at the failure of their evening. She opened the box.

His phone rang again. He said no more than two or three words before hanging up. "The car's here already, there was someone nearby." He got to his feet and walked around to her side of the table. "Enjoy your dinner, have dessert, call a cab, you've had as much to drink as I have. Take your time, and know that I love you." He pulled out his credit card. "I'll tell them to cover anything."

She laughed. "I wouldn't trust that card to pay for a pack of gum. Now get going. I haven't finished my meal yet. Call me when you get a chance."

He bent over and kissed her.

Another promising night ruined. "Sorry," he said.

Eliza Winters watched the man she'd been happily married to for twenty-five years walk out of the restaurant. How much longer, she wondered, would he be able to keep at his line of work? Retirement was getting closer, even as he tried to ignore the passing of time. They'd moved to Trafalgar because he was burning out, fast, in Vancouver. Crushed by the despair of life in the Downtown Eastside. Consumed by guilt at what he saw as failure. Drinking far, far too much. The move had been good for him; the old John was coming back to her. She hoped tonight's call wouldn't amount to anything too serious.

Eliza twisted the necklace around her fingers, letting it catch fire from the candlelight on the table. She signaled to the waiter to bring the bill and dug into her bag for her credit card.

Christa Thompson let all of her frustrations out on the phone table.

"Damn, blast, and hellfire," she yelled. "Leave me alone." The table jumped.

He'd called her again. As always, sweet and kind and considerate. Is there anything I can get you, Chrissie? I'm heading to Nelson. I'll stop at Wal-Mart if you want. Can I pick up anything? Let me help you, let me care for you, let me watch over you, let me, let me….

Why wouldn't he leave her alone?

She buried the phone under a pile of sheets in the linen closet. She knew the routine. He'd call every fifteen minutes, "just checking that you're okay." After an hour or two, he'd suggest coming over with a pizza, or picking up a DVD. She'd tried to be nice, to be friendly. To explain that she'd eaten dinner, thank you. That she was tired and ready for bed. Always being polite, always saying thank you.

But tonight she'd told him straight out not to bother her again, and buried the phone where she wouldn't have to listen to it ring. Would he get the message at last?

She carried a cup of tea into the living room-dining room-study of her apartment and sat down at the computer table. Her essay on the Romantic Poets (20% of the final mark!) was due next week and she'd barely started it. She looked out the window. The lights of town twinkled in the valley and crawled up the lower slopes, getting thinner and thinner until the mountains were nothing but dark shapes against the deep purple sky. Koola glacier was wrapped in darkness.

She sipped at the tea and reviewed her notes. She'd always loved Wordsworth the best. Could his name, perfect for a poet, have contributed to his art? That might be an idea to pursue if she decided to go for her master's in English Lit. She was reading *An Evening's Walk, Addressed to a Young Lady,* settling into the mood and the love of the words, when the loud knocking at the front door yanked her back to her cramped apartment. She occupied the top floor of a house so decrepit it was a wonder that one board still supported another, and her downstairs neighbors could be nasty if she made the slightest noise.

Abandoning Wordsworth, Christa ran down the narrow staircase. She threw open the door.

Charlie stood there. He was well over six feet tall, thickly muscled from hours spent at the gym, with a head as round and bald as a bowling ball. His running shoes filled the mat at her door.

"Gosh, Chrissie, your phone isn't working. It rings and rings but you don't pick up. Suppose you had to call 911 or something. I came over right away."

"Please, please. Leave me alone, Charlie. Just. Go. Away." She slammed the door shut. She leaned her back against it and wept as his fists pounded on the thin wood. "Chrissie. Let me help. I can fix your phone."

"You don't shut your friend the hell up, I'm reporting this to Mr. Czarnecki," the downstairs neighbor screamed through the wall that separated their living room from Chrissie's staircase. "He'll have you out of here on your skinny ass if I have anything to say about it. My kids are tryin' to get to fuckin' sleep." A dull thud as a shoe hit the wall.

"Chrissie? I can't get the door open. You've locked me out by mistake."

She ran up the stairs, blinded by tears.

Everyone called her Lucky, but at this moment Lucy Smith didn't feel lucky in the slightest. She was nothing but disgusted. Disgusted at the pile of petitions on her kitchen table. Disgusted at her husband who appeared to have gone over to the dark side—such a cliché that, but highly appropriate. Disgusted at the people filling her house who were great at rhetoric, but not so good at getting down to solid, productive work.

"This cranberry loaf's delicious, Jane. Can I have the recipe?" Norma McGrath was digging out a pen.

"It's so easy, you won't believe it," Jane Reynolds replied. "Two cups of flour…."

"Please, can we get back to business," Lucky said.

"We have to forget about the Grizzly development and concentrate on the garden," Nick Boswell mumbled around a mouthful of cranberry loaf.

"That Rob Montgomery has to be stopped," Norma said. "His resort will kill the bears."

"Reg. Reginald Montgomery." Lucky restrained a heavy sigh. "But it is a free country, at least for now, and we can't put out a contract on him, can we? So let's concentrate on where we can be most effective. And that's the Commemorative Peace Garden. Once we're sure its future is secure we can turn our attention to the resort development." Sylvester, the big, goofy, good-natured golden retriever lying at her feet, yawned. Sylvester was used to groups of people gathering, and arguing, in the Smith kitchen.

"I agree with Lucky," Michael Rockwell said. "If we fly all over the map we don't make an impression on anything. And so we achieve nothing." He smiled at her and Lucky felt something move in her chest.

"The garden has to come to pass." Barry Stevens choked on the words. Lucky turned away from Michael's friendly smile and looked at Barry. Lines of pain, always there in one degree or another, dragged at his face. His left hand was white against the arm of his chair. His right sleeve hung empty at his side. His eyes, pale, pale blue, filled with water. "It has to. Where's Andy, anyway? I'd expect that Andy, of all people, would be part of this."

"Problems at the store," Lucky said, studying the pattern of the wood in her kitchen table. "He sends his apologies."

"Apology noted," Barry said. "We can start with a letter insisting that the town council stick to its original decision and proceed with the construction of the Commemorative Peace

Garden. To use the estate's bequest to fund the garden, and that the garden be specifically dedicated to Vietnam War resisters."

"Now that the fate of the garden's in doubt, trouble's brewing," Jane said. "Fox News ran a piece on it. I've been told it was nasty."

"Fox News!" Barry's mouth twisted to one side and for a moment Lucky thought he was going to spit on her ceramic floor. "Let the chickenhawks come."

Chapter Three

"I'm sorry, sir, but you can't go that way," Molly Smith said to the staggering drunk.

"Whada ya mean," he mumbled. "I'll go where I wanna go, pig bitch."

She rested her hand loosely on her nightstick. This fellow could barely stand up, much less attack her.

"Police investigation. Please go around, sir."

"What if I say I don wanna go round?"

"Then I'll have to arrest you."

"You and whose army?"

This was ridiculous. She'd been told to stand beside the yellow police tape that had been strung across the entrance to the alley, and stop anyone who might be inclined to ignore it. Detective Lopez had arrived a few minutes ago and was making an initial inspection of the area while waiting for Sergeant Winters and the RCMP forensic crew to arrive. The Chief Constable had rejoined his family at dinner, after posting Smith at one end of the alley, and the second duty constable, Solway, at the other. Smith was hoping to be able to watch what Lopez was doing, but she was stuck arguing with a drunk. Who'd probably pass her on the street when she was out of uniform and give her a nice smile, forgetting that she was a "pig bitch." Trafalgar boasted a population of less than 10,000 people. Smith had lived here all her life, except for a few years at the University of Victoria. It was hard, sometimes, to be a cop in a town where a substantial number of the residents had seen you performing as Number Two Wise Man in the Grade Three Christmas pageant.

"Please, sir," she said, "go away."

He peered at her through unfocused eyes. He was young, not much older than she, thin to the point of emaciation, with a scraggly beard and hair that hadn't seen scissors or shampoo in a long time. Something green was trapped in the depths of his beard. He grinned, showing yellow teeth and exhaling breath so rancid that Smith blinked. "How 'bout we go to my place and have ourselves a party? I'll get a six-pack."

She almost laughed. "I don't think so, sir. You should go home."

A light flashed.

"Meredith Morgenstern, *Trafalgar Daily Gazette*. What seems to be happening here, Constable?"

The drunk slipped away. His hair caught the light from a street lamp and he disappeared.

"Police investigation, Ms. Morgenstern," Smith said.

"I can see that, Molly."

The newspaper photographer took another picture.

"Come on, you can tell me what's going on. For old times' sake, eh?" Meredith tossed a smile so fake it would have elicited boos at a children's play. She couldn't act, but she was beautiful. She was tall, thin and full-breasted at the same time. Her hair tumbled down her back in a river the color of midnight. Her black eyes sparkled in the light from the street lamps. Meredith had been in Smith's class all through school, when her breasts were the size of raisins. Her current lush figure had to be the handiwork of a good doctor. For old times' sake, Smith would cheerfully stuff Meredith's head into the garbage bags behind the convenience store.

"Sorry, Ms. Morgenstern, I can't tell you anything."

"I guess not. Being just a lowly constable. I'll ask that man over there. Come on, Ed."

"This alley is restricted, ma'am," Smith said. She tried to keep her voice level, as she bristled at the sneer in the way Meredith said "lowly constable." What did Meredith think she had to brag about: a second string reporter on the *Trafalgar Daily Gazette,* where the biggest story of the past month was an out-of-control truck careening down the side of the mountain.

"What are you going to do if I go there anyway? Arrest me?"

"Yes."

For the briefest moment Meredith's composure cracked, and Smith relished the thought of snapping handcuffs on her old enemy's thin wrists.

Detective Lopez strolled up. Lopez always strolled; so calm and relaxed, at first Smith hadn't realized that a tough police officer lay under the casual Latin demeanor. She'd seen his hard side when several participants at a weekend-long outdoor rock concert attacked a local girl.

"We've nothing to tell the press at this time. I suggest you go home and wait for an official release."

"But…" Meredith said.

"If not home, then stand on the other side of the street."

Meredith and her photographer complied. Lopez shrugged one shoulder at Smith.

A white SUV pulled up. A blue stripe ran down the side; the city crest and the words *Trafalgar City Police* were painted on the door. Constable Dave Evans drove. Sergeant Winters got out, and Evans remained in the vehicle.

Winters was dressed in a nice business suit, a cut up from the casual clothes he preferred. He nodded to Smith, as if she were the doorman at a fancy hotel, and joined Lopez. They walked toward the black shape that had once been Reginald Montgomery, talking in low voices.

A laughing group of young people came down the Elm Street hill, heading toward Front Street. The women wore long colorful skirts and loose blouses, and the men's hair was either shaved off or gathered into a mass of dreadlocks. They eyed Smith and the police vehicle, and crossed to the other side of the street. One of the boys dropped his cigarette to the ground, and crushed it under his heel. He scooped the butt up and stuffed it in his pocket. The scent of marijuana lingered in his wake. Smith did nothing: this was Trafalgar, where the police pretended not to notice minor drug infractions.

Lopez walked up to her. "Sergeant wants to talk to you, Smith. I'll have Evans take your post."

Winters stood over the body. Just observing. He looked up as Smith approached. The last rays of the summer sun were gone; there were no streetlights in the alley and the light from the restaurant kitchen was poor. His face was full of shadows, his eyes unreadable pools. His black and white hair was cut very short; thin on top but not all gone. He had a well trimmed silver mustache—on him it looked good, rather than outdated. He was tall and lean, with the slightest hint of a middle-aged pot.

"Sir," Smith said, more nervous than she'd been in the presence of the Chief Constable. She'd been working for the Trafalgar City Police for six months. She hadn't said a word to the Detective Sergeant since she'd been introduced to everyone her first day on the job.

Sergeant Winters and Detective Lopez were the entirety of the General Investigation Section. Lopez was one-of-the-boys-and-girls, friends with everyone, loved practical jokes and town gossip. Smith had been to his house for a barbeque earlier in the summer. But Winters kept himself apart. He didn't social-ize, didn't engage in idle office chatter. He'd been a homicide detective in Vancouver, played a prominent role in the hunt for the serial killer who'd been snatching runaway boys from the city's notorious Downtown Eastside for years. Marcus Sanders, a church youth-group leader, had been charged with the crimes, and forensics spent months digging up every inch of his property. Winters quit the Vancouver force shortly after Sanders' arrest and moved to Trafalgar. No one knew why, but speculation ran rampant. Burned-out, some said; disgusted at the long-time official indifference to the fate of the boys, others whispered. Something else, a few said, unrelated to Sanders. Perhaps to do with the Blakeley murder: nasty business that, they all agreed.

Winters never socialized with members of the department. The office administrator, Barb Kowalski, ever cheerful and inquisitive, had made it her mission to find out what she could about his private life. Wife used to be a supermodel, she reported, now does magazine ads for laundry detergent and floor polish. No kids. Fantastic home outside of town, deep in the woods on the side of the mountain.

Winters looked at Smith. "Detective Lopez's daughter is getting married on Saturday," he said.

"Yes, sir." Everyone knew that. Lopez had talked about nothing else all month, and Barb had organized a collection to buy a gift for the happy couple.

"The wedding's in Toronto. He's leaving tonight. Last plane out of Castlegar."

"Yes, sir."

"Bad timing, but it can't be helped. I'll have to conduct this investigation on my own."

"Yes, sir." Smith had no idea why he was telling her this.

Silence stretched through the alley. Restaurant staff threw the odd curious glance out the window—Smith had gone around to tell them, and the solitary worker at the convenience store, not to come out back until further notice—but otherwise the restaurant carried on business as normal.

Winters turned to her. He was quite good looking, for an older guy. "So you'll have to help me."

"Me?" Smith tried to swallow the squeak of excitement that escaped from her mouth.

"Chief tells me you're local."

"Born and bred. My parents live just outside of town. About ten klicks, kilometers, away. Sir."

"There may be some…shall we say sensitive…political aspects to this situation."

"Yes, sir."

"And as I need a partner, with Lopez on leave, and having only been in town for a short while, the Chief thinks you'll be the best one to take me around."

"Yes, sir." Smith was thrilled to bits. The first murder in town all year and she would be assisting the investigating officer.

Her voice had regained some of its strength, so she dared to say something more. "Murder's a nasty business, sir."

"No one's said anything about murder, Constable. Don't rush to conclusions. Accidents happen. And this isn't the army. Stop calling me sir."

John Winters was not pleased at being given this fresh-faced young constable to assist him. Too eager by half, almost panting at the excitement of being involved in a probable-murder investigation, she reminded him of a sled dog at the beginning of the Iditarod. But as the Trafalgar City Police consisted of a grand total of twenty sworn officers, he didn't have much choice. And as the Chief Constable had said, over the phone as Winters had left Eliza and their anniversary dinner behind, Smith was about as local as they came. And local politics, the CC said, might have a major role to play in this investigation.

"Tell me, Molly. What do you make of this?"

She took a deep breath, her chest puffing under the Kevlar vest, trying to make herself look important, wise and knowledgeable. He remembered himself as young recruit to the Vancouver P.D. a long, long time ago. He resisted giving the constable a sympathetic smile. This was a hard job, getting harder all the time. No room for sympathy: if you couldn't cut it, get the hell out of the way.

"I know who he is, sir. Uh, Mr. Winters."

"John will do, Molly."

"Right, sir. I mean John. Reginald Montgomery, owner of the Grizzly Resort. The proposed resort. It hasn't been started yet. He hasn't been in town long—couple of months maybe. Trying to get his development underway. Lots of people don't care for him, or his plans."

Her hair was a pale blond, tied into a neat French braid that fell to the middle of her back. The color was probably natural, as her brows and lashes were the same shade. Her eyes were large, the color of the Kootenay River on a sunny day. She was only a few inches shorter than Winters, and her body looked fit and trim beneath the bulk of her uniform. She was pretty, too pretty to make an effective officer. Her voice was soft—it would have a problem carrying authority—and had the unfortunately tendency to crack under stress.

Tomorrow he'd ask for a more suitable officer, local or not, to help on this investigation.

"What do you make, Molly, of Mr. Montgomery's present situation?" Winters did his best work with a sounding board. The board's opinion didn't matter, but he needed to hear his questions spoken out loud—only when they bounced back at him could he start to formulate answers.

"He didn't kill himself. If he'd jumped out of that window above, he wouldn't have closed the window behind him, would he? And the drop's too short to be sure of a successful conclusion."

"Go on."

"He wouldn't have inflicted that degree of damage to his head had he slipped on a banana peel or something. Well, at least I don't think so."

She was doing okay until she threw in that disclaimer. Never apologize for your conclusions.

"Therefore…?"

"Therefore, someone murdered him. There's enough blood to indicate that he died on the spot. Someone bashed his head in right here."

"He couldn't have fallen from the roof?"

"The roof?"

Winters looked up. The night was clear, no clouds. Stars filled the black sky, looking like the diamonds in the necklace he'd bought for Eliza. The one he'd scarcely had time to slip around her neck before heading back to work. Maybe it was time to toss the job in. For her sake if not his.

"Oh," Smith said. "The roof."

◇◇◇

How could she have been so stupid? The roof was high enough that a fall from it could result in considerable damage to someone's head. She'd been so proud of herself for determining that Montgomery hadn't jumped from the second story, she hadn't even considered the roof. She wasn't cut out for this job. She should chuck it; go back and finish her degree in social work. Her advisor had told her she could return any time. *When you've recovered from this temporary insanity*, he'd really been saying.

"Do you know how we can get up there?" Winters said.

"No."

"Then perhaps," he snapped, "you should find out, Constable Smith."

Smith's mother believed in spirit guides, what some other people might call angels. Smith did not. Until this moment.

Constable Evans walked toward them, a man beside him, wringing his hands.

"Terrible business. Terrible," the man said. He was almost as round as he was tall, and completely bald. His accent was strong, from France, not Quebec. He looked nothing like an angel.

"Mr. Levalle," Smith said. "We need you to take us up to your roof."

Chapter Four

"I could have used you here, Andy," Lucky Smith said. It was close to midnight and he'd only just come in. She took a deep breath, sniffing the air, trying not to appear to be doing so. There was no obvious smell of alcohol, or a woman, on her husband.

"Problems at the store," he said.

What problems could a wilderness adventure store have after closing? Lucky didn't bother to ask. She stuffed the plug of the kettle into the socket. "Tom Maas' death has thrown everything into a fritz. We might have to reconvene the full committee and start the whole business all over again. I don't trust the city council to do the right thing without Tom's guidance."

"Guidance? You mean bullying. Strong arm tactics. Threats."

Lucky rooted through the tea jar. "I mean guidance, Andy. There was a reason Tom was mayor of this town for so long, you know. People liked him, they accepted his leadership. Chai or Earl Grey?"

"Strange as it may seem, Lucky, I don't want tea, okay. I'm going to bed."

She pulled out a satchel of fair trade organic white chai. "The forces opposed to the park are gathering now that Tom's gone."

"Will you listen to yourself, Lucky? The forces of Mordor are not gathering. It might just be that this little garden isn't going to be the salvation of the world."

"Don't mock me, Andy."

"Then stop leaving yourself open to be mocked."

She felt tears gather behind her eyes, and refused to give into them. Once, he would have felt the same way she did.

"This park might not be such a good idea. Come to your senses, Lucky. Tourists are our livelihood. How many locals come into the shop or sign up for an expedition? None, unless they have friends visiting. Maybe thirty, forty percent at the most, of our business is Europeans and Canadians. The rest are Americans. Americans stop coming because they think they've been insulted by a draft dodger monument, we're finished."

Her fingers worked at the tea bag. "You'd forget about what the garden represents to keep Fox News and a handful of hunting goons happy? Okay, suppose all we care about is the business. Most of the people who come to us are looking for blue waters, green hills, wildlife. They're looking for a place of peace. It doesn't matter if they're from the States or Ontario or Lower Slobovia."

"Nice speech, Lucky. Save it for the Chamber of Commerce. I'm telling you that the Commemorative Peace Garden will be the death of this town and thus of our company. All this area has going for it is tourism. Americans won't come if that garden goes in."

"That garden honors you, Andy, and all the men like you. How could you forget?" The bag of tea crumbled to shreds between her fingers. Black leaves sprinkled on the kitchen floor. Sylvester sniffed at them.

"Times have changed. Let the past be past. I don't want to argue any more. I'm going to bed."

"Andy," she said.

The kitchen door slammed shut behind him.

Lucky Smith stared at the tea leaves on the floor. They'd fallen in a black arrow pointing toward the stove. To the heart of her home.

The kettle switched itself off. She released her tears and reached for the phone.

◇◇◇

Tubs of flour, giant bowls, and baking sheets were lined up in Alphonse's Bakery like soldiers on parade, waiting for orders to head into battle. Floor to ceiling racks, empty, filled the back of the room. Everything was as neat and clean and well-organized as one would hope to find in a laboratory handling smallpox virus.

A narrow staircase led from the back of the bakery. Alphonse Levalle led the way.

"What's behind this door?" Winters asked as they reached the second floor.

"Apartment for let. Empty."

"How long has it been empty?"

"One week."

"Do you have the key?"

"Of course, *Monsieur*."

"We'll want to have a look. After we've seen the roof."

Levalle unlocked the door.

"Flashlight, Molly," Winters said.

She flicked it on. The roof was empty, unused. A large, industrial strength spider's web stretched across the doorway at eye level, caught in the light from Smith's beam. A fat fly hung upside down, suspended in the gossamer trap.

"Wait here, Mr. Levalle." Winters ducked to avoid the web. Smith did the same.

The night was clear. Above the bulk of the dark mountains looming over town from all sides, stars filled the sky. White and red lights flashed as an airplane flew toward Vancouver and the Pacific Ocean.

He reached the ledge overlooking the back alley and looked down. Smith stood beside him. Montgomery lay on his back, staring up at them. Evans was standing beside the body. He followed the dead eyes and gave the officers on the roof a salute.

"Shine that light here, across the ledge," Winters ordered. "Do you see any disturbance?"

"Nothing."

"It doesn't look like anyone's been up here in years. Anyone other than birds, that is." Winters rubbed his hand along the surface of the ledge. He held his finger up so Smith could see. It was filthy.

He pulled a handkerchief out of his pocket and wiped his hand. "I'll send the forensics people up here to check, just to be sure. Speak of the devil, here they are now."

The RCMP scene-of-the-crime van was edging its way down the alley. Evans waved them to a halt a few feet short of the mass that had once been Reg Montgomery.

"I want to talk to them first, then I'll have a look at that apartment."

"They shouldn't have to bother coming up here." Smith's voice cracked. She coughed and tried again. "That spiderweb. It proves that no one was up here tonight. At least no one taller than about five feet five. And Montgomery is...was...taller than that."

"Why do you say that?"

"They would have broken the web, wouldn't they?"

"Perhaps our criminal knows the legend of Robert Bruce. Perhaps he, or she, carried Montgomery and isn't taller than five foot five. Lots of people, men as well as women, aren't. You reach your conclusions much too quickly, Constable Smith. Please don't try to be so clever from now on. I'll ask your opinion when I want it. Which won't be often."

Smith's face burned and she was thankful for the darkness. Sanctimonious prick. She'd bet a year's salary that Montgomery and his assailant hadn't been on this roof. And who the hell was Robert Bruce? Some famous detective who'd solved a crime by studying the mating habits of a spider? She'd look him up. In case there was a test tomorrow.

She stood in the doorway to the bakery as Winters greeted the RCMP officers, who were setting up strong lights. Something small and brown, with a long tail, ran out from the garbage bags behind the convenience store and crossed the lane, heading for the safety of darkness on the other side of the fence. Levalle busied himself in the back of his shop, almost falling over trying to see what was going on outside.

The coroner, Shirley Lee, had arrived while Winters and Smith were on the roof. She pulled on thin blue gloves and crouched beside the body. Winters squatted beside her.

"See anything other than the obvious, doc?"

"Define obvious, Sergeant," she said, not looking up. She was tiny, not much over five feet, and thin. Every strand of her black hair was gathered into a stiff bun at the back of her delicate neck. Smith had met her once before, at a traffic fatality, and she'd felt like a lead-footed Sasquatch in the presence of the diminutive, feminine doctor.

"Dead from a blow to the back of the head," Winters said.

"At a guess, I'd agree," Dr. Lee said. "Send him to Trail, and I'll confirm tomorrow. I see no obvious signs of trauma other than the head injury."

"Could he have fallen?"

"There should be injury other than just to the head in that case. I have to see him with his clothes off to be sure. I suppose he could have fallen directly onto his head. Unlikely, though."

She lifted the right hand and leaned over to have a good look.

"Something interesting, Doc?"

"What do you see here, Sergeant?" She ordered a technician to turn a light on their hands, and pointed to Montgomery's fist, clenched tight. Her hand, holding his, looked like that of a child clinging to her grandfather.

From where she stood, Smith couldn't see anything significant.

"Hair," Winters said.

"A few strands. Be sure you bag them."

Lee stood up in one liquid motion, as graceful as a ballet dancer, and pulled her gloves off, one slim finger at a time. "I'll see you tomorrow, Sergeant. Call me in the morning and we'll arrange a time."

"Sure."

"Don't know why they pay her the big bucks," Winters said, more to himself than to Smith, as the doctor walked away. "I've never heard her say anything I hadn't already concluded for myself."

The coroner's van backed down the alley.

He pulled a pair of latex gloves out of his pocket, and pulled them over his fingers. He knelt beside the body and patted Montgomery's pockets. "That's interesting. Nothing here."

"Wallet?" Smith asked.

Winters used the end of his pen to lift the side of Montgomery's suit jacket away. "Nope. No cell phone either. He could have been out for an evening stroll. Left the house without phone or wallet, but at a guess I'd say not. Not dressed in a nice suit like this." He felt both the dead man's wrists. "And no watch." He got to his feet with a stifled groan and pulled off the gloves. A technician held out an evidence bag and he dropped them in.

"You think this might have been a theft?"

"Or made to look like one."

They watched in silence as Montgomery was loaded onto a stretcher and taken away.

"Where's that fellow who owns the apartment?" Winters said.

"Inside."

"Then let's go up and have a look."

The apartment above the bakery was neat and tidy. A thin layer of dust lay over everything, including the floor. The bedroom looked over the alley. Winters stood at the window staring out. Smith glanced around the room. The windows were closed and the day's heat still lingered. It was a spacious apartment, with simple but adequate furniture. The double bed was stripped down to the mattress. It would be nice to wake up to the scent of baking bread and croissants. It was past time for her to get out of her parents' house. The living arrangements were getting tense. When she'd told her family that she'd been accepted by the Trafalgar City Police, her mother couldn't have been more dismayed if Molly'd announced that she was going to take the veil. Or become a lawyer for an oil company, which was what her brother had done.

"Right?" Winters said.

Smith grabbed her head back from thinking about the apartment and her family. "Right," she said, hoping that he hadn't just asked her if she'd killed Montgomery.

He grabbed the window latches and pulled upwards. The window opened with a deep grumble. They could hear Evans talking, someone laugh in response, and the back doors of the coroner's van slam closed. "When were you here last, Mr. Levalle?" Winters said.

The baker was wringing a dishcloth in his hands. "The day the tenants left. Eight days ago. I checked for damage or property missing. My wife cleaned the apartment and then we locked the door. He…he wasn't killed here, was he?"

"Probably not."

Levalle wiped his forehead with the dishcloth. "Good. That would make it hard to rent the apartment. To decent people. Lots of weirdos in Trafalgar." It was an old-fashioned word, but Levalle was right: there were plenty of weirdos in Trafalgar. The small town, nestled deep in the mountains in the interior of British Columbia, was a magnet for drifters. Along with more than its share of artists, the comfortably retired, and Internet workers.

"I said probably," Winters said. "Nothing is definite."

Levalle paled.

"The technicians will be wanting up here. Give me the key and you can go home. They'll call you when they're finished."

Levalle forgot about renting his apartment, and excitement filled his doughy face. "CSI, right. Looking for fingerprints and DNA. They'll be wanting mine, for elimination, yes?"

Winters led the way down the stairs. "That damned TV show again," he muttered.

In the alley a woman was scraping something off the pavement, where Montgomery's head had recently been. Smith's eyes slid away. A flash of sharp white light as a photographer moved in to shoot the scene.

"Is someone going to notify the family?" she asked.

Winters turned to Smith with a smile that didn't quite reach his eyes. "Funny you should mention that, Molly. It's our next stop." He tossed a wave toward the restaurant windows, where staff had their noses pressed up against the glass. Most of them ducked.

He headed toward the street; she hurried to keep up.

"I'll take the car, Dave."

"I can drive you, Sarge," Constable Evans said.

"No need. Keep this alley secure until further notice. The keys." Evans handed them to Winters. He glared at Smith.

"Your chariot awaits, madam." The sergeant bowed toward the marked SUV. "You can drive. Call dispatch and get us Montgomery's address." He tossed her the keys. "I've found that it's always nice to have a female officer on hand when giving news of a loved one's death, don't you agree, Molly?" Winters fastened his seat belt as she started the vehicle.

She picked up the radio and called dispatch. Montgomery's home was within the Trafalgar town limits, they told her. In a prestigious new development high above town. Smith pulled into the slight evening traffic.

"If you think I'm full of shit, you may say so."

"You're full of shit, sir." Smith's teeth ground together. She narrowly missed a cyclist, without lights, crossing an intersection. He was steering so erratically that if he'd been in a car she would have pulled him over for a breath test. "We're not calling upon the widow Montgomery in order to make a nice cup of tea and serve chocolate biscuits while we cluck in pretentious sympathy."

"Too true." He leaned his head against the seat rest. "I really, really hate doing this."

At last he'd given up. Probably because of the downstairs neighbor's threats to "rip your cock off and wrap it around your little finger, which is about as far as it'll stretch."

Christa wiggled the small of her back into the indent of the chair. The screen saver on her computer showed images of Hawaii—lush jungle, tumbling waterfalls, pristine beaches, luxury hotels. Did she have the money for a flight to Hawaii? Those hotels looked expensive. She could empty her savings account, but then she wouldn't be able to afford school in September.

It was all so complicated; she wanted to do nothing but cry.

Christa moved the mouse. Hawaii disappeared, and her essay was in front of her. She read the last paragraph she'd written, trying to get back onto the flow of words and ideas.

But it was gone. William Wordsworth was no longer speaking to Christa Thompson.

She went into the linen closet and dug the cordless phone out. She pressed talk and hesitantly held it up to her ear. All she heard was silence. Christa punched in numbers.

"This is Molly Smith. I'm not available, please leave a message at the beep."

"Call me, Mol. Any time. I'm up."

Christa hung up. She remembered the days when Molly's voice mail had said something like, "I'm either drugging up a storm, having wild sex, leaping into the mosh pit, or studying for my finals. Leave a message and I'll decide if I want to get back to you or not."

But then Graham died and all the fun left Molly.

◇◇◇

It was close to eleven by the time the police arrived at the Montgomery home.

Smith pulled into the driveway, and Winters looked out the window for a moment just to enjoy the view. High on the mountainside, they overlooked the town, the black river, the sprinkling of lights on the far side, diminishing as they climbed up the hill. Where they faded away, leaving nothing but the dark mass of the mountain against the night sky.

He climbed out of the vehicle, and Smith followed. Shrubbery swayed in the night breeze. A man shouted in the hills, and a dog barked. The light over the front door was on. Waiting for someone who would not be coming home.

Smith pushed the door bell. Winters listened, but heard nothing. Smith held her finger to the bell again, longer this time.

Inside the house a dog barked.

"Shush."

A woman peered through the window in the door. Her hair was very black, the dye emphasizing her age, rather than concealing it.

"Trafalgar City Police," Smith said. "Sorry to bother you, ma'am, but we need to talk to you." Her voice was calm, deep, and full of authority. So she could be comfortable, Winters thought, within her area of responsibility.

The lock turned. The door opened a crack. The dog ran out. It was a minuscule thing—looked like a Doberman that had been shrunk in the wash. It barked hysterically and showed its teeth. Couldn't weigh more than five pounds. Winters considered giving it a good kick in the ribs to get it out of the way. But that approach probably wouldn't go down too well with the lady they were here to console on the death of her husband.

"Henry, you shush." The woman scooped the dog into her arms. The beast glared at Winters and Winters glared back. Must be tough to defend your property when you couldn't get out of the grip of a middle-aged lady who looked like she'd fall over in a strong wind.

"Mrs. Montgomery?" Smith said.

"Yes?"

"I'm Constable Smith and this is Sergeant Winters of the Trafalgar City Police. May we come in?"

She looked from one face to another. "My husband isn't home, Officer, although I was expecting him some time ago. Can he call you in the morning?"

"Mrs. Montgomery, ma'am," Smith said. "We'd like to talk to you, not your husband. May we come in?"

The woman stood back. Her face a mask of stoic incomprehension. Winters didn't condescend to smile at her.

The police walked into the house.

The front hall was vast, but mostly empty. A thin-legged piecrust table was the only piece of furniture on the squares of black and white tile. As they passed into the living room, the tiles gave way to thick planks of a rich dark pine. The couch and chairs were white leather, a bad match for the rustic floor. The curtains were pulled back, and the lights of the town winked below. The kitchen was open plan; a long granite counter separated it from the living and dining areas. Everything was as neat, as Winters' mother always said, as a pin.

Mrs. Montgomery was dressed in a pink summer suit, skirt to the knees, matching short-sleeved jacket nipped in at the waist, stockings, expensive-looking pumps. She was very thin, with the look of an expensively maintained body.

"You should have had a better look at my ID before letting me in your home, Mrs. Montgomery," Winters said.

"Perhaps." She gave a nervous laugh. "But this lovely town isn't anything like Vancouver or Los Angeles, is it? Can I offer you a drink? I can make coffee, or tea. We have beer, if you'd like, or something stronger. Juice?"

"Nothing, thank you, Mrs. Montgomery." Not anything like Vancouver, indeed. Her husband hadn't been murdered in Vancouver. "Perhaps you should sit down, ma'am."

She sat. The dog snarled at Winters. He was tempted to snarl back. Instead he said, "Constable, will you get me a glass of water, please."

Smith blinked. "Water?"

It's not for me, you fool, he wanted to shout. "Yes, please. Water." Smith bustled off, her braid flapping behind her. She'd taken off her hat as they came through the door, and tucked it under her arm. He turned to their hostess and settled his face into lines of sympathy. "I'm sorry to have to tell you this, Mrs. Montgomery, but your husband, Mr. Reginald Montgomery, died earlier this evening." Cupboards opened and shut as Smith searched for a glass. He rubbed the face of his watch with his thumb.

Mrs. Montgomery scratched behind her dog's right ear. "That's too bad." Henry wiggled in ecstasy.

Smith returned, carrying a glass full of water. There was no ice. She handed it to him.

"Perhaps Mrs. Montgomery…"

Comprehension crossed the constable's pretty face. "Oh. Right. Mrs. Montgomery would you like a drink of water?"

"Thank you, dear." She accepted the glass and held it out to Henry. The dog drank.

"Do you understand what I told you, ma'am?" Winters said. "Mr. Montgomery was found dead a short while ago."

"I understand, Mr. Winters. Poor Reggie. His heart, I suppose. No matter how I nagged, he simply wouldn't give up fried foods."

"Is there someone we could call to be with you?"

Smith's cell phone rang. She fumbled at the buttons to send it directly to voice mail. Winters glared at her.

"We haven't lived here long," Mrs. Montgomery said. "I don't have close friends or family in town. Except for Henry, of course."

"Of course." Winters had broken the tragic news to many people in his long career. He'd never seen anyone react so stoically. She hadn't even asked him if he was sure, or told him he must be mistaken.

"I'll call my son, Gerald. He lives in California, so it might be a while before he gets here."

"I can arrange for someone from victim services to wait with you until your son arrives."

"No, thank you. I don't care for strangers in my home." She put the glass on the coffee table, scooped up the dog, and stood. "Thank you for coming, Mr. Winters, Miss Smith. It was most kind of you to deliver the news in person. Do you need me to identify the body, or something?"

"That can wait until tomorrow."

"Good. It is late. You can call me any time after ten to arrange a viewing."

Viewing? "Mrs. Montgomery, we should call someone to be with you. Constable Smith can wait until a neighbor arrives."

"I assure you, Mr. Winters, that I will be quite fine until my son gets here in a day or two."

A day or two? "Before we go, can I ask what your husband was doing this evening?"

"Other than getting himself killed?" She laughed.

He heard a strangled sound from Smith, and didn't dare look at her.

"Reginald and Frank were having dinner with potential investors. Japanese fellows, looking for someplace to spend their money. These Asians are buying up the entire province. Someone should put a stop to it before they expect us to eat with chopsticks, don't you agree, Mr. Winters?"

"Who's Frank, and what's his last name?"

"Frank Clemmins, my husband's business partner."

Winters glanced at Smith. She gave an almost imperceptible nod, indicating that she knew who they were talking about.

"Did your husband say where they were dining? Or when he expected the dinner to be over?"

Mrs. Montgomery shook her head. "No. But Reginald never stayed out late. He was almost always home by ten, and never later to bed than eleven. He didn't care for dinners with Asian businessmen. He said they were too interested in having a good time, as long as he was paying. If he didn't get at least seven hours' sleep, Reginald had a tendency to fall asleep in the afternoon, sometimes in meetings, and he disliked that. Made him look old, he said. Poor Reginald. I'll miss him. And so will Henry, won't you, Henry?" The dog barked in agreement. "Now if you'll excuse me, Mr. Winters, it is late."

"Did your husband perhaps forget to take his wallet?"

"I can't imagine him doing so. I haven't seen it around."

"Did he carry a cell phone?"

"Reginald is…was…a busy man. He made phone calls all the day long. He told me many times that he can't imagine how he ever coped in the days before cell phones. I assume you're asking me these questions because his possessions are missing."

"Did he wear a watch?"

"Of course. I told you he was punctual. He lived by his watch. Is that missing as well? It was a good one."

"Can you describe it?"

"It's a Rolex Oyster. His mother gave it to him for his fortieth birthday. Reginald treasured it."

"Do you happen to have a picture of it, Mrs. Montgomery? For insurance purposes, perhaps."

"How clever of you to think of that, Mr. Winters. I believe we do. I'll just be a minute." She put Henry down, and left the room.

Winters walked to the French doors. Hands in his pockets, he stood there, looking over the lights of town.

Smith watched Henry. Henry watched Smith.

"Here it is." Mrs. Montgomery was back, waving paper in the air. "Two photos, front and back. You can see the inscription here." She handed him the pictures. "It says 'To Reginald on his birthday. Love, Mother.'"

"May I borrow these, Mrs. Montgomery? I'll have them returned tomorrow."

"Certainly. Now if there's nothing else?"

"What did you do this evening, Mrs. Montgomery?"

"These Japanese businessmen don't care for the company of wives. As I was on my own, I had a friend over for dinner."

"We may need to speak with you tomorrow."

"I should be here most of the day."

Winters headed for the door.

"Mrs. Montgomery," Smith said. "Was it Dr. Tyler you had dinner with?"

Mrs. Montgomery tilted her head and looked at Winters almost flirtatiously. "I might have told you a little lie." She giggled. "I do have one good friend in the area. I know what you're thinking, young lady, but I assure you that neither of us had reason to wish harm to poor Reginald."

Henry barked in agreement.

Chapter Five

Winters was silent as Smith negotiated the SUV down the steep streets. The lights of the bridge leading out of town shone on the water.

"That's a new one on me," he said, as she pulled into the alley behind Front Street. Constable Evans stood aside to let them pass. "Not exactly the grieving widow. How did you know who her friend is? Her lover, I guess, judging by that schoolgirl giggle. We were supposed to be there in a sympathetic capacity. Deliverers of tragic news and all that stuff. Not that I'm criticizing, mind. You got to the point fast enough."

"Mrs. Montgomery didn't even pretend to be upset at her husband's death. And by the sounds of it, she doesn't expect her son to be too broken up, either. I thought that was sad, so sad," Smith said. "Everyone needs someone to mourn them." Her hat threw shadows across her face and he couldn't read her expression. He waited for her to continue. "I've seen Dr. Tyler's car parked at their house. I sorta guessed why he was there because one of my mom's friends mentioned that the Montgomerys' marriage was somewhat unorthodox. I suppose I paid attention because you don't expect that sort of thing in people of that age. Sorry, John. No offense meant."

Winters grunted. Considerable offense had been taken. "Your mother knows the Montgomerys?"

"No more than anyone else. He's here to build a big resort, the most exclusive resort between Alberta and the Pacific, he calls it. Called it, I should say."

"Some people would be opposed to that."

"You'd be right there. Plus he's, I mean he was, strongly opposed to the peace garden. You know, the park they're wanting to build at the O'Reilly place?"

"I've heard about it." Everyone in North America had heard about the Commemorative Peace Garden. In the 1960s and early '70s Trafalgar and the Kootenays had been the major settling point for young Americans fleeing to Canada because of the war in Vietnam. Draft dodgers, deserters, anyone against the war, had settled in the Kootenay Mountains. A good number never left. War resisters, they called themselves. And now, in the first decade of the twenty-first century, more were coming.

Tom Maas, mayor of Trafalgar for more than twenty years, a Canadian of the same age as the American hippies who'd found refuge in the mountains, had thrown his considerable influence behind the proposed Commemorative Peace Garden. Three acres of prime land had been left to the town in the will of Larry O'Reilly, a one-time draft dodger who'd prospered in Canada. He'd also left money, and the plans, for a fountain to be built at the center of the park. A stream of water flowing from the broken sword of Ares, the Greek god of war, into a reflecting pool. An inscription honoring the war resisters was to be inscribed at the base of the statue.

No one had foreseen any problems with the bequest. At no expense, the town of Trafalgar would have a pleasant park for the enjoyment of the citizens.

But word leaked out to the wider world. Opposition hit the unsuspecting town like an arrow cast by Ares himself. Winters had no opinion on the park one way or the other. But he was probably one of the only people in town on the sidelines. Once the U.S. media had gotten wind of the plan, the town was under siege. Times were not right for a somber reflection of the history and motives of Vietnam protesters. Trafalgar was less than a hundred kilometers from the border, and local businessmen quaked in fear of a tourist boycott.

Reginald Montgomery had not been a calming force. His proposed resort development was facing opposition enough (threat to the grizzly bear habitation, ruination of the bucolic town that was Trafalgar). If the Americans didn't come, his resort would fail for sure.

But Tom Maas, the mayor, had been enthusiastic about the park, talking up its virtues as both a tourist attraction and a moral imperative, convincing everyone that negative U.S. media attention would pass as soon as another pretty, young, blond white woman disappeared.

Anti-park forces retreated; plans for the park went ahead.

And then Maas died. A heart attack moments after he greeted the annual meeting of the Mystery Writers of British Columbia. Linda Patterson, the deputy mayor, thrust into the top job until the next election, was better known for organizing civic functions and speaking at school graduations than for her political skills. She blew with the wind and agreed with whoever was presenting their side at that moment.

"Evening, John. Constable." A large man straightened up from the pavement behind Alphonse's Bakery. A woman was brushing fingerprint dust on the shop doorknob, while a young man rooted through the garbage bags behind the convenience store.

"Anything?" Winters said. Ron Gavin was the lead RCMP crime scene investigator for the entire Mid-Kootenays. They were stationed just outside of Trafalgar, so there hadn't been too much of a delay in getting to the scene.

"At a guess, I'd say the vic was killed where he stood. The doc'll know better, but the amount of blood, brain tissue, and the splatter pattern is consistent with suffering a massive head trauma and falling right over."

"One person? More?"

Gavin shrugged. "Can't say. This alley's well traveled. We've had a steady stream of people wanting to stop by and give us advice on how to do our jobs."

"That damned TV program."

"You can say that again. This alley's a major route for foot traffic. It rained this morning, so we've gotten some nice partial casts of footprints." He nodded toward the entrance to the alley. The pavement was in bad condition, patches of weeds growing between cracks. Anyone stepping in the mud would track that mud in their wake.

"Tell your people I'm interested in locating a wallet, cell phone, and Rolex watch."

"Will do."

"When did the newspaper people leave?" Smith asked.

"Not long after you. They took a couple of pictures of my rear end bending over the bloody residue and called it a night. Hope he wasn't using a wide angle lens."

Winters laughed. Once a player for the Ottawa Rough Riders in the Canadian Football League, these days Ron's imposing size was due more to fast food than exercise.

"Nothing else?"

"Oh, sorry. I almost forgot to mention that we found a message scrawled in blood across the alley. *John W. did it*, was all I could make out." Gavin laughed heartily.

Winters didn't bother to smile. "You'll have a report for me tomorrow?"

"Initial impressions. Details take longer."

"Tomorrow, then."

The Mountie returned to his work.

"Let's head back to the station," Winters said to Smith. "I want to write up some notes, and start sending out feelers on Montgomery."

Smith pulled into Elm Street and turned on Front. Light and laughter spilled from the bars and restaurants. She braked hard to avoid two staggering young women crossing the street, arms wrapped around each other, oblivious to everything around them. She stopped at a red light at Oak Street. A group of drifters in tattered jeans, middle-aged tourists in Bermuda shorts, and two elderly couples in suit and tie, dress and pumps, crossed at the intersection. A young woman stepped off the sidewalk with a cocker spaniel on a lead. She caught sight of the police vehicle, yanked on the leash, and scurried back the way she'd come, dragging a confused dog. Winters had more important things on his mind than enforcing one of the town's more unusual bylaws. No dogs were allowed in the downtown area. At every intersection, the sidewalk was painted with a picture of a dog, in a red circle with a stroke through it. Residents complained, lustily; tourists assumed there'd been some mistake. But the bylaw remained. It was also illegal to play hackisack on the streets of Trafalgar. Winters hadn't figured that one out yet.

The light changed to green, and Smith drove on.

"Give me your home number," he said. "I'll call you soon as Dr. Lee's arranged a time for the autopsy. With luck, it'll be early. Pick me up at home—dispatch has the address. Then we'll collect an unmarked."

"I don't have a car."

"You don't have a car?" She might as well have said she didn't have a head.

"Nope."

"How do you get around?"

"I bike."

"I had a bike in my youth. Got rid of it when Eliza said that if I wanted to marry her, the bike had to go. She didn't trust motorcycles."

"A bicycle, John. I ride a bicycle."

"You do?"

"If I need to go shopping, or somewhere far away, I use my parents' car. I could ask Mom if she needs the car tomorrow." Smith pulled into the parking lot beside the police station.

"We'll take mine." Winters passed her the pen and paper he'd taken out to write down her phone number. "Address and directions."

Smith wrote.

"If they're not ready for us at the hospital in the morning, we'll pay a visit to Mrs. Montgomery's friend. She was insistent that we visit him at his office. As her extramarital affairs were apparently of no concern to her husband, I have to guess that her friend is in a marriage not quite so open. Plus we should have a preliminary report from Ron Gavin to work on."

"Do you have any ideas?"

"Early days yet, Molly, early days. I don't see Mrs. M. bludgeoning her husband with sufficient force to kill him. Arsenic in the coffee maybe, but nothing that would make a mess."

"You could have eaten off the floor in her kitchen," Smith said. "Provided you wanted to."

"Perhaps someone will come in to confess. That would be nice. If not, we'll start looking for a motive tomorrow."

"Suspects," she said. "That'll be about half of town."

Winters got out of the car and they walked through the front doors into the police station.

Smith completed her shift report, signed off duty, said good bye to Ingrid, the night dispatcher, and let herself out the back door. All evening she'd kept her excitement dampened down. Now that she was on her own, she punched one fist in the air and pulled her arm back. "Yes!" She was assisting a detective sergeant in a murder investigation. She was on her way. She'd make detective in no time.

It took a moment for her to realize that she was not, in the literal sense, on her way anywhere. The bike rack at the back of the police station was empty. Her chain lock lay on the ground. Was this a practical joke? Had Evans hidden her bike in pique over her being chosen to work with Winters rather than him? She wouldn't put it past him. Evans had a nasty streak.

But he would not have taken her bike—he might not like her, but he wouldn't dare being accused of stealing. Her bike, her twenty-one speed mountain bike, had been stolen. From the back of the police station.

She went back inside.

"Still here, Molly?" Winters came out of the sergeants' office as Smith was wondering how she should go about placing a complaint of her stolen property. Should she write up the report herself, or phone it in tomorrow? Or forget about it? The chances of the bike being recovered were about nil.

"You offered me a ride, John?"

"Too late to bike? Mountain roads can be treacherous after dark."

"Just tired."

"Offer's still good. The cab'll be here in a couple of minutes. Spoke too soon. It's here now, that was quick. Advantage of living in a small town, eh?"

"Moonlight, is that you? You're early, and was that a car I heard? Is something the matter?"

"I'm early, Mom, because I've been given a special assignment. This is so great, I can't wait to tell you about it. And that was a car because of something that isn't so great."

Her mother struggled to push herself out her favorite reading chair, the one with springs so worn that it was an effort standing up. A book lay open on the table beside her, and her reading glasses were pushed down her nose. Sylvester opened one eye, checked Smith out, and went back to sleep. The house was dark, except for a single lamp over the chair.

At not much over five feet Lucky Smith was considerably shorter than her daughter. Her face was round and soft, with a maze of lines radiating out from the corners of her eyes and mouth; her red hair was heavily streaked with grey and, as always, stuffed into a haphazard bunch at the back of her head. "Sounds like one of those good news, bad news jokes. I'll put the kettle on and you can tell me the bad news first. So it doesn't linger in my mind."

"Why are you still up, Mom? Everything okay?"

"Of course. I'm enjoying this book so much, I wanted to finish it." Lucky went into the kitchen.

Smith picked up the book her mother'd placed on the side table. The corner of page ten was turned down. The novel was the approximate thickness of the phone book. Lucky would be reading into next month if she wanted to get finished in one sitting. Something was wrong between her parents: she'd suspected it for some time. The ground was shifting under Molly Smith's feet, fault lines in the earth's crust preparing to move, and she didn't like the sensation. She followed her mother into the kitchen. Sylvester padded along behind.

Their kitchen was a room well lived in. Light catchers dangled in the window, reflecting nothing of the darkness beyond. Almost every square on the calendar over the phone (a fund raiser for the seniors center—a montage of naked elderly women, tastefully posed) was full of scribbles. Piles of letters, newspaper clippings, and magazines had been pushed to the back of the big wooden table, scarred with memories of family dinners and political protests. Photos of her brother Sam's children, fastened in place by magnets, covered the fridge, and colorful school art was pinned to a cork board set up for that purpose. A shelf, full of cookbooks both well-thumbed and never opened, hung from a loose screw. The screw had been loose as long as Smith could remember. A wicker basket on the counter overflowed with red tomatoes, cherry and beefsteak, interspersed with green peas and yellow beans picked from the garden that afternoon. Several loose sheets of paper had fallen from the pile of petitions, flyers, address books, and notes tumbling all over themselves on the phone table. Lucky picked some of them up.

Smith undid her gunbelt and tossed it on the table. The weapon lay amongst the evidence of a comfortable country mountain home like dog poo on the lawns of Buchart Gardens. Lucky turned her face away in silent disgust. There were some things mother and daughter had learned not to discuss.

"Hungry? There's still some curry."

Smith's stomach rolled over, and an image of Reginald Montgomery's head rose, unbidden, in her mind. "No. I mean, no thanks, Mom. I'm not hungry."

The kettle switched itself off and Lucky busied herself with cups, tea bags, milk and sugar. "Tell me why you got a ride home, dear."

"My bike was stolen."

Lucky stopped, bag of milk in hand. "You park it behind the police station, don't you?"

"Yes."

She burst out laughing.

"It's not funny."

"No, I guess not. You paid a lot for that bike. But it does have its funny side—I'm amazed at the gall of someone who'd steal a police officer's bike from the grounds of the police station itself."

"This isn't some Robin Hood, Mom. Stealing from the fascist police to give to the elderly widow who needs a bike to buy food for her starving children."

"I'm sorry if I made light of it, Moonlight. I'll get home in time to give you a lift to work tomorrow afternoon."

Smith unlaced her boots and pulled them off with a satisfied sigh. The heat had been intense today, and some of it still lingered in the night air. Those boots wrapped her feet in their own private sauna. The heavy dark pants weren't much better, particularly not with all the equipment she wore around her waist. She accepted a cup of tea from her mother. A wrinkled face with prominent nose and bulging blue eyes protruded from the side of the mug—it had been homemade by a family friend and bought at a sale to raise money for the women's shelter. Sylvester nuzzled at her leg, looking for a scratch.

She obliged. "That brings me to the good news. I've been given a special assignment. Detective Lopez is going on vacation, and they need someone to help Sergeant Winters with a murder investigation because he's only been in town a couple of months. This is my big chance, Mom. I'll show them what I can do."

"That sounds nice, dear," Lucky said, placing a plate of raisin and oatmeal cookies on the table before sitting down with her own tea. "But it doesn't seem right that you're so pleased at the murder of some poor soul."

"Let me tell you who our victim is. You have to promise that you absolutely will not say a word to anyone, even Dad, until you hear about it on the news."

"I'm unlikely to tell your father much of anything. But I promise."

"And you can't let anyone know that I told you. Ever."

"I don't gossip, dear."

"You will when you hear this. Promise?"

"I promise."

"Reginald Montgomery."

Lucky Smith's eyes widened, and the slightest of smiles touched the corners her mouth. Then she got herself under control and settled her features into a somber frown. "Is that so? Most unfortunate."

"For him, but not for the peace garden committee, I'll bet."

"Will this be in tomorrow's news?"

"The press listens into the police radio and so Meredith Morgenstern showed up, PDQ. Photographer in tow."

"Perhaps I'll buy a paper on my way into the store. I was supposed to be going to a meeting of the arts council tomorrow evening, but after reading the paper I might call an emergency planning session for the garden committee."

"You didn't hear this from me."

Lucky looked at her daughter. "It's no secret that I don't approve of your career choice."

"No kidding."

"But I would never do anything to harm it."

Smith got to her feet and kissed the top of her mother's head. "I'm going to bed. I have a busy day tomorrow." She grabbed three cookies and her gunbelt.

"Good night, Moonlight."

"Night, Mom."

Moonlight was the name on Constable Molly Smith's birth certificate. Her parents had been hippies, full of ideas about changing the world and not buying into the establishment.

Come to think of it, her mother was still out to change the world, although her father, not so much anymore.

"Have you called Christa?" Lucky called.

Smith stuck her head back into the kitchen. "No, why?"

"She called earlier, said she'd left a message on your cell phone but you hadn't returned it. She sounded distressed, but wouldn't tell me what was wrong."

Smith pulled the cell phone out of her pocket as she ran up the stairs. She'd switched it off at the Montgomerys' and forgotten to check it. She held the phone to her ear with one hand and listened to Christa's message as she pulled her uniform shirt out of her pants with the other.

Chapter Six

"This had better be good," Rich Ashcroft snarled into his bedside phone.

"Oh, I think you'll like it," Irene said. "Are you listening?"

"Of course I'm listening." Rich struggled to a sitting position. The woman beside him groaned and rolled over. Jenny, Joanie…something like that. A generic name for a generic dyed-blonde. "Go ahead."

"You were interested in that stuff about the memorial to the draft dodgers up in British Columbia, right?"

"Spit it out, Irene."

"Word just came in of a murder in Trafalgar. At first I didn't pay it any attention. Killing in small-town Canada, who the hell cares? But I decided to read the whole piece. The dead guy was big in trying to derail the monument."

"You don't say?"

"I say. The report's covered in all sorts of disclaimers, but it's a murder all right."

Jenny, Joanie? reached out a thin pale arm and ran her long red nails across his chest. He slapped it away. Jeannie, that was her name.

"The mayor died couple weeks ago. He was the one pushing hard for the memorial. I did a quick bit of catching up before calling you and this guy, I've got his name right here, Reginald Montgomery, stepped in and tried to stop it. Bad for international relations he said."

"By which he meant bad for business. How'd the mayor die?"

"Heart attack."

"No need to dig into his death. But the other guy? Sounds promising. Pitch it to the bosses, and book me a flight to Trafalgar first thing tomorrow. Get on the phone to the reporter who put out the story. Small town, he's gotta be impressed to have a call from CNC. Sound charming, will you?"

Rich's assistant, Irene, was over sixty years old; she'd had a two-pack-a-day habit since she was sixteen. Her voice was so low and sexy that it, plus the mention of Cable News Corporation, would have any hick town reporter coming in his jeans. Irene laughed. "Aren't I always charming? However, the name on the byline is Meredith. Sounds more like your style."

"Call me with that flight info. I'll be up." Rich switched the phone off, and lay back into the pillows. He grabbed Jeannie's arm. "Finish what you were doing," he said.

John Winters wasn't going to wait until morning to call the Chief Constable.

The taxi had dropped him at his car, still at the resort where he and Eliza had dinner, and he'd driven himself home. They lived outside of town, on a small road clinging to the side of the mountain. The forest grew thicker and the handful of houses dotting the road grew thinner as he drove. His house was the last before the wilderness closed in. A right bugger to get out of in winter, but Eliza loved the solitude and the view. The front porch and wide living room windows looked over the forest to the expanse of the Upper Kootenay River and the mountains beyond, cumulating in a glimpse of Koola, the glacier that loomed over Trafalgar.

Eliza was curled up in the king-size bed under a light summer sheet. The strap of her ivory satin nightgown had slipped down her arm. She smelled of Chanel No. 5. He kissed her on the cheek. She murmured sweet nothings and rolled over, and he went into the kitchen for something to eat and to make the call.

Eliza. It was a wonder she'd stayed with him all these years. In her late 40s, she was still beautiful enough to have her pick of men, yet she stuck with him. Their Vancouver friends had assumed that the move from the city to slow-paced, quiet Trafalgar was to make Eliza happy; more time for her husband to be home, a nice house in the mountains. In reality Eliza had loved their condo on False Creek, loved city life. But he couldn't take it any more. Big-city politics, the sordid Downtown Eastside, filled with hopeless druggies, empty-eyed hookers, and wide-eyed child runaways. Sad lives of sad people for which no one gave a damn. It hadn't been the death of yet another drug-addled teenaged whore or child runaway that had forced him to make up his mind, rather the mess he'd made of the investigation of the murder of a twelve-year-old from a wealthy, highly connected family.

Eliza no longer modeled for *Vogue* or *Harper's Bazaar*, but she still made good money, enough to buy a small apartment in Vancouver where she could stay overnight if she had a shoot in the city. Not only had Eliza been a top model in her day, she was also blessed with the gift of acute financial know-how. Winters could have retired outright, had he wanted. He'd considered it, seriously. But he was a cop. And as hard as the job got sometimes, he wanted to be nothing but a cop.

They'd had packaged-microwaveable roast beef last night. Winters cut thick slices off the leftovers and slapped them between pieces of whole wheat bread. He didn't spare the mustard. After taking a couple of bites, he punched in the Chief Constable's number.

"Sorry to wake you, Paul," he said to the low grumble.

"You find whoever got Montgomery, John?"

"Not yet, I'm sorry to say. It's something else."

"Go ahead."

"Smith. I can't work with her. I need someone with more experience. I'm sure she's a competent beat cop, but for a detective, she's just too green. Leaps to conclusions all over the place, offers her opinion where it isn't wanted, speaks to civilians out of turn. She'll be no good on an investigation until she learns a thing or two on the streets."

"She's been no help at all?"

"She does have some local knowledge which proved useful. But there must be more experienced constables who've been here for a while."

"Are you sure you're not mistaking enthusiasm for incompetence? You must remember what it was like to be young and eager."

"I'm not that old."

"You're as old as me, John. And in this job, that's old. If you think Molly's not up to it, I'll put her back on the street. But it's only been a few hours. And I don't have anyone else who's truly local. This could turn out to be a political incident. And I don't mean political in terms of the Trafalgar town council. International attention's been focused on the peace garden. Why these old lefties have to cling to the past, I don't know. The sixties ended forty years ago, time they got over it. Don't get me wrong, I worked with Tom Maas for many years: he was a good man. I respected his commitment to this town, and I like to think he respected mine. But when he died, I'd hoped that would be the end of this stupid idea. And Montgomery looked like the man to lay the garden thing in its grave."

Winters dug in the fridge for the milk carton. He shook it—empty. Eliza's skill in the kitchen had never been one of the pillars of their marriage. "I understand that, Paul. But what's this to do with Smith?"

"Molly's mother is one of the leading forces behind the park. Everyone who has the slightest interest in seeing the Commemorative Peace Garden become a reality has passed through their house. Lucy Smith, a.k.a. Lucky, is also involved with a group opposed to the Grizzly Resort, Montgomery's place. Lucky and her husband, Andy, own Mid-Kootenay Adventure Vacations, which happens to be located a couple of doors down from where Montgomery met his death."

With milk out of the picture, orange juice would have to do. Winters drank it straight from the carton. "You want Smith to spy on her parents?"

"Certainly not. She'll be able to take you straight to the unofficial center of local politics, that's all I'm saying."

Winters eyed his half-finished sandwich. If he continued to insist that he didn't want to work with Molly Smith, Paul Keller would replace her. But he was getting strong signals from the Chief Constable that he didn't want that to happen. And despite Keller's insistence that he wanted Smith involved because of her local knowledge, Winters wondered if he expected her to rat out her parents, if that became necessary. Smith was ambitious; was she that ambitious?

"Okay, I'll give it another couple of days. Maybe I'll have this wrapped up tomorrow, and all of this political shit won't matter. The wife might be worth looking at—I can't see her doing the deed herself, but she has some proclivities that might lead somewhere."

"That would be good, John. Close to home—a nice neat domestic incident."

Winters' finger moved to disconnect the call; the tinny voice called him back. "Sorry, Paul, I missed that."

"Do whatever you can to keep media attention away. We haven't had a murder here in more than twelve months. If this turns out to be a domestic, it won't look as bad as a political."

"I hear you." Winters hung up. Small-town politics. Not much different than the big city, after all. Maybe a bit worse—after all, the stakes were so much smaller. He made a quick call to the voice mail of a friend from his days on the Vancouver PD to request a peek into the state of Montgomery's business, finished his orange juice, and went to join his wife in bed. Perhaps she'd not be too deeply asleep and he could still salvage something out of their twenty-fifth anniversary.

Smith pulled off her uniform and put on jeans and a T-shirt. She'd love to take her Glock, go around to Charlie's place and blast a few holes in his knees. That would keep him away from Christa, all right. Unfortunately, the Trafalgar City Police frowned on independent thinking of that sort.

She picked up the photograph sitting on her bedside table. Graham smiled at her, trapped forever in an organized scatter of colored dots. It had been taken on the beach at Tofino. The sky was dark—a storm moving in, fast. There was no color in the ocean. A wave reared up behind him. His smile was wide, his teeth white, his body young and full of life. They'd danced in the waves, laughed at the storm, held their arms out to the wind, and their mouths to the rain. They'd run back to the B&B and made love while the storm crashed all around them. When both weather and lovers were sated, they'd gone in search of crab chowder, whole wheat bread, good beer.

She blinked back a tear, returned the picture to its place, and ran downstairs. The light over the chair in the living room was switched off, the kitchen deserted.

She grabbed the keys to her mom's car off the hook by the kitchen door.

Smith drove Lucky's beaten-up old Pontiac Firefly. down the highway and crossed the long black bridge into town. Trafalgar was an old town; old for western Canada. Streetlights shone through the thick leaves of large walnut trees. The pavements were uneven, most of the houses were originals, many in ill repair. So many transients passed through town, and there wasn't much in the way of apartments, that many of the historic houses at the foot of the mountain had been broken into flats. She pulled up in front of Christa's building. A black cat sat on the steps of the house next door, its eyes yellow pools against the dark fur.

Smith knocked lightly, knowing that the neighbors could be nasty if disturbed. Her hand was still raised when the door opened, Christa peeking out from behind it.

The two women climbed a narrow staircase and made a sharp right into Christa's flat.

Christa threw herself onto one of the two bean bags that, along with three milk crates, made up her living room furniture.

"You okay?" Smith asked.

"Why doesn't he stop this? He has to know that he's only making me mad at him. Even if I'd ever considered going out with him, I sure wouldn't now."

"He doesn't know anything of the sort. He thinks he's reminding you of his devotion. And that you'll eventually come around to seeing things his way."

Christa started to cry. Her face was so red and blotchy, it was obvious this wasn't the night's first crying jag. She shifted her right hip to pull an almost worn-through tissue from the pocket of her shorts.

"I'll make tea," Smith said. "Come sit at the table." She held out her hand.

Christa took it and Smith pulled her friend to her feet. She wrapped the other woman in a fierce hug. When they separated Smith said, "My mom believes that tea holds the secret to the solution of all life's problems. And you know my mom's a wise woman."

Christa cracked a smile. "I do. How are your folks anyway? I've been so busy I haven't been over for a visit in a long time."

"Not good, I fear." Smith knew her way around this kitchen as well as her mother's. She lit the gas on the stove and placed the kettle on the element. "I'm trying not to notice it, but they're hardly talking to each other. Mom is so into this peace garden, it's consuming her."

"Lucky's always been like that. You remember when the province removed funding from women's second stage housing? I was surprised she didn't have us all manning the barricades. Like in *Les Misérables*. And when that politician told her it was a financial decision? He was lucky to leave with his head on his shoulders." Christa laughed. "There's a loaf of bread from Alphonse's in the cupboard, and cheese in the fridge. I can't normally afford anything from there—four bucks for a loaf of bread, whew, but I needed a treat."

Not the time, Smith thought, to remember Alphonse's Bakery and the alley behind it. "It's not just Mom rushing to the barricades, to use your analogy, and Dad supporting her. They're on opposite sides on this one. He thinks the park's a bad idea."

"Are they fighting a lot?"

"No. And that isn't good. They've always fought—they're both so passionate about things—but now they're hardly speaking. It's creepy. Kinda like a horror movie when everything goes quiet and you know the monster's about to crash through the walls."

"Bummer." Christa was an only child; her mother had died when she was in primary school, her father devastated by the death. She'd been unofficially raised by the Smith family.

Smith put the loaf onto the table, along with margarine and a pie-shaped wedge of brie. The kettle whistled, and she poured hot water into the brown tea pot with the broken handle. "It's two a.m. and I'm not here to talk about my mom and dad. Spill, kid."

Christa explained about taking the phone off the hook, the knocking on the door, the neighbor screaming at her.

Smith munched on bread and cheese. "If you just wanna talk, go ahead. But if you want my advice, you already have it."

Christa stirred milk into her mug. "I have to get some work done or I'll fail this course."

Smith watched a fly trying to find its way out the window over the sink.

"Okay, I'll make a complaint."

Smith knew how hard this decision was for her: no matter how harshly life treated her, Christa always believed the best of people. "Charlie Bassing might look like a tough guy, but he's a weasly no-account nerd beneath all that steroid-enhanced muscle. No point in calling right now, you'll get night dispatch. Go down to the station tomorrow, that'll be best. You want me to come with you?"

Christa nodded.

"I'm on this special assignment, so I'm busy in the morning. Perhaps we can meet up at the station." Smith was dying to tell her friend about the investigation and her part in it. But Christa was looking out the window at the lights twinkling on the mountainside. For weeks she'd resisted Smith's advice to take a restraining order out on Charlie, convinced that she only had to be firm and he'd go away. Tonight, she'd listen if Molly talked, but her attention wouldn't be on what the murder of Reg Montgomery could mean to her friend's career.

"I gotta go." Smith drained her tea. "If he comes back tonight, call the station straight away. And then me. Got that?"

Christa nodded.

"I'll give you a buzz soon as I'm free. I hope they give me the job of serving the restraining order. I might accidentally bring my truncheon down across the back of his head and knee him in the nuts."

"I don't want that to happen," Christa said. "Maybe I shouldn't make an official complaint. He likes me, that's all. But it's getting to be such a bother."

"I was kidding, Chris. But get one thing straight. He doesn't like you. He wants to own you. There's a difference."

Chapter Seven

Shirley Lee called while Winters was flipping bacon. It was seven a.m. Eliza had to catch a flight out of Castlegar, going to Toronto to shoot a magazine ad for a hybrid car. Something designed to appeal to the "middle-aged, upper-middle-class, environmentally aware woman."

"Aging bags with piles of dough and a guilty conscience," Winters had said when she told him of the assignment.

"Watch who you're calling an aging bag, old man," she'd replied. "And better a hybrid than jail bait and a Camaro."

"Yo, doc," Winters said into the phone, reaching across the counter to press the lever down on the toaster. The twenty-fifth anniversary hadn't been a total washout, and he was in a good mood.

"Good morning, John," Dr. Lee said. "I'm doing the autopsy on Montgomery at noon. It was a quiet night, so I can give him my full attention."

"Glad to hear it."

She hung up without bothering to say goodbye.

"Who was that?" Eliza came into the kitchen, fitting a gold hoop into her ear. "Business?" The weather report was calling for another day of record-breaking heat, and she'd dressed casually for the trip in black capris, white T-shirt, and sandals that emphasized what the Victorians would have called her well-turned ankles.

"Natch. Bacon?"

She shuddered, and reached into the fridge for yoghurt and a jar of blackcurrant jam. She snatched at a slice of toast as it flew out of the toaster and tossed it onto a plate.

"I've got time to take you to the airport, and get back to pick up my apprentice," Winters said, cracking eggs into the hot fat.

"You're driving?"

"Can you believe it, she doesn't own a car. And she calls herself a cop? What is the world coming to?"

"Don't start your relationship with this constable with such cynicism, John. Give her some trust. Paul wouldn't have hired her if she was no good."

"She's too green. Too naïve. She looks like Barbie, all dressed up to play cop."

"I wonder who's being naïve. She can't help what she looks like, but you can help judging her on her looks."

A car horn sounded from the driveway.

"That's my ride. So you have time to consider your prejudice against this young woman before picking her up." Eliza tweaked his earlobe and kissed him firmly on the lips. Her bag was waiting by the kitchen door. She tossed her handbag over her shoulder, balanced her plate of toast in one hand, yoghurt and spoon in another, and somehow still managed to drag the wheeled suitcase out the door.

Winters served himself bacon and eggs and the remaining toast and sat down at the kitchen table. Women, he thought, always sticking up for each other.

"You might be interested in this." Eliza opened the door and threw the newspaper at him.

"Have you seen the day's paper?" Lucky Smith said into the phone. She sat at her desk in the small office behind Mid-Kootenay Adventure Vacations.

"Geeze, Lucky. It's not nine o'clock yet. I haven't seen my face in the mirror. Although that's no great pleasure these days."

Lucky had lain awake all night, while Andy slept stiff and flat, as far to his side of the bed as he could without falling off. She'd debated whom to call first with the news, all the while knowing that the decision shouldn't be a hard one. Barry Stevens had lost an arm in Vietnam. When he was released from hospital, he could have gone home to Tennessee. But he brought his cousin, who'd just received his draft notice, to Canada. The cousin accepted amnesty and returned to the States long ago, but Barry stayed behind. He married a Trafalgar girl, had three kids, and built one of the first computer businesses in the B.C. interior. He never spoke of the war, of his trauma, the father he hadn't spoken to in more than thirty years, or the mother who told her husband she was going to quilting conventions and snuck across the border to visit her grandchildren. He played no part in local politics; Lucky knew him only from mutual friends. Then Larry O'Reilly died, bequeathing his property to the town for the Commemorative Peace Garden, and Barry Stevens came down from the mountains determined to see the park a reality.

"Something tragic has happened," Lucky said, trying to sound somber. "I read about it in the morning paper. Reginald Montgomery died last night."

"You don't say. Goddamn, shoulda bought a lottery ticket." After thirty years in British Columbia, Barry's Tennessee accent was as thick as the day he'd left. "Does the paper say how it happened?"

Lucky didn't know—she hadn't read it yet. But the headline did say something about "tragically." "I'm going to call a meeting of the committee, say seven? My house?"

"I'll be there. After I've bought that lottery ticket." Barry hung up.

Lucky turned her swivel chair to look out the window and propped her feet on the windowsill. It wasn't much of a view, just the alley behind the shop. But the sky was blue, and the vegetable garden of the house on the other side of the alley was dressed in more shades of green than one could name.

She called Michael Rockwell last. He was at his desk in the realtor's office, about to go out, he explained, to show a riverside property to a retired couple from Toronto. He told her the asking price, a million and a half. Not for the first time she wondered what had attracted a prosperous businessman such as Michael to their controversial project.

"Of course I'll be there," he said. "My calendar's empty tonight, so I don't have to make any excuses. You won't have time to fix dinner. Why don't I pick up a few things?"

"That'd be nice. I'll get something for dessert."

"It'll be like a party."

"A man has died, Michael. It's not a celebration."

"I only meant party, as in a gathering of good friends around a meal."

"See you at seven then." Lucky hung up. She alternately read the newspaper article and watched the woman on the other side of the alley moving through her garden, selecting tiny red tomatoes and plump peas.

"No work today, Lucky?"

She started and dropped her feet to the floor. She spun her chair around. Her husband stood in the doorway, a mug of coffee in hand. It saved twenty-five cents at the coffee shop if you brought your own cup. He put the mug down and picked up the paper. "Nasty," he said.

"Very."

"Murder in Trafalgar."

"It doesn't say anything about murder."

"Read between the lines, Lucky."

"I try to take everything at face value."

"And I take it that your committee will be taking over our kitchen yet again. No supper tonight, eh?"

"Michael offered to bring supper."

"Michael has, has he? How kind of him. Will it be enough for everyone, Lucky, or just for two?"

"What does that mean?"

"It means that the council is reconsidering having unofficially given their permission to allow the peace garden to go ahead now that Tom Maas is dead. Some of the councilors want to bring the matter to vote immediately."

"I know that, Andy. They want to kill the park before the organizing committee gets itself back into shape, now that we don't have Tom's support."

"So this town can get on with things."

"So this town can get on with the business of making money, you mean."

"Money. Nasty word, money. This business pays for your house, Lucky, for your car, last year's vacation in Hawaii. Money put your children through university and helps your mother live out the rest of her years in some degree of independence."

She got to her feet. "Don't you dare throw our support to my mother in my face."

"Christ, Lucky. I'm not throwing anything in your face. I'm telling you that if this garden's allowed to be built, family businesses along Front Street like ours, like Rosemary's Campfire Kitchen, like Alphonse's Bakery, will be forced to close down. When the American tourists stop coming, all that'll be left will be the Wal-Mart in Nelson, and a few shops that provide goods for the handful of locals that haven't been driven away."

"There are plenty of people, in the States as well as Canada, who'll be proud and happy to visit Trafalgar, to visit the Commemorative Peace Garden. Not to mention all the people who come here for the wilderness, and do their shopping in this store. People who don't want to sit in air conditioned suites and swim in chlorinated pools and watch cable T.V. at the Grizzly Resort."

"Lucky, you can't...." He turned around. "What the hell do you want?"

Duncan, the company's tour leader, had tapped the pads of his fingers on the open door to Lucky's office. He shifted from one foot to the other, and tried not to look at either of his employers. "A lady's on the phone. She wants to know if we can drop two days off her week's trip, as she has to get back to Vancouver early."

"Of course we can't drop two days. Six other people have paid for a week, are you going to phone them all and tell them they only get five days? Are you, Duncan?"

"Not me, man."

"Sometimes I don't know why I bother." Andy pushed his way out of the office. "I'll talk to her."

Duncan raised one eyebrow toward Lucky.

"You did okay to ask Andy to speak to her," she said. "People like that have to talk to the boss, or they think they're being shafted. He'll arrange for you to leave the group for a few hours and bring her back early." She looked at her computer. The long list of numbers blended into a blur before her tired eyes.

"Lucky?"

"Sorry, Duncan. Not even half past nine and it's already been a long day."

"I have a day trip to meet down at the beach, but I before I go I was wondering how Molly's getting on. I see her sometimes around town. She looks a bit lost, if you don't mind my saying so, as a cop. The boots and the gun seem too big for her."

Lucky rubbed her eyes, and looked at the young man standing in the doorway to the cramped, cluttered office. "Lost," she said, "doesn't half describe my daughter, Duncan."

Smith was ready long before Winters arrived to take her to the autopsy. Truth be told, she hadn't slept at all, excitement building at what the day would bring.

As light broke over the mountains to the east, she took a shower, and waited in her room while her parents moved about downstairs, getting ready for their day. The lack of laughter and friendly chatter spoke volumes about the state of the Smith marriage. They left for work together, as normal.

Lucky and Andy had opened a small camping goods store when their children were small, and, when the eco-tourism industry took off, expanded the size of the store and began running guided trips into the wilderness. In the early days they didn't have much staff, so Andy led the trips himself. When she was in high school, Smith helped her dad on weeklong trips and led day or one-night tours herself. Now Andy ran the front of the store and organized the expeditions, staff led the trips, and Lucky did the books and managed the help. It had always been a good partnership. Smith feared that the business would suffer because of the strain in the relationship, thus adding more strain to her parents' marriage.

She threw an additional spoon of coffee into the pot, to make it extra strong, fixed two pieces of dry toast for breakfast, and ate curled in the cushioned alcove at the wide bay window in the front of the house, waiting for Winters. Ducks swam in the river and birds pecked in the long grasses along the shoreline. The house Molly Smith had grown up in was tucked into a small bay off the river, with a deep sandy beach and a great view over the river to the mountains. Soft, round green and brown mountains crowned the town, but in the background, even in high summer, snow touched the sharp-toothed peak of Koola Glacier.

Many years ago Andy built a dock for Moonlight and Samwise to swim off. They'd owned a boat, for a while. Then the children grew up, headed off to university. The boat's engine died, never to be replaced, and the dock had been allowed to decay until it wasn't much more than a stack of broken logs.

It was time she moved out of her parents' house, bought herself a car. She'd seen the look in Winters' face when she confessed that she didn't own a car. There were some things you simply had to have, if you were to be accepted as a functioning adult in most of North America.

An engine sounded, coming up from the road, the vehicle hidden by the sharp curves in the driveway and the jumble of forest surrounding the property. Smith swallowed the dregs of her coffee, snapped on her gun belt, and placed her hat on her head. She'd already forced her feet into the hated boots. She headed out the door. A black SUV was parked in their driveway, and Winters was getting out of the car.

"Morning," she said.

"Morning, Molly. Nice view you have here."

"I like it."

"You can drive." He tossed her the keys and walked around the car to the passenger side.

Smith swallowed, and got in. She rested sweaty hands on the cool steering wheel. The slightest whisper of good perfume lingered in the soft leather of the seats. "Where to?" She put on her sunglasses and adjusted the mirrors.

"We'll pick up the van from the station, and then pay a visit to the Grizzly Resort site. I want to speak to the staff there as soon as possible. If we have time, we can visit this Dr. Tyler. The autopsy's scheduled for twelve o'clock. The Chief Constable's taking Mrs. Montgomery to make the identification at ten. I don't need to be there: it's not as if a highly skilled detective is required to study the widow's face for emotional clues. I hope that when I die my wife will shed a single tear, at least. Henry the dog was more upset at Montgomery's death than his wife was. Do you know where the resort offices are, Molly?"

"Of course," she said, waiting for an immaculately maintained '60s-era pickup truck to pass before pulling onto the highway.

She headed south along the banks of the wide Upper Kootenay River. They crossed the river and drove through the town of Trafalgar, stopping at the police station to pick up an unmarked van. They they headed to Number 3 Highway, where she turned left, toward Nelson. The road hugged the main branch of the Kootenay River. Before long, she saw a prominent sign announcing *Grizzly Resort,* upon which a red circle with a slash through it had been spray-painted.

The van bucked down the washboard gravel road like a wild horse being ridden for the first time. The development offices were nothing more than a trailer in the center of an acre or so of trampled bushes and raw stumps. A giant billboard, featuring a sketch of the property layout on one half and an architect's drawing of the proposed main building on the other loomed over the trailer.

A middle-aged woman was sitting behind a desk by the door. She looked up as Winters and Smith entered. Her eyes and nose were red, mascara ran down her cheeks like a river of coal, and she clutched a tattered tissue to her face. The morning's *Trafalgar Daily Gazette* was spread out on her desk.

The woman turned her ruined face toward them. "I'm sorry, sir, but the office is closed today." She caught sight of Smith behind Winters. "Hi, Moonlight. Didn't see you there. How's your mom and dad?"

Smith cringed at the casual familiarity. "Fine thanks, Bernice."

"I'm Sergeant John Winters, Trafalgar City Police. Is Mr. Clemmins in?"

"I am."

Smith and Winters turned. There were no tears on the man's face, but his eyes were red, and dark lines dragged his face into sorrow's strokes. He rubbed at his shaved scalp. "I assume you're here about Reg. I simply can't believe it." He gestured toward the open door behind him. "Come in, please. I'll talk to Mr. Yakamoto if he calls, Bernice, but no one else."

Architects' drawings and blueprints, fastened with stickpins, covered the walls of Clemmins' office. His grey steel desk was piled high with papers. A single visitor's chair, orange upholstery stained and ragged, took up most of the remaining space. Clemmins collapsed into his chair. Springs squeaked. He was in his late thirties, much younger than his partner. His hair was shaved down to the scalp, black bristles making a crescent pattern around the naked dome of his head. He was taller than Winters, but thinner. The tail of a snake curled around his bicep and the creature's body disappeared into the sleeve of his white T-shirt. Rattles were drawn on the end of the tail. It was nothing but a drawing, but a chill ran down Smith's back, and she turned her eyes away.

Without being asked, Winters took the visitor's chair. Smith studied the drawings on the walls. They might as well have been written in Greek. A bunch of circles inside squares inside large squares, all of it inside a big circle. She dragged her attention back.

"…how we can go on," Clemmins was saying.

"Can you give me an idea of what your business is, sir," Winters said.

"This'll be the Grizzly Resort one day. A top-of-the-line luxury resort. We're planning a hotel and conference center, surrounded by fractional-ownership chalets."

"Fractional-ownership?"

"People buy a share in a vacation property rather than the property itself. The potential for fractional-ownership is incredible out here. The Kootenays are too far for people to travel from Vancouver or Calgary for a weekend, so it's perfect for vacationing a week at time. Five groups of people—families, friends, complete strangers—purchase one-fifth of a chalet. That entitles them to spend one-fifth of the year here. The resort manages the time allocations, maintains the property, looks after communal areas such as the waterfront and the ski hills. Owners'll be able to come up to the hotel to take advantage of heli-skiing, mountain trekking, horseback rides, a full-service spa. We'll have luxury dining—Reg's negotiating with one of Vancouver's top chefs to headline the restaurant. For nights that people don't want formal meals, the resort will have a more casual kitchen offering gourmet pizza, pasta dinners, sandwich take-out. Of course, every chalet will have its own kitchen, for those who prefer to cook." In his excitement at describing the project, Clemmins had returned Montgomery to the present tense.

"I've heard there's opposition to your plans," Winters said.

"Ignorant fools. This resort is exactly what the Mid-Kootenays needs. Money, jobs, tourists. People in the cities are eager to experience nature in all her glory. And what we're offering here is nature. It's a win-win situation."

Smith shifted from one foot to another. A box air conditioner sat in the single window, pumping out so much cold air that she was surprised Clemmins hadn't suggested polar bear viewing as one of the resort's attractions. The resort was going to be built smack-dab in Grizzly bear territory. Once the first fractional-ownership resident came face to face with the reality of nature, red in tooth and claw, nature would be shot, her cubs left to starve to death, and her carcass dragged off for study. Before long the only Grizzly at Grizzly Resort would be the cute little thing in the company's logo.

Molly Smith considered wrapping Clemmins' face in one of his perfectly executed architectural drawings and dragging him out into the woods where he could experience the true glory of nature. She pushed that picture aside as Clemmins confirmed that he and Montgomery had had dinner at Feuilles de Menthe with two representatives of a Japanese venture capital firm looking to invest in the B.C. tourism industry. They left the restaurant about eight-thirty, quarter to nine.

"Early to wrap up an evening of business entertaining," Winters said. "You didn't suggest going on to a bar after?"

"Once business talk was complete, Reg just wanted to go home to bed. That was his way, and last night was no different. Bit of a stick-in-the-mud, Reg was."

Smith was itching to dive head first into the interrogation. But Winters sat in the visitor's chair, shoulders relaxed, legs crossed, chatting amiably. "So when you left the restaurant…."

"Reg said good night to Mr. Yakamoto and Mr. Takauri, and we arranged to meet at noon tomorrow, today, here. Then he left us, heading for his car, I thought." Clemmins lifted his hands to his face. "This is a disaster. It was hard enough to keep Yakamoto happy once he realized the extent of opposition to the resort. Foreign investors can be mighty shy of controversy. But now—he'll be on the next plane back to Tokyo."

"Someone has added their opinion to the sign out on the highway," Winters said.

"That's the second time this week our sign's been defaced. Bernice has called for a replacement. I might as well place the sign company on stand-by."

Winters changed track so abruptly Smith almost fell off. "After you saw Mr. Montgomery on his way, what did you do then, Mr. Clemmins?"

"Our guests wanted me to show them some entertainment. I'm sure I don't have to explain to you, Sergeant, what they were interested in." He cleared his throat. "If you'll pardon me, Constable."

Smith straightened up.

"Perhaps you could explain it to me, Mr. Clemmins," Winters said.

Clemmins glanced at Smith, and then slid his eyes to one side. She wanted to slap him upside the head.

"They said they'd like to meet women."

"And?" Winters said, as cool and casual as if he were waiting for the Bell operator to connect his call.

"And." Clemmins snatched a tissue out of the box on his desk and wiped at the back of his neck. "I told them that I don't know any unattached ladies I could contact on a moment's notice. I don't think there's a red light district in Trafalgar. Is there?"

Smith said nothing—prostitution in Trafalgar was pretty much limited to casual arrangements. Women didn't walk the streets, and the police had no knowledge of any houses of ill repute. Winters, however, wasn't interested in continuing that line of conversation.

"You saw Mr. Montgomery to his car?"

"No, I'm sorry to say. Perhaps if I had he'd be sitting in his office this morning and you and I wouldn't be having this conversation. We parted outside the restaurant. Reg walked toward Elm Street, and we crossed Front. That was the last I saw of him."

"Do you know where he was parked?"

"Sorry, no. We'd come separately. I'd been here, at the site, and he'd been in town, at a meeting at city hall, or so he told me."

"So he told you. You have reason to doubt that?"

"Of course not. Reg is…was…an honest man. A great partner. We were…I mean I am…going to do great things here at Grizzly Resort."

"What did you do for the rest of the evening?"

"I took our guests to the Mess Hall on Pine Street. They were in the mood for entertainment. They'd mentioned that they liked hard rock, and a good band was playing there. I made my excuses around midnight and headed home. Leaving them behind. God, they're a couple of bores."

"Where are they staying?"

"Hudson House Hotel." Clemmins jumped as the phone on his desk rang. "That's gotta be Mr. Yakamoto. What am I going to tell him?" He buried his face in his hands. "This is a nightmare."

"The truth would be a good place to start." Winters stood up. "You might also tell him that we'll be around to talk to him in the course of our investigation."

Clemmins looked up. His face was even more ravaged than when the police had arrived.

"If you need to leave the Kootenay region for any reason, let the station in Trafalgar know." Winters placed his card on a pile of blueprints. "We'll see ourselves out."

In the outer office, Bernice was clutching the phone in one hand and sopping up tears with the other. "It's Mr. Yakamoto," she said. "Is Frank going to pick up? What am I going to say if he doesn't?"

"I suggest," Winters said, "you tell him that the office is closed for the day. And then tell your boss you're going home."

The two officers crossed the dusty parking lot to their car. Yesterday's rain was just a memory, and the heat continued to build.

"What do you think, Molly?" Winters asked, fastening his seat belt.

She twisted the key in the ignition. Heat burned in her chest. "You want to know what I think? I think this resort will be the death of this community. Not to mention the environment. They might as well buy a vacation home in downtown Toronto. That'll get them as close to nature as they'll get at Grizzly Resort. They want Disney World in B.C. and they can't see the difference."

"I meant," Winters said, "what do you think about Mr. Clemmins as a suspect?"

Smith blew out a lungful of air. That outburst had been a mistake. She could almost see him writing "over-emotional" on her evaluation. "Sorry. I think he's genuinely distressed at the death of his business partner. Not because he particularly cares on any personal level, but because this'll set the cat among the pigeons, so to speak. Mr. Clemmins might do a fine job at pimping for prospective investors, but as for building a resort? Maybe not so good."

"For what it's worth, I agree with you. But if you want to be an effective officer, and I'll go out on a limb and assume that you do, Constable Smith, you'd better learn, fast, to keep your personal opinions under control. I could hear you huffing and puffing behind me like a locomotive running out of coal when Clemmins talked about how much good his resort would do for the area."

Smith concentrated on the track ahead of her. She stopped where the construction road met the highway, and turned the air conditioning up a notch.

"Where to next?"

"We have enough time to meet with Mrs. Montgomery's lover before the autopsy, but we can't be late. Dr. Lee gets nasty when she's left waiting. You know where we can find Tyler?"

"Sure. He's my dentist." Traffic was light, and Smith pulled onto the highway.

Chapter Eight

As Rich Ashcroft expected, Meredith Morgenstern was waiting at the small airport outside the town of Castlegar when he arrived. As he'd also expected, she fell all over herself to welcome the reporter from Cable News Corporation.

But he hadn't expected that she'd be so hot.

"Ms. Morgenstern, a pleasure to meet you," he said with a wide smile and outstretched hand.

"And it is *such* a pleasure to meet you," she said, as if she were greeting Brad Pitt. "This is such an honor. I can't wait to tell my mom that you're here. She never misses *Fifth Column*."

Rich didn't care too much for the mention of Mom, but he let the comment pass. "Perhaps I'll have a chance to meet your mother after I've finished with the story."

"That would be great, Mr. Ashcroft."

"Call me Rich, please."

She giggled, and tossed her mane of black hair, like a filly let out to pasture. "I'm Meredith. Do you have to pick up your bags or anything?"

He gestured to the wheeled suitcase at his side. "I never check luggage if I can help it. It causes no end of bother if things get lost. And in our business, time is of the essence."

She preened, visibly pleased at his use of the word "our." As intended.

Even better than hot, she was young, mid-twenties. This hick town newspaper was probably her first real job.

Young, impressionable, inexperienced. And beautiful. Perfect.

The airport was so small that they only had to walk a few yards to the waiting car. It was an SUV with *Trafalgar Daily Gazette* splashed along the side.

"I thought you'd bring a cameraman," Meredith said, as Rich tossed his bag into the back.

I bet you did. "He's following. I wanted to get here without any delay."

They got into the vehicle and she pulled into the non-existent traffic.

Rich was surprised at how warm it was—he hadn't known it got so hot this far north. "Fill me in, Meredith."

"I don't know much more than I did last night," she said. "It's all in my story that was on the front page of the *Daily Gazette* this morning. Did you read it?"

Of course he hadn't read it. Irene told him what he needed to know. "Great piece," he said. "Powerful writing."

Color touched her cheeks. "I appreciate hearing that from someone of your stature, Rich. But, well, I'm wondering why an important outfit like CNC would be interested in the murder of some middle-aged guy here in B.C."

"It's like the JonBenet Ramsey business. Some stories simply need to be told. You must have found that, Meredith."

"Gosh, yes."

"Tell me about this park. The Commemorative Peace Garden?"

"I don't know why everyone's making such a fuss over it. A bunch of folks want to turn some guy's land into a public garden with a fountain in the middle. Seems like an okay idea to me."

"But it's more than a park, isn't it? I've been told that it's to honor draft dodgers. Do you have any feelings about that?"

"Nope." She pressed a button and the radio blared to life, the music hard and ugly.

"If you don't mind, Meredith, could you turn that down?"

"Sorry." She twisted a dial.

"In the 1960s and '70s some Americans, soft and spoiled, too cowardly to serve their country in Vietnam, ran to Canada. It was a disgrace that Canada let them in and even more of a disgrace when the American government forgave them once the war was over."

"Vietnam," she said. "My mom went there on a tour last year. She said it was nice."

"When their country called upon them to do their duty, they ran like rats from the light. And now this so-called peace garden is going to honor their cowardice. That can't be allowed to happen, Meredith. I'm here to ensure that the people of the United States know the real story of this garden."

"I thought you were here because of Mr. Montgomery being murdered?"

"Just between us, Meredith, I suspect his death has something to do with the park. He wanted to put a stop to it, right?"

"Yeah."

"And now he's dead. Murdered. Doesn't that make you wonder?"

She took her eyes off the road. "Seems like a bit of a stretch to me."

"How many murders were there in Trafalgar last year, Meredith?" he asked, although the answer had been in Irene's briefing notes.

"None."

"Wow, that's impressive. A good journalist looks for anything out of the ordinary. Always think outside the box, Meredith, that's my advice to you."

"You think someone who supports the garden killed Mr. Montgomery?"

"I don't *think* anything, Meredith. I'm here to investigate, that's all. We'll let the truth speak for itself. What the hell is that?"

On the side of the hill someone had spelled out a word in stones painted white: *Marywuana*.

Meredith shrugged. "It appeared about a week ago. No one knows who did it or what it's supposed to mean. Some people think it's code, and some think the writer can't spell."

"I'm guessing it's supposed to say marijuana."

"Probably."

"The police haven't removed it? You can see that sign for miles."

"The police don't much care who smokes up now and again. As long as no one's selling to kids, or there are hard drugs involved."

"What the hell. Am I in Oz?"

"Australia? Of course not, this is Canada." She slowed down as her lane took them off the highway and into town. Small businesses lined the street; the sidewalks overflowed with pedestrians and colorful flower boxes. Trafalgar looked like any one of a hundred, a thousand, small towns Rich had been to in his long career. Except for the surrounding mountains and the misspelled advertisement for marijuana.

They passed a building built of aging red stone. *1888* was carved above the door, and the modern sign over that said *Trafalgar Daily Gazette*. Meredith turned left, left again, and pulled into a parking space. "Here we are," she said, redundantly.

Dr. Louis Tyler looked nothing like a lothario. He was very short, with a round belly that made him resemble one of Santa's elves. Long strands of grey hair were draped from left to right, a failed attempt to cover his bald spot. Winters knew diners in Vancouver that could have made use of the grease from his hair. But the dentist's eyes twinkled with good humor and he greeted Smith with warmth.

"Molly, my dear, here in your official capacity, I see. In that case, I won't embarrass you by mentioning that it's been more than six months since your last visit. You want to keep that gorgeous smile, now don't you?" The dentist looked at Winters. "Is that smile not a testament to the quality of my work, sir?"

Smith's face turned as red as the silk roses on the receptionist's desk.

There was one patient in the office, a freckle-faced young woman with straight brown hair, parted in the middle, a long colorful skirt, red eyes, and a clump of tissues held to her right cheek. She glared at the interlopers.

"If I could have a couple of minutes of your time, Dr. Tyler," Winters said. "On a police matter." He smiled at the young woman, obviously in dental distress. "We won't be long, Miss."

Tyler escorted them to the back. "You see how much we need subsidized dental care. That woman should have been to see me months ago. But she couldn't afford it and now she's in for a substantially larger bill. Don't you agree, Mr. uh, what did you say your name was?"

"I'm Sergeant Winters, and you know Constable Smith."

"Please sit down. Let me ask Rachel to bring in another chair, I won't be a moment." He headed for the door.

"That's not necessary, Doctor. I'll stand," Smith said, pulling out her notebook. "This isn't a social visit."

"I suppose not." Tyler settled himself behind his desk. His office was small, tucked behind the examination rooms. The practice was decorated in soothing shades of peach and pale green; soft music came from hidden speakers. "What can I do for you, Sergeant?"

"Have you read the paper this morning, Doctor? Or listened to the news on a Kootenay radio station?"

"Never do. Nothing but shootings and stabbings and wars and famine. I'm from Manhattan originally. I fled the urban jungle and moved my bride and my practice more than twenty years ago. My family tells me that New York has improved a great deal since then, but I don't know whether or not to believe them. My mother is always trying to entice me back. More her grandchildren than me, I suspect."

Winters stepped into the flow of words. "You're unaware there was a death in town last night?"

The cheerful expression drained from his face. "Someone I know? It must be, because you're here. My daughters and my wife, I saw them at breakfast not an hour ago. Don't tell me…."

"Your family's fine, as far as we know," Smith said from her place against the wall.

The dentist blinked. "Then who?"

"You're friends with Mrs. Eleanor Montgomery?"

"Ellie? Not Ellie?"

"Mrs. Montgomery is in perfect health. Can you tell me what your relationship is with her?"

A curtain closed over Dr. Tyler's face. "We're friends."

"Good friends?"

"How do you define good, Sergeant? I meet a lot of people due to my practice and my participation in community affairs. I have good friends in New York I haven't seen in years, but there are people in Trafalgar who I dine with on a regular basis without even knowing if they have children."

"Stop prevaricating, man." The fellow couldn't say one word if a hundred would do. "I asked you a straightforward question. Answer it."

Tyler looked at a framed picture on his desk. Winters couldn't see what it contained, but he could guess. The happy Tyler family, no doubt. "Mrs. Montgomery told me that you and she were having an extramarital affair. Would you dispute that?"

Color drained from Tyler's face. Winters could almost feel the heat of Smith's interest hitting him in the back.

"Ellie can be blunt at times, Sergeant. She has scant interest in common social conventions."

"Is that a yes or a no?"

"Perhaps you could wait outside, Molly?"

"Constable Smith isn't going anywhere, Dr. Tyler, at least not until we're finished here. Did you have dinner last night at the Montgomery home?"

"Yes."

"What time did you leave?"

"Eight forty-five on the dot."

"You're sure of the time?"

"Ellie likes to keep a regular schedule."

"What time did you arrive at their home?"

"Four. I close the practice early on Thursdays and Fridays."

"That was a long dinner."

Tyler looked up. "Why are you asking me all this, Sergeant?"

"Reginald Montgomery died last night. Shortly before nine o'clock. It takes, what, five minutes to drive from the Montgomery home into town?"

Tyler leapt to his feet with such force that his chair fell to the floor behind him. The long strands of his comb-over flapped to one side of his head. "Are you accusing me of killing him?"

"Should I be?"

"This is ridiculous. Get out of my office, now. I'm calling my lawyer." He snatched up the phone.

Winters remained seated. "It is, of course, your privilege to call counsel. Although I'm asking you a simple question. What were you doing at the Montgomery home between four and eight forty-five, Doctor?"

"Fucking, Sergeant. Fucking. I was far too busy to murder anyone. My wife spends most of her time worrying about whether or not she'll ever have grandchildren, and Ellie is an open-minded, fun-loving woman." He slammed the phone down. Spittle flew from the corners of his mouth. His face had turned bright red, and a vein pulsed in the middle of his forehead. "We fucked before and after dinner. Although in my wife's favor I will admit that Ellie's cooking is barely palatable. Perhaps I should have dinner at home and then go round for dessert with Ellie, eh? I've considered it. I've started taking Viagra. It does wonders for an older man's stamina. You might want to try it, Sergeant Winters. Now unless you intend to arrest me, I have a patient waiting."

"What did you do after leaving the Montgomery home?" Winters asked, with no change in his tone of voice. Tyler clearly had anger-management problems, but so did a lot of people. Not all of them killers.

Tyler fell back into his chair, the bluster leaving him as quickly as air escaping from a balloon pricked by a needle. "I went home, Sergeant. To my wife."

"I'll need to confirm that with her, Doctor."

"You won't…you won't tell her where I was, will you? She thinks that I go to Dental Association meetings some nights. She…well, my wife is a highly strung woman. My marriage is important to me."

But not important enough to withstand the benefits of Viagra. Winters got to his feet. Hard to believe anyone could be more highly strung than the doctor himself. "Your activities prior to eight forty-five may not be relevant. If they're not," he leaned heavily on the word *if*, "we can probably avoid involving Mrs. Tyler in that discussion. Thank you, Doctor. We'll see ourselves out."

The receptionist and the patient watched with round eyes and drooping jaws as Smith and Winters strolled though the waiting room.

They took the stairs in silence. They both reached for sunglasses as they stepped out into the street.

"I think," Smith said, "it's time to find a new dentist."

"I'd like to plunge head first into the story and start interviewing people around town." Rich said to Meredith. "People who knew Montgomery. Was he married?"

"Yes."

"A grieving widow makes a great story. Set up an interview, ASAP. Then we'll tackle the peace garden angle. I'd like to meet these traitors who abandoned America when she called them. I'm counting on you to take me to them, Meredith."

"I'm not sure," she said, studying her long pink fingernails. "People don't like outsiders interfering."

"We're not interfering. We're just telling their story. I can assure you that I want to hear what everyone has to say. *Always Impartial*, that's the motto of CNC, right, Meredith?"

"I don't want to take sides."

"Nor do I. *Always Impartial.* I can tell from the story in the morning's paper that you're a good reporter, top notch. You've got your ear to the ground. I need your help on this Meredith, do I have it?"

Indecision moved behind her lovely dark eyes.

He didn't give her time to make up her mind. "We'll make a super team. Now tell me, who's the best person to talk to about this Commemorative Peace Garden?"

"Lucky Smith probably."

"Can you set up an interview with him?"

"Lucky's a woman."

"Even better. Give Lucky a call. I guarantee she'll be pleased to tell her side of the story to the audience of CNC. Early this evening would be good. My cameraman'll be here by then. Tell her that I'll have a photographer, women love that."

"I can talk to her, sure, but there might be a problem."

"Come on, Meredith, you're a journalist. Explain to this Lucky woman how important it is that America understands what she's trying to achieve here."

"It's not that, Rich. It's just that Lucky's daughter, Molly, found the body."

"How horrible for her. She needs an outlet for her stress. We'll interview her along with the mother. Play up the shock of discovering the deceased to add a human interest angle."

"That's not it. Molly's a cop. I thought she was just a beat cop, but she's assisting the sergeant in charge of the investigation. I went to high school with Molly. I'm pretty sure she'll tell her mom not to talk to anyone."

If Rich Ashcroft believed in God, he would have fallen to his knees in the parking lot behind *Trafalgar Daily Gazette* and raised his hands in thanks.

"Kootenay Boundary Regional Hospital in Trail. The autopsy's scheduled for noon. We should just make it, which will put us in Dr. Lee's good books. She hates being left waiting." Winters leaned against the headrest and closed his eyes. "Wake me when we get there."

Communities in this part of the province were small, with long stretches of undeveloped land between them. Trail was about an hour from Trafalgar but less than half-an-hour from the border with Washington State. Smith had driven down this road many times. Lucky, Samwise, and Moonlight visited family in the States. They never visited Andy's side of the family, and he didn't often come with them. When Smith was fourteen, her parental grandfather, whom she had never met, died. After that her grandmother traveled to Trafalgar every second Christmas, and sometimes Andy's sisters and their families came with her. No one ever spoke about the old man, and his years of bitterness at the son who'd abandoned not only his country but the legacy of generations of a proud military family.

The sky was blue, and the temperature indicator in the van already read twenty-nine degrees Celsius. She switched on the car's air conditioning. American tourists sometimes ran into difficulties with the change in the temperature scale as they crossed the border, thinking that twenty-nine degrees meant scarves and mittens, rather than the shorts and sunscreen required by the equivalent of eighty-five Fahrenheit.

Houses and property sporadically broke through the heavy pine forest stretching back from the road. She passed everything from tumble-down shacks to luxury mansions, sometimes less than a hundred yards apart. At the lights for the turnoff to Castlegar, a young woman, hair wrapped in a red scarf, heavy pack at her feet, stood on the other side of the intersection, her thumb out. She raised her eyebrows as the light turned green and the unmarked police van, the only car on the road, accelerated. There weren't many places you saw hitchhikers these days, and certainly not women. Other than the Kootenays, that is.

It was five minutes to noon when they arrived at the hospital. Smith found a parking spot close to the entrance and switched off the engine. When she turned to wake up Winters, he was looking at her. There was no trace of sleep in his dark eyes or the muscles of his face.

"Here we are. Trail."

"So I see. Thank you, Molly."

Smith cursed herself for an idiot. Did she always have to point out the obvious? Of course they were in Trail. Winters must have been here hundreds of times.

They walked across the parking lot, heat rising from the asphalt. One of the advantages of being a woman is summer clothes—cropped pants, light cotton T-shirts, naked arms, barely there sandals, acceptable even at work. But now that she was a cop, Smith's feet sweated in boots and thick socks, her pants clung to her legs, and her gunbelt dragged her down. She'd made the mistake of wearing a new bra, and beneath the Kevlar vest the underwire dug into tender skin. Winters, by contrast, was dressed comfortably in brown pants and a perfectly ironed cream shirt, open at the neck. The shirt wasn't tucked in, and Smith knew that it concealed his gun and handcuffs.

The hospital was quiet on a pleasant Friday morning. Her boots were loud on the freshly polished floors.

"Have you attended an autopsy before, Molly?" Sergeant Winters asked, pushing through the door marked *No Entry*.

"No." A flock of small birds searched for a place to nest in her stomach.

Dr. Lee was waiting for them. Her unbound hair fell in a sleek black waterfall. The too-large white lab coat covered her dress, and she held a Styrofoam coffee cup in her right hand.

"We're ready to begin." Lee turned, and her stiletto heels tapped like a marching band down the bright white corridor. She tossed her cup into a wastepaper basket without giving it a glance.

Smith swallowed.

"There's no disgrace in being sick or feeling faint. Leave if you have to," Winters said. He pulled a small tube out of his pocket and rubbed it above his upper lip. He held it out. "Menthol. Kills some of the smell. This body isn't old, so it shouldn't be too bad, but it's never pleasant. Take it."

Smith took it. She smiled at Sergeant Winters. *Deep calming breaths*, she said to herself, applying the balm. *Take deep calming breaths*. This couldn't be any worse than the guy who flew off his motorcycle and hit the side of the mountain head first going a hundred kilometers an hour. After having a lot to drink and telling his buddies that only pussies wore helmets.

They followed Lee through the swinging doors.

The room was filled with white light, like someone's idea of heaven's waiting room. However, unlike what Smith might hope to find in the heavenly vestibule, a slab of meat that had once been a human being lay on the table in the center of the room. He was naked, and in the indignity of death and the lights of the morgue his skin was the pale blue of skim milk. His mouth gaped open. His belly was flabby, the muscles of his arms and legs shrunken to pinpricks, genitals withered to insignificance. The table he lay on wasn't like any table Smith had ever seen. A gutter ran all around it. She tried not to think of what might be the purpose of the gutter.

A young man stood against the wall, beside an array of instruments that would have done a medieval torture chamber proud. He was almost as pale as Montgomery, and a scattering of whiskers on his chin struggled to make a goatee. He nodded greetings.

"Russ," Winters said. Smith dared not say anything.

Dr. Lee walked to Montgomery's head. She pulled an elastic band out of the pocket of her lab coat and, with one twist, bound her hair. Then she held out her hand, and Russ handed her a saw. "I've made a visual examination of the exterior of the body, and am now going to penetrate the skull." The doctor held the instrument over Montgomery's head. "If you think you are going to be sick, Constable Smith," she said, "leave immediately." The saw roared to life. "It messes up the chain of evidence if I have to pick an observer's vomit out of the cadaver's brains."

Smith put both hands to her mouth and fled.

"That wasn't nice, Doctor," Winters said, once Lee had finished her task and they'd left Russ to clean up.

"Constable Smith?" the doctor said. "Next time, she'll be better prepared. She'll last a good five minutes before running out the door. And before you know it, she'll be as cool as a cucumber, just like you."

"There's something to be said, Shirley, for people who vomit at the sight of violent death."

"Not in our professions, John."

"Probably not. Tell me what you think, before I fetch our embarrassed constable."

"Killed by a series of blows to the back of the head. No doubt by the proverbial blunt instrument. I don't see any traces of the instrument itself in the wound, which almost certainly rules out wood. Something metal, probably, and clean. Death was instantaneous or as good as. There are no wounds, other than to the head, that I can see. No defensive wounds, no sign of restraint—bruising around the wrists or ankles, for example. His last meal had been steak and potatoes and Caesar salad. Why men of your age persist in believing that a few leaves of lettuce, if they're coated with high-fat dressing, sprinkled with chunks of bacon and deep-fried bread cubes, is at all healthy, I hesitate to guess. He'd eaten less than an hour before death." Lee shrugged thin shoulders. "My report will be ready before the end of the day."

"Thanks, doc." What the hell did she mean by *men of your age*? First Tyler suggested that Winters should try the delights of Viagra and now Shirley Lee was lumping him in with the overweight Reginald Montgomery.

"Time of death?" he asked.

"Less than an hour before I got there. He was very fresh."

Lee walked away without another word. Back to her strange world of the dead.

Winters went in search of his constable.

She was sitting on a bench by the front doors of the hospital. The smokers, some of them in wheelchairs, or taking in liquids through IVs, watched her from the corner of their eyes.

"Ready to go?"

Her eyes were dry, but tinged with red. She held her hat in her hands. Strands of pale hair had escaped from the braid and caressed her face. Despite the blue uniform, the badge and gun belt, she looked like a high school cheerleader who'd just found out that her boyfriend, the captain of the football team, had been making merry behind the stands with another girl.

An ambulance sped past, under full lights and sirens.

"We have work to do back in Trafalgar," Winters said. "Let's go."

A woman edged toward them; her ears might well have been flapping. The details of her face were concealed in a camouflage of cigarette smoke.

"Can I help you, madam?" he asked.

"Just bein' friendly," she chuckled. Some of the smoke cleared, to reveal a face that was a hundred and twenty if it was a day.

Winters walked away, heading for the van. Smith would follow or not. And if not, he would be well enough rid of her.

Heavy boots fell into step behind him. "I thought I'd be ready for it. But I wasn't. I'll get used to it, soon."

"Pray you don't get too used to it, Molly. I want to drop in on Mrs. Tyler. Officers have been visiting the businesses backing onto the alley to ask what time they closed up last night, and if anyone saw anything out of the ordinary. I'm hoping that people in Trafalgar will be more accommodating to our enquires than they were in Vancouver."

"You were involved in the Sanders case, I've heard," she said, her voice and eyes filling with interest.

"The depths to which humans can fall," he said, shaking off many memories. "Alleged, of course."

"Of course. Do you want me to drive?"

The color was back in her face, and her shoulders were set and her back straight.

"I do."

Winters' phone rang as they settled into the car. He listened briefly, before hanging up with a thanks. "A wallet and cell phone matching the description of Montgomery's were found in a flowerbed a couple of blocks from the site. There was no cash in the wallet, but lots of credit cards. They're on the way to the lab for fingerprinting. Too bad, I was hoping our perp would use the cards or make a call."

"The watch?"

"Still looking. That watch is valuable. Might be that he couldn't bring himself to toss it. If he tries to sell it we'll have a good lead—I've had the description circulated to pawn shops and second-hand jewelry stores all across the province."

"Someone else might have picked it up."

"That would be a complication we don't need."

"Hi, Lucky," a voice said from the doorway. "I'm glad to find you in. Have you got a minute to chat?"

Lucky Smith glanced at her watch. Past two o'clock, and she'd missed lunch once again. The better the business did, the harder she had to work. She'd thought it would be the other way around. She pushed her glasses down her nose and rubbed her eyes. "Meredith. Hello. What can I do for you?"

Meredith's face shone with excitement, and her black hair swung as if a strong wind was behind her. "I'd like you to meet my colleague, Rich Ashcroft."

A man, too handsome by half, crossed the room and extended his hand. Lucky rose from her office chair. He was short, with a large head. Close to Lucky's age, maybe a bit more, but the lines around his eyes and the corners of his mouth were stretched tight, the effects of surgery, perhaps. His hair was thick and black, and his perfectly straight teeth were a shade of white rarely found outside of a fashion magazine. Lucky shook his hand, and her skin shivered at the damp touch of his fingers. She sat back down.

"Rich is here to do a story about the peace garden," Meredith said. She dragged a chair out of the corner and offered it to Ashcroft.

"A story?" Her interest caught, Lucky settled into her own chair. When the Commemorative Peace Garden had first been proposed, media attention had risen to a fevered pitch, to the surprise of everyone in town. Reporters from the national newspapers, even from the *New York Times* and Fox News, descended on town. But, as is the nature of media attention, they'd gone away as soon as something else captured their interest. The mayor had made it clear that he intended to approve the Peace Garden, and Lucky's committee had collapsed with a contented sigh like the master of the house settling into his lounge chair after Christmas dinner.

But it was all in turmoil again. Tom Maas died, taking his support for the gardens with him, and Reginald Montgomery looked under every rock he could find to locate embers of opposition—of which there were plenty. Linda Patterson, the interim mayor, couldn't fight her way out of a paper bag. The entire pro-park committee was expecting Lucky to do something. And she was just too darned tired.

She picked an invoice off her desk and waved it in front of her face. Would this damned heat never let up?

"What paper are you with, Mr. Ashcroft?"

"Please, call me Rich. May I call you Lucky? I'd love to know the story behind that name. Is it what your parents christened you?"

"My legal name is Lucy. Many, many years ago, I was in the drama club at the University of Washington."

"My sister went there. I wasn't so lucky. Oops, that wasn't meant to be a pun." He grinned at her, and she found herself smiling back.

"I was second string." She hesitated, but Ashcroft was looking at her with interest, as if he wanted to hear the story, and so she drifted into memories. Of when she was young, and the world was electrified with the possibility of change, and she'd been head-over-heels in love with a math major with radical opinions by the name of Andy Smith. "Just a stand-in. But the lead actor in *The Glass Menagerie* caught a dreadful cold the day of our opening. She could barely breathe, never mind project. So I took her place. And for some strange reason, I was a hit. So they called me Lucky, and it stuck." Andy Smith had been in the audience that night, leaping to his feet and cheering when Lucy

Casey took her bows. "Lucky Lucy. Lucy Lucky," her castmates had chanted when the final curtain fell. "Lucky Smith," Andy said later as they watched the lights of the city twinkling in the distance. Then he'd told her that he'd received his draft notice and was going to Canada. He wanted her to come with him. She had never acted again.

"You're interested in the Commemorative Peace Garden?" she asked.

"It's an incredible story. After all these years, you people are still looking for approval."

A warning bell rang in the back of Lucky's mind. *You people?* "The garden isn't about *us.* It's a memorial to everyone who's stood up to oppose war. Many at great cost to themselves."

"I have a cameraman due in town soon, and if we act fast I can get this story out tomorrow. Prime time. So why don't we…."

"Cameraman? You mean a photographer?"

"Yeah, a fellow who takes pictures. He's good, one of the best. He'll do your face justice."

Lucky looked at Meredith. "The local media covered this story in depth. Why the renewed interest?"

"Rich isn't…" Meredith said.

"I'd like to talk to you at the place where the garden's going to go. Get some visual background. Seven okay, Lucky?"

"Sorry, but it isn't. The death of Reginald Montgomery has changed the dynamics a bit, so the committee's meeting at my house at seven. Tomorrow morning?"

"You're getting together tonight? That's a perfect opportunity. How about I bring my photographer around and interview you all at once? The *Daily Gazette* has your address, right?"

"It's in the phone book."

"How about seven thirty, then. Hey, I've had a great idea. Let's make my visit a surprise, Lucky."

"Why?"

"You know what people are like soon as they think their face'll be on TV. Or in the papers. They'll come all dressed up, and look unnatural. I want to get the feel of a real salt-of-the-earth, middle-America planning committee."

"This is Canada."

He laughed. Lucky didn't like his laugh; she couldn't see much, if any humor in it. "I meant," he said, "America as in the generic North America sense."

"You said you're from B.C. right?"

He stood up. "I'm looking forward to this, Lucky. We can do a great story."

And he left, Meredith following with such enthusiasm that Lucky wondered why a tail wasn't wagging on her skinny behind.

She snatched up the first piece of paper that came to hand and fanned herself again. Why was the *Daily Gazette* treating this as if it were a new story? The whole thing had been hashed out for months. It was so damned hot. How could she think straight when she was so hot?

"Lucky." Duncan stuck his head into her office. "Someone from the police is here. He wants to talk to you, about when you left work yesterday. It's not Molly." His voice was tinged with disappointment, and Lucky hid a smile. Duncan was obviously smitten with Moonlight, and Moonlight blind to anything but her police career. It might be up to Lucky to do something about setting them both straight.

Ruth Tyler was delighted to receive visitors from the police. Sergeant John Winters had been the subject of gossip ever since he'd moved to town. Involved in the infamous Sanders case, it was said. So handsome, and married to Eliza Winters, the model!

Ruth showed her visitors into the living room. Winters was accompanied by the Smith girl, Moonlight. Such a ridiculous hippie name. But then Lucky Smith had always been a dreamer. And middle age didn't seem to be mellowing her one bit. Lucky's daughter was a pretty thing; Ruth would give her that, although the uniform didn't suit her. Well, it wouldn't, would it—it had been designed for a male body, and quite right too. Ruth insisted that Sergeant Winters take a seat beside the patio doors, in the best leather chair, with a view over the river.

She'd offered tea, which he politely refused. Moonlight pulled a notebook and pen out of her pockets. The girl's boots were enormous; Ruth had wanted to ask her to remove them at the door, but somehow that didn't seem a proper thing to say to the police.

Investigating the death of Mr. Montgomery, John Winters explained. Had she heard about it?

"Of course; it's all the talk in town. I'd love to help you with your inquiries, but I've never met Mr. or Mrs. Montgomery."

"Sometimes the smallest of details can help us, Mrs. Tyler," he said. "Were you home last night, say from seven o'clock on?"

"Thursday's the regular meeting of the Kootenay Kwilters Klub." Ruth spelled out the unusual spelling precisely for Moonlight to write in her notebook. "The meeting finished at seven. I stopped to rent a video, and came straight home."

"Was your husband here?"

"Louis is rarely home for dinner Thursdays. It's the Dentists Association meeting night."

"They meet once a week? Seems a lot for a professional group."

Ruth shrugged. She didn't care what Louis got up to on Thursdays. It was the one night of the week she looked forward to, when she could toss together a casual dinner, serve herself a glass of wine, or three, and settle in front of the TV to enjoy a movie he scorned as a chick flick. Louis found his Thursday meetings exhausting, and always went straight to bed once he got home.

She looked at Winters. He was a most attractive man. She smiled at him, and he smiled back. "The association does charity work, as well as discussing how to best serve the dental needs of the community."

"Highly commendable. What time did your husband get home last night?"

Ruth scrunched up her forehead and thought. Something about last night had been different. "That's odd," she said.

"Odd? How so?"

"I put on *Pride and Prejudice* while having my dinner, and, do you know, the movie was almost over before Louis came in."

"What time would that be, Mrs. Tyler?" he said. Moonlight's pen scratched against paper.

"Ten? Louis is normally quite punctual, and gets home on Thursday nights around nine. Yes, I'm sure it was ten. I didn't have to pause the movie to greet Louis and ask him how his day had been. It had just ended when I heard his key in the door. Perhaps it was an exceptionally short movie, although I don't remember it being so when I saw it in the theatre."

Ruth looked at her guests. John Winters was sitting straight in his chair, and Moonlight had stopped that annoying scribbling. "What could my movie viewing possibly have to do with Mr. Montgomery's death? I rented the video from Mike's Movie Mansion, where I always go." She stuck the index finger of her right hand into her mouth. "Oh, my god," she whispered.

Moonlight stepped toward her. "Don't be too concerned, Mrs. Tyler. We're only just beginning our inquiries. Isn't that right, Sergeant Winters?"

"Thank you for your professional opinion, Constable," he said. "Now, if you'll return to your corner and continue taking notes."

"I don't believe it," Ruth said. "You think Mike killed Mr. Montgomery. He couldn't have. I rent movies from Mike at least once a week, sometimes more. He was in his shop when I arrived, and he's always open until ten. So there. You'll have to look elsewhere for your killer, Mr. Winters."

"I'm sorry to have disturbed you." Winters got to his feet. Moonlight stuffed her notebook and pen into a pocket in the leg of her baggy pants with the blue stripe running down the leg. Winters headed toward the door, but stopped in the entranceway. "One thing more, Mrs. Tyler. I'd appreciate it if you could keep our conversation to yourself." He smiled at her while Moonlight fumbled at the doorknob. "It is highly sensitive police business, you understand."

"Of course." A shiver passed through Ruth. She would die before betraying John Winters' confidence. "I won't tell a soul. Cross my heart."

Chapter Nine

"You're back on the beat, Smith. Effective immediately."

"I only thought…."

"You thought too damned much. That woman appeared to be on the verge of telling us that she suspected her husband of murder and you decided to let her know that it didn't really matter."

Smith clenched the steering wheel. Tears gathered behind her eyes, and she blinked as rapidly as windshield wipers in a hurricane, trying to keep them from spilling over. Traffic was heavy as they drove through town. It was a summer's Friday afternoon; weekenders were pulling into town, and locals leaving work early. Her father stood in front of Mid-Kootenay Adventure Vacations, chatting to passers-by. "Mrs. Tyler didn't say a word about her husband. She thought we were after the video store owner." She'd been only trying to help. To be a good cop, and a good citizen.

"So you thought. Tell me, what would you have done if she'd admitted that her husband was the killer? Offered her a cup of tea, a shoulder to cry on?"

"With all due respect, sir, that's most unfair. Mrs. Tyler did not finger her husband. In fact she didn't even realize where your rather obvious questions were heading." Smith plunged on, realizing that she was heading for a cliff, but, like a lemming, unable to stop. She pulled into the police station parking lot, not quite understanding how she'd managed to get here. She shoved the gearshift into park. "I'd suggest, Sergeant, that if Mrs. Tyler had a single ounce of guile she'd have been onto you in a moment and be stringing us a line that would stretch all the way to Kootenay Lake." Molly Smith watched her career take wings and fly off into the clear sky. "She was so infatuated with you, she'd have admitted that Santa Claus visited last night, if that's what she thought you wanted to hear."

Winters turned in his seat. "How many years of expertise do you put behind that opinion, Constable?"

She took a deep breath. Oh, well, if she was fired from the police, she could always find work in her parents' store. "Twenty-six years. Unless you think that we spring fully formed as if from the brow of Zeus the day we leave police college. In that case I have less than one."

Winters looked out the window. Smith pulled the keys out of the ignition. She didn't know whether to get out of the car or sit here and wait until he spoke to her. Always easier to do nothing. So she sat.

"The Chief Constable seems to think you've the potential to make a competent officer," he said after a pause so long she wouldn't have been surprised if it'd started to snow. "I'm aware that you know these people, some of them very well. That's a complication I rarely came across in my years in Vancouver. But you're a police officer first. You'll arrest your grandmother if you have to. Think you can do that, Constable Smith?"

"I've thought about that. When I first decided to apply for the force, and almost every day since." With an activist mother like Lucky, Smith knew that the possibility of her arresting her own mother wasn't idle speculation. "But I want to be a police officer, Sergeant Winters, and a good one. And I want to live in the Kootenays, at least for now. So yes, I will arrest my grand-mother, should she be caught digging up a neighbor's perennial she's had her eye on, or hitting a young man with her cane if he's shown her what she thinks of as disrespect." Smith looked at her hands, twisting the car keys over and over.

"Remember your place, Molly, in the course of this investiga-tion. I'm looking to you for local commentary, not intervention. You are not replacing Detective Lopez. Do you understand?"

She understood all right. It was he who didn't. This was not the big city, where everyone kept rigidly to their assigned roles. In a town the size of Trafalgar, you had to give and take a bit. "I understand."

"I'm hoping that the preliminary report from the forensics team'll be ready, and we can hear what the officers who visited the shops backing onto the alley found out. Let's go."

As she climbed out of the car, she lifted her eyes to the mountaintops. Sunlight sparked on the snows at the top of Koola Glacier. Winters might be an overbearing jackass, but he'd kept her on the case. And that was all that mattered.

Constable Jim Denton was at the front desk. A solid, reliable cop of the old school, happy to remain a constable and to staff the desk while watching the calendar flip toward retirement. He gave Smith a smile as they came in. She tried to smile back, but it felt weak.

"Who was out questioning the shopkeepers this afternoon?" Winters asked.

"Evans, Sarge."

"Ask him to come in, will you."

"Right away, Sarge."

"Anything I need to know?"

"Several folks dropped by. Lady that lives up the mountain, name of Jenny Jones, you know her, don't you, Molly?"

Smith nodded. Everyone knew Ms. Jones, or at least knew of her.

"She came into the station."

"Wow," Smith said. "And it's only July." For more than thirty years, Jenny Jones had come into town every November, did some Christmas shopping, mailed her parcels to Montreal, and retreated back into the mountains for another year.

"She hitched a ride down," Denton said. "Came straight here because she'd seen Reginald Montgomery killed."

"I'm guessing by your lack of urgency that Ms. Jones' statement was none too reliable," Winters said.

Denton chuckled. "Saw it happen in the flames in her fireplace, she did. The killer was a dark-skinned man with dark eyes, a black beard, and a cloth wrapped around his head. Shot Montgomery in the heart."

"She had a fire," Smith said. "In this heat?"

"Old bones, she told me."

"Most amusing. Is there anything more reliable I could be working on?" Winters asked.

"A couple of calls from the people who always let us know that they're on hand to help if we need it. And that's it, I'm afraid, Sarge. The Vancouver papers called, but the CC handled them. A bike theft this morning. Lady didn't bother to lock up her bike before going into the co-op for milk, and when she came out it was gone."

Smith blanched. She'd forgotten to report her own stolen bike.

"Send Evans in when he gets here. Molly, write up your notes. Come to my office when Dave arrives."

She watched Winters head down the hall to the office he shared with Detective Lopez. Then she turned to Denton. "Speaking about bike theft, I have something to tell you."

A shout of male laughter followed Winters down the corridor. The detective's office was barely large enough for two battered antique desks. A beautiful painting of a child playing in a yellow meadow hung over one wall, a long-ago gift from a grateful citizen. Otherwise the beige walls were covered with official notices and wanted posters. A bookcase, crammed full of papers, coffee mugs, manuals, and family photographs, separated the two desks. Having worked here longer, Lopez had the desk beside the window, where he tended a row of African violets on the windowsill. They needed watering. Winters threw himself into his chair and switched on the computer.

There was an e-mail from Ron Gavin, the RCMP scene-of-the-crime officer. The report was very preliminary: they'd found nothing to indicate that Montgomery, or anyone else, had been either in the apartment above Alphonse's Bakery or on the roof in at least a week. No sign of the murder weapon, nothing in the bags of garbage behind the shops in the alley. Heavy foot traffic complicated the scene—lots of shoe and boot and paw prints, cigarette butts, marijuana butts, a coffee container, residue of dog poop. A bicycle had rested up against the door to the bakery recently—there were no footprints on top of the treads. Strands of hair had been found between Montgomery's fingers. Short hair, about an inch long, brown, no dye or hair spray used. A couple had roots still attached, so they might be able to make a DNA identification. If they could find something to match it with. Montgomery's wallet and cell phone: wiped clean.

A whole bunch of nothing.

Winters' friend in Vancouver had sent him an initial assessment of Montgomery's company, M&C Developments. Apparently a solid business, they'd built condos in Vancouver, homes in the suburbs, a small resort near Golden, a slightly bigger one in Radium Hot Springs. The Grizzly Resort development was bigger, in terms of luxury and cost, than anything they'd tried before, and they'd put themselves very far out on a limb for it.

The CC had given him Molly Smith because he thought that this killing had local political ramifications. Winters had largely dismissed the CC's initial evaluation as an attempt to cover his ass and had decided to concentrate on Dr. Louis Tyler. The man was screwing the wife of the deceased; he'd lied to the police about the time he got home the night of the murder, and he had, according to his wife, a good hour unaccounted for. The very hour at which the murder was taking place. But perhaps there was something to the political situation, after all. M&C Developments wasn't some faceless international corporation, with unlimited backing, for whom the death of an executive would be a minor speed bump on the road to riches. The death of Reginald Montgomery might well derail the entire project.

Would someone kill a man to save a bunch of Grizzly bears? This was British Columbia. Of course they would.

Winters eyed the list of numbers pinned to his wall, grabbed the phone, and punched the buttons. "Molly, get in here."

How humiliating. Someone had been murdered last night, and before she could write up her notes on the investigation she had to fill out a report on the theft of her own bike. Denton had laughed as if it were the funniest thing he'd heard in ages. It could have happened to anyone—actually it did seem to happen to just about anyone these days—but she'd look like an incompetent fool who couldn't even look after her own property at the police station, of all places. And if the press got wind of it, the Trafalgar City Police would be made to look mighty incompetent as well. The Chief Constable wouldn't be best pleased at that. Not to mention that it might be the nudge Winters needed to get rid of her.

The Ride of the Valkyries announced that her cell phone was ringing. "Molly Smith."

"Hey, Mol."

"Christa." Something else she'd forgotten. Her promise to help Christa.

"I was expecting to hear from you, Mol."

"I am so sorry. It's this case I'm working on. Montgomery. Did you read about it in the paper?"

"Yeah. I guess you're busy, eh? Never mind, it was a stupid idea."

"No, it wasn't. Charlie won't leave you alone unless you do something about it. I'm here now. In the station. Are you at home?"

"Yes."

"I'll be waiting at the front desk. And we'll put a stop to Charlie Bloody Bassing and his nonsense right now. Okay?"

"I'm working on my essay. I have to get it finished."

"You need to do this now, Christa. How's the essay going? Not well, I'd guess, right?"

"I keep thinking about Charlie."

"Move it, Chris. Now's the time. I'm waiting."

Christa gave a weak laugh. "You are so tough, Molly. You make me feel tough. I'll be right there."

As Smith pressed the button to disconnect the call, the phone on her desk rang. She didn't even have time to say her name before Winters barked into her ear.

It was mid-afternoon, but Christa was still in her pajamas. All she wanted to do was work on her essay. All she wanted to do in her life was to finish her degree.

She'd loved to learn but had hated school. And so she'd dropped out and headed for Vancouver the day she turned sixteen. After a few years of drifting between one McJob and another, she heard about distance education and correspondence courses. She knew that she could study, if she didn't have to sit behind a desk, or walk the corridors with leering boys and jeering girls. She came back to Trafalgar, leaned on her father to pay her tuition and rent and supply her with a good computer. Now she was on the verge of getting her B.A. After that, Christa was determined to go for a master's, and maybe a Ph.D. She'd find a way to make education appealing to all the lost girls like she'd been.

She ran down the stairs two at a time. The first floor brats were yelling that they didn't want grilled cheese. Their mother screamed something back about starving children in India who'd be thrilled to be offered grilled cheese. They were quick enough to threaten Christa with eviction if she so much as stepped on a loose floorboard, but didn't seem to notice that the tone of their own family would wake the dead. She threw open the door to the street.

"Hi, Chrissie. I was just passing by."

"Go away, Charlie."

She pushed past him and walked down the road, trying to keep her stride long and determined. Forceful, the way Molly walked.

He fell into step beside her.

She stopped walking. "Go away, Charlie. I do not want you around me. Never. Do you hear what I'm saying?" Most of the houses on this street were very old, some in very bad repair, broken up into flats, some gentrified to Victorian perfection. The street was moving up in the world. It was more likely that the run-down homes were being fixed up than allowed to fall further into decay. Large walnut trees cast cooling shadows onto cracked sidewalks. A fat marmalade cat streaked across the street to disappear under a crumbling front porch.

An elderly man was watering a profusion of white and purple annuals in his front garden. He watched them, water streaming from the hose in his hand like a classical statue of a peeing cupid.

"Don't talk to me like that, Chrissie," Charlie said.

Christa resumed walking. "Get lost, loser."

Charlie stopped. She turned around. The smile on his face had died.

Blotches of red began to pop up on his face. His eyes opened wide, showing too much white, and a vein pulsed at his temple. He reached out.

Christa took a step back and looked around her. At the far end of the street a car started up and drove away. The gardener had dropped his hose and gone to the back of his house. There was no one else in sight. The sun was hot on the back of her neck.

Charlie's fist closed around her arm. He pulled her close, his breath sour in her face. "Molly put you up to this, didn't she? That bitch."

"You're hurting me. Let go. Please, Charlie." All her bravado had fled, and she hated the sound of pleading in her voice.

"What's going on there?" The gardener had returned, carrying a pair of pruning shears. "Let go of her, you young punk." He held up the shears.

Charlie dropped his hand. "Mind your own business, Grandpa. We're just having a friendly chat, right, Chrissie?"

"I'm calling the police," the man shouted.

"All right, I'm leaving. I've got better things to do than stand here arguing. Tell Molly to butt out of what doesn't concern her, or the Trafalgar cops will be short one officer."

Christa watched Charlie saunter up the street, moving in and out of the dappled sunlight. His hips swayed under his oversized jeans as if he owned the neighborhood. He pulled an iPod out of his pocket and fitted it into his ears.

"Do you want me to call someone, Miss?" the gardener asked.

She let out a deep breath, and blinked away tears gathering behind her eyes. "No, thank you. He's gone."

"Punks today. Wouldn't have bothered a girl on the street in my day." He snapped a dead cane off a rosebush.

Chapter Ten

Winters had barely replaced the receiver before Smith ran into the detectives' room. She'd taken off her hat and strands of hair escaped her braid, flying around her head like the golden halo of a mischievous angel. The scowl she'd worn in the parking lot when he'd reprimanded her was gone, and in its place her face was bright with anticipation and enthusiasm. Winters scarcely remembered what it had been like to be that excited about the job.

"You called, John?" He almost expected her to snap her heels and salute.

"Take a seat and tell me everything you know about the Grizzly Resort and the Commemorative Peace Garden."

She sat in Lopez's chair and wheeled it across the room, pushing her heels into the floor. "Some people think it's a bad idea to build a big resort in that area. There's a creek runs right through there, so it's kinda like an animal highway. Others say we need the jobs and the resort'll bring in lots of tourists. Most of those people aren't from around here."

"Do you think the people of Trafalgar are mostly opposed to the resort?"

"I'd say so. But nobody would kill Montgomery to stop the resort. No point, is there? He's just the front man, right? These giant corporations have plenty more executives ready to step up to the plate."

"Remember that I've only been in Trafalgar for a couple of months, Molly. Tell me more. You're opposed to the resort?"

"We don't need more wilderness destroyed, and we don't need more outsiders coming just 'cause there are jobs here. Oops, sorry. I mean some outsiders are okay." Her cheeks turned pink. If she was to be an effective officer, Winters thought, she'd have to control that blush.

"What about the peace garden?"

"I guess I can can see people coming to blows over that. The town's divided pretty much in half about the park."

"Will Montgomery's death have any effect on negotiations for the property?"

Smith looked out the window at a cruiser pulling into the parking lot. "It might make it easier for the garden to go ahead. My mom was worried that Montgomery was influential enough to derail the plans, once the mayor died."

"Your mother?"

"She's uh…well, she's one of the people in support of the garden."

"I'd like to meet your mother."

Smith's eyes flashed blue. "My mother didn't kill Montgomery."

He raised his hands. "I didn't suggest she did. I only meant that I'd like to meet your mother to talk to her about the political situation."

"That'd be okay, I guess."

"You wanted to see me, Sarge." Dave Evans' head popped around the door.

Winters glanced at his watch. It was long past three and he was starving. "You went to the shops and homes on the alley this morning?"

"Yes." Evans looked at Smith, sitting in the detectives' office chair, her hat off, her hair mussed. His lips tightened with disapproval.

"I need to hear what you found out, but it's long past lunch time. Have you eaten, Dave?"

Evans shook his head.

"Let's go then." Winters got to his feet. "We can pick up sand-wiches on the way. Molly, get your hat. We might not be back."

Smith drove and Evans sat shotgun. She found a parking spot in front of the sandwich shop that doubled as an Internet café, and Winters ran in. Smith and Evans looked out their respec-tive windows, watching people on the street, not saying a word to each other. She knew he didn't like her. He thought she was getting ahead because of reverse discrimination. She thought she was getting ahead because she was a hard worker, whereas Evans was lazy and flippant. He was the son and grandson of senior RCMP officers, but the Mounties hadn't been hiring when he was looking, so he'd joined the Trafalgar City Police. He made sure that everyone, short of the Chief Constable, knew that he considered this job to be a stopgap on the way to something better. He looked like Dudley Doright, the stereotypical cop: tall, muscular, strong chinned, prominent cheekbones, clean shaven, short haired. Good-looking and he knew it.

The back door rattled as Winters pulled it aside and climbed in. He carried two brown paper bags, bulging under the weight. "My house, Molly. The only place in town where we can be sure of not being overheard."

Winters hadn't asked them what they liked in a sandwich, but when they settled around his kitchen table, and he unloaded the bag, Smith grinned with pleasure. Corned beef on rye. Pastrami on pumpernickel. Roast beef on a kaiser. Ham and Swiss on white. Turkey and cheddar on a baguette. Bags of potato chips and cans of pop accompanied the meal.

"My wife's out of town for a few days," Winters explained, pulling sections of paper towel off a roll beside the sink. "I have to fend for myself."

He joined them at the table. "Tell me what you found out, Dave."

"Not a lot. No one seems to have seen or heard anything. The lady who lives behind the bakery, Mrs...." He put down his sandwich and pulled out his notebook. He flipped the pages. "Mrs. Morrison, had been in her garden around five. She washed up and went to her sister's for the meeting of their bridge club. She got home around ten, and went straight to bed."

"The restaurant?" Winters ripped open a plastic packet of mustard and applied it liberally to his pastrami sandwich.

"Not all the staff working last night were there when I dropped in at lunch time. The head cook said he went out for a smoke around six thirty. Didn't see anything out of the ordinary, and after that everyone says they were too busy to even look out the window. I don't buy that."

"I sure do," Smith laughed. She swallowed a hunk of her sandwich as well as her words at the expression on Evans' face. "A busy restaurant is a busy restaurant. Once dinner service starts they don't have time to go to the can much less take a peek out the window."

"You know this, do you," Evans said, barely disguising a sneer.

"I waited tables when I was a student."

"I bow to your superior knowledge."

She wanted to slap him. Or, if not that, at least slap the sandwich out of his hand.

"What about the rest of the businesses?" Winters said. "Come on, Dave, that's a busy alley, and there was a bit of daylight left before nine."

Evans shrugged. "The bakery closes at six, the bookstore at seven. Everyone says they were gone a few minutes after. The convenience store was open at the time we're interested in, but you know that. The same guy, the Chinese fellow who was there last night, swears that he didn't go out the back and heard nothing until the police arrived. At Mid-Kootenay Adventures," Evans looked at Smith, "Mr. Smith closed at eight, stayed for a while to rearrange stock, but didn't hear anything. The same story, up and down the alley." He studied the pop selection with care, before grabbing a Coke.

"Have a bag of chips, Molly," Winters said. "My wife finds them and I'll be done for."

"Thanks." Smith licked mustard off her fingertips, wondering, not for the first time, why middle-aged men couldn't take responsibility for their own health. Her father was just as bad. His weaknesses were frozen sausage rolls and pizza pockets. He'd been known to devour entire packages at one time. Lucky kept watch over the freezer and guarded against sausage rolls as she might a cockroach.

Smith folded up her sandwich wrappings and grabbed a bag of salt and vinegar chips. While she tore the bag open, her mind pulled up a map of the alley behind Front Street. "What about Rosemary's?"

"Who?" Evans said.

"Rosemary's Campfire Kitchen. It's just off Elm, between the bookstore and Mid-Kootenay Adventures. Did you talk to Rosemary? She works all hours of the day and night. Before and after the shop's closed, Rosemary's usually there cooking."

Evans shrugged. "The girl behind the counter," he checked his notebook, "Emily Wilson, said she left at eight, soon as they closed. Rosemary locks up." He tilted his head back, and sucked at the last drops of his drink.

"So where," Winters turned from the trash can, where he'd been about to deposit the sandwich wrappings and chip packets, "is this Rosemary person?"

Evans crushed the can in his right hand. "Gone to Kelowna to visit friends. It's the busy season so she won't be gone for more than a day, Emily said."

"She left when?" Winters' voice was low. Evans sorted through the remaining chip packets.

"This morning. She did enough cooking to last the day, told Emily to look after the store, and said she'll be back tonight. Nice girl, Emily, pleased to be left in charge."

"You didn't think we need to talk to Rosemary?"

"I got a description of her from Emily. She's a middle-age widow. You know what they're like, Sarge. If she'd seen anything she'd be in a lather to report it."

Smith considered hitting Evans over the head with her truncheon. Instead she watched Winters. He didn't appear to have been all that impressed at Evans' suggestion that he would know what middle-aged women were like. By the way he spoke of her, Smith guessed that Winters was a man very much in love with a wife of many years. Sort of like she'd imagined her own parents marriage to be—until recently.

"Why," Winters asked casually, "would she be in a lather, as you put it?"

"Enjoying the excitement, of course. Nothing better to make you the center of attention than finding a murder victim on your doorstep. What?"

"Find Rosemary…what's her last name, Molly?"

"Fitzgerald."

"Find Rosemary Fitzgerald, Dave. Your friend Emily should have a number for her. I want a report of what she has to say before five."

"If she'd seen something, she'd have told us…."

Smith's cell phone rang, and she turned away from the table to answer. It was the station.

"Smith."

"Molly, there's a young lady here. Says you were supposed to meet her."

She'd forgotten Christa. Smith glanced at Winters. He was looking at her, one eyebrow raised. "I'll be right there, Jim."

"What's up?"

"I have to get back to the station. A woman's come in to make a complaint about a stalker and she wants to speak to me."

"We're ready. I want to pay another visit to the dentist. His wife's failure to provide him with an alibi puts him firmly in the frame. Meanwhile, Constable Evans, you'll be making a phone call, am I right?"

Evans mumbled something.

"Go back to the restaurant at six to question the dinner shift," Winters said. "And in the meantime, you might pay another visit to some of the shops and houses backing onto that alley. Middle-aged women can be highly observant, I've found."

Chapter Eleven

Rich wanted lunch. Meredith suggested a French place in the center of town. From what he'd seen of Trafalgar, Rich figured that everything was in the center of town. They walked a few blocks from the paper, past George's Diner, which looked like somewhere locals went for a reasonably priced home-cooked breakfast or lunch, to Feuilles de Menthe, a perfect tourist trap. He'd asked Meredith to take him somewhere that would give him a feel for the town. Plop this place down in New York, and he'd get a good feel for Manhattan.

At three thirty, the patio was almost empty. The waiter escorted them to a table for four in a back corner.

"Nice," Rich said. The restaurant was located on the town's main street. The patio jutted out into the street, cutting off a section of parking. Windowboxes overflowing with petunias and variegated ivy spilled down the freshly painted white picket fence enclosing the patio. Vehicles moved slowly and the sidewalks were heavy with foot traffic. Sunlight and small boats played on the blue water. The mountains surrounded the town in every direction, making it feel as if they were sitting in the bottom of a wide-bottomed, green and blue pasta bowl.

Two young women walked by, long straight hair parted in the middle, hanging loosely down their backs. Brightly patterned skirts flowed around their ankles. Their sandals were thick and practical.

"Haven't seen outfits like that since the Sixties," Rich said.

"This is Trafalgar."

The waiter arrived with the menus. "Hey, Merry," he said. "How's it goin'?"

"I'll have a glass of white wine, please," she replied, obviously mortified at having been recognized by what was probably some nerd from her high-school days.

"Ice water." Rich studied the menu. "One thing I'll say for the surrender monkeys, they know how to cook."

"The what?"

"The French. This is a French place, right?" The printed menu was large and ostentatious, the selection small and select.

"The chef's from Los Angeles. The paper did a spread on him when he arrived."

"I'm going to have the paté followed by lamb shanks." He closed the menu. "Order what you want, the company's paying."

Rich's phone rang. He pulled it out, said a few words and snapped it shut. "That was Greg, my cameraman. He'll be landing in an hour. He'll grab a car and meet us at my hotel. Plenty of time to meet up and head out to the Smith place for the interview."

A dark van pulled to a stop in the line of cars waiting for the lights at the corner to change. The driver wore a cop's uniform, but she was one pretty girl. Two men, one in uniform, were with her. She half raised her hand in greeting to Meredith. The light changed and she drove away.

"Let me guess," Rich said. "That was Smith."

"Wow. How'd you know that?"

"Observation and experience."

His paté arrived, pink and plump, served with browned toast points.

"I have to ask." Meredith glanced around to ensure no one was listening, before taking a hearty swig of her wine. "You sort of suggested to Lucky Smith that you were local. Like from the Kootenays."

Rich coated toast with paté and took a bite. Liquid velvet spread across his tongue. "That was to make her more comfortable. Trust me on this, Meredith. CNC has such an enormous audience that people, not the elite political types who crave the attention, but salt-of-the earth folks such as Mrs. Smith, get scared at the idea of such exposure. I find it works better to gradually lead them to understand what a wide audience they'll be getting from me."

"I guess," she said. But she drew out the last word in such a way that he knew she wasn't totally convinced. Her glass was already empty. A sign of nerves. Rich snapped his fingers to attract the waiter's attention, and ordered another.

"It's like this, Meredith. You go running in there, thrusting the CNC logo in their face, and people draw back. Heck, once upon a time I'd have been afraid of CNC too. How would you feel if you were just a common-and-garden housewife about to be featured on a program like *Fifth Column*?"

"Intimidated."

"Right. Mrs. Smith and her friends would be intimidated if I told them straight out that I'm with CNC. I decided to ease into it, introduce my cameraman, explain that we want to capture their story so all of America can understand. She'll be much more relaxed that way. I'm sure you've found, Meredith, that a comfortable interview goes so much better, not only for the benefit of the interviewer but for the subject. And that comfort transfers itself to the audience. What business are we in, Meredith?"

"What?"

"You and me. What's our business?"

"Reporting?"

"The truth is our business. Our job is to dig until we arrive at the truth. And then we continue with our job to ensure that the American citizen is informed of the truth. The truth, the true story. There is no higher calling." Sometimes Rich Ashcroft impressed himself with his rhetoric. He'd go into politics if it didn't pay so badly.

"I guess. But this is Canada."

Okay, that was a mistake. Easy to rectify. "The average Canadian's included in that, of course. I meant all the citizens of the world."

Meredith leaned back to allow the waiter to put their plates on the table. "I hadn't looked at it that way. It's great working with you, Rich. I'm learning so much already."

"Will you look at that," Rich said. A man with a sarong wrapped around his waist passed them. His feet were bare, he carried a guitar, and his head bobbed to music that no one else could hear.

Meredith dragged spinach leaves through the dressing at the bottom of her bowl. "That's Trafalgar," she said. "Do they have any job openings at CNC?"

By the time they got back to the station, Christa had left.

"She looked mighty steamed," Denton said, "when I told her you weren't here."

"How long ago was this?"

"Fifteen minutes maybe."

"Call Tyler's office, Molly," Winters said. "Tell him we're coming around to talk to him."

Smith had tried to get her friend to come in and report Charlie, and when Christa did, she, Smith, blew it. Christa could have said something to Jim Denton, but she didn't: sometimes she depended too much on others to tell her what to do. "I need to call my friend, John. It's police business, really."

He looked at Denton. The desk constable shrugged.

"Get Tyler's office, first. You can call while I'm checking my e-mail."

Dr. Tyler, Smith was informed, had just begun surgery. He'd be occupied for at least an hour, probably an hour and a half. "Is everything all right, Constable Smith?" the receptionist asked, trying to sound helpful, but pretty much fishing for gossip.

"Tell Dr. Tyler that Sergeant Winters will be around at five thirty to speak to him. If he finishes surgery earlier than that, have him call us." Smith rattled off the number of the police station.

"I will, Molly. Perhaps I can help you in the meantime. Are you interested in Dr. Tyler's schedule for yesterday?"

"Not at this time, thank you," Smith said.

She hung up. "Dr. Tyler's reputation in this town is toast." She told Denton what happened at the dentist's office earlier. "If the patient in the waiting room doesn't run and tell her friends every juicy detail, his receptionist certainly will."

Denton laughed.

Winters came out of the back. "Let's hit the road."

Smith explained that the dentist was operating. Pretty much the only time the police couldn't march in and arrest someone was when a doctor had a patient sliced open in front of him or her.

"In that case, I'm going to see Lucky Smith, and you, Constable Smith, cannot sit in on that interview. Where can I find your mother?"

"She's probably at work."

"Where's that?"

"Mid-Kootenay Adventures. My parents own the store."

"There wasn't anything in my e-mail on Montgomery. While I'm out, call Vancouver and ask for Rose Benoit, mention my name, and ask her to find out what they know about him. Clemmins as well. Then start digging into the both of them. I need to know if they've ever been in any trouble. Clemmins looks like he has a past with a bike gang, but appearances are not always meaningful. Check on Tyler while you're at it. He's from New York. It'll take a while to get an answer, but see if there's anything to find there."

Smith groaned without making a sound. Back to the desk work. "About Tyler?"

"Yes?"

"Don't you think someone should go over there and wait outside the surgery? He might make a runner."

"He's on my suspect list, for the moment, but I can't see him taking off. Too much the solid citizen. Private practice, family, house. If he's the guy we're after, he'll be counting on me being too dumb to figure it out, and if that fails, a first-class lawyer to get him off. Tyler will be waiting for us at five thirty, highly indignant at having his life disrupted. I'll walk to your mother's place. Be ready to go to Tyler's at five twenty. Jim, call me if Tyler calls earlier, but I doubt he'll be considerate enough to let us know when he's free."

Winters stepped back to allow a woman through the door. Her deep black hair clashed with the network of heavy lines running across her face. She wore a pink and green shorts and T-shirt set and a straw hat with a pink band. She carried a small white dog under her right arm and waved a piece of paper in her left hand. An indignant dog owner fined for bringing her pet into town. Tourists were usually let off with a warning, but Dorothy Blanchard insisted on breaking the law, and at least once a week she marched into the station, waving her ticket in the air, pretending she'd never seen such a thing before.

"Can I help you, madam?" Denton said, pretending he'd never seen her before. Smith made her escape.

The constable's room was, as always, a jumble of coffee cups, pop cans, papers, and computer equipment. A stack of binders on top of a bookcase threatened to tumble onto the floor. Someone's dry cleaning, a dress uniform wrapped in plastic, hung on a filing cabinet. The TV mounted high on the wall showed the front door—where nothing was happening. The office was empty, as usual. Constables were expected to be out on the road, using the computers in their cars, not leaning back in chairs, feet up.

The window looked out onto George Street. Sunlight and dust mites performed a waltz in the air. Smith pulled up a chair and logged onto a computer, thinking about Winters' interview with her mother. Time was, she'd heard, Lucky Smith wouldn't have given a police officer the time of day. But Lucky had mellowed with the years, and the times, as her hair lost its fiery red and her face settled into lines of responsibility, and Molly Smith was sure, well, as sure as she could be, that her mother would do what she could to answer Sergeant Winters' questions.

She called the Vancouver Police, identified herself, and asked to be put through to Inspector Rose Benoit. A surprisingly strong New York accent answered on voice mail. Smith left her message and disconnected.

Christa. Oh, for heaven's sake, she'd forgotten. Again. She dialed Christa's cell. The phone rang four times before it was answered.

"Mol, is that you?"

"Sorry I missed you, Chris, but I got called away. I hoped you'd wait for me," Smith lied.

"I understand you're busy. What with such an important job and all. But so am I, you know. I can't hang around waiting for you all day. I have to get back to my essay. It's going to be the best thing I've ever done. I'll send it to you when it's finished and you or your mom can check it over before I submit it."

"Come back. I'm here, at the station, and we'll get the restraining order started."

"No, thanks Molly, but I've heard that restraining orders are useless anyway. Ideas are filling my head, and I have to get them down before they decide that I'm not interested in them and fly away."

"Chris, please. Let us help."

"You know what I'm going to treat myself to? Butter chicken with dhal and rice. Just the thing for an all-nighter, finishing up that essay. Look for it in your inbox tomorrow, Mol."

"You're making a mistake, Chris, and if I could tie you up and stuff you in the back of the cruiser and drag you here, I would. But as I can't, enjoy your dinner. Call me if you need anything."

"You'll be there, right, Mol? Like you were an hour ago when that fat cop told me you'd left and he didn't know when you'd be back."

"That's not fair." But Smith knew that it was perfectly fair. She'd failed Christa. Again. "I was out on a call."

"A more important call than me. Hey, I understand. I still expect you to edit my paper. Bye."

The dial tone rang in Smith's ear.

◇◇◇

At first glance Lucky Smith looked nothing like her daughter. The Smith Winters knew was tall, slender, a pale blue-eyed blond. The mother was short and plump. Her curly red hair, as fluid as a river in flood, crossed by streams of gray, flowed every which way around her head. Green eyes, a cluster of freckles spilling across the bridge of her nose. But when he looked again, the resemblance was there. The high cheekbones, the firm set of the chin, the shape of the eyes.

Winters had identified himself to a young man lounging behind the cash register, flicking through a mountain biking magazine. The boy was darkly tanned, short brown hair streaked from the sun. He wore a sleeveless T-shirt and baggy surfer shorts. His eyes widened; he dropped the magazine and lifted up his hands. "Hey, man," he said. "I ain't doin' nothin'."

"What's your name?"

"Duncan. Duncan Weaver. I work here. I was out on the river with a tour. Just got back."

The boy was so nervous, he probably had a stash of marijuana in his back pocket. Not Winters' concern. "I'm looking for Mrs. Smith."

Weaver let out a sigh that would have filled a child's birthday balloon. "You're here about the murder, right? I already spoke to the cop who came around asking about it. I was wondering why you've come, that's all."

"Is Mrs. Smith in?"

"She's in the back. How come Molly didn't come?"

"Who?"

"Molly Smith, you know her, right? I was thinking that Molly'd be the one to come in and ask us questions. She's the beat cop around here, you see."

"Yes, I see. Mrs. Smith?"

The bell over the door tinkled. A man headed for a display of water bottles.

"If you see Molly, can you tell her to drop in? I don't know anything about that killing, but if she lets me play with her handcuffs, I'll make something up."

Winters looked at him. "Is that supposed to be funny?"

The boy shrugged. "Can't you understand a joke, man? Lucky's office's through that door." He pointed. "Knock first."

Winters knocked.

Lucky's desk was piled so high with papers that the whole mess threatened to tumble onto the floor. John Winters was almost psychopathic in his hatred of paper. He had to keep his own desk in perfect order or he'd break into a panic. When he was a rookie Vancouver cop, he'd had a situation: a man who hated heights so much that when he somehow found himself on Capilano suspension bridge, he'd tried to throw himself off, simply to get the terror over with. Looking at Lucky Smith's desk, Winters understood what the man had been going through.

"I don't know if I can help you," Mrs. Smith said, after offering her visitor a chair. Winters tore his eyes away from the mess of papers. "Dave Evans was here earlier. I told him I left shortly after four yesterday, long before closing."

"Mr. Montgomery was known to be opposed to the Commemorative Peace Garden, to which, I've been given to understand, you're a prominent advocate."

"Did my daughter tell you that?"

"It seems to be common knowledge."

"No reason for it not to be. I want to see the park become a reality. Tom was about to sign the papers. But he died, and the town council said they wanted to reassess the situation. Cowards, all of them." Lucky's eyes burned with green fire. "I won't pretend that I liked Reginald Montgomery. Foul man. Comes out of nowhere, and tries to tell people who've lived here most of our lives how to run our town. His horrid resort was bad enough, but then he decided that the peace garden would be an impediment to investment."

"You're pleased at Mr. Montgomery's death, then, Mrs. Smith?"

"Don't put words in my mouth. I'd have been pleased if he'd taken his foolish project and gone home. I am not pleased when a man dies prematurely." She gathered stray tentacles from the back of her neck and stuffed them into the clip holding her hair in place. "No one calls me Mrs. Smith. I'm Lucky. Or Lucy, if you prefer to be more formal, John." She picked a piece of paper off the desk and waved it in front of her face.

Winters hid a smile. The room was cool, the windows shaded, a large fan spinning in the corner. Younger officers might take Lucky's sudden rise in temperature as a sign of a woman with something to hide, but he knew she was having a hot flash. Although Eliza was several years younger than Lucky, she'd begun to suffer from them. They got worse, she told him, under stress of any sort: difficulty screwing a light bulb in would have her drenched in sweat.

Not for the first time, he thanked his stars that he hadn't been born female.

"You know everyone involved in planning the peace garden," he said. It wasn't a question.

"I do. And I can assure you that we're not going to bump anyone off to achieve our objective."

"Pardon me, Lucky, but I think we both know that there are people in many situations who will go to almost any length to get what they think's right."

"So I've heard."

"I'm ready to believe you'd do everything possible to promote the park you so obviously care about. Within the bounds of the law. Am I right?"

Now it was Lucky's turn to try to hide a smile. "Not entirely, John. The bounds of the law as defined by a bunch of white men in suits don't mean too much to me. But the bounds of morality and living together in what we call civilization do."

"Do you know anyone who'd step outside those bounds, Lucky, to stop Montgomery?"

"Will this heat never end? You've been honest with me, John. So I'll be honest with you. In my own circle of citizens, those opposed to the Grizzly Resort and those in favor of the Commemorative Peace Garden, and they're pretty much one and the same, I'd be astonished if anyone committed an act of physical violence against people opposed to our aims."

Winters settled back into the uncomfortable chair facing Lucky Smith's cluttered desk. This woman knew how to choose her words.

"And people outside of your circle of citizens?"

She grinned. She was attractive, in an earth mother sort of way, her hair un-dyed, her face un-made up, her nails chewed to the quick. Clothes chosen for comfort rather than style. "I'm not going to accuse anyone, nor am I going to name names based on rumor and conjecture."

"Which tells me that rumor and conjecture have something to say."

"Trafalgar is a strange town. It attracts a lot of strange people. There probably are people in town who'd consider killing Mr. Montgomery over his resort, although maybe not over the peace garden. Most of the people who favor the garden are aging hippies like me, long past days of violent resistance. Even some of the men Larry O'Reilly wanted his garden to honor, men like my husband, men who had the courage to abandon all for their values rather than be sucked into the war machine, want to let it go. Let the past be past, they say.

"Environmental issues, however, may be another matter. I'll admit that some people might be prepared to go to extremes."

"You know these people?"

"I know of them. I know of a lot of people, including those who claim they've been abducted by space aliens."

As a boy, Winters had been considered a good chess player, usually beating his dad and Uncle Joe, and most of the members of the high school chess club. But when he'd joined the club at University he soon dropped out: he couldn't begin to outthink the people he was expected to compete against.

Talking with Lucky Smith gave him the same feeling.

"If you think you know someone who might have killed Reginald Montgomery in a dispute over his resort, you need to tell me. I'm not looking to railroad anyone."

"Fortunately for you, John, whether or not I believe you is irrelevant. My daughter's assisting in this investigation?"

Winters nodded.

"I believe in Moonlight's integrity," she said.

Winters felt himself veering off track. Was this competent, intelligent, skillful woman about to turn airy-fairy on him? "Please don't tell me that your astrology readings have advised you to cooperate, Lucky. The light of the moon has nothing to do with any of this."

The edges of her mouth turned up. "My daughter's name is Moonlight. As I may have mentioned, I'm an aging hippie. When she was born, the light of the moon outside my window shone on freshly fallen snow. She was so fair, as if reflecting the scene outside. Do you have any children, John?"

"No."

"A blessing and a curse, all at the same time. Two outsiders arrived in town a couple of months ago. Stuffed full of rhetoric about animal rights and the spirituality of the untouched wilderness. The sort who talk about the noble Native Canadian but have never bothered to actually meet one. They were quick to badmouth citizens' groups, such as I belong to, as too arthritic to accomplish anything." Lucky fanned the back of her neck. "There are people who believe in fighting for animals against people. I may not always disagree with them, but one can cross the line."

Winters said nothing.

"You understand I'm making no accusations. Just chatting."

"Why are you not a lawyer?"

Winters meant the question to be rhetorical. Lucky didn't take it so. "Because I got pregnant with my son Samwise, and because Andy was on the run from the Selective Service and without government-sponsored child care and…."

"Please, Lucky. The point."

"Kevin Sorensen and Robyn Goodhaugh. Very, very passionate animal rights types, although I suspect he's just following her lead. Robyn's been heard to say, or so I've been told, that the Grizzly Resort is equivalent to the opening of the earth down to hell. The Hellmouth, she calls it."

Chapter Twelve

"Your mother told me your full name."

"Oh for God's sake." Smith slapped the steering wheel. She was trying to make her way through the world as a competent adult. A cop, no less. That god-awful name haunted her. "It's completely embarrassing."

"I thought it was nice," Winters said. "The exhausted, but thrilled, young mother looking out her window and seeing the light of the moon reflecting onto freshly fallen snow."

"Moonlight's not so bad, I guess. But they had to follow it up by a ridiculous name from *The Lord of the Rings*."

She could tell by the look on his face that she shouldn't have mentioned it. "My mom didn't tell you my middle name, did she?"

"No." He was smiling now; it made him look almost likeable.

"Legolas." She practically spat out the word. "A fey elf. One of the Fellowship of the Ring. Utterly humiliating. In school one of the teachers suggested that I try out for the archery team. I considered showing her an arrow, all right."

Her parents had been *Lord of the Rings* fans back in the day. Smith's brother Sam was a hotshot corporate lawyer in Calgary. She wondered if his blue-blood wife knew that his proper name was Samwise. When the *Lord of the Rings* movie came out a few years ago, Smith had been horrified to see that the actor playing the elf Legolas bore a strong resemblance to her. Tall, lean, thin face, high cheekbones, long, straight blond hair the texture of corn silk. She had not gone to see it.

Sergeant Winters laughed. It was a deep, hearty laugh, straight from the diaphragm. She felt a smile tug at her mouth.

"We all have our crosses to bear, Molly. I had a classmate who gloried in the name Robin Hood. His parents should have been shot."

When they walked into the dentist's waiting room, the wide-eyed receptionist buzzed the doctor without a word.

All of two seconds passed before he made an appearance. The dental hygienist peeked out from a side room.

"I'll be making an official complaint about this harassment." Dr. Tyler was puffed up and full of his own self-importance. Smith decided on the spot that he wasn't guilty of the murder of Mr. Montgomery. If he were, surely he'd be a bit more ingratiating.

"That is, of course, your privilege, Dr. Tyler," Winters said. "But if it would make you more comfortable, we'll continue this discussion down at the station."

Tyler deflated slightly. "I wouldn't want to take up your time." He turned on his receptionist. "Shouldn't you be going home, Gloria? It's past closing."

She yanked at a drawer in search of her handbag. It fell to the floor with a clatter. Pens, highlighters, markers, a stapler, packets of brightly colored Post-it notes, and a heavy-duty tampon spilled out. The hygienist laughed.

Tyler spun around. "The office is closed," he yelled. "If you repeat anything you heard here today, you'll be fired, the both of you."

The women grabbed lunch bags and purses and scrambled for the door. Smith's brother had once briefly dated Rachel, the hygienist. They exchanged glances, and Rachel tripped over a loose bit of linoleum.

"Common gossips, both of them. It's difficult to get competent help in this damned town," Tyler said.

Smith pulled her notebook out of the pocket at her thigh.

Winters got to the point. "I spoke to your wife earlier."

Tyler threw himself into the receptionist's chair. He didn't offer his visitors a seat. "A boring conversation, I'm sure." He spun the chair around in circles.

"Don't make too much fun of this, Doctor. Murder is a serious business."

Tyler studied his nails.

"You told me," Winters said, "that you were with Mrs. Montgomery until eight forty-five and then you went home."

"Which is what happened."

"Your wife says you didn't get in until after ten."

He stopped spinning. "She's mistaken."

"She seems sure. Do you agree, Constable Smith?"

"Ten it was, sir. She was positive."

"Some evenings, when I'm not home, my wife enjoys more wine than perhaps she should."

"What did you do after leaving Mrs. Montgomery, Doctor?"

The dentist stood up. He patted his comb-over and wiped his hand down the side of his trousers. He looked at Smith.

"Dr. Tyler, can you answer the question?".

"Nothing. I did nothing. I went for a drive. I was emotionally unsettled."

"What caused you to become emotionally unsettled?"

"Can't you just accept that I went for a drive and got home around ten-ish?"

"I can't just accept anything. If you don't tell me where you were between eight forty-five and ten o'clock last night, I will consider you a suspect in the murder of Reginald Montgomery."

Tyler blanched. "I drove up the mountain. It was a clear night. I like to look at the lights from Eagle Point Bluffs when I have things to think over. I sat in my car at the side of the road for a while."

"What were you thinking over?"

Tyler shook his head. "Personal problems."

"Nothing's personal, I'm afraid, in a homicide."

Tyler blew out a breath of air. "You won't tell anyone, will you?"

"Not if it's not relevant to the investigation."

"Molly?"

"Get on with it, man." Winters' patience snapped like a rubber band loaded with a spitball. "Constable Smith is not here to collect gossip."

"I was considering asking Ellie to leave Reg and come with me. We have children, Ruth and I. It's a big decision."

"If you have to leave town, Doctor, call the station and let us know. We wouldn't want to have to try to locate you. We can find our way out."

"You're not arresting him?" Smith asked as they walked to the van. A shiny grey Mercedes SUV was the only other car in the lot.

"I don't think he did it. The man was having an affair with the wife of a prominent businessman. An affair that you yourself told me was common knowledge. Probably to everyone but the husband and wife of the participants. I'll bet he did have a lot to think about."

Smith flicked the door opener of the van and the inside lights came on. She glanced at Winters. His face was tight and drawn. "I've made mistakes," he said, "more than a few. But unless Doctor Tyler won an Academy Award that he's keeping secret, he isn't that good an actor. When we spoke to him earlier, he didn't seem to have a clue what we were there for. Said he hadn't heard of the Montgomery killing." He fastened his seatbelt. "I'm not dismissing him as a suspect, but I see no reason to drag him, and what'll probably be an excellent criminal lawyer, down to the station. Not yet anyway. Call in and find out what Tyler drives, Molly. That fancy new Merc, I'm guessing. I'll send someone up to Eagle Point later to ask if any of the dog walkers saw him there last night."

A group of barefooted, dreadlocked, tie-dyed-T-shirt-wearing young men and women had gathered in front of Big Eddie's Coffee and Bagel Emporium at the corner of Elm and George streets. A man squatted on the pavement, pounding on a home-made drum clenched between his splayed knees; a tall, lithe woman shook a tambourine, her hair moving with the rhythm.

Two people of indeterminate gender swayed to the music, and a white dog looked very bored.

Winters rubbed his eyes.

"You okay?" Smith asked, not sure whether she should appear to have noticed. She didn't know what her relationship with Winters was, and was afraid of making a misstep. Winters, she suspected, liked to work alone.

"Just tired. It's been a long day, and it's nowhere near over yet. I need to talk to the gentlemen Clemmins and Montgomery had dinner with last night. Highly unlikely that Clemmins would use business acquaintances as a fake alibi, but no stone unturned, eh?"

He gave her a weak smile, but the cloud behind his eyes didn't go away. He turned his face toward the window.

For the nineteenth time in the past twenty minutes, Lucky Smith looked out her kitchen window.

"I've never seen you like this," Michael said with a chuckle. "Calm down, Lucky. You told them seven thirty. It's not even quarter past."

"Don't know why I'm so nervous. It's not as if we haven't spoken to the press before." She turned from the window. They were sitting around her scrubbed pine kitchen table, exchanging nervous glances. "Perhaps it's because Barry isn't here," she said.

"Barry's not coming?" Jane Reynolds said. "What's happened?"

"He called me just before you got here. Marta was seeing him to the door, and she tripped over a dog toy and fell down the stairs. She might have sprained her ankle, so they've gone to the hospital."

"Is it a problem? That Barry isn't here?" Norma McGrath asked.

Several voices murmured. They were ten, and Lucky's kitchen table was large enough to accommodate all of them with room to spare.

Lucky said nothing. It was Barry who'd left an arm in Vietnam. Barry who gave their group the gravitas it needed in the face of the media. Jane had a half-century of activity in the peace movement, but age was quickly overtaking her, and she looked and sounded too much like someone's dotty grandmother. Joe had escaped the draft, but he was so tongue-tied that the press didn't bother with him. Michael never talked about his past, and Lucky didn't quite know why he was here. She hadn't told Andy the press were coming to interview the group—he would have just told her to let it go. Tonight, it was up to Lucky Smith to make their case. Vehicle lights washed across the driveway. She swallowed a glass of wine in one quick gulp.

It was long after midnight when Winters dropped Smith off. They'd spent the night moving between the alley south of Front Street and Eagle Point Bluffs, looking for someone who'd seen either a disturbance behind the bakery or Dr. Tyler brooding alone in his car.

No one they spoke to had been in the alley at the time in question. The restaurant staff was kept under such tight control, by a chef so tempestuous that he'd been fired from Food TV that they didn't dare so much as to take a breathing break. The dog walkers had all been either early or late yesterday. On Thursday night, the alley behind Alphonse's Bakery might well have been on the far side of the moon as far as the good citizens of Trafalgar were concerned.

At the park overlooking the lights of the town far below and the black shapes of the mountains all around, courting couples had been busy with their own interests—watching the stars twinkle overhead, apparently.

All in all, it had been a fruitless night. But Smith did allow herself to get her hopes up, just a smidgen, that she was making some headway with Sergeant Winters, proving to be a good detective. Or, at least, a competent detective's assistant.

Her mom was sitting at the kitchen table, dressed in the loose tank top and cotton shorts she wore as pajamas. Her head was cradled in her hands, and her shoulders shook.

Smith fell to her knees and grabbed Lucky's hands. They were as cold as the snow on Koola Glacier. "Dad," Smith said, "where's Dad?"

"The hell I know." Lucky lifted her head. Tears ran down her face. "Did you see it?"

"See what?"

"The program."

"Help me here, Mom. I don't know what program you're talking about. I was working, not watching TV."

"He set us up, Moonlight. Like lambs to the slaughter. And Meredith Morgenstern sprinkled bread crumbs to show him the way."

"Mom, please. I don't know what you're talking about. Who set who up, and what does Meredith have to do with anything?"

Lucky pointed to the door leading out of the kitchen. "Go watch. I taped it. It's bad, Moonlight. I've been a fool."

Smith scrambled for the small TV in the family room that was older than she. A tape was in the VCR player. She rewound it for a few seconds and pressed play. "Good night from Rich Ashcroft, in Trafalgar, Canada." A commercial for a North American car began—the car, and the ad, indistinguishable from every other. Smith rewound the tape for about fifteen minutes' worth.

She watched in increasing horror. The last portion of *Fifth Column with Rich Ashcroft* featured the town of Trafalgar.

Which, the viewer was told, was the scene of a brutal murder. A still shot of Montgomery throwing a fishing line into a river appeared on the screen as the narrator talked about Montgomery's love for the Mid-Kootenays. The camera pulled back to reveal Ellie Montgomery holding her husband's photograph. She was beautifully made up, her blouse a match to the solid black of her perfectly arranged hair. "My husband," she said, wiping away a tear, "said it wasn't right that a small group of people should be allowed to tie Trafalgar to the past." She lifted a pure white handkerchief to her eyes. "He believed in looking to the future, Reginald did. Always." It was the first bit of emotion the widow had displayed over her husband's death.

The coroner told Winters that Ellie identified the body with as much feeling as if she'd been picking out a steak for supper.

Lucky Smith was photographed from below in poor light. All dark shadows, wild grey hair, wrinkles, hooded eyes. Normally, Lucky talked in compound sentences, thoughtful pauses, deep ideas. The film was so chopped up she sounded like a lunatic. The other members of the committee weren't treated much better: Norma McGrath said something about the importance of listening to spirit guides, and a man grimaced into the camera and shouted about the resurgence of fascism, while displaying bad teeth. Scenes of Trafalgar interspersed the interviews. Then a handsome, dark-haired man came onto the screen. The lights of the city twinkled in the background, and the Upper Kootenay River flowed toward the sea. "Here," he said, spreading his arms wide, "in this bucolic community, on the banks of this peaceful river, are the sad remnants of men who abandoned their country in wartime. And now they want to build a memorial to that shame. The city council's doing all it can to stop it."

Deputy Mayor Patterson popped up on the screen. She was at a barbeque lunch at a children's summer camp. "The Peace Garden," she said, accepting a hot dog from a smiling volunteer, "has to be stopped." Several bites of the hot dog had disappeared between one half of her sentence and the other.

"They need," Ashcroft said, his voice low and serious, his eyes intense, "your help."

"Whoa—kay." Smith flicked the video off. She turned to see her mother in the doorway. Lucky's arms were wrapped tightly around her body, her face drawn. Tracks of tears ran down her cheeks.

"That is seriously bad stuff. Where's Dad?"

"I. Do. Not. Know."

"Have you tried calling him?"

"His phone's off. He might be out of town."

"Did you leave him a message?"

"No."

Smith dug her cell phone out of her pocket.

"What channel was that program on?"

"CNC."

"CNC! Mom, what were you thinking? Anyone could have told you that they wouldn't be at all fair. They're so right wing, you can't even see them from where you're standing." She punched in the number for her father. The tinned female voice of the operator came on immediately. Smith hung up.

"How was I supposed to know that? I've never watched it."

"Didn't anyone in your group tell you?"

"He implied that he was from Vancouver, and Meredith didn't contradict him. Michael was a bit suspicious, but we were rushed into it. It's all my fault; I insisted on going through with it. I assumed that any news program would present both sides."

"Oh, Mom."

"They didn't interview anyone on the other side. He said tomorrow he'll set up a meeting so that we can discuss the issue with the local businesspeople and veterans' groups who're opposed to the gardens." Her voice fell. "Talk things over, agree to disagree. I'm guessing that won't happen."

"There is no agree to disagree in their world, Mom. There's only their side and the bad guys."

"How do you know this?"

"Graham watched CNC some of the time. He believed that you had to listen to what everyone was saying. I never had the stomach for it."

Smith crossed the room, rested her chin on the top of Lucky's head, and wrapped her arms around her mother. "Let's go to bed, Mom. I've got to be ready at seven tomorrow."

Lucky hugged her back. Her chest heaved. They stood for a few minutes, saying nothing. The windows were open and the scent of the warm night air filled the house. A cat howled.

"Never thought the day would come when I'd hug a person carrying a gun," Lucky said, pulling herself out of the embrace. "Are you getting anywhere with finding who killed Reg?"

"You'll have to read about it in the papers, Mom. Just like everyone else. All you can do is leave this. Don't be writing letters of indignation to the network. That'll play into their hands. Do you hear me?"

"I hear you." Lucky looked up and almost smiled. "The program aired at ten o'clock Pacific time. Not many people would have been watching, and no one on the east coast. It'll all blow over. Good night, dear."

"Night, Mom." Smith climbed the stairs. Lucky was such an optimist. This wouldn't blow over. Not if Rich Ashcroft had anything to say about it—and he almost certainly did.

She pulled off her uniform, freed her toes from the heavy boots, locked her gun in the safe, ran a toothbrush over her teeth, and fell into bed. She felt like killing—Rich Ashcroft first, her dad second. Meredith Morgenstern would be a distant third.

When the phone rang at three o'clock, she reached for it instantly, her heart pounding. Dad. He hadn't come home. In her job, she herself had made some unwelcome early-morning phone calls.

Instead of a solemn-voiced officer asking to speak to Mrs. Smith, it was Sergeant Winters. "Be ready in fifteen minutes," he said. "We've got a situation."

Chapter Thirteen

The building was a smoldering ruin. Firefighters were rolling up hoses and packing away their equipment when Smith and Winters arrived. Curious citizens had gathered across the street in an assortment of summer sleepwear. A police cruiser blocked entrance to the park, and Constable Dawn Solway stood beside it.

Winters had said nothing to Smith when he picked her up, thirteen minutes after his call. She hadn't known if she should put on her uniform, so dressed in jeans and a T-shirt, with running shoes on her feet, and her gun and badge tossed into a fanny pack. She hadn't had time to braid her hair, just stuffed it into a clip as they drove. She'd been pleased to see her father's car parked in their driveway.

A firefighter met them as they got out of Winters' car.

The men shook hands and the firefighter nodded to Smith. "Joe Matthews," he said. His helmet was tucked under his arm, and soot streaked across his face.

They walked toward the scene of the fire, the smell of smoke heavy in the air, wet grass soft underfoot. "I'll bet my son's university tuition that this was arson," Matthews said. "Not the slightest attempt to hide it."

"No one on the scene when you arrived?"

"Long gone. It was called in by a lady who lives across the street. She was up feeding her baby, looked out the window before settling it back to sleep, saw flames and called us."

"Is it safe to poke around?"

"Long as you don't go into the structure itself, and don't pick anything up. Arson investigator's been called."

"Thanks."

Matthews walked away, the orange stripes on his bunker gear glowing in the lights from police car and fire truck.

The building wasn't more than seven or eight feet square. Charred gardening implements and workmen's tools littered the blackened ground. Water soaked into Smith's running shoes.

This property was owned by the town of Trafalgar, as much as some citizens might not want it. It had been left to the town in the will of Larry O'Reilly—the site of the proposed Commemorative Peace Garden.

"I haven't heard of an arsonist active in this area, have you, Molly?"

"No."

"Ineffectual building to want to burn to the ground."

The fire truck drove away, its big tires digging trenches through the grass.

Across the street, people began to disperse.

"But symbolic," Smith said.

"How so? It's a garden shed. I have a bigger one in my back yard."

"My mom has a draft of the plans." Smith waved her arm. "This is where the fountain's supposed to go. As there isn't anything else to burn, I guess they figured this shed would have to do. The house is over that ridge. The garden was separated from the property immediately around the house, and left to the town."

"You think this was a political act? Not a couple of drunk teenagers with nothing better to do?"

Smith shrugged. "Why else would you call me out?"

"Because I think this was a political act related to the Commemorative Peace Garden and the murder of Reginald Montgomery. What I'm wondering, though, is why it happened tonight. There hasn't been any real trouble, criminal trouble, over the park. Just a lot of yelling and shouting at town council. Did the murder of Montgomery bring troublemakers out of the woodwork?"

Smith laughed without mirth. "That TV trash certainly didn't help." She felt something squish under her foot, and knew she'd stepped into a pile of dog dirt. Made nice and moist by water from the firefighters' hoses.

"What TV trash?"

She rubbed her shoe on the grass. "CNC, the cable news channel, sent one of their most incendiary so-called journalists to town. They ran a piece earlier, totally one-sided. It said, if I remember correctly, that people opposed to the park need help."

Winters blew out his cheeks. "They might have found it. You saw this show, Molly?"

"My mom taped it. It makes her look bad."

"Let's go."

"Where?"

"To your house. I want to see this program."

As they walked across the lawn, a man stepped out from behind the cruiser. The end of his cigarette glowed in the dark. "I'm thinking that this isn't a juvenile prank getting out of control," the Chief Constable said.

"It might be," Winters replied. "That sort of thing happens. But tonight? The day after the Montgomery murder? Have you seen the CNC program, Paul?"

"What program? I went to the movies with my wife. Some fool thing with women in long dresses and men bowing and scraping to everyone in sight."

"Perhaps you should come with us. Molly's about to give me a private showing. Will there be popcorn, Constable?"

She didn't bother to reply.

The CC tossed his keys to Solway. She caught them in one hand, and looked pleased with herself. "Have someone take my car home," he said.

"Hard to imagine it could be much worse," Paul Keller said.

"Come to Trafalgar and help us create strife and mayhem. That's pretty much what he's saying," Winters said.

They were in the Smith living room. Not only the Constable, the Sergeant, and the Chief Constable, but also Mr. and Mrs. Smith, who'd come downstairs at the sound of the door opening and boots hitting the floor. It was five o'clock and neither of them looked like they'd gotten a minute's sleep. They gathered nightclothes around them and joined the police in the family room. The room was casual and comfortable, with wood-paneled walls, colorful furniture, and an overflowing bookcase. The coffee table was piled high with magazines and empty mugs, and cushions were scattered across the floor. Photographs decorated the walls. Winters studied Constable Smith growing up while Lucky gathered up the dishes, all the while apologizing for the mess. Many of the photos also featured a freckled red-headed boy, several years older than his sister, looking the dictionary-definition of mischievous. A golden retriever, thrilled to have company at this time of night, weaved itself around everyone's feet.

Andy Smith was a tall, heavy-set man, muscle collapsing to fat. His cheeks were puffy, and his grey hair was interspersed with a scattering of remaining blond strands. Lucky, much shorter and darker, looked like his shadow. But the analogy wasn't perfect. He was the washed-out one, his face stoic, revealing nothing, whereas she, without saying a word, radiated righteous indignation. She returned, wiping her hands on the seat of her housecoat, and started to offer her guests refreshments, but Paul told her no one wanted anything.

Constable Smith rewound the tape, and they took seats to watch the program.

"Trouble," Paul Keller said, as Ashcroft's show ended and an ad for deodorant began. "This'll bring nothing but trouble."

Andy Smith jumped up. "I don't see how you could possibly have agreed to that, Lucky. I thought you had more sense."

"Leave it, Dad," Smith said. "You think Mom doesn't know by now it wasn't a good idea?"

"You don't think anyone will watch it, do you?" Lucky smiled weakly at Keller, seeking confirmation.

"Probably not," the Chief Constable said. "Don't you worry, Lucky." His face was flushed, and Winters wondered what on earth the man could be thinking. Of course the program would be seen. As far and wide as Ashcroft wanted it to be.

"Christ," Andy said, "are you in dreamland? Molly smells of smoke. She's brought her boss to our house at," he checked his watch, "five o'clock in the morning to watch you make a fool of yourself, and you're hoping no one will see it."

"Whether anyone will or will not see that program," Winters said, "is out of our control. Molly mentioned that she had a copy of the video at home, and I wanted to see it."

"We were at an arson earlier," Keller said. "No one harmed, fortunately. Thank you for your hospitality, Mrs. Smith." He smiled at Lucky.

"You come out in the middle of the night to investigate every crime, Paul?" Andy snorted.

Lucky said, "I'm going to make tea. Anyone want some? Sergeant Winters?" She looked like hell. The circles under her eyes were dark and deep, the eyes themselves filled with the ghost of tears. She didn't look any older than when he'd interviewed her this afternoon, but her air of good humor and enjoyment of verbal combat was gone.

"Another time, perhaps."

"I for one am going to bed," Andy said. "So should you, Molly." He left the room.

Smith's cheeks were pink, and her eyes threw thunderbolts at her father's retreating back.

"Night, Molly, Lucky," Keller said. "John, I left my car behind. You'll have to take me home."

Smith walked them to the door and stood watching as they climbed into the car. Before Winters switched on his lights, she was briefly lit from behind, standing in the doorway like a museum exhibit. *Homo constableus* in her natural environment. He backed out of the driveway.

"That program was bad, John, very bad."

"I agree."

"It'll bring every troublemaker within a thousand miles to town." Keller pulled a cigar out of his shirt pocket. Winters considered telling him that no smoking was allowed, but decided against it. He and Keller went back a long way. But the man was still the Chief Constable. A lighter spat out a thin flame of red and yellow.

"I can't see the connection between the show, the arson at the park, and Montgomery's murder," Winters said, as much to himself as to his boss. "Montgomery was openly opposed to the garden. The program was clearly on his side, and so, I'll assume for now, was our arsonist. If someone killed Montgomery because of his opposition to the park, I'd expect them to make a statement about it." The road back to Trafalgar was winding and treacherous. A cliff rose up on the right, and a sharp drop to the river was on his left. Occasionally he caught a glimpse of brilliant eyes reflecting his headlights. A scattering of house lights twinkled across the river.

"I'm thinking of calling in IHIT."

Winters let out a breath. "I don't think that's necessary, not yet."

The Integrated Homicide Investigation Team was an RCMP unit out of Surrey, prepared to help local forces throughout the Lower Mainland and the B.C. interior with murder cases.

"In the past, I'd have called them right away. But you were a homicide detective in Vancouver for a long time, John, so I figured you could handle it. Tell me why you don't need them now."

The undercarriage of the car clattered as they crossed the bridge into town. There was no other traffic. "Scene of the crime evidence isn't telling us much. In fact, it isn't telling us anything. The wife and her lover would be the obvious suspects, but she, contrary to what you saw on TV earlier, is so bored by her husband's death, that I can't imagine her getting fired up enough to have caused it. And her lover—he's either the world's greatest actor, or he's innocent. Or a complete psycho—I've sent some feelers out to ask if he's been brought to the attention of the police before, but so far nothing. The business partner is another possible suspect. His alibi is rock solid, but the killing might have been contracted. I won't commit to that line until I've found out a bit more about their company, M&C Developments. If there's particularly hefty partnership insurance involved, I'll be notified. It could be a random thing—a druggie coming across a well-dressed man in a dark alley. But you know better than I do, that's never happened in Trafalgar."

"There's always a first time."

The Chief Constable's home was new, a sprawling bungalow, situated high on the hillside. Far below, yellow lights outlined the bridge and danced on the black waters of the river.

"So what are we left with?"

"Lucky told me that a couple of radical environmental types are in town, aiming to put a stop to the Grizzly Resort. Some of those environmental activists can be ruthless."

Keller puffed on his cigar. "I'll tell the Yellow Stripes that we have the matter well in hand." Winters grinned at his boss' use of the not-always-polite nickname for the RCMP, derived from the color of the stripe on their uniform pants. Keller pulled the unused ashtray open and ground out the half-finished cigar. "Karen'll have my hide if I bring that into the house. Look into the resort, that's my advice, for what it's worth. The situation seems to be all tangled up with this damned peace garden, but my gut tells me the resort's where you'll find the answer, John. I don't see that bunch of old hippies killing anyone over their garden. She's a good person, Lucky Smith. If she was the slightest bit suspicious that someone would kill to stop her beloved park, she'd tell us. I tell you that in the strictest of confidence, John, as Lucky and I've been at loggerheads more than a few times over the years. I'd have loved to have been a fly on the wall the day Molly told her parents that she was joining the Trafalgar City Police." He opened the door, and the interior lights came on.

"How's she doing anyway, Molly?"

"A bit more self-control and she might make a detective one day."

The Chief Constable and Lucky may have been at logger-heads, but Keller couldn't hide the fondness in his voice when he spoke of her. He chuckled as he stepped out of the car. "Glad to hear it, John. Glad to hear it. Let me know what you hear from the arson investigator."

Winters glanced at the dashboard clock as he crossed the bridge. Six thirty. Time was he loved nothing more than to work all night, pop home for a quick tumble with Eliza, followed by a grease-laden breakfast, another rush to the marital bed, and back on the road as the commuter traffic began to build. But Eliza was in Toronto, and if she were at home, she'd be dishing up muesli and yoghurt for breakfast. Although the twinkle might occasionally still be seen in her green eye, when he'd been up all night, John Winters wanted nothing more than a couple of hours of uninterrupted sleep.

He'd told Keller he could handle the case without IHIT. But could he? Even after what happened in Vancouver, was he still arrogant enough to be overconfident of his own abilities? He'd screwed that one up royally: too sure of himself, too proud, too wrapped up in his own prejudices to listen to the words of caution his partner had been trying to give him.

Maybe it was time he did throw the job in. Live a life of leisure as a kept man.

Or maybe just recognize that he wasn't all-powerful and that even he needed help now and again.

He pulled to the side of the road before taking out his phone and calling the programmed number.

"Huh?" was the reply.

"Breakfast at George's. My treat. We've a lot to talk about before the day starts. Half an hour. Be ready." He disconnected the call.

Chapter Fourteen

Molly Smith cut into her *huevos rancheros*. Almost good enough to be dragged out of bed after an hour of sleep. Almost, but not quite.

George's was a Mid-Kootenay tradition. There was a real George, who'd cooked at the place for more than thirty years. He enjoyed playing with the menu, offering fashionable fare, such as tofu scramble and buffalo sausage, but still sticking with the basics: eggs, bacon, and home fries for breakfast, tuna sandwiches and hamburgers for lunch.

"I'm going to have a chat with the Japanese guys who're in town to look into the resort," Winters said, dragging a slice of fat sausage through a puddle of egg yolk. "Although I don't expect to get much out of them. Seeing as how they're inscrutable and all that."

She looked up.

"Just kidding," he said. "I don't care what their nationality might be, but no savvy business type's going to be all that thrilled at having the main guy knocked off in the midst of negotiating a deal."

It was just past seven; the restaurant was full and a line snaked out the door. Wait staff shouted orders, cooks cursed, eggs and bacon sizzled on the grill, someone shouted for more toast, and the patrons raised their voices so as to be heard over the buzz.

"Today," he said, "we're going to split up. I'm taking Evans to meet with the business partners." He held up his fork, glistening with egg yolk. "I need you to find out where I can find Robyn

Goodhaugh, and then poke around a bit more. Go to the alley, go to back to the garden shack at the park."

She opened her mouth to protest, but he spoke first.

"Every time you visit a crime scene, Molly, there's something new to be found. Usually it's nothing more than a branch that was broken a week ago, a paw print in the flowerbed, nothing significant. But sometimes, sometimes, you see something important. Like a neon light you didn't notice the night before, and today it's all you can possibly see."

"Wouldn't forensics have seen the neon light?"

"I'm speaking in tongues, Molly."

"I know," she said, inwardly steaming. There was no reason she shouldn't go along to question the men from Japan, in Trafalgar to do business with M&D Developments. No reason, except for simple sexism.

She mixed the last of the refried beans into a pool of hot salsa.

"There's something in that alley we missed." He rubbed his thumb across the face of his watch. "I know it."

The waiter slapped their bill on the table. "Hey, Moon," he said. "Long time no see. You look great in that uniform. Does your gun work?"

Winters paid in cash. He didn't think the smart-aleck waiter deserved a tip.

The early morning light was soft in the alley, and the air aromatic with fresh baking. Yellow police tape still blocked off the spot where the body'd been found and the back door to the bakery.

Smith kicked at a stone, her enthusiasm for the task diminishing. What could she possibly find here that Winters, the pathologist, a team of police, and countless curious citizens hadn't? She climbed over the tape. Nothing of Reginald Montgomery remained; even the dirt that had soaked up his lifeblood had been scooped up and taken away for analysis. Tracks of a bicycle were outlined against the wall beside the bakery door, reminding Smith of her own bike. Maybe it was time to get a car. She'd seen a great little car in town the other day. A dark blue Mini Cooper convertible. Too cute.

She looked east down the alley, wondering how much one of those cars might cost. The tourist information office was on the other side of Pine Street, not far past Mid-Kootenay Adventures. A bike rack sat outside, one bike parked in the rack—a top-of-the-line men's red mountain bike. When she next got a day off perhaps she'd go to the dealer. Find out how much a Mini would cost and if it could manage mountain roads in the snow.

As she admired the red bike, and thought about buying a car, a man walked up to the bike rack. He pulled something out of his backpack and bent over the front wheel. A long, thin, red coil fell to the ground. He stuffed the equipment back into his pack and grabbed the bike. He jumped on it and was pedaling up Pine Street while Smith's brain was registering what she'd seen. The red coil lying on the ground like an embarrassed snake was a bike lock cable.

He'd stolen the bike.

Smith ran.

◇ ◇ ◇

"Conflict, Meredith. Television is all about conflict. No conflict, no good TV."

"I can see that, Rich. But isn't there enough conflict in the world without making stuff up?"

"What did I make up, Meredith? There wasn't a word in that program that wasn't true. People talk to me, I report what they say. At the end of the segment, after everyone's said their piece, I try to summarize the situation as best I can. Because, to be honest, some of my viewers aren't that swift on the uptake."

Meredith sipped at her coffee, still looking dubious. Rich poured maple syrup generously over his pancakes.

This hotel was second-rate, not the sort of place he liked to stay when traveling for a story. But there didn't seem to be anything much better in this primitive backwater. Now the Grizzly Resort, from what he'd heard, might have promise.

"I had a phone call from my editor. He's never called me at home before. He thinks your show put Trafalgar in a bad light."

Rich snapped his fingers at a passing waitress and pointed to his empty glass of orange juice. "Rubbish. My assistant called this morning to say the show was well received. If anything, it'll be good for the area. Bring Trafalgar to the attention of people who wouldn't hear about it otherwise. And that can only be good, right?"

She lifted her cup to her lips and looked at him over the rim. "You'll have to convince me of that, Rich."

Stupid bitch. But she was pretty enough, and he needed someone to help him navigate around this insular town. He'd only been here one day and was already feeling claustrophobic. The small town, the mountains on all sides. He gulped at his coffee. Dreadful. Trafalgar was probably the only community in North America that didn't have a Starbucks.

"Morning, folks." Greg, the CNC cameraman, pulled up a chair. The waitress hurried over with Rich's orange juice and another menu.

"Good program, I hear," he said. "How's the pancakes?"

"Adequate."

Greg shut the menu with a snap and smiled at Meredith. "How are you this morning?"

She smiled back. Rich bristled. Greg was in his early thirties, muscular from carrying camera equipment everywhere, darkly tanned from an assignment in the Middle East. Rich had invited Meredith up to his room last night, to watch the program and have a drink. She'd refused.

"I'm interested in this Grizzly Resort," he said. "The place Montgomery was developing. It has potential to be a good story. I called Irene last night, and asked her to find out what she can about the company. Two-man operation, sounds like. Trying to bring jobs and development to this area. Of course, the local animal rights hysterics are up in arms."

"I don't think," Meredith said, "hysterics is the proper word. People in Trafalgar are concerned about the environment, that's all."

Rich stuffed a slice of pancake into his mouth.

"We'll get all sides of the story," Greg said. "Don't worry about that."

Rich swallowed. "I need someone who knows this town, who knows the people, to help me out. You were a great help introducing me to Mrs. Smith, Meredith. I wouldn't have met her without you. If your bosses don't want to help us anymore, then why don't you take a couple days leave and work for CNC? I'll bet the network pays a hell of a lot better than your provincial newspaper."

She chewed the lipstick off her mouth. Indecision moved behind the expressive dark eyes.

Rich pushed his plate aside. "I don't want to pressure you, Meredith, but I have to know now. Time's important in this business. There's a job opening coming up at CNC. No promises, but I am not without influence."

"Really?" Meredith whispered. Indecision retreated and her eyes shone.

Rich wiped his lips with his napkin, tossed it onto the table, and stood up. "Sign the bill, will you, Greg. Are you coming, Meredith? I'll understand if you'd rather finish your coffee before going to your office."

She leapt to her feet. "We'll have to take my car. I can't use the paper's car."

"Before we pay a visit to the surviving owner of the Grizzly Resort, tell me something about Lucy Smith's daughter. You said she's a cop here in town. That might make an interesting human interest angle."

◇◇◇

"Two cancellations. A party of five from Idaho and a couple from Calgary. And it isn't even nine o'clock yet." Andy stood in the doorway to Lucky's office.

"We'll get other bookings," she said, not at all sure of herself. "Don't worry."

"Of course I'm worried. This publicity's going to kill us. I can't imagine what you were thinking to allow that TV hack into our house."

She stood up. "I was thinking, Andy, that I'd tell our story. Your story, if I remember correctly. Too many people have forgotten what men like you sacrificed for your principles. They need to be reminded, once again. Perhaps you yourself need to be reminded."

"The world's moved on, Lucky. No one cares anymore about what happened back in the '60s. No one but a bunch of aging war resisters who've spent the last forty years hibernating up in the mountains."

"The people in this town care. They want the garden. I care. Barry and Michael, Jane and Norma care. And all the rest of the group."

"I doubt if Michael even knows where Vietnam is."

"What the hell does that mean?"

"It means that Michael is more interested in getting you into the sack than building a statue."

"I'll not dignify that comment with a response. But you, you of all people, how can you say you don't care?"

"The past is past, Lucky. Times have changed. We've lost. The military-industrial complex is stronger than ever. The empire is on the march."

A heavy glove closed over Lucky's heart. "I'll never give up," she said.

"Hello? Anyone here?" a woman called from the store.

Andy turned.

"Let Duncan take care of it," Lucky said. "We have to finish this. Where's Duncan anyway?"

"Getting coffee." He walked out of the office, a miasma of bitterness and resentment trailing behind him.

Smith reached Pine Street; he was still in sight, pedaling uphill. If he'd headed down, toward the river, she wouldn't have a hope of catching up with him. She ran up the hill, yelling into the radio at her shoulder for assistance. Vehicular assistance, she emphasized.

He didn't look back, just kept pedaling.

"Stop, police," she yelled. An elderly gentleman out for his morning constitutional looked at her. A smartly dressed businesswoman walking a Pomeranian turned to stare. The Pomeranian barked and lunged toward Smith. Her gun slapped at her hip, her boots weighed her down. The uniform was hot, even in the mild morning sun.

He turned onto the street at the crest of the hill and disappeared. She heard sirens behind her. The cruiser slowed down. Smith wrenched the door open and jumped in.

Dawn Solway pressed her foot on the gas. "What's up?"

"Next left," Smith gasped. A stitch dug into her side. "Guy on a bike. Move it."

They took the corner on two wheels. Nothing but morning dog walkers and people heading to work. The only cyclist was a toddler on a tricycle, colorful ribbons on the handlebars blowing in the breeze.

Smith pounded the dashboard. "He has to be around here somewhere. That alley, turn down there."

Solway turned, but the alley was empty. She switched off the siren.

"Back up, back up."

Solway backed up. At this end of town the roadway was a maze of twists and turns; roads went up the mountain, and down again. Or not. One-way streets turned into throughways, and major roads dwindled into nothing. There were streets that ended at sheer cliffs and others that changed name or direction without warning. And because the roads were so unpredictable, walking paths jutted off in all directions.

"Where to?" Solway asked.

"How the fuck am I supposed to know?" Smith hit the dashboard again. "Keep driving."

"What'd he do?"

"Stole a bike. Stole a goddamned bike while I stood there watching, thinking it was a nice bike. You laugh and I'll have your guts for garters."

"I wasn't laughing."

"Christ, I can't believe the nerve of the guy. He didn't even look around to see if anyone was watching, just snapped the chain and took off."

"Recognize anything about him?"

"Too far away. Might not have even been a guy, now that I think about it. All baggy pants and oversized T-shirt."

They drove around, Smith shouting at Solway to stop at every pedestrian they passed, to ask if they'd seen someone on a red bike. No one had.

"Could be anywhere by now," Solway said. "Holed up in someone's back yard, most likely. Watching us driving around in circles."

"Go back to the tourist info center. See if we can find the bike owner. This'll make the Trafalgar City Police look good—hey, I saw someone steal your bike but couldn't catch him."

"You tried, Molly, don't sweat it. You were on foot, he was on a bike."

"I just can't get over the gall. He must have known I was chasing him, or her, but he didn't even look back when I yelled."

"Maybe he knew you'd recognize the face."

"That's a thought. Which means someone local, or who's been brought to our attention recently."

A man was standing outside the tourist info center, looking at the empty bike rack, incomprehension on his face.

Smith's cell phone rang as Solway pulled up beside him and got out of the car.

"Are you missing something, sir?" Solway said.

"Moonlight, where are you?" Lucky's voice was tinged with panic.

"Right near you, Mom. I can see the store from here. What's wrong?"

"Can you come by for a minute?"

"Is Dad okay? Are you okay?"

"I need you in your professional capacity, Moonlight."

"I'm coming." Smith jumped out of the car. Solway was making soothing gestures to the wildly gesticulating bicyclist.

"I have to go. Something's wrong at my parents'."

"You," the bicyclist shouted. He was older than she'd thought at first—probably into his forties. His hair was cut short, his face clean-shaven. Sleek black and red bike shirt and shorts on a well-toned frame. He threw his red helmet to the ground. "She said you saw it happen. Was it your coffee break or something? Wrong time of the month to make an arrest?"

"Go, Smith," Solway said, "I'll help this gentleman make a statement." She bent down and picked up the bike chain. "Cheap," she said. "Easy to cut. I would've thought that you'd get better security for such a nice bike."

Smith left him sputtering his indignation, and sprinted down the street.

No one was in the store. "Mom? Dad?"

"In the back," Andy Smith called.

She went into the office. Her parents stood together, their arms wrapped around each other. Lucky's red and grey head was tucked into her husband's chest. For a moment Smith was happy just to see them together. Then Lucky pulled away. Her face was pale beneath her freckles and tan.

"What's happened? Sam?"

Andy's cheeks were red, his mouth set in a tight white line.

Lucky picked a piece of paper up off her desk, holding it by the tips of her fingers as if it were covered in dog dirt. She handed the note to Smith, her hand shaking.

Smith took it. The paper was badly crushed.

Boom, boom
Too bad this isn't a bomb
But I don't have enough fertilizer
Yet
Remember Oklahoma
That's what we do to traitors and deserters
Boom, boom

Chapter Fifteen

Smith let out a long breath. "When did you get this, Mom?"

"It was pushed under the door," her father said.

"When?"

"It was there when I opened up. I figured it was someone local paying a bill, so I tossed it on your mother's desk. People in town sometimes don't bother with the post office, you know that."

"Where's the envelope?"

Lucky nodded toward her desk.

Smith looked at the envelope but didn't pick it up. *Mrs. Smith* and the name and address of the store printed in neat black letters. There was no return address and no stamp.

She punched numbers into her phone. Andy gathered his wife back into his arms and looked at his daughter over Lucky's shoulder. His eyes were wet.

"Winters."

"Can you meet me at my parents' store, John? It's important."

"I'm just leaving the Hudson House Hotel. Be there in five."

The bell over the front door jingled cheerfully. Footsteps crossed the wooden floor.

"Tell them we're closed, Moonlight, please."

But it was only Duncan, carrying two coffee mugs with snap-on lids. He was dressed in baggy surfer shorts and a sleeveless T-shirt, with Tevas on his feet. "Sorry I took so long. You wouldn't believe the crowd at Eddie's." He smiled at Smith. "Hi, Molly, you look really good today. Doesn't she always look great in that uniform, Andy?" Finally he appeared to notice their faces. "What's up?"

Smith held out the letter. "Don't touch, but have you seen anything like this before?"

Duncan put the mugs down and read. His cheerful smile faded. "That's awful. It must have been delivered here by mistake. Why would anyone want to bomb our store?"

Lucky gasped.

"Duncan, would you please make my mother a cup of tea," Smith said.

"I don't want tea."

"You need one. Duncan?"

"She can have my coffee."

"I said tea." Lucky didn't drink coffee, and right now she needed sugar. "Dad will have one too."

"Okay, sure. Tea all around." The kettle was set out beside a half-sized bar fridge in one corner of the office. Duncan had to go to the washroom to fill it.

The bell over the door rang again. "Molly, where are you?"

"In the back," she called. Duncan returned with the filled kettle. "After you've plugged that in, go and lock the door," she said. "And turn the sign to closed."

"Yes, ma'am. Whatever you say, ma'am." Duncan saluted. Smith didn't think the situation was particularly amusing. He passed Winters on his way out of the office.

Smith held the letter by the corners for the sergeant to read. Lucky would have opened the envelope, taken out the letter, read it, crushed it in her hands, and tossed it in the garbage. Then Andy would have pulled it out and uncrumpled it. Later, it had been passed to Smith, who'd accepted it without a thought. It was unlikely that the fingerprints of the author would be identifiable. But there was never any harm in being careful.

"Nasty," Winters said.

"Gee, you think?" Andy said. "This is a direct threat to my family and our business."

"I agree with you, Mr. Smith. Constable, find a bag for the letter and the envelope."

The kettle switched itself off. Duncan began gathering cups and tea bags, milk and sugar.

"I'll get a forensic examination started on this right away," Winters said. "It's a threat all right, but it's unlikely that this person has either the inclination or the knowledge to carry it out."

"You can guarantee that, can you, Sergeant?"

"Of course I can't, Mr. Smith. But I can guarantee that the Trafalgar City Police will be keeping an eye on your property until we find this person."

"My property, fine. What about my family? What about my wife?"

"Oh, stop, Andy," Lucky said. She walked around her desk and sank into the chair. She adjusted the back support. A bit of color was returning to her face. "They'll do what they can."

"We'll close the store for the rest of the day," Andy said.

"We'll do nothing of the sort. I won't be chased out of our business by a poisoned-pen writer." She took a deep drink of her tea. "Duncan, unlock the door."

Winters said, "You'll let us know if anything even the slightest out of the ordinary happens?"

"Yes." She began rummaging through the mountain of paper on her desk.

Duncan preceded the police to unlock the door. "Do you have a moment, Mol?" he asked, flipping the sign to Open.

"My car's right outside," Winters said. The bell jangled as he left.

"If you know something about this letter, Duncan, you need to tell Seargant Winters, not just me."

"It's not about that. I've been wanting to ask you a question for a long time, Mol."

She looked outside. The lights of Winters' SUV flashed as he flicked his remote. "So ask."

"I'm going to Vancouver on Tuesday. I've got tickets for the Pearl Jam concert. Do you wanna come with me?"

It took Smith a good few seconds to understand what he was saying. "You want me to go to a concert with you?"

"It's been sold out for months. Get outa town, see Pearl Jam, eh? Sound good?"

"Duncan, I'm here, right now, as an investigating officer. I can't make a date with you." Winters was drumming his fingers on the steering wheel. She wouldn't put it past him to drive away without her. "I have to go."

Duncan's face tightened and the lines between his eyebrows came together. "It'll be fun, Molly. You can stop being a cop for a while."

"I don't want to stop being a cop."

"You're acting as if I've insulted you. And I don't want you to stop being a cop, anyway. Tell me you'll think about it."

"I can't think about anything but this case. And now my family's been threatened." He was pretty cute, Duncan. Usually easygoing, cheerful. But right now he just looked angry. Some guys just couldn't take rejection. "BC-DC's playing at the Regal on Saturday. If, and it's a big if, I'm free, I'd like to go. If I do, do you want to come?"

"Pearl Jam's the real deal, Molly."

"Pearl Jam isn't going to happen."

Winters leaned on the horn.

"I have to go," she said. "See you, Dunc."

"Okay. Saturday then."

She ran into the street and jumped into Winters' vehicle, instantly forgetting Duncan Weaver and the BC-DC concert.

"It's most likely an empty threat, you know that, don't you?"

"Oh yeah. Fuckin' coward's threatened my mom, my dad, their livelihood. And I've got to pretend it doesn't really matter."

"I'm not asking you to pretend anything." Winters pulled into the parking lot at the police station. He switched the car off, but didn't move to get out. "But I have to ask you if you can be a professional about this. And give me the help I need."

"No one's ever challenged my professionalism before, John."

"So I've been told."

"But no one's ever threatened my mom before!" The red and white maple leaf flag above the police station snapped in the warm breeze.

"Anyone dropped a poisoned-pen letter addressed to Eliza, my wife, through my mail box, I'd be out for blood too, Molly."

The leather headrest felt cool against the back of her head. Smith closed her eyes and remembered that she hadn't had much sleep last night. "You think this had something to do with that god-damned CNC TV program. What's it called, Filthy Column?"

"*Fifth Column.* Strange name for a program that follows the governing party's line so closely. Anyone threatened your family before?"

Smith's eyes flew open. "Of course not. You think I'd keep that a secret?"

"Just asking, Molly. Just asking. I'm just a dumb cop, but even I have to wonder. An incendiary TV program mentions both the Commemorative Peace Garden and your mother. Remind me, did the show say anything about your parents' business?"

"There was a shot of the sign and the front windows. It might as well have been captioned, 'Aim your rocks here.' Bastards."

"And within hours of the program airing we have arson at the project site and a threatening letter to one of the sponsors. Coincidence? Unlikely. Let's get this letter to forensics, perhaps they'll find something. You'd be surprised at how stupid most criminals can be. We wouldn't catch many of them if they had half a brain cell to rub together."

"Half of anything can't rub against nothing."

Talk at the coffee shop was all about the CNC program. It had been rebroadcast across the United States that morning on the network's breakfast show.

"I wouldn't of thought many people in town watched CNC." Christa joined the conversation in the bagel line.

A young woman with hair cropped to her scalp, a short T-shirt, and low-slung cut-off jeans shrugged. "Word got around that there was going to be a piece on Trafalgar, so people tuned in. Hoping to see themselves in the background."

"Fellow came in already," Jolene, behind the sandwich bar, said, as she sliced a pumpernickel bagel, popped it into the toaster oven, slipped an onion one out, and slathered it with cream cheese. "Told me he'd driven up from Oregon and wanted to know where he could go to protest the peace garden."

"What'd you say?" the short-haired girl asked.

"Sent him to Nelson."

Everyone laughed.

"Dill and garlic on whole wheat, please." Christa shuffled down the line. She'd been up all night, working on her paper. As the sun touched the top of the mountains, she'd pressed the Outlook Express send/receive button and sent it on its way. She'd done a good job and deserved a treat. On a nice morning like this sometimes it seemed as if everyone in Trafalgar passed through Big Eddie's.

"Excuse me," a middle-aged woman said from the back of the line, "but are you people talking about the Commemorative Peace Garden?"

The line ground to a halt as the locals turned and looked at her. Even Jolene stopped in the midst of slicing a bagel.

"My friends and I flew in from Vancouver. We heard about the program and wanted to let you know that you have our support."

Like an assembly line that had been re-started after an accident, the bagel line shifted into motion again. "That's nice of you," a tall young man said. "But the show was only on last night."

"We can move quickly when we have to. I'm with the Vancouver Women's Peace Alliance."

"Not everyone's going to be happy to see you." A man walked past, balancing coffee and bagel bag. He was dressed in a suit and tie. You didn't see that much in Trafalgar, and certainly not in high summer. "O'Reilly donated the land and asked for a park to be dedicated to him and his buddies, so I figure they should respect his wishes. But we don't need strangers stirring up trouble." He glared at the woman from Vancouver.

Christa poured herself coffee and moved further down the line to pay.

"Some people aren't in favor of the garden," a woman in tennis whites, pushing a stroller, said. "Like the old World War Two vets. They say it disgraces their memory."

"But the garden has nothing to do with World War Two. My grandpa lost an eye in Italy and he…."

Eddie took Christa's money. "I don't take sides," he said, handing Christa her change and the warm bagel bag. "Have a nice day."

The tables inside and out were all taken; people were propped on the short brick wall around Eddie's's property, and the line snaked down the street. With one or two exceptions there were no North-American-wide fast-food restaurants or coffee chains in Trafalgar. The citizens were active and vocal, and kept the corporate biggies out.

Christa sipped coffee through the hole in the lid. Perhaps she'd go to the beach later, spend a lazy day in the sun. It would be nice if Molly could come, but she was probably working, unless they'd solved this murder. In a million years Christa would never have guessed that Moonlight Smith would become a cop. But when Graham was killed, a lot of things changed with her friend. Molly had been working toward her MSW, Master of Social Work, at University of Victoria. Graham had finished ahead of her and had a job in Vancouver. Their wedding date was set for the following summer. But he'd been killed days before Christmas, stabbed and left to die in a garbage-strewn alley in the Downtown Eastside by one of his spaced-out clients. The doctor told Molly, foolishly in Christa's opinion, that if someone had just called 911, Graham would have lived. But people passed him in the alley all night and no one called for help until morning. Molly quit the MSW program, came home to Trafalgar and wrapped herself in mourning and loneliness. She took an office job in Calgary, at her brother Sam's law firm, two days before what should have been her wedding day. Six months later she was back in Trafalgar, and shortly after that announced that she'd been accepted as a recruit by the Trafalgar City Police. Her parents, Lucky in particular, were vehemently opposed to the very idea. But Molly didn't argue, simply told them that she'd decided this was what she was going to do and they could accept it, or not. Sensibly, they accepted it.

Christa fumbled in her pocket for her key. A day at the beach would do Molly a world of good. It had to be tough, working on this murder case. She was still a rookie, and although she hadn't said so, Christa sensed that Molly wasn't getting on with the sergeant guy all that well. Even if she were working all day, she should be able to get away for a couple of hours later. They'd borrow Lucky's car, take fold-up chairs, big straw hats and trashy magazines, and wine hidden in a thermos, and have fun. Like when they were kids.

The key slipped out of her fingers. She balanced the coffee cup, tucked the bagel bag under her arm, and bent over to retrieve the key.

"Let me help." An arm knocked her against the wall, and long fingers grabbed the keys.

"I can manage, Charlie."

"I'll just help you take your things upstairs, okay?"

He unlocked the door.

"I don't want your help. Good-bye." She held out her hand. "Give me the key."

"Don't be like that. I'm trying to help you, aren't I?" He reached for the coffee cup.

She pulled it out of the way. The brown bag fell to the ground. "I'm calling the cops." She thrust her hand into her shorts pocket seeking her cell phone. Oh, no. She'd left it behind, thinking that it wouldn't be needed on a quick walk to the coffee shop on a pleasant summer's day.

He pushed his body up against hers, forcing her inside. His breath was rancid, like he'd been drinking all night and hadn't brushed his teeth. The front hall was small, barely large enough for one person. He slammed the door behind him and they were plunged into near darkness, the only light coming from the small, dirty window in the top of the door. Christa fell onto the bottom step and scurried up the stairs, backward, on her butt. Hot coffee soaked the front of her tank-top.

"I've had enough of you and your shit," Charlie yelled. "What the hell's the matter with you, Chrissie?"

White hot pain streaked across her face. Her head felt as if it were flying off her neck.

"I don't want to do this, but you just won't listen to reason." He lifted his foot.

Chapter Sixteen

"Call for you, John. Rosemary's Country Kitchen."

"Sergeant Winters."

"Hi, Mr. Winters. It's Emily here, from Rosemary's Country...."

"Have you heard from Mrs. Fitzgerald?"

"Constable Evans told me to let you know soon as she called. Her son in Toronto's had a heart attack. She's flying straight there. She said it sounds bad. I don't know how I'm going to manage this store on my own. I've been run off my feet this morning."

"Did you tell Mrs. Fitzgerald that I want to speak with her?"

"She said she can't be bothered with that now."

"Did you tell her why?"

"I didn't get a chance. She said she wondered how you'd heard what'd happened, but she'll phone the station when she gets back."

Winters spluttered. "How I'd heard....Do you have a number where she can be reached?"

"She told me to call her on her cell phone."

"What's the number?" He jotted it down on a pink Post-it note.

"Something up?" Smith stood in the doorway.

"Fitzgerald's left the building." He dialed the number. A pleasant voice answered, asking him to leave a message at the beep. He did so. If she was in the air, then rushing to her son's side, perhaps in the hospital all day, she might never turn her phone on.

"You think Rosemary's got something to do with this?"

"No, I don't. But it bothers me to have stones unturned. She said something odd to her assistant, although I suspect the assistant got the message mixed up. If she doesn't call by tomorrow, I'll ask the Toronto Police to track her down; her son's in the hospital, so they should be able to find him. Oh, God, I hope the son's name is Fitzgerald. It might not be. Whatever happened to the days when a son could be expected to have the same last name as his mother, eh, Molly?"

"You mean the good old days when there was no divorce because people died in their twenties and thirties, and so the surviving spouse, provided they were healthy enough, and lucky enough, might live to be widowed several times over?"

"Right. The good old days." He dug his knuckles into his eyes. He needed some sleep. "Let's go."

"Go where?"

"Back to the park. The Mounties'll be there, doing their thing. I'd like to have a look around in the daylight."

◇◇◇

Rich Ashcroft untangled himself from the front seat of Meredith's car. He'd seen bigger sardine cans.

The Grizzly Resort was a sorry sight. A single trailer on a muddy patch of dug-up forest.

"Not too photogenic," he said.

"Oh, I don't know," Greg said, looking away from the building, toward the forest. "There's always something."

"I want promise. I want hope. I want to see the future here. I want to see nature in all her tamed and pacified glory, kneeling before the authority that is the modern American man."

"This is Canada, Rich," Meredith said.

"Whatever." She was starting to get tedious. But he needed the local help. At first he'd tried to keep a low profile, didn't want to be spotted by too many fans on the street. But as no one seemed to recognize him, he became bolder. Still no luck. He hadn't been recognized anywhere he'd gone. So Meredith was pretty much the only talent he could draw. He couldn't wait to get back to L.A.

They climbed the steps of the trailer. Greg followed, lugging his camera.

The eagerness on the receptionist's face as she welcomed them brought joy to Rich's heart. Either she dressed every day as if the Queen would be dropping by, or she'd gone home to change after Meredith called to make the appointment with her boss.

"It is *so* nice to meet you, Mr. Ashforth." Flecks of lipstick stuck to her prominent teeth.

"Ashcroft."

"Sorry. Hi, Meredith."

A man came out of the inner office. He crossed the floor in two strides and held out his hand. Rich shook it.

"Thank you for agreeing to talk to us, Mr. Clemmins. It was good of you to take time on such a sad day."

"No problem." Clemmins waved toward his pokey office at the back of the trailer. "Come in."

Clemmins looked like a biker gone soft. Not the image of a respectable businessman that Rich wanted, but there was nothing he could do about that.

"Why don't we step outside? It's a nice day, and the woods'll give us plenty of atmosphere."

"Sure. Bernice, hold all my calls. Unless it's Mr. Yakamoto or Mr. Takauri."

"You wouldn't like to take a few pictures in here first?" Bernice looked like a dog whose bone had been snatched inches from its drooling jaws.

"Great idea," Rich said. "Greg, get some footage of the office. I want the feel of a busy organization, lots of paperwork. Would you mind, Bernice, is it? if Greg gets you in the shot? Talking on the phone, or working at the computer."

"If you think it would help," she said, whipping a brush out of a cavernous handbag.

"It'll add background. Thanks, Bernice. Join us as soon as you're finished in here, Greg."

Rich posed Clemmins against the side of the trailer. He asked a couple of introductory questions, waiting for Greg to finish taking useless footage of Bernice wasting her time and join them. Meredith watched.

Greg and his camera clambered down the trailer steps. "Not there," he said. "Too many shadows. How about if you stand over here, Mr. Clemmins. If I shoot high, I can catch the color of those trees against the blue sky. That'll give us the pristine wilderness look I think you're looking for, Rich."

Everyone moved into position. Rich settled his face into serious lines. "This is a beautiful spot you have here, Mr. Clemmins, looks like the perfect place for families to enjoy the wilderness."

Clemmins cleared his throat. "Sorry."

"Don't worry about it, just keep talking. It's normal to be nervous. Pretend we're interested investors." The cough could be edited out. Along with anything else that Rich's audience didn't want to hear.

"You're correct, Mr. Ashcroft."

"Rich. Say it again, but this time call me Rich."

"You're right, Rich. What we want to build here is a place to which people can bring their children, and those children will, in years to come, bring their own children. Far from being an attack on the wilderness, I see the Grizzly Resort as a place where generations can be introduced to the true meaning of nature, a meeting of two worlds, if you will."

"Sounds perfect to me, Frank. Let me congratulate you on having such foresight. But someone murdered Reginald Montgomery, your business partner, two days ago. How might that despicable act threaten this resort you both worked so hard to bring to fruition?"

Clemmins squinted into the camera. "It's made some of our investors understandably nervous. But I'm confident that they're aware of the value of this project and we'll be able to continue."

"Some people are saying that the cold-blooded killing of your partner, Mr. Montgomery, was committed by activists associated with the Trafalgar Commemorative Peace Garden crowd. What are your feelings about them?"

As they drove to the site of last night's fire. Winters told Smith what he'd learned from his earlier meeting with the businessmen from Japan.

"Nothing."

She refrained from telling him that she'd seen that one coming.

"They are, quote, shocked and horrified, at the sudden death of Mr. Montgomery. We already know they were with Clemmins for a couple of hours after Montgomery left them on the night in question, so they're not in the frame. But I wanted to get a feel for how this'll affect their business plans."

"And?"

"And, if the police don't solve this in a hurry, and prove that it has nothing to do with M&D Developments, they might, just might, suggest to their bosses that M&D isn't a good investment opportunity at this time. All of which I learned by reading between the lines, you understand."

She drove past Big Eddie's coffee shop. The French doors across the front were open wide, and a line-up spilled down the street. A neatly dressed middle-aged man appeared to be having an intense conversation with a dreadlocked young woman. People were gathering around. Smith watched them in her rear view mirror.

"Get someone heading this way in case that scene grows," Winters said.

She picked up the radio.

She stopped at an intersection in one of the leafy residential streets in the original part of town, not far from Christa's place, to let an elderly lady with a walker cross the street. A face loomed up in her side window, and knuckles tapped at the glass.

It was Charlie Bassing, as mean and ugly as ever. A few red spots dotted the front of his sleeveless white T-shirt: it looked as if he'd had a nosebleed.

Smith pushed the button and the window rolled down. "What do you want, Charlie?"

"Just sayin' hi, sexy cop. This old guy your boss? Gotta go down on him to keep the job, eh?"

She wanted to punch his smug face in. Or perhaps shoot his knees full of bullets. He wouldn't be so tough if he couldn't walk. Instead she rolled the window back up and stared straight ahead. The old lady was now directly in front of the van. She waved like the Queen on parade and moved a centimeter further.

Charlie rapped on the glass again. Smith ignored him. They were only a couple of blocks from Christa's. She'd told Christa to call next time Charlie bothered her. But Trafalgar was a small town, and Christa's apartment was centrally located; perhaps Charlie really was only passing by.

"Roll down the window," Winters ordered.

"Bet you loved it when the cops let girls onto the force, eh, man." Charlie turned his bullet-shaped head and spat into the street.

"Do you want to accompany us to the station?" Winters said. "I can think of several reasons to keep you a guest of the city overnight."

Charlie raised his hands and backed onto the sidewalk. "No thanks. Have a nice day, pal."

The woman and her walker had barely cleared the front bumper of the van. Smith drove across the intersection anyway.

"You know that gentleman?" Winters said.

"Sadly, yes. He's after my friend, won't leave her alone. I've tried to persuade her to get a restraining order, but she won't do it. Figures that if she politely explains that she isn't interested in going out with him, he'll get the hint and go away."

"Nothing we can do then," Winters said. "I don't understand why women put up with men like that. Can you explain it to me?"

She would like to explain to him, all right, about power-imbalances, about being raised to be a good girl, about the embarrassment of explaining to a stuffed-shirt, condescending, middle-class *male* police officer like John Winters what it felt like to be stalked, humiliated, threatened.

"Tell her that he won't be talked into seeing her point of view," Winters said. "Tell her to come in and lay a complaint. It might save her life."

As if she hadn't done all that many times over. "She doesn't live far from here. I don't like it that he's so close."

"Worry about that later," Winters said. "Ron Gavin's at the park. I need to find out what he's discovered. Perhaps our arsonist will have dropped his driver's license in the mud."

There was no one in front of her: Smith put her foot on the gas.

It suited the bulk of his audience to think that Rich Ashcroft was a good, religious man. Today he was almost ready to believe it himself.

As they were pulling away from M&D Developments, with plenty of good footage in the can, something even better came his way.

A white SUV blocked the entrance to the work site. The logo on the side was of a man on a horse, holding a lance upright. The RCMP. Americans loved the Mounties. It reminded them of the Old West, the frontier. Of which there was nothing left in America. Not much left in Canada, either, but a Mountie driving an SUV would do. Unfortunately, the officer wasn't dressed in red serge. Just a brown uniform with a yellow stripe running down the pant leg.

A ragged bunch of protesters marched in the dirt in front of the entrance to Grizzly Resort. They wore an assortment of animal costumes that might have been stolen from their baby sister's Halloween get-up.

"We'll play it real friendly," Rich said. "Get it all, Greg. Meredith, stay in the car."

Cop and protesters stopped what they were doing at the sight of the car.

"Hey, officer, what's going on?" Rich put on his friendly face. Greg tried to be as noticeable as possible—not difficult for a man with a camera on his shoulder.

"Stop the animal killers!" The protesters ran forward.

Rich saw a grizzly bear, a wolf, a tiger, a moose or two, and what might have been a Maltese poodle. Horns and antlers wagged, big ears waved. "What's going on?" he asked.

"If you'll be on your way, sir," the Mountie said.

"A minute, please. These people are here for a reason. I'd like to hear it. You, sir, Mr....uh...bear. I'm Rich Ashcroft, CNC." He ran the letters together, trying to make them sound like CBC, the government-owned Canadian broadcaster that had the reputation of being left-wing. "Can you tell me what you're protesting here?"

Mr. Grizzly Bear pulled off his head. Underneath he was a clean-shaven, short-haired, mid-thirties man with frameless round glasses. He might have emerged only this morning from the cube farm of a bank. "We, uh," he mumbled.

"This abomination will kill the animals that count on this ravine for passage around the filth of human settlement." The speaker wore a wolf's head, as threatening as a Care Bear. The voice was muffled under the mask, but the big breasts could only belong to a human female.

Rich stepped closer, signaling to Greg to zoom in. "This looks like a nice family place to me. Wide open spaces, not too crowded, plenty of room for children to experience nature."

"They might as well go to a theme park in Florida for all the nature they'll experience here. It has to be stopped." The pack mumbled their agreement. The cop was looking edgy. He spoke into the radio on his shoulder. Time to move this on.

"What do you mean, stopped? The company has the proper authorization, doesn't it?" Rich asked, his eyes wide open and innocent. Innocent was his best look. They fell for it every time.

"Authorization," the wolf yelled. "We don't care about authorization." The group behind her shifted from foot to foot without much enthusiasm. Rich signaled to Greg to focus on the wolf-woman.

"You want the real story?" she asked.

"I'm here to listen."

Whereupon the wolf-woman told him that they would do whatever was necessary to stop the development. The grizzly bear, the moose and the tiger shuffled away. Rich could almost feel Greg's camera closing in.

"Whatever's necessary?" Rich said. "What do you mean by that?"

"An animal in the wild kills only because it has to."

"I'm sorry, but I don't understand. Are you comparing yourself, your group, to an animal cornered by its enemy? As if you're being put into the situation of kill or be killed?"

"Exactly," she said, as if she'd thought up the idea all by herself. She punched her fist into her hand. "We will stop the Grizzly Resort. Kill," she said, as Greg zoomed in on her masked face, "or be killed."

Chapter Seventeen

Ron Gavin's generous butt stuck out from the lower branches of a dense cluster of shrubbery.

The ground, sodden from last night's hoses, squelched beneath Smith's boots. The park entrance was blocked off with yellow tape, and the curious and bored peered through the decorative iron railing around the property, watching the investigators work.

"I've got reserve constables going door to door," Winters said as they crossed the lawn. "Asking if anyone in the neighborhood saw anything suspicious last night. Morning, Ron."

Gavin got to his feet with a low moan and a hand to the small of his back. He wore blue latex gloves. "John, Constable Smith. Hold on a mo. Over here!" His two assistants came running. Gavin pointed to the bush. A scrap of blue cloth was caught on a thorn. "Bag it," he said, "and you, Rebecca, are the lucky one who gets to go into that thicket and see if there's any other goodies to be found." The woman groaned good-naturedly, and the man carefully eased the cloth off the branch and into an evidence bag.

"Can you tell how long that's been there?" Smith asked.

"I can make an educated guess," Gavin said. "My thermos is in the van. Let me go and get it. That bush faces south, and there are no big trees close, so the sun is on it most of the day. There's hardly been a cloud in the sky for weeks, except for some rain Thursday morning. That cloth doesn't show any signs of fading. At a guess, and this is strictly off the record because we have tests to run back at the shop, I'd say it might have been put there yesterday."

"That's great!" Smith said.

"Not much to go on," Winters said, stomping all over her enthusiasm. "Anything else?"

"Lots of footprints. Too many footprints. Firefighters all over the place, laying down hose, spraying everything in sight. Plus this is a public park, anyone's prints being here don't mean a thing."

Gavin's small pile of belongings lay on the ground beside the RCMP's scene-of-the-crime van. He picked up his thermos and twisted the cap. "Sorry. No spare mugs."

"Not a problem," Winters said. "Have you seen the arson investigator's preliminary report?"

"Nothing surprising. Gasoline poured around the outside of the building and lit."

"I'm thinking this is an outsider," Winters said. "Good chance he," he glanced at Smith, "or she, arrived in town in the last few days. It's possible they didn't bring gas in a can ready to do the job. They would've needed to scout out the area first before coming up with a plan. I'll get someone checking gas stations asking if anyone came in for a can in the last little while."

A shout came from the RCMP investigators beside the bush. Gavin threw his cup down, and coffee ran into the ground. "Looks like they've got something."

Rebecca's face was scratched, and there was a tear across the shoulder of her shirt that hadn't been there a few minutes ago. But she was smiling broadly. She flexed her fingers in the blue gloves. "A lighter," she said. "One of the long ones that you use to light barbeques or firelogs with."

Gavin pulled a fresh set of gloves out of his pocket. "You don't say. Show me the way." And without another word they plunged into the bush. Smith could hear them thrashing about. Gavin swore lustily.

"I want pictures of that lighter as soon as they bring it out," Winters said. "I'm going up to the street to see if our people are getting anywhere with the neighbors."

She watched him walk away. He was dressed in beige chinos and a loose navy blue shirt. His walk was light, easy, his arms swinging loosely at his sides, and she guessed that he was a runner.

"So that's John Winters, eh?" Gavin's male assistant said.

"You know him?"

"Know of him. Bad business."

"What's bad business?"

"Whoa! You don't know—I'm not gonna be the one to tell you."

"I have to work with that guy. If there's something wrong with him, I need to know."

"Nothing wrong, Constable. Rumor, that's all."

"Tell me the rumor."

"I heard it like this." He lowered his voice. Smith stepped closer.

"You better not be telling tales out of school, McNally." Gavin had come out of the bush, soundlessly. Did he put the creaky old man bit on as suited him?

McNally jumped. "Not me."

"Keep it that way." A line of fresh red blood ran across Gavin's cheek—doubtless from an encounter with a thorn. He held up an evidence bag. Inside was a long grey and green metal tube with a trigger at the base, looking like an exceptionally thin gun.

"The camera's in the car," Smith said. "I'd like a picture of that, can I run and get it?"

"Sure. It's the sort campers use." Gavin held the bag up and turned it around so he could see all angles. "Judging by the camouflage coloring. Looks newish. Should be able to tell if it was bought strictly for this purpose by the fuel level. Something's stamped on the handle. My eyes aren't as good as they used to be." He held the bag out. "Can either of you see what it says?"

"Looks like an eagle and the letters MKAV," McNally said. "Probably the manufacturer."

"No," Smith said. "It means Mid-Kootenay Adventure Vacations."

Chapter Eighteen

A pickup truck that had not been young when the first Bush was president was parked at the side of the road a hundred yards from the entrance to the Grizzly Resort development. A head was silhouetted in the driver's seat, but Rich gave no more than an idle thought as to who it might be. Cop backup, maybe someone from the local paper hoping things would get interesting.

The truck turned around as Rich, Greg, and Meredith got into her car. Rich watched it in the side mirror, as Meredith pulled away. The truck came closer. The headlights flashed; the horn tooted. Greg turned around. "Guy wants to pass, Meredith. Idiot, there's plenty of room."

"Pull over," Rich said.

"Huh?"

"I said pull over. He doesn't want to pass. He wants to talk to me."

Meredith guided the car to the side of the road.

"Have the camera ready," Rich said.

"Never would of thought of that all by myself," Greg mumbled. Rich ignored him.

The truck pulled up behind them, so close that it almost touched the bumper. A man got out. He was Rich's height, around five foot seven, and scrawny. A blue ball cap advertising a brand of beer perched on his head; strands of greasy hair touched the back of his neck. His jeans were too large, his T-shirt could use a wash, and his running shoes trailed muddy laces across the ground. His left eye jerked under the force of an out-of-control twitch.

Rich stood beside the car and waited for the man to approach him.

"Recognized you back there. Ashcroft, right? From TV?"

He was in his late twenties, maybe younger.

Rich said nothing.

The man held out his hand. Rich looked at it. "Can I help you?" he said.

The man took his hand back. He didn't look offended at having it rejected. "No. But I can help you. I've been here a while, laying low, checking things out. Wondering what I can do to put an end, once and for all, to this peace garden idea. I saw your show last night. I figure you want the same thing I do."

"I want," Rich said, "to report the truth."

The man laughed. "Yeah, right."

"What's your interest in the park?"

"My dad was U.S. Army. Died in Vietnam. December of '72."

Rich whistled. "Only a couple months before the U.S. pulled out."

"I was born six months later. This monument, they might as well spit on my dad's grave."

Rich held out his hand. "What's your name, pal?"

They shook. "Harris. Brian Harris. And I'm proud to say that was my father's name."

"Greg," Rich said, "set up the camera."

Smith's parents' store stocked hundreds of those lighters, maybe thousands. They'd had the store logo stamped on them because they gave the lighters out as promotional items, freebees with the purchase of camping stoves or kerosene lamps.

And one of those lighters had, apparently, been used to set fire to the gardening shed at the peace garden site.

Coincidence, or was someone sending a message to the Smiths?

Smith switched off the camera. "I'd better go find the boss."

"I'll walk with you," he said. "I haven't finished my coffee." From inside the bush, Rebecca squawked in pain. "Must be what an iron maiden was like," Gavin said.

Smith didn't know what an iron maiden was, and didn't want to look foolish by asking.

"I've known John Winters for a lotta years," Gavin said, apropos of nothing. "I was with the Vancouver P.D. when I started my career, before switching to the more noble calling that is the Mounties."

The group of the curious had grown since their arrival. A Jack Russell made a lunge for a German shepherd about ten times its weight and, believing that discretion is the better part of valor, the shepherd retreated behind his owner's legs. These days everyone and their dog had an interest in police forensics.

"Lots of rumors floating around about John Winters," Gavin said. "Some of which aren't true."

"By which you mean that some of them are."

"Good cop, John. Always was, still is. He worked the Downtown Eastside. You know where that is?"

Where Graham died. "Yes."

"Tough beat."

She said nothing.

"But not as tough as Grey Point."

"Grey Point? In Vancouver? That's pretty much the opposite end of the social scale to the Eastside. Can't imagine much happening there."

"Which, I suspect, was the problem. I don't know the whole story, but John screwed up. Enough that he was about to end his career all by himself because his confidence in his own judgment had been shaken. I only know this because, as I said, we're old friends, and he called me when he heard there was an opening in the Trafalgar Police and he wanted to know what I thought of them."

He picked his cup off the ground. "Drat, that was the last of my brew."

"I can go and buy you one."

"Nope. No one makes it strong enough around here." Smith shivered at the idea as he put the cap back on the thermos and tucked it into his backpack.

"So, what was the problem?"

"He's waving at you, Smith. Better get going."

"Why did you tell me that story, if you're not going to finish it? This isn't the Downtown Eastside, or Grey Point either."

Gavin waved at Winters, letting him know Smith was coming. "I wouldn't have said nothing, if McNally hadn't shot off his fat mouth. I don't want you looking for problems where there aren't any, that's all. Partners have to trust each other. In my mind that the first rule of policing."

Partners, Smith thought, crossing the lawn toward their vehicle. Were she and Winters partners? She'd kinda thought they were boss and lackey. When she got a chance, she'd get on the Internet, see if she could find out more about this incident her "partner" had been involved in.

"Plenty of nothing," Winters said, once they were in the car. "No one saw anything. In Vancouver that'd be code for not wanting to get involved, but here, considering it was the early hours when the fire started, and everyone except new mothers was tucked up in bed like good citizens, I'll buy it. Did you get a picture of that lighter? I'll tell the people asking about the gas purchase to mention the lighter as well."

"No need." They pulled into traffic, the spectators watching, the Jack Russell barking as if it would attack their car, if not for that inconvenient leash.

"What do you mean, no need? Are you conducting this investigation, Molly?"

"No, of course not. I just meant that I can tell you where the lighter was purchased."

"Are you going to?"

"My parents' store. It had the store logo on it."

"I hope you're going to tell me that they produce one lighter a year and award it to a special individual."

"They give them out to pretty much anyone who wants one."

"I was afraid of that. Okay, next stop, your parents' store. Let's at least ask if they remember anyone getting a lighter in the last couple of days."

While Winters went into the store, again, Smith waited in the car. At his request, she called Rosemary Fitzgerald's number, and got voice mail. She left a message, again asking Rosemary to call the Trafalgar City Police. While the Fitzgerald phone rang, Smith accessed the car's computer and entered a report of their visit to the arson site, with details of the blue shirt fabric and the lighter. She also filed a report on Charlie Bassing, mentioning that he'd been insulting and potentially threatening to police officers.

She called Christa next. The phone rang, and once again she was put through to voice mail. Her parents had told her that there was a time when phones simply rang until someone answered or the caller hung up. She only half believed them.

Shoppers and tourists packed the sidewalks, and the street was heavy with traffic. The patio of Feuilles de Menthe overflowed with patrons and flowers. A steady stream of people walked in and out of Alphonse's Bakery, those leaving carrying bulging paper bags. It had been a long time, Smith thought, since those *Huevos Rancheros* at George's. A truck pulled into the parking space beside her. A kayak was loaded on top, and a family of four tumbled out.

"We have one possibility." Winters got back into the car. "A family from Montana bought a camp stove yesterday. Theirs died in Banff. Your father gave them a complimentary lighter."

"He usually does."

"Dad's a lawyer for the town of Billings, Mom's an oncologist. The kids were aged around three and five. Sounds like your radical arsonists to me. I'll drag them in for a session under the bright lights, starting with the three-year-old. Does your father always know so much about his customers?"

"He likes people."

"He's going to try to put together a list of everyone whose name he recorded as having been given one of those lighters in the last few months. Fortunately your parents believe in the value of building up an e-mail list. No stone unturned, eh, Molly?"

"Not a one."

"The lawyer slash oncologist family's staying at Valhalla Provincial Park. I'll have the Horsemen send someone to talk to them. They just might have given the lighter to a tall, dark stranger who told them his name and address as he stopped by the campfire for a cup of coffee brewed in a tin pot."

"Are you always this cynical, John? Isn't detailed investigative work the keystone of policing?" Out of nowhere, Smith felt a surge of anger, as hot and painful as heartburn, deep in her gut. All this man ever did was mock their profession. He had a good reputation, and, so she'd recently learned, a lot of gossip behind him, but if he was too old to cut it, time he stepped out of the way to let the young ones take over. "Should I forget about questioning people, following up clues, all that boring stuff and pull people off the street because I don't like the look in their eye or the set of their jaw?"

He turned to look at her. A very long few seconds passed.

"I can be cynical, Molly, yes. But I assure you that I believe in the value of good, solid police work. It doesn't hurt to laugh now and again, you know." He looked out the window. The kayak-owning family opened the trunk of their car. They threw in several bags marked with the logo of Mid-Kootenay Adventures and went next door to Rosemary's Campfire Kitchen. "You've got a nice town here," he said, "nice people mostly. Stay here, Molly. Stay out of the cities; they'll rot your cop soul. Let's head back to the station."

Maybe she should learn to lighten up a bit. But she was afraid that she might lighten up at the wrong moment. And, in this job, the wrong moment could allow something very bad to happen. Instead of thinking about that, she changed the subject.

"If you don't mind, John, I'd like to stop at my friend Christa's on the way. She's the one being stalked by that guy we encountered earlier. She isn't answering her phone, and it bothers me that he was close to her house. I can drop you first, if you want."

"I'll come with you. Then we can call on Robyn Goodhaugh, and I'd like to pay another visit to the not-grieving widow. I don't see her as her husband's killer, or even the instigator thereof. But I've been wrong before. I'm telling you that in the strictest of confidence, Smith. Don't let it out around the station."

He was a strange guy, Smith thought as she shifted the van into reverse. Best buddies one minute, rude and officious the next. When people blow hot and cold, she'd learned, best to avoid them altogether.

A green Neon blocked her exit, Meredith Morgenstern at the wheel. She couldn't quite make out the man beside Meredith. Then the light changed and Meredith pulled away and Smith caught a glimpse of him. She'd last seen that head when it had leaned toward her mother, his low, seductive voice asking her to explain the purpose of the Trafalgar Commemorative Peace Gardens.

"Hell and damnation," Smith said.

"What?"

"It's that TV guy. Rich Ashcroft. Being squired around town by Meredith Morgenstern of the *Daily Gazette*. And I'd bet anything the fellow in the back was their cameraman. I was hoping they'd have scurried back into their rat hole after last night's show."

"Which car?"

"The Neon. Two ahead."

"Turn that way. Let's see where they're going. But do it unobtrusively. I don't want any police harassment accusations."

The journalists went no further than a parking lot behind Front Street. Smith glided into a vacant spot on the side of the street and watched as Meredith, Ashcroft, and the unidentified man left their vehicle. The man put his equipment into the trunk, and they walked up the street. Meredith's eyes flickered as she saw Smith and Winters sitting in the unmarked van, but otherwise she didn't react.

"I don't think Meredith's too happy with her fellow journalists," Smith said.

"Why so?"

"Her body language. She's holding herself all stiff and tight. Look how much distance there is between her and Ashcroft."

"Maybe that's just her way."

"I know Meredith. Her way is to get in the face of every influential person who arrives in town."

"You don't like her?"

"Ambitious small-town journalist. Dedicated cop. Both products of the hate-factory that is a district high school. What's not to like?"

"Stay here. I don't want them to spot that uniform." Winters unfastened his seat belt and got out of the van.

Smith called Christa again. Voice mail again.

Molly Smith turned her phone off when she wasn't working, but Christa lived by her cell.

Smith punched instructions into the van's computer and pulled up the number for Christa's dad. Maybe she'd gone to visit him, as unusual as that might be. Cell phone reception in the mountains was pretty much non-existent outside of the handful of towns nestled in the valleys and the highways connecting them.

"Hello?"

"Hi, Mr. Thompson. This is Mol…uh…Moonlight Smith, Christa's friend. Remember me?"

"I certainly do, young Moonlight. It's been a long time. Are you as pretty as ever?"

Mr. Thompson always did think of himself as a charmer.

"Is Christa there?"

"No. Why do you ask, dear?"

"Nothing important. She isn't answering her phone. She's probably out of range, so I thought of calling you."

"I'm pleased to hear from you, Moonlight, but I can't say I've seen Christa in the last few weeks. Why don't you come up and have lunch one day."

"Hold that thought, Mr. Thompson. Sorry, I've gotta run." She hung up. Perhaps Christa had found a beach somewhere. It was a perfect day for the beach, and after a month of sunshine and temperatures in the mid thirties, even the glacier-fed lakes would be inviting.

But Christa didn't have a car. Hard to get to a beach out of town without a car. A ride with a friend? Christa didn't have many friends. Just Molly Smith. She might have made new friends, which she hadn't told Smith about. Nothing wrong with that.

"Nothing," Winters said, getting back into the car. "They went to India Delight for lunch. I'm not happy to know that rabble-rousing TV scum is still hanging around. Speaking of lunch, I'm starving. I'd love Indian, but that might be considered police harassment. Chinese instead? My treat?"

"Chinese is always good in my books."

The proprietor acted as if he were delighted beyond belief to have a uniformed police officer in his establishment. Smith gave him a tight smile: at least it was better than the people who metaphorically spat as she passed. Winters asked for whatever would be the fastest, and they were soon served plates piled high with hot, scented food. Winters used chopsticks, but Smith went for a fork.

"I like to eat," he said. "But aside from that, I find that it gives me time to slow down and think. What do you make of all this?"

She was trapped with a snow pea halfway to her mouth. "Huh?"

"Montgomery. Are we any way toward solving this? The CC wants to call in the IHIT. I told him that I…we…can handle it. Was I wrong?"

He was asking her?

She lowered her fork. "You seem to have abandoned the dentist and the not-grieving widow."

"Because I think they didn't do it. I have an appointment with her at three. She graciously managed to fit me in between nail and hair appointments. I've never seen a woman so unimpressed by her husband's death. But I have to believe that if she were in any way responsible, she'd be throwing up a smokescreen of inconsolable grief. Your dentist lied about where he was at the time in question. That's a black mark against him. I'd like to find someone who saw him on the bluffs at the time Montgomery was dying. The business partner is in the clear, as are the business associates, unless they acted together, which I can't see. Or hired out the killing. But it wasn't a professional job—too up close and personal. Unless it was made to look unprofessional. So I'm left with…."

"The peace garden proponents or the resort opponents."

More food arrived, serving platters overflowing.

"Do you think," Winters said, "that we're being provided with more than the standard fare? Perhaps we should pull them in for attempting to bribe an officer."

She worried that one day she'd mistake one of his jokes for a serious suggestion, and really mess up. It was not a pleasant thought.

"Let's not," he said. "That would make it hard to find a good, cheap meal."

They ate the rest of their meal in silence.

The bill arrived and Winters said, "Let's get back to the station."

Smith dialed Christa again as they left the restaurant. Four rings and then voice mail. "I'm sorry, John, but I'm worried about my friend. It's probably nothing, but seeing him so near her place, and her not answering, has me concerned. I'd like to stop by, check everything's okay."

He looked at her over the roof of the van. The sun was high in the sky and it cast a shadow over his face. He put on sunglasses. "Let's go," he said.

◇◇◇

Meredith was no longer the bubbly cub reporter Rich Ashcroft had met yesterday. This was a small town; she'd have friends and family on the other side. He didn't care in the least if she was happy or not, but she was the only local contact he had, so he wanted to keep her sweet.

"That footage is going to be great," he said. "What a story. We've got the solid, respectable business man, looking like Charles Manson, but I can't do anything about that, talking softly about the death of his partner, and the loonies outside, ready to destroy his business, screaming abuse. And then Harris, all wet eyes and honoring the father he never got the chance to know. I want to go to someplace with a good view and record my closing comments. I'll run this segment at the top of the show tonight, and we'll get major exposure on the East Coast tomorrow morning."

Greg grinned and wiped his face on his napkin.

"But I need something more," Rich said. "I need a local touch. It's one thing me telling the viewers what I've found here in your pretty town, but I need help. Think you're up to it, Meredith?"

"Up to what." She leaned back to let the waitress remove her almost untouched plate.

"Reporting for CNC. A first step toward a regular job."

Fire shot through her eyes. *Gotcha*, he thought. She sucked in her breath.

"Me?"

"You've got what it takes to report for TV, or I wouldn't ask. I need local color. How about it?"

"I'd appreciate the opportunity."

Greg tossed his company credit card onto the table.

"Can I go home and change?" Meredith said, as they left the cool of the restaurant for the sunbaked street.

Rich stood back and studied her body. She had a good figure: long legs, trim waist, and adequate-sized tits. She wore a short jeans skirt that showed a good portion of her long, bare, brown legs, a blue tank top, and sandals with thin straps. Her dark hair hung in loose curls around her shoulders. She put her sunglasses on. "No need," he said. "That outfit's perfect for a woman-in-the-street reporting style. I'd like to get an interview with that cop friend of yours, Smith's daughter. When can you arrange it, Meredith?"

"Molly? I can't see her agreeing to an interview."

"There's no real hurry. I'm going to stay on for another couple days. Get the town's reaction after they see that once people have watched my show, there's going to be a lot of controversy over this so-called peace park. The power of the press. You okay with two or three more days, Greg? Nothing on at home?" As if Greg had a life other than behind that camera. He probably jerked off against it every night.

"Not me. I'm good, boss."

"We'll get the lady cop later. Right now, I'd like a shot of you, Meredith, walking past that store, the one the Smiths own."

"Why?"

Rich wasn't used to underlings who asked why. He swallowed a sharp reply. Keep her sweet. "The store gives the feel of what this place is like. Small town, family-owned businesses. Footage of you in front of it will locate you, Meredith, in this place at this time."

"The bridge is usually used as a backdrop for Trafalgar," she said. "It's quite distinctive."

"Usually. That's exactly the word, Meredith. I'm not here to do what's usually done. But if you're…."

"Hey," she said, "let's go."

Chapter Nineteen

Winters waited in the car while Smith went to the door. Her friend's apartment was in an old house divided into two apartments. In this town of transients, there were a lot of houses broken up to be rented out.

It was a nice street though. Some of the homes were well maintained, restored back to their heyday of Victorian gentility. Unlike the suburbs, the street was busy with people walking or gardening, and children played on neatly maintained front lawns in the shade of large and aged trees.

He missed Eliza. This case was proving to be more difficult than he'd expected, and the political angle was throwing him off. Eliza was an astute observer of human nature, and he'd sometimes done his best thinking while bouncing ideas off her. If she hadn't been in Florida for six weeks last year, helping her parents out because her mother had broken her leg, he might not have screwed up the Blakely case so badly.

Someday he might come to trust Smith enough to throw his more outlandish ideas at her and see if they'd stick. But she had a lot of growing up to do first.

A brown bag lay on the front steps. Smith paused, touched it with her foot, picked it up, and looked inside. The frown on her face deepened. She knocked on the door a few times, before pulling out her truncheon and banging at it. A woman stuck her head out of a downstairs window, all ready to give her hell. But she stopped at the sight of the uniform, and Smith walked over to her. The woman shook her head. Smith took out her phone and dialed, listened for the length of time it took the phone to ring four times, and hung up with a grimace of disgust. Tonight, he'd phone Eliza in Toronto. They'd been married for twenty-five years, and he still couldn't manage a couple of nights without hearing the purr of her voice.

Smith went back to the door and leaned up against it, standing on tiptoes and holding her hands in front of her face to peer in the high, dirty window at the top of the door. Her body jerked back with such shock that before she could turn and call for help, Winters was moving.

"What?"

"I see someone." Her face was white, her blue eyes wide, breath short and choppy. "On the floor. She's not moving. Chris!" Smith banged at the door. "Chris, it's me. Open up."

"Ask the lady next door if she has a key."

Smith ran, yelling, and Winters took her place at the window, stuffing his sunglasses into the front of his shirt. He could see a woman's legs, bare, the feet wrapped in sturdy sandals. The upper half of her body disappeared into darkness. He studied the door. It was old, made of thick, solid wood. It wouldn't be easy to kick down.

"Got it." Smith waved the key. The neighbor followed her, trailed by two sticky-faced children.

Smith moved to push him out of the way. He held out his hand. "I'll take that." For a moment he thought she was going to refuse. But she passed the key over.

"Call this in. Get an ambulance. Keep that woman and particularly those children out of the way. Half the street'll be here in a minute. Constable Smith, I gave you an order. Do it!"

She blinked, took a deep breath, and he could almost see the cop flooding back into her, the way that in old horror movies you could see the demon taking possession of the body of the white-limbed maiden.

She straightened her shoulders and fingered the radio at her collar. "I need you to take your children inside the house ma'am," she said. "There's nothing to see here. Dispatch, this is Smith, I need…."

The hallway was very small and very dark. The woman on the floor took up most of the space. "Bring me a flashlight," Winters yelled. The legs were curled across the floor, in a semi-fetal position, but her head and shoulders were draped across the stairs, face down. The step was wet. The small, enclosed space smelled of released bladder, blood, and fear.

Winters dropped to his haunches and touched the exposed neck. Warm skin moved. His fingers came away wet and he looked at them. Definitely blood.

He heard sirens, the squeal of brakes, doors opening, Smith's strong voice telling them where to go.

"She's alive," he said to the paramedics. There wasn't room for all of them in the landing. He walked outside and left them to do their job.

He blinked in the bright sunshine. "She's alive," he repeated to Smith. "Finished at the park or not, I want Ron Gavin here now. Call it in."

People began to gather on the sidewalk across the street. Paramedics talked in low, professional tones. Another siren and a marked police car pulled up. Dave Evans parked half on the sidewalk.

"Keep those people back," Winters told him. "Too many people with nothing better to do. You can sit in our van now that Dave's here," he said to Smith.

"Charlie fucking Bassing. When I get my hands on the god-damned bastard," she said.

"You will escort him to the station with all due formality and have him questioned as per procedure. Do you hear me, Constable Smith?"

Her blue eyes looked like storm clouds moving in on a sunny day. Her mouth twitched.

"Otherwise you will be seriously compromising a legal case. Is that what you want?"

"No." She buried her face in her hands. Her shoulders shook.

"Go and sit in the van," Winters repeated.

"I'm okay." She looked up. Her eyes were dry. "Dave needs some help over there." Evans was arguing with the downstairs neighbor, the one who had a key.

"I have to see if anything's been stolen," she shouted.

"Evans can handle it. Get in the van, Constable Smith."

A dark blue uniform backed out of Christa's doorway, holding the end of a stretcher. A second paramedic followed, holding a plastic bag and an IV line over a thin shape under a white sheet. Christa's head was streaked with blood, and blood soaked the front of her shirt. The crowd fell silent while she was loaded into the ambulance.

"Have you room for my constable?" Winters asked the medic, his hand on the floor of the vehicle, ready to jump in the back with the patient.

"Yes."

Smith was in the van, as ordered, watching. Winters gestured to her, and she leapt out. "Accompany the patient to the hospital," he said. "You're off duty for the rest of the day." She clambered into the ambulance, rejecting a hand from the paramedic, and the doors slammed shut behind her. Evans forced onlookers aside to make a path for the retreating vehicle.

At the hospital, they wouldn't tell her anything. Christa was rushed away, but a nurse stopped Smith at the reception desk. "You can wait here, Officer."

"I'm not an officer. I mean, I'm not here as an officer. I'm her friend."

"Then take a seat over there." The nurse nodded toward the waiting area. The room smelled of disinfectant, floor polish, grief, and pain. A woman about Smith's age wept silently into the shoulder of a much older man. He patted her back and his lips moved, but no sound came out. People flicked through dusty magazines. Some of them looked up to see what was going on. A TV was suspended from the wall, turned to a headline news channel. Either the sound was off or Smith couldn't hear it over the screams of blame and recrimination bounding around the inside of her brain.

She pulled her phone out.

"No cell phones," the nurse said.

Smith punched in the number as she ran outside. "Mom?" she said. "I need you, Mom." And the tears fell.

Lucky Smith splashed cold water across the back of her neck. God, she'd decided, was not a woman.

This could not be happening. A bomb threat, of all things, and now the police were questioning them about the barbeque lighters they used to promote the store. Barbeque lighters. John Winters hadn't said why he wanted to know. He hadn't had to. There'd been a fire last night. Burned the gardening shed that was all the Commemorative Peace Garden consisted of, so far, almost to the ground.

Had someone happened upon a Mid-Kootenay Adventure Vacations customized lighter, or was it a direct threat? It had to be the latter. They sold and gave away a lot of those lighters over the course of a year, but nowhere near the numbers that would be bought at the Wal-Mart in Nelson, or any retail outlet.

She studied her face in the mirror. Water dripped from the tendrils of grey hair at the back of her neck. Lines of worry and stress pulled at the corners of her eyes and the edges of her mouth. *When,* she thought, *did I get so old? About the same time my husband abandoned all our ideals, my daughter became a cop (a pig, as I used to say) and my son graduated from law school, and instead of taking on pro-bono cases for the poor and dispossessed, joined an oil company.*

The phone rang. Lucky considered not answering it. A supplier explaining that they were backordered. Another supplier wondering why they hadn't been paid (because the check is in the mail, goddamnit!). A booking calling to cancel. Duncan reporting that they were still waiting for the last of the overnight group and had she heard anything.

Who would care? It would just go into the ether that was voice mail. Where she'd answer it or not, as she chose.

"Lucky, phone," Flower, the weekend employee, called. "Can you get it? I'm with a customer."

She took the call. "Welcome to Mid-Kootenay Adventure Vacations."

"Mom? I need you, Mom."

Lucky ran out of the store so fast that the customers thought a hurricane was blowing through. "Christa's in hospital," she shouted. "Tell Andy I'll call soon as I know anything."

As worried as she was about Christa, who had pretty much grown up in the Smith house, Lucky was just as worried about Moonlight. The cry in her voice was so sharp that Lucky knew her daughter was reliving the morning she'd rushed to the hospital in Vancouver. Too late. Because Graham was already dead.

Rich had planned to have Meredith walking down the street, through the slowly moving crowds, passing Mid-Kootenay Adventures while Greg got a long shot of the store frontage. He positioned her at the corner of Elm Street and stationed Greg on the other side, to get a wide view before narrowing in on Meredith and the store through the traffic. Rich hadn't bothered to wire Meredith. She'd never make it outside of print journalism; she was pretty enough, but her voice was too high pitched. He'd let her say something on camera and tell the producer to edit almost all of it out. He'd blame the network for cutting her best lines.

He fastened a mike to his own shirt front and stood with Meredith. He'd walk behind her, just out of camera range. A few passers-by glanced at Greg and his camera, but most people were preoccupied by their own affairs.

"Okay, babe," he whispered to Meredith. "Show time."

She walked. Her hips swayed under the denim skirt; her heels tapped on the sidewalk. An old lady, all purple dress, sensible shoes, slate gray hair and pearls, smiled at her. Perfect local color.

As Meredith reached Mid-Kootenay Adventures the door crashed opened and a tiny red tumbleweed fell into the street.

"Lucky," Meredith said, forgetting that she was supposed to keep walking. "Are you okay?"

Lucky Smith was clearly not okay. Her face was flushed, her eyes showing so much white she looked like a horse smelling smoke in the barn. "Meredith," she said, "hi. Gotta run."

"Mrs. Smith." Rich broke from his planned scenario and ran forward. He tapped at the mike fastened to his lapel as if it were a talisman. "Do you have a moment for our viewers, Mrs. Smith?"

"You," she shouted, "how dare you come anywhere near me?" A section of red-and-gray hair broke free of its clip.

He stepped directly into her path. "I'd like to ask you a few questions," he said, using his calm interviewer voice.

"Get the fuck out of my way," she shouted. Spittle flew from her mouth. He hoped Greg was focused good and tight. She stretched out both arms and pushed Rich in the chest, with as much force as butterfly crashing into him. He grunted and staggered backward.

"What's the matter?" Meredith said.

"My daughter," Lucky yelled, "I have to get to my daughter."

"Molly? What's happened to Molly?"

"Please, Mrs. Smith," Rich interrupted. He placed his foot firmly on top of hers. "Get yourself under control."

"I'll get you under control, you fucking monster, if you don't get out of my way."

Crowds were gathering. Rich heard a voice call his name in recognition. It was not a friendly voice. Several people asked Lucky, by name, what was happening. Rich backed away and put up his hands, palms outward. "I don't want any trouble here. Just doing my job."

The crowd parted to let a tall, chubby man through. "What on earth?" He recognized Rich. "My God, it's you. Haven't you done enough harm to my wife?"

Rich ran across the street, dodging cars as if a mob were chasing him, rather than just Meredith. The onlookers remained behind to suggest that someone call the police, or an ambulance, or to ask Lucky if she needed help.

Perfect.

Chapter Twenty

Big Eddie's Coffee Emporium was empty. John Winters had walked up from the station, needing time to think. He was still surprised at how many people he passed knew who he was, and how many of them smiled a greeting. Sometimes, after the anonymity of the city, it felt nice to be part of a community. Nice, until you were with your partner when she found the battered body of her childhood friend. He ordered four coffees to take back to the station.

"Is Christa gonna be all right?" the black woman behind the counter asked him. Her accent made him think of the late Princess Diana. "She was in here just this morning."

Amazing how fast news traveled. "She was here? When?"

The woman shrugged. "Morning rush. I can't say for sure, it gets so busy."

"I'm John Winters, by the way." He put his hand across the counter.

She shook it with a flash of white teeth. "Jolene."

"Was she with anyone?"

"No. Christa's always on her own."

"Anyone seem to be paying her any particular attention?"

Jolene passed him a take-out tray for the coffees. Her hair was a mass of braids sprinkled with beads so colorful they might have been selected from a child's toy box. They flew around her face as she shook her head. "No. People were talking about that

TV program last night. This isn't a town where people keep their opinions to themselves."

He smiled. "So I've noticed. In your opinion what was the general feeling about the show?"

She tilted her head to one side and thought before speaking. "Sixty percent maybe were upset about it. They thought it put the town in a bad light, regardless of their thoughts about the park. Twenty percent thought that any attention to the garden was a good thing, as it will get support moving again. Another ten percent said that if it helped stop the park it was a good thing. What am I up to?"

"Ninety percent."

"And at least twenty percent felt bad for the park committee, saying that it made them look like fools."

"You're over one hundred, Jolene."

"I haven't even counted those who agreed with everyone," she said, placing Styrofoam cups into the tray.

"Nor those who disagreed with everyone," the bulky man behind the cash register said. "There are always folks who just like to get up everyone's noses. So what's the story about the fire, eh? Not an accident, I'm suspecting, not after that TV show. I'm Eddie by the way. Welcome."

"Thanks. John Winters." He balanced the tray of coffee and shook the outstretched hand. "The full report on the fire isn't in yet." He pulled a handful of coins out of his pocket. "Did you notice Christa Thompson here earlier?"

"I might have. But before you ask, I didn't see anything that made me sit up and pay attention. Too busy."

"If you remember anything, either of you…."

"I'll call you," Jolene said.

"We care about our customers here," Eddie said as he rang up the charge. And somehow it didn't sound to Winters like an advertising slogan.

He walked back to the station. He handed out the coffees and was told that Rose Benoit had called. His former partner, Rose was an inspector now, in charge of the commercial crime section. Which suited her—there was not much Rose loved more than getting her head around a set of books.

He returned the call, and caught her at her desk. They exchanged pleasantries before Benoit got to the point. "There's no reason to believe the resort's in any trouble." Winters put his feet up on his desk and took a sip of his coffee. "Unless…." He straightened up. "Unless opposition to the resort, which opponents claim will disrupt prime grizzly bear territory, finds focus and draws enough attention to the environmental dangers that people hesitate to buy into the resort. In addition, if the proposed Commemorative Peace Garden is built in Trafalgar, the nearest town, and vacationers from the U.S., to whom the company is aiming sixty percent of their marketing efforts, avoid the area because of the political implications, the Grizzly Resort could be in deep financial trouble. It's unlikely that M&C Developments could survive the collapse of Grizzly."

"Partnership insurance?" he asked.

"Seems straightforward. Enough to help Clemmins and the business absorb some of the blow caused by the death of Montgomery, but nothing excessive. By the look of things, John, I'd say Montgomery was the drive behind the partnership. Clemmins dug up the start-up costs and worked to get investors interested in putting up more money, while Montgomery negotiated with construction companies and townships. I also took a peek at the Japanese firm negotiating with M&C. They seem to be squeaky clean. From what I've learned, without Montgomery M&C Developments is hanging on by its fingertips. Clemmins has more to lose with the death of his partner than he has to gain. Although…."

"I like the sound of that, Rose," he said. "Carry on."

"Just rumor and conjecture."

"Rumor and conjecture to a detective without a lead is like mother's milk to an abandoned kitten."

"Whatever. The business community's buzzing with talk about Montgomery and M&C. There was some strain between

Montgomery and Clemmins. They were overheard not long ago having an intense discussion."

Winters had no idea where Rose got all her information. But it was always reliable.

"Seems that Clemmins was getting cold feet. The Grizzly Resort was pretty much the sum total of M&C the last few months. Montgomery even rented a house in Trafalgar to be near the action."

"Clemmins didn't like that?"

"He was worried that they were getting too deep into the resort. With local groups and environmental activists opposing the development, and the possibility of an American boycott of the town if this monument to Vietnam draft dodgers is built, the risk of losing it all was climbing."

"So he decided to cut his losses and take out a contract on his partner?"

"Been done before. But both Montgomery and Clemmins have clean reputations. For developers in this market, anyway. If you want my off-the-record opinion."

"I do."

"Clemmins might bash Montgomery's brains out, or visa versa, in an argument over the resort. But you say he's got a good alibi, so it would have to have been a contract killing. And I can't see that. There might be something I haven't found out, but I'd say Clemmins has too much to lose from Montgomery's death."

They hung up with the promise of dinner when he was next in Vancouver. Eliza enjoyed the company of Rose and her husband, Claude, who was, of all things, a sculptor. One of his pieces had been bought by the city for a prominent square. It was a minor scandal, as everyone thought that the sculpture was a stylized giant penis about to penetrate a woman. It was, Claude had sniffed, the arrow of truth breaking into the cave of narrow minds.

Even now Winters laughed when he thought of it. He tossed his coffee cup into the trash. Time to head off to a visit with Ellie Montgomery. That would surely be a waste of time.

"Tell me you've heard from Mrs. Fitzgerald," he said to Denton at the front desk.

"No can do." Denton was still nursing his double-double. "The Horsemen called. They talked to the Baxter guy."

"Who?"

"Got a lighter from Andy Smith's store yesterday?"

"Right."

"Waved it in front of their faces."

Yet another dead end. "Anything from the people checking gas stations?"

"Not yet."

"Bassing?"

"Not at his place. His car's gone, which is good news. We've sent his license plate number to the border guards, all across B.C. and down to Washington State. That girl was in here only yesterday, asking for Molly. Any word from the hospital?"

"Not yet."

◇◇◇

As expected, Winters learned nothing new from Mrs. Montgomery, but driving back to town, Ron Gavin called to tell him that the entrance to Christa's apartment was a gold mine of forensic evidence—evidence up the wazoo, he said. Her key was on the floor, two sets of fingerprints on it. Two sets on the door knob. The neighbor had been watering his lawn that morning, and had also watered the sidewalk. Muddy footprints too large to be Christa's had stomped up the path, overlaying a smaller set that was probably hers, and went through her front door.

Dave Evans called next to say that he'd found a neighbor who'd seen Christa in the company of a man only steps from her door. And the neighbor was sure he'd be able to identify the guy.

Winters heard nothing from Smith at the hospital nor from the hospital itself, and he hoped that no news was good news. They should be able to get Bassing well and good. Now all they had to do was to find him.

Time to head home, change and go for a good long run. Something to clear the cobwebs out of his brain.

And maybe he'd have a flash of insight about the Montgomery case while pounding the pavement.

Andy Smith was sitting at the kitchen table in the center of a puddle of yellow light when Lucky and her daughter got home. Sylvester leapt to his feet and greeted them as if they'd been away for months, trekking in the Himalayas. Lucky pushed him aside. She wasn't in a mood to endure his usually joyful greeting.

"Christa?" Andy asked.

"She'll be okay." Lucky collapsed into a chair. Sylvester kept nuzzling her, until she relented and gave him a half-hearted pat. "A couple of broken ribs, a lot of bruising on her face. A cracked cheekbone." Christa had been wrapped in bandages, her right eye swollen and blackened, her lips thick and cut. She'd been sleeping when Lucky and Moonlight were allowed a minute in her room. Her breathing sounded harsh and ragged. Lucky kissed her lightly on the cheek, her heart breaking, and Moonlight had clenched her own hands together until her knuckles turned as white as the face of the moon, and they left.

Moonlight tossed her boots onto the mat beside the door. She filled the kettle. "She was starting to regain consciousness when I found her. She could have lain there for days calling for help before that bitch of a neighbor did anything other than hammer on the wall and scream at her to shut up."

"Can I visit tomorrow?" Andy asked.

"You should be able to," Lucky said.

"Good. I want to catch the late news."

Moonlight tossed her gun belt on the table. Lucky winced at the sight of it, as she always did. At least it was her daughter who carried a gun, not her son. She didn't know why that seemed preferable, but it did.

A loose floorboard creaked under Andy's footsteps. He hadn't reached out to comfort her. These days they seemed to interact like two bubble people, each confined to their own private world. It would have been nice if he'd sat with them for a while. Had tea and cookies around the kitchen table, and talked over their troubles. Like they used to.

"It's my fault," Moonlight said, taking mugs off the drying rack and bags of tea out of the canister on the counter.

"Nonsense," Lucky said. "It's the fault of Charlie whatshisname. And don't you dare forget that."

"I told her to take out a restraining order. But when she came to the station, I wasn't there. I had more important things to do. I forgot her. She could have died."

"Look at me, Moonlight," Lucky said. "Look at me."

Moonlight turned her head. Outside the sun was setting, and the shadows of the trees were as long as those across her high cheekbones. She tucked a strand of hair behind her ear.

"You did all you could. You tried to warn Christa. You told her to make a complaint. You couldn't force her to go in front of a judge, could you?"

"No, but…."

"No buts about it. I've seen it before." Lucky accepted a cup of tea. Moonlight threw herself into a chair. The gun belt lay on the table between them. The Great Divide—tearing the one strong river that had been their family into two. "A nice young woman like Christa, she can't believe in the violence of the world outside."

"That's the point, Mom." Moonlight hit the table so hard the sugar bowl jumped. "I know! I knew she was in danger. I wasn't there when she turned to me. I was too busy."

"Too busy," Lucky said, "trying to find the person who murdered a citizen of this town. I may have disagreed with Montgomery, profoundly, but I want his killer to be caught. Don't make it sound as if you were smoking a joint and reading *Cosmo*, Moonlight."

Lucky's daughter stared into her tea cup.

"You're an officer of the law. A policewoman. Moonlight Smith can't make Christa's choices for her. But Constable Smith can do something about bringing that…person…to justice. Not only Christa, but Montgomery, and the people of this town need you. Are you going to be there for them?"

"I don't know, Mom." Moonlight lifted her head. Her eyes were blue pools in a face touched with sunburn. She was so fair, like her father, that she didn't take the sun well. "The job. The responsibility. Sergeant Winters thinks I'm a schoolgirl. Christa needed me and I forgot her. Graham would have told me what was right." She ground her knuckles into her eyes until fireworks exploded behind her lids.

"Well, Graham isn't here," Lucky said, sounding as firm as she could. "And you're on your own, Moonlight. Molly. But think of this…if you'd been working as a clerk in your brother's law firm, or helping out at the store, or teaching at the university, would you have found Christa today?"

"No, but…."

"Lucky, get in here!" Andy bellowed from the family room.

Mother and daughter looked at each other. Had his favorite baseball team scored?

"Now, Lucky!"

They ran.

"Not him again."

Rich Ashcroft was interviewing Frank Clemmins. Lucky caught the tail end of the interview as Clemmins, trying to hide a tear at the corner of his eye, talked about his business partner, so cruelly cut down. He hoped, he said, with a deep sigh, to be able to continue the project that was Reg's vision. He said something about families enjoying the wilderness. Then he was gone and Ashcroft pontificated for a few seconds. An ad for a luxury SUV came on. Somehow the advertisers had been able to associate their product with saving the environment.

"That wasn't much," Moonlight said. "Forget him. He's had his fifteen minutes of fame."

"Sit down, both of you," Andy snapped. "He isn't finished. The whole first segment of the show, he said at the beginning, is about Trafalgar. And didn't I see him this afternoon, in front of our store?"

The family sat in silence waiting for the program to resume. Lucky picked a copy of the *Utne Reader* off the coffee table and fanned her face. A hot flash was coming on.

A group of people wearing animal masks appeared on the screen, and for a hopeful moment she thought the program had gone to an early Halloween segment.

"That sounds like Robyn Goodhaugh." Moonlight was sitting on the arm of her father's chair. She touched his shoulder, and for a moment Lucky had a flush of hope that they could be a loving family again. Or was it just another hot flash? She fanned harder. Damned house—they should have gotten air conditioning years ago.

On TV, the wolf head said something about kill or be killed, and they broke for a commercial.

Lucky groaned. Robyn had joined the Commemorative Peace Garden committee and worked like a demon organizing petitions and letter-writing campaigns. At first Lucky thought they were fortunate to have her. But Robyn's rhetoric quickly turned to threats of violence if she didn't get her way, and Lucky and Barry decided that she had to go.

The parting had not been easy. Robyn was now quick to disparage the park committee at every opportunity.

"Didn't you have that fool of a woman here, in our house, Lucky?" Andy said. "I'd have expected you to have better sense."

"Stop bickering." Moonlight threw herself onto the floor in front of the TV. If not for the dark blue uniform and the shoulder patches with the town crest and the words *Since 1895; Trafalgar City Police,* Moonlight might have been a kid, pleased to be allowed up late to watch a special program.

Ashcroft interviewed a young man next. He'd been born after his dad died, he told Rich, in Vietnam, only a month short of the end of the war. He spoke about growing up without a father, full of pride of the man he'd never known. The skin at the corner of his left eye twitched. And now this garden, he said, this monument to cowardice, made him wonder if his life had been a lie and he should be ashamed of his father's sacrifice.

"Never," Rich said, struggling to keep his voice under control. "Never." He gripped the boy's shoulder.

Another ad.

"He was in the store yesterday," Andy said.

"Ashcroft? He's everywhere, like the smell from clogged drains."

"Not Ashcroft. The young guy, Harris."

"Why?"

"I don't remember him buying anything. Browsed around, not really looking at the merchandise. He doesn't look much like the outdoors type, so I kept an eye on him."

"Shush," Lucky said, "they're back."

Meredith Morgenstern sauntered down Front Street as cars flashed in front of her and the summer crowds flowed around her like a river coming to a slow-moving branch. Mrs. Alexander from the United Church Women greeted her.

And Lucky knew that this was going to be bad. Very bad. She wanted to run from the room. But she was trapped in her chair as if she were wearing leg irons.

The camera focused on Meredith's bouncing bosom in a thin T-shirt. Then it jerked and the screen was full of Lucy Casey, known for the past thirty-five years as Lucky Smith.

She scarcely recognized herself, screaming, swearing, looking like a child's idea of a witch, missing only the pointed black hat and the broom.

Sylvester sensed her distress and nuzzled up against her leg, trying to offer comfort. He was ignored.

The program ended with a close-up of Meredith standing at Eagle Point Bluffs. She mumbled half a sentence about conflict in a peaceful community, before the camera cut to Rich Ashcroft.

Trafalgar was laid out behind him. White glacier, green and brown mountains, blue sky behind, blue river in front.

His closing commentary didn't call for viewers to descend upon the town with pitchforks and torches. But it might as well have.

"We are so fucked," Andy said. "This is all your fault, Lucky."

"Mine! I've heard enough today about fault and blame."

"Maybe you've heard enough, because you're the cause of it all."

Moonlight jumped up. "Dad, slow down. Mom didn't want any of this to happen."

Andy struggled out of his La-Z-boy. His face was red and his pale blue eyes the shade of glacier ice. His jowls quivered. Lucky had never before noticed just how much weight he'd put on around his face. "You and your sixties sentiment's going to destroy my business."

"My sixties sentiment? What the hell does that mean, Andy? Are you telling me that you missed the sixties? And what do you mean *my* business? Last I looked it was *our* business."

Sylvester barked and ran from one person to the other, his lush tail low. Sylvester never took sides.

"Calm down," Moonlight said. "Mom? Dad?"

"It's time," Andy said. "We recognize that we've come to a parting of minds, Lucy. I'll sleep in the den tonight, and tomorrow, I'll move myself out. Get yourself a lawyer. Night, Molly."

He left the room, Sylvester trotting behind.

Moonlight looked at her mother. "I do not want to know," she said. "I do not want to know a single thing about this. You will patch this up. Do you hear me? I refuse to hear the 'D' word."

"The 'D' word," Lucky said. She hadn't moved from her place on the badly sprung couch. She was so hot she might set fire to the chair; she'd been shown as a screeching harridan to half the population of the United Sates, and probably most of her own family, who already thought her crazy. Her daughter, precious Moonlight, was a cop. Her dream of something to recognize Andy and Barry and all the men like them was crumbling to dust. And Andy himself didn't give a fig.

"What's the 'D' word?" she said.

"Divorce. I won't allow you to even consider getting a divorce. You are the most perfect parents in all the world."

Lucky looked at her daughter. Tears glistened in Moonlight's eyes like stars reflecting off a mountain lake.

"You think so, dear?"

"Yeah, Mom, I do."

Lucky stood up. She was a good six inches shorter than Moonlight. She wrapped her daughter—hard cop, loving child, beautiful woman, fragile human being—in her arms.

"Do you suppose," Moonlight said, "Harris snatched one of the store lighters out from under Dad's nose?"

Chapter Twenty-one

Duncan was at the hospital when Smith arrived. He clutched a bunch of daisies, looking as if they'd been picked from a roadside ditch, in one hand, and she thought the gesture was sweeter than had he brought a dozen perfect long-stemmed red roses.

"The doc's with her," he said. "They said we won't have to wait for long."

She sat beside him on the overused visitor's couch. Badly painted little girls dancing through fields of wildflowers hung on the walls. A tiny white fridge stood in the corner underneath a bulletin board instructing them as to the location of the emergency exits as well as how to wash their hands after using the bathroom. Duncan slipped his arm over her shoulders. Smith settled into it.

She allowed him to stroke her shoulder. He took a deep breath, and she felt his ribs move. His lips touched the top of her head, and his hand lightly brushed the gun at her hip.

She pushed herself away. "Don't do that. I'm in uniform."

"You look great." He coughed. "That is, you always look great, Molly."

Smith studied the pictures on the wall.

Once Lucky had phoned the hospital and confirmed that Christa hadn't taken a turn for the worse during the night, Smith called Winters to let him know she'd be back to work.

He sounded neither pleased nor disappointed. Just told her to call after she'd visited Christa and he'd pick her up.

Smith and Duncan leapt to their feet as the doctor came into the waiting room.

"I'm sorry, Officer, but I don't think that Ms. Thompson is up to being questioned at this time."

"I'm not here for that," Smith said. "I'm her friend—her best friend. My mom's sorta like her foster mother."

"Then you can go in. She's awake, although on heavy medication. You have five minutes at the most."

Smith hesitated at the door to Christa's room. She took a deep breath, trying to gather enough strength to pass some on. Duncan took her hand, and she didn't pull away. He pushed open the door.

Christa had a double room, but the other bed was empty. A huge bunch of flowers, peach roses and white baby's breath, was on the windowsill, enjoying the cheerful sunshine streaming through the windows.

Christa looked bad, but no worse than Smith expected. The hair on the right side of her head had been shaved off and a white bandage was stuck to her scalp. Her face was a painter's palette, and her breathing was rough.

Christa's left eye flickered at the sight of Smith and Duncan holding hands. The right was so swollen it was unlikely she could see much of anything. Smith pulled her hand away and forced out a smile. "Hey, sweetie," she said. "You need a makeover."

Duncan held out the flowers. Christa's arms were tucked under the snowy white sheets and she made no move to accept them.

"Why don't you grab a water glass out of the bathroom," Smith said.

She leaned over the bed and kissed Christa on the cheek. Her friend's smile was like Sylvester's when he approached a strange dog in the park. The left incisor was broken. Rage boiled up inside Smith's chest. Rage so hot and fierce that she knew that if Charlie Bassing walked into this room right now, she'd beat him to a pulp. She wanted to shout questions, ask Christa how this had happened, if she knew where Charlie'd gone. To get confirmation that it was, in fact, Charlie who'd assaulted her.

But she wasn't here to interrogate the victim. She was here to visit her friend.

After five minutes of one-sided chatter—greetings from the Smith family, news that Lucky would stop by later, admiration of the flowers, a funny story from Duncan about the group he'd taken camping yesterday—and their time was up. A chubby-cheeked nurse told them to leave.

Smith reached under the sheet for Christa's hand. Her friend's grip was as insubstantial as fairy dust. "We'll get him, Chrissie. Fucking Charlie Bassing. I'll see him locked up and…."

"Officer, I said visitation is over," the nurse said.

Duncan took Smith's arm. "Let's go, Molly. See you later, Christa. Get strong, eh?"

Once they were back in the corridor, Smith leaned against a wall. She wiped her eyes with the back of her hand.

"You wanna go for a coffee or something?" Duncan asked.

She pulled her cell phone out and headed for the exit. "Thanks, but I can't. My boss said to call when I'm done here, and he'll come get me."

"Why don't I drive you? I'm going to the store. I've a parents and tots trip at noon."

"Great, thanks." She put the phone away.

Duncan walked her to a black Ford F-150. Expensive wheels for a guy who worked as a kayaking guide. Extravagant for a guy who called himself an environmentalist.

"My dad owns a Ford dealership in Victoria," he said with a shrug. "It was a gift when I graduated." He unlocked the doors with a flick of the remote. "Jump in."

Smith jumped.

"You saw *Fifth Column*?" Winters said as Smith walked into the sergeants' office.

"Oh, yeah."

"Trouble in River City."

"Huh?"

"Before your time. The deputy mayor's been on the phone to the chief. Demanding a solution to the Montgomery murder. Half the good citizens, and a sizeable portion of the not-so-good-ones, are also demanding that we do something. I'd suggest that we get in my car, drive for, say, ten minutes, and then arrest the first person we pass on the right. How's that sound to you?"

He was joking. *Wasn't he?*

Molly Smith hadn't slept much last night, between worrying about Christa, thoughts of Charlie Fucking Bassing's prick on the chopping block and a cleaver in her hand, and despair at the state of her parents' marriage. Plus trying to come up with a solution to the Montgomery killing that would have everyone, Winters in particular, singing her praises and her future in the Trafalgar City Police secure.

"You don't look too well, Molly," Winters said. "Christa?" His face settled back into lines and wrinkles, and she realized that when he was joking his expression let go of some of its usual seriousness.

"She's gonna be fine."

He tossed his coffee cup into the waste basket. "Turns out that Mr. Bassing has a record. Purse snatching in Vancouver. He wasn't armed, first offense, so he got off without jail time. But his fingerprints are on file. Lots of nice clear prints were found at the scene."

"So now all we have to do is find him."

"Punk like that. Piece of cake. I suspect it's a dead end, but we have two cases in three days. I want to ask Clemmins and Mrs. Montgomery if they know Bassing. Looks like Goodhaugh and Sorensen are in the clear. I spoke to them yesterday. Lots of smug looks and talk about how he'd deserved it, but they were in Calgary on Thursday evening, at a wedding. Robyn was her sister's bridesmaid. I'm checking, of course, but she looked like a smart cookie, not the sort to come up with an alibi that easy to confirm if it isn't true. I'm glad Christa's going to be okay."

"Me too," Smith said as they left the office.

"How do you stand it, John?" she said. "The job. Seeing the worst the world has to offer. Day after day. All the pain, the misery." She stopped talking, horrified at what she'd said. It was the 21st century, but even so, there were still impediments for a woman on the job. And she'd thrown herself into the biggest trap of them all—going all emotional.

Instead of running back to his desk where he kept a big black ledger to record every female constable's moment of weakness, he turned to look at her. "You have to find that out for yourself, Molly. But think of it like this. You're driving down the street one night. Been at a party, had a good time and you're feeling great—not intoxicated, of course. You see a dog ahead, lying in the street. Someone hit it and drove on, perhaps didn't even know what he'd done. Do you turn your head to one side and drive on, wanting to keep that after-party glow? Or do you pull over, grab a blanket out of the back to protect your hands, and wrap the dog up to take him to the all-night vet?"

"I'd pick the dog up, of course," she said. "We're dog lovers in my family. But if I found out that the person who'd run him down got away without any consequences, and the dog died anyway, then maybe I'd regret spoiling my party mood."

"We each have to find our own way, Molly. But now, I want to find my way to Frank Clemmins."

She let out a deep breath. Find her own way. Wasn't that the problem in a nutshell? What was her way? Between her mother's outdated hippie pacifism, her father's keep-your-head-down ethics, her brother's make-all-the-money-you-can-fast-as-you-can morals, Graham's aggressive push-everyone-forward style, and Christa's quiet optimism, Molly Smith no longer knew what was her own way. And then there was John Winters. Tough cop or local clown?

"Hold up, John, Molly." Jim Denton lifted a hand in the universal stop gesture as Winters and Smith headed for the door. A car pulled away from the station, under full lights and sirens.

"Big fight on Front Street. Scarcely eleven o'clock on a Sunday morning."

"You think this is something to do with my investigation?" Winters asked.

"It's at 345 Front Street."

"Christ." Smith headed for the door. "That's the store."

"Think this is related to our case?" Winters asked, taking the steps two at a time beside her.

"There's never been a fight there in all my years," she said. "Last night it was revealed to the massive CNC audience to be the heart of darkness. You decide." She headed for the parking lot. She would not even entertain the idea that the fighters might be her own parents. That could not be happening.

Winters passed her, running. "Move it, Smith," he said. The headlights of the plainclothes van flashed as he flicked the remote.

A large crowd had gathered in front of Mid-Kootenay Adventure Vacations. A blue and white police vehicle was pulled up, half on the sidewalk. The red light went round and round, but it didn't throw much of a glow, sitting in the full summer sun. Dawn Solway was standing in front of the shop doors, ordering the crowd to keep back.

Smith leapt out of the van while Winters was still bringing it to a halt. Solway looked up, relief crossing her face at the sight of reinforcements.

Dave Evans had a man up against the counter. He pulled handcuffs off his belt as Smith ran in. Andy Smith was lying on the floor, on his back, rolling from side to side, blood gushing from his nose. Lucky held a heavy-duty flashlight in one hand, over the head of a man backed against the wall with his hands lifted in front of his face. A woman screamed, and Duncan spoke to her as he would a newbie facing whitewater for the first time. The display table in the center of the store was overturned, legs turned toward Smith as if pointing out that this was all her fault. The table's contents—tourist and orienteering maps of the area, guide books, nature guides—were scattered across the floor.

"What do you need?" she said, her training kicking in. This wasn't her parents' store—it was a police situation.

Evans snapped the cuffs shut and jerked the man around. He was about five seven and very thin, hair cut short to his scalp, face pitted with acne scars and a sprinkling of fresh spots. He wasn't much over twenty. He wore tattered jeans, heavy boots, and a loose jacket in a camouflage print. "Escort the other guy out, Smith," Evans said. "And we can all go down to the station."

"Everything okay here?" Winters sauntered in.

"You can step back, Mom, uh, Mrs. Smith," Smith said to her mother. Lucky lowered the flashlight. She barely came up to her opponent's collar bone. Like the other guy, he was dressed in semi-military clothes, but he was much bigger and had a scrap of mustache across his upper lip. He wore a short-sleeved T-shirt that revealed heavily tattooed arms. "Commie bitch," he said, letting loose a plug of phlegm.

Lucky ignored him and ran to Andy.

Smith said, "Let's go, buddy."

"We didn't do nothing. That old guy," he pointed to Andy, being helped to his feet by his wife, "attacked my friend." Andy leaned his head back and Lucky pressed a tissue up against his nose. The front of his white shirt was spotted with blood.

"Looks like a real tough guy to me," Winters said. "Gotta be, what, twice your age?"

"You weren't here, man. He's a lunatic. And as for that old broad…."

"Watch your mouth," Winters snapped. "We'll sort it all out at the station."

The screaming woman had finally shut up, and Duncan was patting her arm, making soothing, sympathetic noises. He saw Smith watching them and rolled his eyes.

"Did you see what happened here, ma'am?" Winters asked.

"He," she pointed at the smaller man, "hit him," she pointed at Andy. "They were arguing about the peace garden. I read about it in the paper. He asked him to leave and she said that she was going to call the police, and then he hit him and if it hadn't been for her he would have joined in. I see my husband outside. I'd better go."

"If I could bother you for more of your time, ma'am," Winters said. "I need you to come to the station and make a statement."

She was well into her forties, well-preserved fifties perhaps, with perfectly cut and highlighted blond hair, khaki shorts, and a matching T-shirt embroidered with big wooden beads. She almost preened under the force of Winters' attention. "I'd be happy to be of help."

"Constable Smith, help Constable Evans with these two gentlemen." Another siren sounded outside. The ambulance. "Mr. Smith," Winters said, "do you need to go to the hospital?"

"No," he mumbled. A gush of blood soaked Lucky's tissues and ran over her fingers. The customer having calmed down, Duncan reached under the counter and handed a box of tissues to Lucky. "I wanna come wif you," Andy Smith said. "Lay charges."

"You and Mrs. Smith can ride with me."

Smith looked at her mother for the first time. Still holding her hand to her husband's face, Lucky raised one eyebrow. Her face was flushed and there was a smile tugging at the edges of her mouth, a smile which Smith didn't like one bit. Lucky had been arrested at the infamous 1968 Democratic Convention in Chicago for jumping on the back of a police officer who was either attempting to subdue an offender or beating the shit out of an innocent protester, depending on one's point of view. She recalled the incident fondly whenever she had the chance, and Smith feared her mother was reliving her glory days. Lucky put the flashlight on the counter. "After you, Sergeant," she said.

Smith grabbed the big guy by the arm. "Do I have to cuff you?" she said.

"Hey, babe, I'm easy. What are you doin' after work?"

"Move."

Approximately half the population of Trafalgar had gathered outside Mid-Kootenay Adventures. Solway had been joined by another constable and they had their hands full trying to keep everyone back. Traffic was at a halt, as onlookers spilled off the sidewalk and drivers stopped in the middle of the street trying to get a glimpse of what was going on.

"Nothing to see, folks," Evans said, as he walked out of the store with his handcuffed prisoner. "Go about your business."

Smith thought that Evans had seen one too many cop movies.

She followed with the big one who was asking her if she had plans for dinner.

"What's the matter with you people?" the scrawny guy yelled. "Are you gonna stand by while these terrorist sympathizers erect their monument to cowardice and treason?"

"Let him go," someone deep in the crowd shouted. "Lucky Smith won't be happy until every business in town's shut down."

Voices rose, some shouting their agreement, some throwing counter-arguments.

"Are you losing your minds?" a woman shouted. "When did Trafalgar become about censorship and silencing citizens? I never would have believed the day would come."

"We have to stand up for peace," someone else shouted.

"My father died in Vietnam. He died doing his duty. Unlike that fat scum." Smith recognized the guy from last night's TV program. In the soft morning light, rather than the shadows cast by the TV camera, she could see that he was no older than she. If his father had died in 1972, Brian Harris been conceived from frozen sperm.

"Get moving," Winters yelled.

Smith and Evans bundled the men into the car. She had to push hard on her prisoner's thick head to get him to duck. She took shotgun and Evans turned on the siren. People in the crowd were still murmuring, but they began to move off the road. Evans negotiated around the ambulance—the paramedics were talking to Andy—and edged into the street.

Sunlight caught on glass, and Smith looked across the street. Standing outside the hardware store was a man with a camera on his shoulder. Meredith Morgenstern was beside him, summer-fresh in a short yellow skirt and matching T-shirt. Rich Ashcroft was on the other side of the cameraman, his mouth moving. He watched while Evans executed a three-point turn, although he could just as easily have gone around the block. When he knew she was looking at him, Ashcroft lowered one eyelid in a slow wink, and lifted his right thumb.

Chapter Twenty-two

While Smith and Evans escorted the two men to the booking room at the back of the station, Winters went to brief the Chief.

"I'm not happy about this, John." Paul Keller took a hearty gulp of one of the ten or twelve diet Cokes he'd consume over the course of the day.

"I didn't think you would be."

"The last thing we need is outside agitators arriving to stir the pot up. We don't need any more oars dipping into our community's problems."

Winters ignored the badly matched metaphors. "That TV guy, Ashcroft, filmed the whole thing."

"Tell me you made that last statement up."

"I don't suppose we can run him out of town on a rail."

"This is only the tip of the iceberg, John. There'll be more folks arriving. I'm not fond of this garden myself. It's unnecessarily divisive, and it's like flicking the finger to our American neighbors."

"The two guys we arrested at the Smiths' store are from Creston."

"Oh, goodie. Local thugs. That makes me feel so much better." The Chief crushed the can in his fist and tossed the remains into the trash, where the day's Coke graveyard was beginning to build.

"Don't suppose you want to have a word with this Ashcroft fellow, John? Suggest he go cover more important things. Like the trade in nuclear weapons or a war brewing somewhere."

Winters didn't smile. "Not my job, Paul. Not my job. And I'm glad of it."

"I've called the Yellow Stripes. Told them we may need help if this keeps building." The Chief looked out the window. "Did you, uh, bring the Smiths in?"

"They're in an interview room. Peterson'll take their statements."

"Perhaps I should pop in, make sure Andy's not too traumatized. He's not as young as he used to be." His laugh sounded more like a dog with kennel cough. "And Lucky as well, of course."

A drop of sweat slid off Keller's forehead, and Winters realized that the Chief Constable had been, perhaps still was, in love with Lucky Smith.

The phone on the desk rang. Keller looked at the call display. "The deputy mayor. I guess she's heard there's trouble in town and's calling to demand that I put a stop to it. Never would have thought of that myself. Do you want to take it, John? Tell her I'm on the beat, rounding up troublemakers."

"Not my job, Paul." Winters pulled the door shut on his way out.

He went to the booking area in the back. The little guy was yelling something about terrorist sympathizers, and the big one was asking Smith if she'd go out with him. Neither of them seemed to be concerned that they were about to be locked up.

Evans had read them the caution and was starting on the paperwork.

"Leave this to Constable Evans, Constable Smith," Winters said. "I need you on the road."

"Woo hoo," the big guy yelled. "Aren't you the lucky one?"

"Shut the fuck up," Smith said.

"Hey, she can talk. What else can you do with that mouth, sweetie?"

She walked out of the room. Winters followed. Her face was set into firm lines, and a spark of red coal blazed behind the blue eyes. A small vein pulsed in the side of her neck. *Women,* Winters thought, *did sometimes have it hard.*

"My mom and dad?" she said, visibly gathering her self-control.

"They're in an interview room. Staff-Sergeant Peterson'll take their statements. We've a witness to talk to."

"I'd like to check that they're okay."

"Your parents are okay. You can't take part in the interview, Molly. You know that."

"Where are we going?"

"A man called the station in response to our asking for anyone who'd been at Eagle Point Bluffs on Thursday night to come forward."

They walked to the parking bay. Heat radiated off the asphalt and into the bottom of his shoes. The sky was as blue as in a brochure for Caribbean vacations; a single tuft of white cloud hovered in the west, no larger or more substantial than a cotton ball. "We could use some rain. I haven't had time to water the impatiens beds, and if they're dead when Eliza gets back, she'll not be pleased."

"The whole area is on extreme fire alert," Smith said.

They got into the van, and Winters switched on the computer.

"Where to?"

"Hold on, computer's slow." He typed, waited for a response, then gave her the directions.

She pulled onto George Street. "What happened at the store?"

"Two guys walked in. Started trouble right away. Asked the clerk, what's his name?"

"Duncan."

"Duncan, if he was a deserter. He didn't know what they were talking about. Your mother heard them, came out. They recognized her from TV and started with the insults."

Smith sighed. "So my dad intervened."

He coughed. "Not at first. There seems to be some, if I may say, conflict between your parents around this business." That was an understatement. The van was so chilly with the Smith parents in it, Winters hadn't needed to turn on the air conditioning.

"Tell me about it." She stopped at a light to let a hugely pregnant woman cross. She was pushing a baby carriage and dragging a toddler by the arm. Her skirt was pulled down low and her T-shirt didn't extend far enough to cover the round belly.

"Your dad tried to reason with the guys. Told them that the TV program was a pack of lies, and everyone in Trafalgar just wants to get along with everyone else."

"I bet Mom loved that."

"She basically told them they'd come to the right place and what did they want to do about it. One of them threw the table over and threatened to wreck the store. A customer ran out into the street, yelling for help. Mrs. Smith picked up a flashlight and threatened to bash their heads in if they didn't leave and Mr. Smith stepped in front of her. And got hit."

"What a mess. Who are they, anyway?"

"Your parents said they'd never seen them before."

"Neither have I. Outsiders."

"We can expect more to arrive. As long as that Ashcroft guy's in town. I saw last night's show. He's upping the ante. Getting nastier. The war hero's posthumously born son was a nice touch."

"We can't do anything to stop him?"

"Not as long as he doesn't trespass onto private property. You noticed that he didn't try to come into the store, get the fight in action so to speak."

"He was at my house the other night."

"Invited by your mother."

They had to drive by the park entrance on their way to their meeting. People were lined up on both sides of the street. One group was mostly middle-aged women with grey hair either clipped close to their scalp or cascading down their backs, men with unkempt beards, and youths in T-shirts and sandals. The other was neatly dressed middle-aged or older people, with a few younger ones in ugly shorts for the men and pastel short-sets for the women. A man in the second group waved a small flag in each hand. The Stars and Stripes and the Maple Leaf.

A TV van with the logo of the Canadian Broadcasting Corporation was parked further up the street. A woman walked through the crowd, carrying a tape recorder. Smith couldn't be sure, but with scraggly blond hair and big glasses, she looked a lot like the picture of the *Globe and Mail*'s human-interest columnist.

A single Trafalgar City Police officer watched over it all.

"Chief has the Mounties on standby," Winters said.

"Hope it doesn't come to that."

◇◇◇

Lucky Smith was still exhilarated when they got back to the store. It was like when she was young, back in the Sixties. When anything and everything was possible. Sometimes she thought that the street battle with the cops outside the Democratic convention in Chicago was, aside from the birth of her children, the most exciting day in her life.

She looked at Andy, his nose swollen, drops of blood drying down the front of his shirt, and thought that perhaps she shouldn't have gotten such a rush out of the fight. But, hey, she'd shown that two-bit punk, hadn't she?

Nice of Paul Keller to check on them. She'd always liked the Chief Constable, although they'd had their differences over the years. She remembered when he was a newly promoted sergeant, fresh from the big city, full of his own self-importance, trying to face her down over that water-access issue. Paul might be The Man, but Lucky had always thought they respected each other. She'd been secretly pleased that he'd hired Moonlight; she expected that he'd turn the girl down because her mother was a known agitator.

"I'm going home to change," Andy said.

"Okay," she said. He hadn't actually moved his things out, as he'd threatened to do yesterday.

He headed for the door. Duncan watched them from behind the counter.

"Andy," she said.

He turned around. "Yes?"

She swallowed what she'd meant to say. Poor Andy, as he got older he mellowed and wondered why she didn't. He was no longer happy with a firebrand for a wife. All he wanted was a peaceful life. But when that foul young man had threatened her, he'd jumped in front of her, quick enough. "Don't be long," she said. "Duncan has a trip to take at noon, and Flower isn't in until two."

"I know my staff's schedule, Lucky."

"Just reminding you, dear."

Andy may have mellowed, she thought. But the world hadn't. And until it did, neither could she.

Duncan had put the table back on its feet and picked books and pamphlets off the floor. But he'd done nothing about the blood on the wide pine flooring. "If you can mop that mess up, Duncan," she said, "I'll be in my office."

The phone rang before she'd fully settled into her chair.

"Lucky, what the hell's going on there?"

"Hell's the word, Barry. Where are you?"

"Home, at last. Marta broke her foot, as it turns out. Badly. Doc said he'd rarely seen such a mess. We got in a few hours ago. I settled her onto the couch, went for some groceries and beer, made lunch, ate lunch."

Lucky drew circles on her desk blotter. Barry did sometimes talk in lists.

"Only then did I access my e-mail. Everyone on the committee has been sending frantic notes back and forth. My nephew in Tennessee wrote to ask what's going on. Said he'd seen something on TV about Trafalgar."

Lucky explained the situation. She could almost feel the steam coming down the phone line as Barry got angrier and angrier.

"I'm on my way," he said, when she stopped talking.

"That might not be a good idea. That CNC guy's hanging around, spoiling for a fight. Let it all calm down, and he'll be on the next plane out. And his viewers' attention will follow him. They'll never think about us again."

"This means a lot to me, Lucky."

"I know, Barry, I know. Let's keep our heads down and wait until the shit has stopped flying, shall we?"

"Keep me posted."

"I will."

She had only just opened the letter on the top of her mail pile when the phone rang again. She looked at the call display: Barry again?

"What, you couldn't you keep your fool head down for longer than ten seconds?"

"The town council's going to discuss the garden at tonight's regular meeting. They're going to decide once and for all whether or not to approve it."

"How do you know?"

"An e-mail. Sitting in my in-box since yesterday. Unsigned, from an anonymous hotmail account."

"The sneaky bastards are trying to do a run-around without anyone noticing."

"So it seems."

"Feel like going out tonight, Barry?"

"It's a date. I'll pick you up at seven thirty."

"I'll call the others."

"You know, Lucky, I'd rather not involve them."

"Why?"

"Tempers are at fever pitch, judging by the contents of my in-box. Just you and me, Lucky. We'll ask the council to recognize us, and say what we have to say. I'm the one who was there, in 'Nam; you're the one with the silver tongue. All the others—they'll just clutter up the scene."

"I don't know, Barry."

"Will Andy come?"

She snorted. "Easier to get him to a bridal show."

"Thought so. Be nice if Dwayne Washington could come, but he's laid up with his back again. Robbie Colman's gone to Arizona for some sorta family reunion. Most of the rest of us old guys are scattered, too hard to get to with half a day's notice. Or not interested, like Andy. It's you and me, Lucky."

"One for all, eh?"

"And all for one. See you at seven thirty." He hung up.

Lucky looked out the window into the alley. A woman dragging a Yorkshire terrier on a leash passed by. The dog strained to sniff under a bush, but the woman kept on walking. Lucky could feel her heart beating. The fight earlier had ignited a spark that had been burning deep inside her, like a single ember buried in a mountain of coal. She punched her fist into the air.

"Bring it on," she said.

"That puts Dr. Tyler out of the frame," Smith said.

"Perhaps."

"Seems conclusive to me. The old guy was walking his even older dog and they passed Tyler's car at the side of the road. And he was still there when man and dog came the other way half an hour later."

"The car," Winters said. "But not necessarily Tyler himself."

"Mr. Johnson was positive that there was someone in the driver's seat. You think Tyler arranged for someone to sit in his car at the top of the bluffs for an hour or so while he dispatched Montgomery?"

"Don't laugh, Molly. I've seen stranger things."

And he probably had. "Sorry."

"If I were investigating organized crime in, say, New York City, I wouldn't think that scenario to be at all out of the ordinary. But in pleasant little Trafalgar, a middle-aged dentist who's screwing the wife of the deceased? Probably not.

"Tell you the truth, Molly, I'm pretty much stumped on this one. Someone in the family's usually the perp. Business associates a distant second. Strangers last of all."

"Random?" she asked.

"Always a possibility. Damned hard to nail down, if it is, if the guy doesn't do something stupid or have an attack of the guilties and turn himself in."

Winters' jacket rang. He pulled out his cell phone, as Smith drove down the mountainside. She took a short cut down Sycamore Street. Several young people were lounging in front of Happy Tobaccy, which sold hemp products, posters calling for the legalization of marijuana, drug paraphernalia and, under the counter, the finest B.C. pot.

As long as the product wasn't sold to minors, wasn't waved in anyone's face, and nothing harder than pot graced the premises, the Trafalgar City Police pretty much pretended not to notice. A woman waved cheerfully at the van as Smith drove past. She'd hadn't taken to the stuff herself. She'd used it once in high school, but it made her so nauseous she didn't want to try again. A second attempt when she was at University had the same result.

If she'd liked pot, would she have become a cop? She'd never know.

"Find a spot to pull over," Winters said.

She eyed a parking space just ahead and began to slow down.

"Preferably not in sight of Happy Tobaccy. I'd rather they not come over to ask if we're staking the place out."

She turned the corner. "Who was on the phone?"

"Peterson. I sent the Toronto police out searching for Rosemary Fitzgerald. They found her first try—her son, James Fitzgerald, was in Toronto General last night."

"That's good." Smith pulled into a church parking lot. Luxurious beds of pink and white petunias lined the walkway leading to the wide wooden doors. Moisture glistened off green leaves.

"Not entirely. James had a bad case of heartburn. Because he'd had a heart attack less than a year ago, everyone panicked. He was discharged at six thirty this morning. Toronto time. Whereupon, as you might expect, the family left the hospital."

"Oops."

"They were long gone by the time the Toronto cops tracked her down. They called the son at home and were told that Rosemary headed straight to the airport." He pulled a scrap of paper out of his pocket, referred to it, and punched in another series of numbers. Smith could hear the tinny sound of voice mail answering.

Winters snapped his phone shut. "What the hell is the point of having a cell phone, of having voice mail, if you don't pay any damn attention to it?"

"You think Rosemary's important to this case?"

"Not at all. But it bugs the hell out of me that I can't talk to the damned woman. That I can't, as they say in the English crime novels, eliminate her from my enquiries."

"If she's heading home, she should be here by the end of the day."

"Unless she decides to take a last-minute vacation in Hawaii. Back to the station, Molly. This case is going nowhere."

Christa was sitting up in bed reading *People* magazine when Molly Smith arrived, balancing flowers, a fantasy paperback, two coffees, and a bag of croissants, warm from Alphonse's oven.

Smith dumped everything on the tiny bedside table. "I thought you'd be ready for something yummy." She gave her friend a cheerful smile. But it was hard. Christa's face was various shades of blue, black, and yellow. Her lip was cut and her right eye swollen almost shut. "How ya doin', sweet thing?"

Christa closed her eyes and lay back against the pile of white pillows. "I hurt."

"I thought you might like something to eat." Smith gestured to the bag. The scent of warm baking was almost strong enough to override the usual hospital smells, disinfectant and body fluids.

"I'm not hungry."

"I'll leave them for you to eat later. Coffee?"

"No."

"Even if I help you with the cup?"

"Fuck off, Molly. I said I don't want coffee."

Smith felt as if she'd been slapped. She dropped into the visitor's chair. "Did someone from the police come and interview you?"

"Yeah. A cute young cop."

"Nice."

"A cute young female cop."

"I should have told them to send Dave Evans."

Smith struggled not to ask the obvious questions. *Was it Charlie who did this to you; did he say anything; did he give you any clue as to where he was going; do you know where he might be now?* She was here to visit her friend, not interrogate her. Dawn Solway would have done that.

"Has your dad been in?"

"Yeah, he stopped by."

"My mom?"

"Not yet."

"She got tied up." Smith told Christa about the incident at the store. Christa nodded in all the right places, but didn't seem too interested. The drugs, Smith guessed.

She sat in the hard visitor's chair, overwhelmed with anger. At Charlie, of course, but also at herself. For failing Christa. "I bought you a book. I thought you'd want something to read."

"Thanks." Christa's eyes closed.

"I'll let you get some sleep."

"I'm afraid to sleep. What if I'm asleep when he gets here?"

"Who?" Smith asked. Although she knew.

"Charlie, of course."

"He's long gone. Run away with his tail between his legs like the coward he is. The hospital's been told to be on the lookout for him, and to call us right away if he shows up."

"And by the time you get here, I'll be dead."

"Jesus, Christa. Don't talk like that."

Her eyes remained closed. She took a shallow breath through cracked ribs, and grimaced with the effort. "Go away, Molly. Just go away."

"Everything'll be okay. You'll be out of here soon, and Charlie'll not bother you again."

Christa opened her eyes. They were very wet, but she wasn't crying. "Whatever you say, Molly." She turned her head toward the window. "Nice flowers."

"Yup."

"Who're the daisies from? There's no card."

"Duncan. Remember, he was here first thing this morning?"

"Duncan who?"

"Duncan Weaver, of course. Works at the store."

"Never met him," Christa said, closing her eyes once again. "I wonder why he brought me flowers."

Chapter Twenty-three

Rosemary Fitzgerald shifted in the uncomfortable chair, and flicked through the pages of "O" magazine. What a god-awful day. It was mid-July, height of the travel season. She'd spent all day trying to get across the country without airline reservations. Never mind what this wasted trip to Toronto was costing her. Heartburn. She'd abandoned her business, flown across three time zones, because her son had an attack of heartburn. She snapped the magazine shut. She'd better give Emily a call. She hadn't even checked into the store since leaving for Toronto. She dug her cell phone out of the depths of her bag and flicked it open. The call waiting notice beeped. She'd never managed to figure out how to get her messages.

"Rosemary's Campfire Kitchen."

"Hi, Emily, it's Rosemary here."

"How's your son?"

"It turned out to be nothing. What's happening there?"

"I'm run off my feet. We're running out of the soup packages. The chili and stews and stuff that you made? They're almost all gone. If you don't come back soon, I don't know what I'm gonna sell. My mom said she'd try to make some batches of stew or curry, but she doesn't know anything about health regulations and all that stuff."

"I'm in Vancouver. I was stuck in Saskatoon for ten hideous hours. One plane after another left full, and when I finally got on one, it was cancelled because of mechanical failure. I could have driven faster. But I've got a seat on a flight to Castlegar that's leaving in fifteen minutes. I'll grab the shuttle to Trafalgar and should be there by seven. We can look over the stock before closing. Can you wait, if I'm delayed?"

"Gee," Emily whined. "I have a date."

"They're calling my flight now. Wait there until you hear from me. I'll pay if there's overtime."

"I guess. Oh, the cops have been really keen to talk to you. They told me to tell you to phone Sergeant…something or other…I have the name here somewhere."

"I have to go, Emily."

"You're to call Sergeant Whatever, immediately."

"Seems like a lot of fuss over a bike. But maybe the police in Trafalgar don't have anything more important to worry about. That's a nice thought. I'll call them when I get there. Bye."

Rosemary Fitzgerald stuffed "O" into her bag and ran for the gate, waving her boarding pass in her hand. She was the last one through.

Meredith Morgenstern dropped her phone into her black and green Nine West bag as Rich Ashcroft returned from the washroom. He didn't like the look on her face. She'd been about to fold, he knew it, to follow him upstairs because she wanted the chance of a job at CNC so much she'd prostitute herself to get it.

"That was interesting news," she said, licking at the drops of Drambuie that had collected on the rim of her liquor glass. They'd spent the day filming and interviewing the growing numbers of protesters (for and against) gathering outside the site of the proposed peace gardens, and talking to people on the main street. He'd weeded out most of those who approved of the park (except for one or two that were almost certainly certifiable), and prepared the rest for broadcast. An elderly couple who'd lost a son in Vietnam had driven up from Boise, Idaho, after seeing Rich's Saturday program, to voice their indignation at the very idea of a dedication to men who'd avoided that service. They'd been featured prominently on tonight's show. He'd done another interview with Brian Harris, just strolling around town, listening sympathetically as the boy talked about how his mother had mourned her husband for the rest of her life, never remarrying, turning their home into a shrine to his memory. It had taken Irene about two minutes to find out that no one named Brian Harris had died in the last months of the war. Not as part of the U.S. military, anyway. Rich didn't care what Harris was up to—just trying to be part of something bigger than his miserable little life, probably.

"Are you going to tell me about your phone call, or do I have to find someone else to fill me in," Rich snapped.

The pretty face collapsed into an unbecoming pout.

"Sorry, Meredith," he said. "That was uncalled for. Another drink?"

"Sure."

He raised his hand to call the waiter. People at the other tables kept looking at him out of the corner of their eyes. Rich noticed that he was served while tables who'd been waiting longer were still waiting. It had taken long enough, but at last the citizens of sleepy little Trafalgar were starting to wake up and recognize him.

Greg had looked to be happy to settle in for a long night downing expensive shots, on Rich's expense account, and trying to get Meredith to drop her pants. But the first time she excused herself to go to the washroom, Rich had told him to get lost. Greg pushed his chair back and stood up with a smirk. "If you need me, boss, I'll be in the fleshpots of Trafalgar. Oh, wait. There aren't any. So I'll be in my room watching porn movies. Oh wait, there aren't any of those either. Hope there's a Bible in the night table."

Rich watched him cross the room. Greg had far too smart a mouth on him; if he wasn't such a goddamned good cameraman, Rich would have gotten rid of him long ago.

"Interesting goings on at town council tonight," Meredith said.

Rich's sixth sense ticked in, the one that had taken him to the top of the cut-throat world of TV journalism. He knew that the balance of power had shifted; he could smell it as a dog could smell a bitch in heat miles away. He was no longer the one with all the cards. Meredith knew something, and she knew he'd want to hear it. A candle sat in the middle of the table, throwing a single tall flame between them. She touched her glass to her lips.

"I can't guarantee you an interview," he said. "I can only recommend."

She dug in her bag and pulled out a notepad and pen. She pushed them toward him. "So recommend," she said. "The words dedicated, competent, highly qualified, come to mind. And anything else you might want to throw in."

He wrote. She leaned back in her chair and lifted the liquor glass to her nose. She breathed in deeply. And he knew that this was going to be good.

She read what he'd written. "You forgot to sign it."

He signed.

She stuffed the notepad into her cavernous bag.

"Eleven a.m. Day after tomorrow. Our esteemed deputy mayor is going to stand in the street and declare that the town has decided, for definite, absolute sure, the fate of the park."

"How do you know?"

She lifted her glass to her lips and grinned. "It was discussed at a town council meeting tonight, but the room was cleared before they took the vote. My pal from the paper was there, as is part of his job."

Rich laughed. "So this will be in the *Daily Gazette* tomorrow, for every reporter with half a brain to read?"

"It will. There was one member of the public who spoke to the councilors."

"Who?"

"Lucky Smith. She put up quite a fuss when the public gallery was cleared so the council could debate *in camera*."

"I have to get to the cop daughter," Rich said, crushing a cube of ice between his teeth. He was drinking ice water. He drank nothing but ice water when he was working. And Rich was always working.

"I might be able to arrange a meeting," Meredith said, leaning back into her chair. She was wearing a low-cut blue summer shirt and tight jeans. She dipped a finger into her cleavage. The restaurant was almost empty: two couples and a raucous group of six women remained. The lights had steadily been turned down, encouraging lingering patrons to leave. The waiter brought Meredith's fresh drink.

"A meeting with Constable Molly Smith. That might be worth something." Meredith grinned at him across the table. She looked like a cat at play with a particularly stupid mouse. "A nice angle: aging hippy, kid who rejects those values and becomes a cop. There might be something there."

"Get to the point, Meredith."

"The point." She placed her Drambuie glass onto the table with an audible thud. Her eyes were clear and alert and Rich saw that this girl could hold her liquor. "Is that I can get to Constable Molly Smith, whereas you, on your own, wouldn't be able to approach her with a ten-foot pole."

"A disturbing metaphor. Get to the goddamned point."

"I will," she said, "arrange for you to meet with the elusive Constable Smith. It's up to you what you get out of her. If anything. That has nothing to do with me, because I'd guess that Molly's a good deal smarter than you."

"Are you here to insult me, Meredith?"

"Not in the least. I'm pointing out a few truths, that's all."

"What do you want in exchange?"

"A personal introduction to the producer of *North America Tonight.*"

"You're a crafty little bitch, aren't you?"

"I've spent the last three days watching you at work, Rich. Deal?"

"Deal. And just so you know, I'm going to mean it."

She laughed.

The bill was sitting on the table between them, the charge already run through. Rich signed the receipt with a scrawl.

They stood up and headed for the door. The group of elderly women whispered to each other as he passed, watching him out of the corner of their eyes. He gave them his publicity photo smile.

Three of the women turned away. Two stared. And one woman lifted her middle finger.

Get him the hell back to L.A., where women who looked like your mother didn't make obscene gestures.

They stood in the street. The night air was warm and dry.

"So," Meredith said. "Let's go to your hotel, eh?"

The freezer at Rosemary's Campfire Kitchen was almost empty. Tired as she was, she'd now have to spend the night cooking. "I'll pay time and a half if you help me in the kitchen tonight, Emily."

"Okay." The girl answered so quickly that Rosemary suspected there hadn't been a date on tonight's plans after all. "I can't cook, though," she said.

"I'll tell you what to do. First, go to Safeway. I'll prepare a list."

"You'd better call the cops. They really have been bugging me about you."

"All right, all right." Rosemary looked in the pantry. No onions, almost out of rice, enough tins of tomatoes and beans.

When she emerged from the pantry, list in hand, Emily was holding the phone. "Call the police, Rosemary, please. The cop who keeps coming around is really cute, and I wouldn't mind if he dropped by off duty, understand, but I'm afraid that he's going to arrest me and throw me in jail for killing you and burying the body in the cellar." She exchanged the phone for the shopping list.

"You are such a nag." Emily had saved Rosemary's Campfire Kitchen these last few days. A less reliable assistant might have taken the opportunity to close up, and say that business had been slow. She owed Emily something. "What's the number?"

"911."

"I can't call 911 if it isn't an emergency."

"Well, if you listen to the dishy Constable Evans, it's like there's a terrorist attack threatening Trafalgar and only you can stop it." She dug into the pocket of her jeans and pulled out a card. She handed it to Rosemary. "Be back soon."

The bell over the door tinkled as Emily left on her errand. Rosemary looked at the card. All this fuss over a bike. In Toronto they could hardly be bothered to talk to you if you called to report a stolen bike. She punched in the numbers.

"Mrs. Fitzgerald. Sergeant Winters has been trying to get in touch with you," the person who answered the phone said in tones that might be used to admonish a child who'd failed to return their signed report card.

"I've been out of town on a family emergency."

"Where are you now?"

"At my shop. 343 Front Street in Trafalgar."

"Hold on please, Mrs. Fitzgerald."

Rosemary hung on. She'd start with beef stew. And then make vegetarian chili and macaroni and cheese. Why had she thought cooking for a living was going to be easy?

"Mrs. Fitzgerald?"

"I'm here."

"Sergeant Winters requests that you remain in your shop until he gets there. He'll be about ten minutes."

"I'm not going anywhere. But I don't understand. It's only a bike, why is all of this so critical?"

"A bike?"

"The bike that was stolen Thursday. I didn't even report it—I didn't think you'd much care."

"Please wait for Sergeant Winters, ma'am. He's on his way."

"Okay." Rosemary hung up. There were some wilting vegetables in the back of the fridge. Soup was always a hit with campers.

John Winters also had his head in the freezer. There had to be something in here he could eat. He'd told Smith that tomorrow she would be back on regular duty. Her face had sort of crumpled in on itself, but she recovered and said something about happy to be back on the streets.

There was no point in dragging a constable around after him any longer. A constable who'd be needed for crowd control if this business got any more intense. Rich Ashcroft's program was on at ten. By ten thirty there might well be barbarian hordes descending upon Trafalgar, British Columbia. Lopez was due back in a couple of days. Maybe he'd bring a new perspective to the Montgomery murder. Winters studied a package of frozen pizza. The best-by date was six months past. How reliable was that date, anyway? Did it mean he was going to die if he ate it one day late, or was it a marketing gimmick to get him to buy another pizza? He ripped open the package and threw the frozen circle of dough into the microwave. If he died, at least he wouldn't have to worry about the Montgomery case any more.

The microwave pinged and he took out his dinner. He grabbed a bottle of beer from the fridge and went into the study. Tonight was a night for a good solid action flick. If he couldn't solve the Montgomery murder, he could at least watch a tough cop mow down the bad guys. In the movies it was easy to sort out the bad guys from the good guys. The bad guys had greasy hair and wore good suits or baggy trousers and smoked a lot. People who had nice, normal middle-class families, stable jobs, were the good guys.

They didn't use their own children as sex toys and blame an itinerant gardener if something went wrong. It was always there, in the back of his mind. Samantha Blakely, daughter of a vice president of a major bank, had been murdered, in her home, the day after her birthday. As she'd turned twelve, her mother decided that she didn't need to go to the babysitter's after school, as long as she came straight home. Manuel Estavera, the gardener, discovered the body, raped and strangled, stuffed into the shrubbery beside the pool like a bag of autumn leaves. The investigation, led by John Winters, immediately focused on the gardener. There was no DNA on the girl's body; the killer had worn a condom, nowhere to be found, but the gardening gloves were bloody. Numerous strands of the girl's hair were found in the gardening shed. She liked to watch him work, Estavera explained through a Spanish translator. He'd been wearing his gloves when he found her, and he tucked her dress around her lower body. To preserve her modesty, even in death. The autopsy revealed that abuse had been going on for some time. The bank VP was a good-looking guy, dressed in two-thousand-dollar suits; his wife was a tall, blond stunner who worked two days a week in an art gallery and did charity work the rest of the time. She was home by five on her gallery days, and she'd thought that Samantha could handle the responsibility of two hours on her own. Because of the prominence of the family, and the luxury Grey's Point community where the crime had taken place, press attention was relentless. Columnists called for stricter immigration controls; others took the opportunity to bay for their favorite hobby horse—the return of the death penalty. And John Winters, charmed by the gracious wife, admiring the perfect home with the perfect view, maybe a bit jealous of the quality of the suit, zeroed in on Manuel Estavera, the gardener.

Winters had been in his office, about to leave to charge Estavera with the murder of Samantha Blakely, when his partner called. He'd found someone from Blakely's gym, where he'd supposedly been at the time, who thought that he'd seen the man leave much earlier than he'd said. Once Winters turned some of his attention from the gardener and started to dig into Blakely, the case came together like the wheels of a Swiss watch. Richard Blakely was now doing life in Kingston Penitentiary; the glamorous wife was doing life in therapy. And John Winters was wrapped in the guilt of how close he'd come to railroading an innocent man.

His prejudices and arrogant confidence in his own judgment had almost seen an innocent man convicted, and a guilty one left free.

The phone rang, and he lunged for it, glad of the chance to shake off his memories.

"Rosemary Fitzgerald's back, Sarge," Ingrid, the night dispatch officer, said.

"Where is she?"

"At her store. It's called Rosemary's Campfire Kitchen at…"

"I know where it is."

"I've got her on the line. She mumbled something about a bike. You think maybe she knows something about a motorcycle gang?"

"God only knows. Tell her to stay put until I get there."

"Will do."

Beer and pizza forgotten, Winters headed for the door. When he'd arrived home, he'd changed into shorts and a Vancouver Grizzly T-shirt. He stuffed his gun and handcuffs into the belt of the shorts and pulled a flannel shirt on to cover them. No need to let Mrs. Fitzgerald think he'd come to arrest her at gunpoint.

Winters drove into town. People strolled up and down Front Street in the warm evening air, and light and music spilled from the town's many bars and restaurants. He couldn't find a place to park close to his destination, so he ended up at a lot several blocks away. He jogged toward Rosemary's Campfire Kitchen.

The Closed sign was on the door. He knocked, grateful for the chance to control his breathing before he had to talk. He was getting old.

A woman opened the door. She was as lean as whippet.

"Mrs. Fitzgerald?"

"The one and only. Come in. But please understand that I'm so backed up, what with rushing off to Toronto for absolutely no reason at all, that I have to keep cooking."

He stepped into the shop. The smell of frying onions and garlic reminded him that he'd abandoned his dinner.

"It was grayish blue, ladies' style, no distinguishing characteristics. Cost me four hundred and fifty bucks. That might not be a lot to some people, but it sure is to me. The deductible on my insurance is five hundred. I'd have to give them fifty dollars to make the claim, eh? It was taken on Thursday sometime before I left after closing. Whoa, my onions are burning. Got to get to them. No one likes burned onions in their chili."

Winters' head spun, and not only from the scent of burning onions. Rosemary disappeared behind a red curtain. He followed. The back of the shop was about the same size as the front. A freezer lined one wall, an oven and range were set against another. The shelves were piled with kitchen implements.

"I'm sorry, Mrs. Fitzgerald," he said. "But I'm not following you. What was grayish blue?"

She stirred the onions, while reaching for a spice bottle.

"Why, my bike, of course. That's why you're here, right? Can you pass me that green bottle? Second on the right."

"No, I cannot. Mrs. Fitzgerald, please. I see that you've a business to run. But I must insist that you sit down and talk to me."

"This isn't about my bike, is it?"

"The theft of your bike, perhaps not. But I'm interested to hear that it was taken on Thursday."

"Would you like a coffee?"

"No, thank you. Your bike was stolen on Thursday. What time did you notice it missing?"

"A few minutes before nine."

Winters' heart took a jump. When dispatch had called to tell him that Mrs. Fitzgerald was back in town, he'd almost asked them to send the beat constable around to talk to her. But his pizza had been so unappetizing, and Rosemary had been so elusive, that he decided to come himself. That was looking to be a wise decision. "Are you sure of the time?"

She shrugged. "Roughly. The store closes at eight. Some nights I stay and cook for the next day, but last week I had plenty of stock, thank goodness for that as it turned out, so I left after cleaning up."

"When did you notice your bike was missing?"

"Right away. I park it just outside the back door."

"Can you show me?"

"Sure." She unlocked the door and stepped out into the alley. Winters followed. Looking west he could see the rear of Alphonse's Bakery. The shadows were long, but the alley was fully visible. A dog sniffed at the garbage bags at the rear of the convenience store.

"What did you do when you realized your bike was gone?"

She shrugged. "Went back inside. My lock was lying on the ground, right there." She pointed. "The cable was cut through, so I knew it had been stolen. No point in looking around, was there?"

"Did you see anyone while you were out here?"

"You mean behind my store? No."

"I mean anyone at all. Anywhere in sight." He pointed west. "That way perhaps."

"What's all this about, Mr. Winters?"

Rosemary had been out of town since Friday morning; it was possible she hadn't heard about the Montgomery murder. "I'll explain in a minute," he said. "Take your time, just look around. You were probably pretty angry when you realized someone stole your bike."

"Damn straight," she said. "Perhaps I didn't go right back inside. I might have stood here and stewed for a few minutes." A car drove down Elm Street, windows rolled down, hip hop music cranked up. From the houses behind the alley someone called "Buster," and the dog at the store lifted its head. It took one last sniff of the garbage before trotting away.

"There were two men down that way, on the other side of the street. I often see the staff from the restaurant out in the alley at this time of night, having a smoke or getting some fresh air."

"Two men? Did you notice anything about them?"

"They were arguing."

He let out a breath he hadn't realized he was holding. "How do you mean?"

"They weren't exactly yelling, but their voices were raised, sharp, you know?"

"Could you hear what they were saying?"

"Sorry, no. Just the tone of voice? I'm guessing that something happened there that night, am I right?"

"In a minute, Mrs. Fitzgerald."

"Call me Rosemary."

"Can you describe them at all?"

"The light was poor, like it is now. So they were in shadow. And I was only thinking about my bike." She closed her eyes. Winters said nothing.

"One was large, fat, big pot belly. The other taller and much thinner. I think. Well, I don't want to guess."

"Go ahead and tell me what you think, Rosemary. Your impressions are important."

"I thought that the fat one was older, and the thin one younger. He had that sort of wiry body that young guys have. You only see that on middle-aged men if they run marathons or something."

Instinctively Winters sucked in his gut. No one would ever call him wiry.

She opened her eyes. "I'm sorry, but I didn't notice them all that much. I was upset about my bike."

"You've been a big help, Rosemary, thank you."

"Now can you tell me what all this is about? And while you're at it, I'll put the coffee on, and I have a couple of double chocolate cookies left."

"It's a deal. But first I have to make a call." He pulled his cell out of his pocket. Rosemary ground beans and ran water into the coffee maker; Winters could almost see her ears flapping as he talked into the phone.

"Call Ron Gavin of the Mounties." He recalled bike treads in a patch of concrete against the back of the bakery. And that Alphonse said he didn't own a bike, nor did any of his staff ride one to work. Was it possible that Rosemary's bike thief had gone that way, and perhaps seen Montgomery and his killer? "I need a full ident team behind 343 Front Street in Trafalgar ASAP. Tell him I want them to see what they can find in the way of bicycle prints. It's been a long time, but at least there hasn't been any rain. Let me know when they'll be here." He hung up.

"Cookie?" Rosemary said, holding out a plate piled high.

Chapter Twenty-four

Molly Smith didn't have to be on duty until three in the afternoon for the start of a twelve-hour shift. But on Monday she was up early, restless and troubled.

She and Sylvester trudged through the bush along the banks of the Upper Kootenay River. Sylvester chased noises in the undergrowth and Smith kicked at leaves and small, helpless plants. Off the case. Sent back to the beat. Without a resolution to the case anywhere in sight. Her chance to make an impression, to show them that she could cut it, gone. Finished. Back to the beat with the likes of Dave Evans. It was another hot day, but the woods were cool. The bush ended about twenty yards short of the river, opening into sandy flats. The mosquitoes were bad, and she waved her arms in the air around her head and neck like a human windmill. Sylvester leapt into the river, and Smith smiled as she watched him lapping at the water while swimming, his pink tongue working hard. Watching a happy dog could always make her troubles fade, for a little while.

When she got home last night, she'd found her father rooting around inside the fridge.

"You're still here," she'd said.

Andy straightened up and turned. He was holding a bottle of beer. "Where else would I be?"

"Last I heard, you were leaving Mom, abandoning me, and heading off to an ashram in Tibet."

"Adult children should be living on their own," he said, twisting the cap off the bottle. "Your mother and I have our disagreements. You never noticed that before?"

"Seemed like more than a disagreement to me."

"You want a beer, Molly?"

"Okay." She accepted a bottle and popped the top. "Cheers."

"Bottoms up," he said, taking a long drink. He scratched at the label on the bottle. "I love your mother, Molly. I love her with all my being. Thirty years together and I don't feel any the less for her than I once did. I hope that someday you find someone to love as much."

An image of Graham flashed behind her eyes. They were on a kayaking trip in Desolation Sound. She'd left the campsite, stepped over the rocks and logs, and rounded the cove, seeking someplace private to go to the bathroom. When she'd returned, she stopped, and for a long time simply watched Graham's profile outlined against the orange flames of their fire. He leaned forward and pushed a log with his stick, and then, sensing her presence, looked up with a smile.

"But she drives me crazy," Andy said. The image of Graham faded. "She can't let go of the past. You'd think it was still the Seventies, that we all had long hair. Well, me anyway." He rubbed his thinning scalp. "And bellbottoms and were protesting Vietnam, to hear her talk sometimes."

"Perhaps Mom just cares about things that haven't changed. War, for example."

"Fine when we were twenty, young and innocent," he said. "But we have a business to maintain, employees who depend on us, children, as old as they might be, to worry about." Sylvester barked. "And dogs to keep in the style to which they have become accustomed."

"Where's Mom anyway?" There was something most uncomfortable about learning the details of your parents' marriage. Next he'd be telling her about the night she was conceived.

"Another meeting of that goddamned committee. I just hope that rabid idiot from CNC doesn't get wind of it. He'll egg your mother on until she loses it, and then display her as a model of radical lunacy." He looked at his watch. "It's almost ten. Time for the program. I'd better watch it just to see if Lucky's making a display of herself once again."

Smith had pulled a chair up to the scarred kitchen table. One scratch, among many, cut through the surface. As a teenager she'd smashed her plate, containing her entire dinner, into the table. The plate had shattered, food flown everywhere. Lucky had done the same. Sam had grabbed his own plate and fled for the comparative safety of the family room.

She picked up one of Lucky's political magazines and flicked through it. She heard Andy switch off the TV (there hadn't been any swearing or throwing of things, so presumably the program hadn't been too bad) and the light from the living room was extinguished.

"Same rubbish," he said, "A lot of people gathering in town to protest the garden. That young jackass, Harris, was on again. You wouldn't know from watching that show that there are reasonably sane people in favor of the park. Your mother's late, probably stayed to watch Ashcroft's program. You'll let Sylvester out before going to bed?"

"Sure. Night, Dad."

She returned to the magazine.

Lights flooded the kitchen as a car pulled into the driveway. She recognized the out-of-tune engine of her mother's car, and Sylvester recognized his footsteps of his beloved.

He was at the door, tail wagging, when Lucky came into the kitchen. Long strands of hair had come out of the clip, and lines of age and stress radiated from the corner of her mouth and the edges of her eyes. But those eyes shone with determination, and Molly Smith had known, without a word being said, that the battle was on. Once again.

A bug zoomed in under her flailing hands like a fighter plane and hit the back of her neck. She swatted it and her finger came away with a streak of red blood. She called Sylvester to get out of the water and they ran for home.

She was online, looking at cars and their prices, and scratching the back of her knee, when the phone rang.

"Molly Smith."

"Hi, Molly. I'm glad I caught you. How are you doing?"

That squeaky voice was unmistakable. Why would she be phoning here? "Meredith?"

"It's been a long time since we talked, about anything aside from our professions that is, so I wanted to give you a shout. Did you hear that Darla Wozenk is pregnant? Again? What's this, her third? My mom figures that she's keeping herself preggers so she can stay on welfare."

"Meredith, why are you telling me this?"

"Maybe just for old times' sake, Molly. I miss the high school days sometimes, don't you?"

Like I miss the time I had a root canal. "Yeah, sure."

"I called the station. They said you weren't due in until three. Why don't we have a late lunch, say around one thirty? A quick bite, a place just down the road from the police station, and then you can pop on over to work after. How's that sound?"

As appealing as that root canal. There had to be some reason that Meredith Morgenstern wanted to have lunch with Molly Smith. And it certainly wasn't for old times' sake. If this was April 1, Smith would suspect an elaborate joke. Meredith the reporter could have called Smith the cop and asked for a meeting, if she'd wanted. All this let's- do-a-girls'-lunch joviality—which must have Meredith wanting to vomit up her breakfast—had to be for an audience.

Who else but Rich Ashcroft.

"Okay," Smith said. "I'll bite. Where?"

Meredith laughed. "Flavours at one thirty?"

Flavours was the hottest new restaurant in town. Very, very expensive.

"I can't afford Flavours on a cop's salary. We don't have expense accounts, you know."

"My treat, Molly."

"Well, okay. I can change into my uniform at the station."

"That's not necessary. Everyone in town knows who you are. And your uniform suits you so well. That blue is perfect for your coloring."

Smith wondered if she'd fallen though a wormhole into a parallel universe. "I'm not having lunch with you as a police officer, Meredith. You said it was a chance for us to get together."

"Sure it is. I don't want you to be inconvenienced, that's all."

"I'll see you at one thirty." Smith hung up.

Something was up. And that something almost certainly had to do with Rich Ashcroft and his interest in the peace garden. But what Meredith hoped to learn from Molly Smith, who knew nothing more than anyone who'd read this morning's edition of the *Daily Gazette,* Smith couldn't imagine. Meredith probably knew more about what Lucky's committee was up to than Molly did.

She'd have lunch with Meredith, order the most expensive stuff on the menu—too bad she had to work right after and thus couldn't select something outrageous from the wine list—and listen to her hostess make small talk. As long as she said nothing about police business, what would it matter? If she kept her ears open she might even learn a thing or two.

She turned back to the computer. Half an hour looking for cars, get dressed for work, and she'd have time to visit Christa in hospital, and then meet Meredith. Her parents had gone into work together so she could take Lucky's car. She looked at the computer screen. A new Mini Cooper convertible was looking to be outside her budget. But Toyota had some nice deals on almost-new cars.

Once again the alley behind Front Street was closed off. Ron Gavin and his team arrived, ready to go over every inch of ground, one more time. Brad Noseworthy was with them. He was the only qualified crime scene investigator on the Trafalgar City Police, and mighty pissed off at having been out of town and thus missing the initial investigation of their first murder in more than a year.

"A bicycle was stolen from over there." Winters pointed to the back of Rosemary's store. "At almost the exact time our Mr. Montgomery was on his way to meet his maker."

"Coincidence?" Gavin said.

"Probably. But it's possible our bike thief saw something. If he's the witness I need, he's not going to come forward and say 'Hey, Man, I was like, lifting this bike the other day, and I, like, saw this dude killing this old guy.' So I have to find him."

"Don't give up your day job," Gavin said. "You do not have a career on TV."

"Follow those bike treads to my witness' back door, and you'll make me a happy man, Ron."

Winters stood to one side and watched them work. This had to be the break he needed. Fitzgerald had seen two men arguing in the alley behind the bakery shortly before nine o'clock. One overweight with a good-sized beer gut—the description fit Montgomery. It also fit half the men in Trafalgar, but half the men in Trafalgar had not been murdered in that place around that time. The other fellow was young, probably, tall and wiry. Definitely not the short, chubby Dr. Tyler.

He called Paul Keller. "I need someone to pull together everything we have on bicycle thefts in town, going back, let's say, six months as a start."

"Why?"

Winters explained about Fitzgerald's bike. "It's possible that the thief saw Montgomery arguing with his killer. Even if he just saw someone else in the alley, it'll be a lead we badly need."

"I'll get someone on it. You know that most bike thefts don't get reported?"

"I am aware of that, Paul, thanks."

"Just reminding you. Start with Molly Smith."

"Is she in charge of bike theft investigation?"

Keller laughed. "Her bike was stolen from the back of the station a couple of nights ago. Fortunately the press didn't get wind of it. They would have made us look like the Keystone Kops."

Winters remembered Smith telling him the first day she'd worked with him that she'd decided it was too late to bike home, and was looking for a ride. "I'll talk to her. This is a priority, Paul."

"Good thing I have officers sitting around with nothing to do all day. I'll put someone on it right away."

Winters hung up and stuffed his phone in his jacket pocket. He had to talk to that bike thief.

Chapter Twenty-five

Christa Thompson stared at the flowers on her windowsill, listening without interest to the murmur of a busy hospital. Footsteps sounded in the hallway. Three nurses stopped to talk in front of her door. A child yelled, and was hushed. The meal cart clattered. Someone cried out, in pain or sorrow, Christa couldn't tell. Nor did she care.

She'd pushed her lunch tray away, without touching the unappetizing mess. Her father had come in last night, not long before the end of visiting hours, bearing fat cream roses in a crystal vase. He sat in the visitor's chair and talked about the weather and federal politics. At last the nurse came in to check on her before turning out the lights, and her father had left.

She heard Molly's voice in the corridor, saying hello to someone. Christa closed her eyes and settled her breathing.

"Hey, girl. How ya doin'?"

Christa breathed.

"Oh, sorry. Are you asleep, sweetie? It's me, Molly."

Christa breathed. Why couldn't fucking Molly Smith just leave her alone? She'd gone to the police station, like Molly had told her, but Molly wasn't there, was she? More important things to do. More important people to be helped.

Behind her eyelids, she saw the rays of sunlight dim. Molly was standing at the window. Christa cracked her right eye open. Molly bent over and sniffed at the roses. She was in uniform, looking tough and imposing in the dark uniform, bulletproof vest, trousers full of pockets, blue stripe down the pant leg, belt jingling with equipment.

"Hey, you're awake. Good. I can't stay for long. You won't believe who I'm having lunch with."

"I don't care."

"What's up? This is good."

"Just go away, will you. And don't come back."

Now Molly didn't look so tough. Underneath the uniform, she was small and female. Vulnerable. Like Christa.

Early afternoon on a Monday, Flavours was pretty much empty. The hostess, hair a shade of orange that existed nowhere in nature, not even on an orange, waited at the door to greet her. "Constable Smith, so nice of you to join us. Ms. Morgenstern is just this way."

She followed the orangehead through the empty restaurant. Meredith occupied a table at the back tucked into a small alcove. "Hi, Molly. Have a seat. This is so cool."

Smith sat. The table was set with crisp linen, silverware so shiny it reflected light, and wineglasses you could drown a small dog in.

A bottle of wine sat in a silver ice bucket beside the table. Meredith's glass was half-empty. "Wine?" she said. "It's a California chardonnay. Very good."

"No thanks. I'm on duty in an hour."

"Then we'd better go ahead and order. Have anything you like." Meredith lifted her hand.

A good-looking young man came up to their table and gave them a warm smile. He was dressed formally in a black suit, starched white shirt and thin black tie. But his hair was gathered into a ponytail and a cluster of earrings outlined his left ear. The marks of a piercing ran through his eyebrow.

Smith would have loved a steak, rare, with a baked potato piled high with sour cream, but she had a twelve-hour shift ahead of her, and a meal like that would have her asleep on her feet. She ordered a spinach salad. Meredith went for the salmon.

"So, Molly, how's your family? How's Sam? I don't mind telling you that I had a bit of a crush on him when we were in school. He was so much older than us, seemed so sophisticated to me." Meredith giggled and downed the rest of her glass in one gulp. She poured herself another.

"Everyone's fine," Smith said, as the waiter brought her a bottle of San Pellegrino. He opened it with a great flourish and poured a glass as if he were pouring liquid gold.

"I guess you heard that my sister, Andrea, graduated top of her class in law school. Mom and Dad are so proud of her. Of course...."

"Look, Meredith, as interesting as the doings of your family are, I'm afraid I have trouble believing that you're wanting to catch up on all we've missed. Why don't you get to the point?" Smith was not in the mood to spar with Meredith. She'd chewed herself out all the way, stinging from Christa's attack. In her gut she knew it was her fault that Christa had gotten beaten up; Charlie Bassing may have done the beating, but Molly Smith hadn't been there to protect her friend.

Meredith took another slug of wine. Her eyes darted around the room and settled back on the woman sitting across from her. "Okay. The point is that I need your help, Moonlight. Never thought I'd say those words but there they are. First, in all honesty, let me tell you that I always envied you that name. I was named after my maternal grandmother. I have the name of an eighty-year-old."

Smith was momentarily taken back. Everything Meredith had said rang as false as Rich Ashcroft's concern for the wellbeing of the town of Trafalgar. Except for this sudden confession. Meredith showed Smith her sparkling white teeth as she twisted the stem of her wineglass in her manicured fingers, and Smith remembered who she was talking to. Meredith Morgenstern might have liked the name Moonlight, but she'd certainly never liked the person.

"I'll tell my parents you said so. Spit it out, I haven't got all day."

"You are having lunch at my expense."

"True. So if you want me to tell you about Sam and his wife Judy and their two lovely children, Ben and Roberta, I'll be happy to. Where to begin? They live in Calgary. Sam's a lawyer with Western Canada Petrol, and Judy is a producer at...."

She stopped talking as the waiter put their lunches on the table. He pulled a gigantic wooden phallic symbol out from under his arm, waved it in front of their faces, and asked if they wanted fresh ground pepper.

They declined.

Smith stabbed her fork into a pile of helpless spinach.

"...a radio station," she continued. "Ben's in the rep hockey league and Sam's making plans to manage his career in the NHL. While Roberta excels at piano."

"Oh, look who's here," Meredith said with a smile so sharp that her salmon might have turned into shark.

A middle-aged man, trim, well dressed in comfortable casuals, enjoying his own self-importance, was walking toward them.

"Meredith. I've been looking for you. But don't let me interrupt your lunch." His smile was broad and as false as his mouthful of teeth.

Smith dropped her fork. "I'm outta here." She pushed her chair back.

"Don't leave on my account," Rich Ashcroft said. He grabbed a chair from another table, swung it around, and sat down. "Constable Molly Smith."

"You know who I am?"

"As you obviously know who I am. So let's not beat about the bush. I'm here to do a profile of your lovely town. I had no idea that you were friends with my colleague, Meredith, but now that we've met, I'd like to interview you for my program."

Smith looked at Meredith. "You must be out of your mind, to think you could trick me into something like this."

The waiter and the hostess hovered, watching. "Perhaps you could give my viewers background on Trafalgar," Ashcroft said.

"Hardly." She headed for the door. What on earth was Meredith thinking? That she'd give a TV interview while dressed in full uniform? She might as well hand in her resignation on the spot. Could Meredith and Ashcroft possibly have believed that she wouldn't have seen, or even heard about, the CNC program on Trafalgar?

She stepped onto the sidewalk. The sun was bright and in her eyes. She fumbled for her sunglasses.

"I understand that your mother, Mrs. Lucy Smith, who everyone calls Lucky, is one of the leading organizers of the Commemorative Peace Garden, Constable Smith." Ashcroft had followed her out. He was standing close to her. Much too close. Perhaps she'd pull out her handcuffs and cuff him. That would shut the pompous bastard up. Instead she took a couple of steps backward. He followed her. She could smell his breath, all mint and mouthwash. "As someone charged with the maintenance of law and order you must be concerned about your mother and her group. How does that affect the performance of your job?"

"It doesn't affect it at all," she said, aware that she shouldn't be saying anything. "The Trafalgar City Police have no opinion on the garden."

"Some folks have suggested that the Trafalgar City Police has an interest, for some twisted reason, in town council approving the peace garden. With your mother agitating, causing trouble, does that put you in a conflict of interest, or are you representing her to the police department?"

"Certainly not." She had to get the hell out of here. People walking past recognized Ashcroft; they pointed at him and whispered among themselves.

She turned and walked away.

"Constable Smith, please," Ashcroft called. His voice was low, soft, charming.

She turned.

He stood no more than a couple of feet away from her. He was her parents' age at least, but still a good-looking man, tanned and fit, with a haircut that probably cost a hundred bucks or more in California.

"Yes?"

"Some might think that your mother and her friends are attempting to actively interfere with the U.S. political situation as it is today. Or is it simply that they can't let go of memory of things long past?"

Meredith had come out of the restaurant. She held her hands to her mouth, and her face was pale.

"Fuck you, Ashcroft," Smith said. "How dare you come to our town and try to tell us what to believe. And fuck you too, Meredith," she yelled, "for all your let's-remember-the-good-old-days."

"Please, Constable," Ashcroft said. His smile was as friendly as those of the gargoyles adorning town hall. "Calm down. Is it true that your father was a draft dodger?"

"He came to Canada because he didn't believe in the Vietnam War, yes. But, as you said, that was a long time ago. Before I was born, in fact."

"How much support does your mother, Lucky Smith, have from the Trafalgar City Police?"

"Don't be ridiculous. The police don't take sides on matters such as this. Leave me alone." She started to walk away.

"Do you object to the actions of your mother, Constable Smith?"

Smith turned again. Again Ashcroft was standing in her private space. Rage boiled up behind her forehead, and she fought to keep her eyes from filling up like a pothole in the road in a sudden rainstorm. "Will you leave my mother the fuck alone," she yelled. A small crowd was gathering. A man spoke to Meredith, and she shook her head.

"No need to get upset, Constable. I'm only asking you some simple questions."

"You don't back off, buddy, I'll arrest you for harassing a police officer."

"I'm not harassing you, Constable Smith," he said, in a voice as smooth and sweet as honey. "I only want to know if having a communist, terrorist-supporting harridan for a mother is compromising your ability to serve and protect the people of this town."

She'd faced down drunks spoiling for a fight after the bars closed, irate motorists who figured that doing a hundred miles an hour on a winding mountain road was well within their rights, and an abusive husband who'd decided that as his wife was out of battering range, a female cop would make a suitable replacement. And she'd handled them all, calmly, as she'd been taught.

She took a step forward, expecting Ashcroft to retreat. Instead he smirked. "Closer, Molly," he whispered, staring into her eyes. "Come closer. Your mother's a washed-up old hag trying to relive her glory days, and as for your father, they used to hang…."

A black SUV careened across the street. Brakes protested as it came to a halt, facing the wrong way. A man jumped out, leaving the engine running. Ashcroft's gaze broke and he stepped back. John Winters pushed his way between them. "What's going on here?"

Ashcroft gave Smith a long, lingering look, and then turned to Winters. "Sorry," he said, "I don't think I've had the pleasure."

Smith was shaking all over. This close. She'd been this close to assaulting a journalist.

Winters pulled his wallet out and flashed his badge. "Sergeant John Winters, Trafalgar City Police. If you're looking for an official statement from our office, the station is around that corner. Otherwise, please be on your way. You're creating a disturbance."

"I might pop by later, thanks," Ashcroft said. He looked at Smith. His eyes were as cold as the water in Meredith's ice bucket. "We'll talk again later, Molly. Count on it."

"Anything else we can help you with?" Winters said.

"Winters, I'll remember that name."

They watched Ashcroft saunter away.

Meredith's face was white and she tossed Smith a look somewhere between pain and regret and embarrassment before running after Ashcroft. A fat woman stepped out from the group of spectators and handed Ashcroft a pen and scrap of paper, which he signed with a flourish. He looked around, but no other fans approached him. The crowd began to disperse, a few people muttering. Ashcroft waved, and a man stepped out from an alley. He carried a camera on his shoulder; it was pointing at Smith and Winters.

"Oh, God. They were filming it."

"Get in the car."

"I'm okay. I can walk."

"Get in the car, Constable Smith, or that cameraman will get a good shot of you being forced into it."

She ran around the SUV and wrenched open the passenger door. Winters hit the gas and pulled away with a speed that should have had her giving him a ticket.

He didn't take her to the station, as she expected; instead, he drove toward the river. He pulled into the parking lot beside the city hall park. "Get out."

"I'm on duty."

"Not for another half an hour. Get out."

"I don't want to."

"Get out of the car, Constable."

She opened the door and stepped out. The sun was warm on her face. As if she were watching a movie, she saw herself pulling out her truncheon and knocking Ashcroft to the ground. She stood over him and kicked him in the ribs. Maybe a kick to the head as well. And it would all have been captured on camera.

Winters walked into the park. Smith followed, because she could think of nothing else to do. The public beach was about two hundred yards away. Parents sat in fold-up chairs and watched children playing in the sand or paddling in the water. Two boys chased a squealing girl, splashing water on her, while their father yelled at them to behave. They paid him no attention and he went back to his book. The benches at this end of the park were empty. Winters sat down and watched the families enjoying the beach.

Smith joined him. Her misery shrouded her like a *burka*. Except that she didn't even have eye holes to see out of.

They sat in silence.

A mother called her children out of the water to come and eat. They ran toward her, screaming with pleasure.

"What happened there?" he said at last.

"I'd rather not talk about it." It was bad enough just watching the scene play over and over in her head, never mind having to tell him about it.

"I'm not asking, Smith. I'm ordering you. What happened there?"

She swallowed bile. "I was set up. Meredith Morgenstern from the *Gazette* invited me to lunch. I knew her in school."

"Yes, you told me, go on."

"It was a trap. That Ashcroft asshole arrived, all false charm. I walked out. I don't think Meredith paid the bill."

"If not, they'll find her. Go on."

The tears that had been building up behind her eyes ever since her best friend had told her to leave the hospital began to flow like the river at break-up. She sat on the park bench, hot salty tears running down her face. She made no move to wipe them away. "I screwed up, okay. I screwed up big time. Christ, I can handle the tough guys, but that smarmy bastard." Her chest closed up, and her shoulders shook, and regardless of how hard she might try not to let it happen, she sobbed. Winters made no attempt to comfort her; he didn't put his arm around her shoulders, mutter platitudes or even offer her a tissue. And she knew that her career was finished.

"Lots of smarmy bastards in the world, Molly," he said at last. "And I'm sure you've met some of them. Why'd this one get your goat?"

She dug in her pocket for a tissue and blew her nose. "My mom. He said things about my mom. And my dad. My parents are good people. Really good people. Dad only wants to keep the store going, and to get along with everyone. Mom might be living in the past sometimes, but the things she believes in are so important to her."

"I thought as much. It's tough, doing our job in a town this small. Where everyone knows everyone else. Where we have family, childhood friends, neighbors. But we're still the police and we have a responsibility."

The word "we" sounded nice in her ear. But it wouldn't be long before she was no longer part of Winters' *we*. She started crying again. A young couple passed, holding hands, smiling at each other with that stupid smile that told everyone in the world that they were newly in love. They paused in front of the bench and then scurried on. In other circumstances, Smith might have laughed to imagine what they must be thinking to see a police officer crying her heart out in the summer sun.

"He filmed it," she said.

"I noticed. It's going to be bad, Molly. Probably very bad. I'd tell you that you shouldn't have said a word and just walked away, but you know that. If someone like Ashcroft insulted Eliza, and I knew he was planning on slandering her all over national TV, I'd probably deck the guy. So I won't criticize you."

"Thanks," she mumbled. She twisted her sodden scrap of a tissue between her fingers.

"It's ten to three. Mop your face and gird your loins, as I believe they say in the classics. You have to tell the chief what happened."

"I can't."

Winters stood up. "Whether you can or not is irrelevant. You will tell him the moment you walk into the station. You want him to see you on TV tonight without being prepared?"

"No." She got to her feet. Her boots felt like lead weights holding her down. Perhaps she should just go home now. Crawl into bed, grab Jenny, the Cabbage Patch doll she'd been given for Christmas when she was ten, pull the covers over her head and never come out. *Why, why did I ever think I could be a cop?*

"Let's go," Winters said.

She wiped her nose on her sleeve. "I would have punched that asshole into the ground if you hadn't shown up. They're going to show it tonight, so what does it matter what I say to the Chief. You can prepare him."

"If that's what you want," Winters said. "I'm going back to my car. I have work to do. I'll drop you at home, or I'll take you to the station. Or I'll leave you here. Your choice, Molly, your choice."

He walked up the hill to the parking lot. A colorful beach ball tumbled across the lawn toward him. He scooped it up and tossed it to a little girl with her finger in her mouth. She grabbed the ball and ran.

Smith took a deep breath and followed him. Might as well face the chief today. He'd be firing her once he'd seen *Fifth Column*.

Chapter Twenty-six

A list of bike thefts in the area was waiting on his computer. Smith had stopped crying on the drive back and had scuttled off to the washroom to wash her face and compose herself before going to see the Chief Constable. Jim Denton had given her a quizzical look and been about to say something, but Winters shook his head behind Smith's back, and the question changed to a greeting.

Winters didn't wait to see if she knocked on the CC's door. She would either confess, or not. If she ran from this, her career would be finished. And that was up to her. Stupid thing to do, let the press get to her, but she was young and very green.

He settled down to read incident reports. He'd also asked for reports from the Mounties and other towns in the Kootenays. It didn't take long to see that in the last four months the number of bike thefts in Trafalgar was sky high compared to a year before, and compared to other towns nearby. He sifted through the reports, looking for something, anything, to focus on. There was nothing obvious—bikes were snatched pretty much any day of the week, any time of day. Almost always from the downtown streets, though, very few from the newer residential areas higher up the mountain. He picked up the phone. "Jim, is Molly still in the station?"

"No. She was in with the boss for about twenty minutes, then left for her shift. You gonna tell me what that was about?"

"You'll find out soon enough. Ask her to drop in next time she passes this way, will you."

"Sure."

Winters turned back to the reports. Detective Lopez had worked hard on this file, but bike theft was notoriously hard to solve. Bicycles were easily transportable, easy to hide, and there was an eager market for the stolen goods in Vancouver.

"You wanted to see me, John."

He looked up. Smith stood in the doorway. Her face was pale and her eyes tinged with red. People would think she had a slight cold. "Your bike was stolen the other night. Tell me about it."

She wasn't expecting to have been called in off the street for that. "Why?"

"I've been staring at the damned computer for too long. My head hurts." He rubbed his eyes. It was getting increasingly hard to read small print if the light was poor, and the computer monitor was giving him headaches. He feared that he was going to need reading glasses soon: reading glasses, and before you knew it, it was a walker and spilling soup down your shirt front. "Let's go pick up a coffee. My treat. We can talk on the way." He stood up, trying to ignore the slight twinge in his lower back. "I've read the report on the loss of your bike, Molly, but I'm wondering if there's anything more you can add."

The equipment on her belt jingled as she walked. "It was gone, that's all, the cable lock cut right through. If you don't mind my saying so, John, as much as I'd like to get it back, I can't see why you've been called away from the Montgomery murder to worry about my bike."

He explained about Rosemary Fitzgerald and his search for the person who'd stolen her bike close to the time Montgomery was murdered.

There were no customers at Big Eddie's. Eddie was behind the counter, reading the newspaper. Winters ordered a large coffee, strong. Smith asked for a hot chocolate with whipped cream and chocolate sprinkles. They carried their drinks outside.

Cars drove by, but there were few pedestrians on the streets. It was the dinner hour for those with regular jobs.

"You saw a bike in the process of being pinched," Winters said, "from the Tourist Info Center."

"Yeah. Arrogant bastard. I can't believe he didn't see me in that alley."

Winters stopped walking. "What did you say?"

She licked at the tower of whipped cream. "He was so cool, he didn't even bother to look around to see if anyone was watching. Just broke the lock and took off."

"When you found Montgomery, you were on your regular rounds, right?"

"Yes."

"Do you normally check out that alley?"

"Of course."

"Round about the same time, every shift?"

"You can't set your watch by the time I'm at the corner of Elm and Front. But I'll usually go down that way sometime between eight thirty and nine thirty, if it's a quiet night."

"Goddamn it. You're the common denominator, Smith."

Comprehension dawned, her blue eyes opened wide and her pretty face settled into angry lines. She threw up her hands. Chocolate splashed over the rim of her cup. "Hey! I'm not pinching bikes. Ask Solway, she saw me chasing the guy."

"I'm not accusing you of stealing them, Molly. Just of being in the vicinity when it happens. Look, we know of three bikes being stolen in the past week. One—Rosemary Fitzgerald's around the time you could be expected to pass by on your rounds. Two—your own bike. And three—when you saw the guy in action." He threw his half-finished coffee into a trash can. "I want to see your shift records for the past six months, and check them against the bike theft reports. And while I'm at it, we'll look at other minor crimes. Stuff stolen from unlocked cars, for example. See if there's a spike when you're working."

"Please, no," she said. "You don't think I'm in enough trouble without creating my own private crime wave."

"You're creating nothing, Molly. But if I'm right, someone's watching you."

Smith and Winters watched the program in the chief's office. It was not quite as bad as they'd feared.

"Makes Ashcroft look like a bully," Jim Denton said, giving Smith a smile that was meant to be encouraging.

"Makes me look like a storm trooper," she said.

"The bully impression isn't doing us, or Molly, any good," Winters said. "It implies that the big bad wolf is bullying sweet little red riding hood who happens to be a female officer."

Keller pressed the remote and the TV went black. "Not a wolf, nor a storm trooper." He leaned his elbows on his desk and folded his fingers into a pyramid. "But a public relations disaster no matter how you look at it."

"I'm sorry, sir,"

"Never apologize, Molly," Keller said. "I'd have thought that your mother would have drilled that into you as you lay in your cradle. 'Never apologize. Never explain. Get the job done and let them howl.' I think the quote goes something like that."

John Winters looked out the window. The blinds were drawn but one of the slats had not met with its neighbor and there was a good-sized gap. A laughing crowd passed under the streetlights.

"It might not be as bad as you think, Paul," Winters said. "Ashcroft looks unhinged to me. First he's trying to get Molly to speak against the garden, and thus by implication her mother, and when that doesn't work, he tried to rile her up by insulting her parents. He doesn't show the baiting, but the way in which his interview flies from one point on the compass to another makes him look like a man desperate to get whatever angle he can."

"His fans won't see it that way," Keller said.

"I don't imagine there's anything that could make them see the situation any other way than how he intends them to see it."

"Probably not. Good of you to stay, Jim. Molly. A couple of minutes of your time, John."

The office door clicked shut behind Smith and Denton. "When's Lopez back?" Keller asked.

"Next week."

"You getting anywhere with Montgomery?"

"No." Winters decided to keep his suspicions about the bike thief and his apparent relations with Molly Smith to himself for now. They'd found a correlation between the times she was on the beat and the stealing of bicycles from the downtown area. Unfortunately, not only did that not bring him any closer to finding the thief, there was no guarantee that even if they found the guy, he'd know anything about the Montgomery murder.

"I have to ask the Yellow Stripes for help with this park business, John," the Chief said. He picked a pen off his desk and ran it between his fingers like a baton twirler. "People have been arriving all day, taking one side or the other. There's likely to be serious trouble on Wednesday when the damned fool we have for a deputy mayor announces the council's decision. And as long as I'm asking for the Horsemen's help, I'm going to ask them to send someone from IHIT as well. We need fresh eyes on the Montgomery case, John."

"I agree," he said. Although it burned him, deep inside, to say so. He was supposed to be the hotshot homicide detective from the big city. Blessing the minuscule Trafalgar City Police with his presence. And he couldn't solve the first murder that had happened in this backwoods town all year. He'd come here to escape from the memory of his own failure. And now he'd failed again.

The wheel of the shopping cart caught in a rut in the parking lot. Lucky wrenched it free with a curse. When she looked up a man was standing beside her car, arms crossed, watching her. Her heart leapt into her throat. It was a midweek afternoon; the parking lot was full, people were coming and going with their groceries. A red-faced woman dragged a little boy by the hand. He was screaming and trying to fall down. She swatted him on the bottom.

Lucky stopped walking.

"Mrs. Smith," the man said.

"Yes?"

"Do you know who I am?"

"Of course I do, you're Brian Harris. Come to Trafalgar to make trouble."

"The way I see it, Mrs. Smith, you're the one making trouble. You and that ridiculous committee."

"What do you want?"

"To talk," he said with a smile that didn't touch his eyes. He wore a blue baseball cap and the corner of his left eye twitched.

"We have nothing to talk about. I have to get these groceries home before the ice cream melts." She tried to calm her breathing. Surely Harris wouldn't attack her? In the middle of town in the middle of the day. He stepped toward her. She gripped the handles of her shopping cart and made sure it was between them: the shield of a twenty-first century warrior.

"No one wants trouble, Mrs. Smith."

"Then go away and leave us alone. This is our town."

"You're part of a larger world. Although you peaceniks don't seem to be able to see the big picture. Peacenik—isn't that what they called you back in the day, Mrs. Smith?"

"And we were proud, still are, to be on the side of peace." She felt some confidence returning. It had scared her, badly, to see him watching her, arrogance written all over his pinched face, letting her know that he could find her any time he wanted. But she was on her own ground, and he was just a young punk who thought he was tough because he didn't know the meaning of the word.

"Get to the point, please."

"The point, Mrs. Smith, is that you've lost. My contact on the town council tells me that they've voted to end the project outright and return the property to O'Reilly's estate. What happens to it then will make a lot of lawyers rich."

She tried not to let her dismay show. Could she believe him? He might have someone on his side in the town council, just as Barry had been anonymously warned about the meeting last night. "We'll await the formal announcement," she said.

He grabbed the front of her shopping cart and leaned forward. Shocked, Lucky stepped back; he moved in tandem. She was aware that the toddler was no longer screaming, that traffic in and out of the parking lot had stopped, that no one was chatting to their friends or talking on cell phones. In all the world, there might only be Lucky Smith and Brian Harris. Facing each other across a cart piled high with a week's worth of groceries.

"Now that I've got your attention," he said with a laugh, releasing the cart. "As I said, no one wants trouble. You've lost, so give up before someone gets hurt."

"*I'm* not about to hurt anyone."

"Dangerous job, a cop. Should be left to men and women who look like men. Not pretty girls with delicate bone structure and long blond hair."

"Are you threatening my daughter?"

"Just making an observation. In anticipation of tomorrow's announcement by the town council, we'll be gathering tonight to express our support. Better if you and your bunch aren't there. Because I don't want anyone to get hurt. Remember this, that uniform is designed to make the wearer stand out in a crowd." He winked at her, shoved the shopping cart toward her, hard, and walked away.

Lucky's knees buckled. Surely the bastards weren't going to harm Moonlight? She was a police officer; if anyone came after Moonlight, they'd have every cop in the British Columbia Interior, in the whole province, to deal with.

Her hand shook as she fumbled in her purse for her cell phone and punched up the number. Voice mail answered. "Barry, it's Lucky. There's going to be trouble tonight at the site of the garden. Call me."

She hung up. She looked at her hands. She was gripping a shopping cart. It was not a shield.

Who was she kidding?

Chapter Twenty-seven

Why anyone would think that a name like The Potato Famine would attract bar patrons, Molly Smith couldn't imagine. But everything Irish was fashionable in the world of imitation pubs.

A group of men tumbled out of The Potato Famine, a cheap bar at the far end of town. One of them caught sight of her, and shouted to his friends. They whistled and made obscene gestures. She stuck her thumbs through her gun belt and stared them down. They carried on up the road, leaning on each other for support, shouting drinking songs into the night. She let out a puff of breath and her fingers loosened their grip on her belt.

The radio at her shoulder crackled. "Report of a disturbance on Primrose Street," the night dispatcher said. "Constable Smith, report your location."

"Outside the Potato Famine on East Street."

"Wait there. A car will be around to pick you up."

She didn't have to wait long. A marked SUV pulled up beside her. Dave Evans was driving. She jumped in. "Trouble?"

"Looks like it. Saw you on TV, Molly. You shouldn't let them get to you."

"I'm sure you'd have handled being ambushed by the press much better, Dave."

"Natch," he said, flicking the switch to bring on lights and sirens.

She clenched her teeth. He'd been in the constables' room when she arrived for the start of her shift. Barely able to control his smirk at seeing her returned to the beat.

"You've got to try not to be so emotional, Molly." He turned into Front Street, barely managing to keep two wheels on the road. "This is a tough job. It needs tough players. No one else need apply."

She looked out the window. The stores and restaurants of downtown turned into late-nineteenth-century houses, then, as they climbed the hill, the big old houses changed into compact Fifties bungalows, larger Eighties homes, and finally twenty-first-century edifices of brick and glass. They might have been traveling in a time machine rather than a police car. By "tough players," Smith knew that Evans meant men. "No one else" was, of course, women.

"You would've punched his lights out, eh?" she said.

"If he insulted my mother like he did yours, count on it."

She had a moment of silent satisfaction thinking about Evans being kicked off the force for beating up a journalist.

They could hear the disturbance before they saw it. A low murmur, growing as they drew closer. An RCMP car blocked the road. Evans slammed his foot onto the brake pedal and avoided a collision by inches.

Macho idiot, Smith thought, getting out of the vehicle.

There were about a hundred people on the sidewalk in front of the park. And maybe three times that across the street. A single Trafalgar City cop stood between them. It was Dawn Solway, and her face lit up at the sight of reinforcements.

Two Mounties got out of their car. Streetlights reflected on the yellow stripe running down their trouser legs, the source of their nickname. "We just got here," one of them said. "I'm Tocek and this is Chen."

"Evans and Smith."

"Looks like there might be trouble," Tocek said.

Solway came over. "I'm so glad to see you. The mood's getting ugly." It must, Smith thought, have been terrifying being the lone cop standing in the middle of the street between the two factions, listening to the murmuring discontent grow.

Lucky Smith was beside the park gates. Her hand tucked into the right arm of her friend Barry, his left arm an empty sleeve. Faces Smith recognized from around her kitchen table stood behind them. Michael Rockwell held Lucky's other arm. He said something into her ear. Lucky looked into her daughter's eyes.

Smith returned the look. *Strength,* she thought, *Mom's sending me strength.*

As if orchestrated by an invisible conductor, the crowd across the street began to chant. "Cowards" and "traitors" were some of the words Smith caught. She turned away from her mother. "We need more people," she said to Tocek.

"Yeah, you do, but right now we're it. You handled a riot before?"

"No."

"You?" he asked Evans.

"No."

"I have, so until help arrives I'm in charge." He didn't look to be much older than Smith or Evans, and he was only a constable, like them. She didn't know what Evans thought, this guy barging onto their patch and taking over, but she was glad that someone was.

The five officers fanned out across the middle of the street. Smith's heart was beating so hard she feared it might burst out of her chest, like the alien in *Alien*. She touched her nightstick, just to feel its solid weight under her fingers. She felt her mother watching her.

"I saw her on TV," someone screamed. "That cop. The blond one in the middle. She said she'd do whatever was necessary to see the garden built."

It took Smith a moment to realize he was talking about her.

"You're crazy," a voice shouted from the garden side, "if you think the cops are with us."

Something broke on the pavement beside Smith's feet. She looked down to see thick brown glass. A beer bottle. *What the hell am I doing here?*

The line of protesters edged forward.

"Do you think they'd laugh if I held your hand, Molly?" Solway said in a small voice.

"Not as much as if I ran for my mommy. Who, unfortunately, is standing right behind us."

Tocek stepped forward. "Why don't you folks all go home."

"Go home. Go home." The garden side began to chant. Smith thought that she could hear her mother's voice, but she couldn't be sure. What would she do, if it broke into a riot? Save her mother and abandon the other citizens of Trafalgar? This couldn't be happening. She saw Rich Ashcroft's cameraman at the edges of the crowd. The red light in the front of his camera glowed. Ashcroft himself was nowhere to be seen, but she didn't doubt he was moving through the crowd, whispering agitation, rustling up good footage.

Her radio crackled. Dispatch was asking every officer to report in immediately to the station and pick up control gear. The Mounties' Emergency Response Team was being called. That unit was too far away to be of much immediate help, but some Mounties lived in Trafalgar; they'd come. Just knowing that all available resources were on the way helped to quell some of the panic churning through Smith's stomach.

"Disperse," Tocek said, in a voice so calm he might have been instructing a toddlers' swimming class. "There's nothing more to be gained here." He turned and faced the group at the park entrance. "And you too. Go home. Nothing can be settled tonight."

Smith was facing the anti-park group. They shifted and muttered amongst themselves. People at the back began to slide away, trying to look as if they hadn't really been part of all this. The pro-park people, including her own mother, for heaven's sake, were behind her. She heard similar mutterings, people suggesting that they just leave.

Tocek's shoulders relaxed. Chen let out a healthy breath.

"Stay in your place!" Brian Harris stepped to the front of the line. His right hand was buried deep in his pocket, ball cap low over his eyes. "You heard that pig bitch on TV. The cops are on the side of the appeasers' park." He grabbed the shoulder of a man who was retreating back into the crowd. "Are you running away? Like they did?"

The man looked at the line of police—all five of them, young, inexperienced, terrified, trying hard not to show it—then he looked at Harris. "No way," he said. He spat in the general direction of Solway's feet.

"Peace now!" someone yelled. It might have been Barry Stevens, Lucky's friend. "Come on," he said, "show us. Are you on the side of peace or war? Only one way will get us all killed."

"Killed. I'll kill you, you traitor."

A rock flew over Smith's head. A woman cried out.

A stone, about the size of a pea, hit Chen in the chest. He watched it bounce off and fall into the street. A brief shower of pebbles fell on them. Smith lifted her hands to shield her face. Somewhere behind her, glass broke.

The front line was swaying, moving from one foot to the other. All they needed was a reason to rush forward.

She turned to look at the line in front of the park. Robyn Goodhaugh, who'd protested at the Grizzly Resort in a wolf mask, jumped up and down, like a baby confined to a Jolly Jumper, throwing torrents of verbal abuse across the street.

"Mom," Smith yelled. She looked at the row of faces. Most scared, some exhilarated. "Mom?"

"I'm here." Lucky stepped out from behind a bush. Michael was holding her arm.

"Please, Mom," Smith said. "Go home. I do not want to have to worry about you."

Lucky's eyes moved.

"Mom?"

"She's right, Lucky," Michael said. "We've made our point."

"Barry, Jane, everyone," Lucky called to the people surrounding her. "This is out of our control. Let's go."

"Retreat is not always a dishonorable action," Barry said. Michael tugged on Lucky's arm, and she turned to follow him.

Now all Smith had to worry about was protecting the citizens of this town and herself.

"See that guy," Tocek said. "In the blue cap. He's inciting them. Follow me, Solway. Hey, you," he called, walking forward. "Let's talk, buddy. Time to calm this down."

"Talk is appeasement," Harris shouted. He waved his left hand toward the people behind him. His right was still in his pocket.

Smith heard sirens coming from all directions. Vehicles pulled up and doors slammed, men shouted and dark shapes were all around them. Cops with helmets, riot shields, tear gas.

Smith ran her eyes over the crowd. Fucking Ashcroft's fucking cameraman was filming everything.

She turned back to the mêlée. People, those with a sliver of common sense, were running in all directions. A good number of the anti-park crowd held their line. Rich Ashcroft came into sight: he said something to his cameraman, and the red light of the camera turned toward her. All Smith could do was to ignore it.

Robyn ran across the street, straight toward the camera. She threw something. The cameraman ducked, pulling his equipment with him, and a brown beer bottle shattered at his feet. A couple of demonstrators from her side followed her, and people who'd been standing in Ashcroft's vicinity surged forward to meet them.

Relieved that, for once, her mother'd seen reason and was hopefully well out of the way, Smith gathered what scrap of courage she could find and gripped the handle of her truncheon. Before she could make a move to try and separate the warring packs, her radio crackled. Police not wearing riot control gear were being called back. She couldn't see the two Mounties nor Solway. Evans was slightly behind her, telling park supporters to go home. A line of police in black riot uniform moved toward the protesters, banging batons on shields, trying to be as intimidating as possible.

Streetlamps and lights from police vehicles lit up the protesters' faces. A man threw a punch at Robyn Goodhaugh. Blood streamed from a cut on his forehead, and his face was contorted with rage. She staggered back, but didn't fall, and a man dodged in around her to deliver an uppercut to the bleeding man's jaw. They clashed and twisted and turned, pulling at each other's clothes, scratching at faces, like dancers gone mad. Goodhaugh charged toward the TV camera.

On the radio, Sergeant Peterson was yelling for Smith and Evans to state their location. She didn't know what to say. *In the street?*

She began to back away. Leave this to the people with the right equipment. "There's the cop bitch," someone yelled. "Get her."

Were they talking about her? Smith saw people she knew. People she passed on the street every day, who shopped at the Safeway or Alphonse's Bakery, and greeted her with a smile. But most of them were strangers, outside agitators. Like Brian Harris.

As if she'd conjured him up by the force of her own thoughts, he was there, standing behind a fat man in a sleeveless T-shirt. The fat man screamed at her. But Harris just stared. Through eyes as blank as the bottom of the Kootenay River.

She spoke into her radio. "I've got the leader in sight."

"Describe him."

"Blue shirt, blue ball cap. Standing no more then ten feet from me."

"Someone's coming your way. Point him out and then retreat, Smith. You're not wearing control gear."

Harris lifted his right hand and curled his index finger, moving it back and forth, beckoning her.

Screw him; she wasn't looking for a fight. She turned. Time to retreat.

Chapter Twenty-eight

Jane Reynolds had been a pacifist and anti-war activist all her adult life. One of the first women in North America to make full professor of physics, she'd raised three children while mentoring hundreds, perhaps thousands, of young people. She'd joined the ban-the-bomb movement in the '50s, and traveled throughout the States in the '60s protesting the Vietnam War. In the '80s the family lived in England for a few years while Jane was a visiting professor at Cambridge. She went to Greenham Common as much as possible, in support of the women protesting the nuclear weapons based there. She was comfortably retired now, her husband long dead, her children scattered across the continent. Her health was poor, and not getting any better. But her passion for the peace movement still ignited her life.

Someone knocked into her; she stumbled on the worse of her two bad knees and her glasses fell off. She didn't dare try to lower herself to the ground to feel around for them. She peered myopically into a blur of sound and movement. She'd heard Lucky's voice a few moments ago telling everyone to retreat. "Lucky?" Jane cried. "Barry, Michael, where are you?"

People were screaming in anger or yelling in fear. A steady *thump, thump* came from the left; a bullhorn called everyone to disperse. A body bumped into her from the right; she would have fallen had not someone been in her way and inadvertently kept her upright. She didn't know which way led to safety, or to her side of the fracas. If there were sides any more. She was turned around, confused. People were running in all directions. She realized, to her horror, that she was crying. She cursed under her breath—but only at herself. For getting old. Feeble and helpless. This wasn't the first demonstration she'd been in that had turned violent. She'd been in far worse situations. But back then she could see what was going on, and she could count on her strong, quick body to take her out of the way of danger. Embarrassed, humiliated, angry, in pain, she cried even harder. She fumbled in her pocket for a tissue and wiped at her face. It came away streaked with blood.

A deep voice reached her out of the wall of noise, and a large hand touched her arm, pulling her out of her circle of chaos. She blinked up at him. It was young constable Evans.

"Come with me, ma'am, please."

"Never thought I'd have to be escorted away from a protest." She allowed him to take her arm.

A space cleared in front of them. Lucky's daughter, Moonlight, was only a few feet away. "Smith," Evans called. "Let's get the hell out of here."

Moonlight turned and began to head toward them. Her face was very pale, the bones of her face almost visible through translucent skin. She looked as small and breakable as one of the antique teacups Jane collected.

Amongst the cacophony shattering the night air on this normally peaceful, tree-lined street—people yelling, a woman screaming, glass breaking, sirens, police shouting, truncheons striking shields—Jane heard a roar of rage.

The young man who'd been stirring up trouble ever since he arrived in town ran toward them. He pulled a small bottle out of his left pocket. The neck of the bottle was distorted as if something had been stuffed into it. The fingers of his other hand flicked, and a small flame illuminated the darkness. He pulled his arm back as if he were standing on the mound, ready to pitch the last inning in the final game of the World Series. He was looking directly at Dave Evans.

Jane screamed a warning. Moonlight turned.

Jane looked at Evans, still holding her by the arm. His eyes filled with fear, as he saw Harris coming toward him. He shoved Jane away from him, hard. She went down, hearing, as much as feeling, the arthritic bones in her arm snapping. She wanted to just curl up in a ball and stay there. But she forced herself to look up, and all she could see was Harris' homemade bomb lighting up the night.

Chapter Twenty-nine

Like almost every Canadian kid, from the daughters of business tycoons to the sons of immigrant laborers, Molly Smith had played soccer. She'd been fast on her feet, and was usually the goalkeeper. She sometimes thought the position had helped to prepare her for the life of a cop: ninety percent hanging around the goalposts watching the activity at the other end of the field, ten percent the center of the action.

Harris' attention was focused on Evans, standing over the fragile body of Jane Reynolds. When he saw Smith barreling toward him he tried to pivot, but his foot slipped and he stumbled. Smith struck Harris full on, her whole body colliding with his. He yelped and the object he'd been holding flew out of his hands. Glass broke and liquid spread across the pavement. The air filled with the smell of gasoline. It ignited with a whoosh and flame raced in a thin, deadly river across the street.

Smith's head spun; she stared at the pavement, inches from her face. Harris lay on the ground beside her, momentarily stunned.

Feet and legs ran past. A woman screamed, the sound so fierce it might be heralding the end of the world. "No, no," a man yelled.

Smith was jerked roughly to her feet. Her body shook as if an earthquake was ripping through the Mid-Kootenays. Dave Evans gripped her upper arms. He shook again. "Damn it, Smith, you okay?"

"Yeah," she said. "Get that lady the hell out of here. I'll handle him."

"Okay." Evans released her. He pulled Jane Reynolds off the pavement, and, without a backward glance, carried her away from the disturbance. She sobbed into his shoulder.

Harris struggled to get to his feet. Smith pushed him back down and dropped to her knees beside him. She slammed his face into the pavement, pulled her handcuffs off her belt, and wrenched his arms behind him. "You are so under arrest, asshole."

He let out a scream of pain. She stood up, dragging him with her. His nose was pushed to one side, and blood flowed like a red river out of it. His blue cap lay in the road.

He kept screaming, "My arm, my arm, you've broken my arm."

"If you goddamned stop pulling on it, it might not hurt so much."

A camera was shoved into her face.

She ignored it.

"Good job, Molly. I'll take him." John Winters grabbed Harris' other arm. The man screamed.

"Thought it was your left broken," Smith said. "Guess you got them mixed up."

◇◇◇

Smith, Evans, Solway, and Chen pulled up chairs in the constables' office. Tocek leaned against a wall. They held hot drinks in hands only just beginning to stop shaking.

"Hope there isn't any trouble in town tonight," Solway said. "With no one on the beat."

"We've had enough trouble for one night," Tocek said, giving Smith a soft smile. He was well over six feet, with the bulk to match. His black hair was shaved almost to his scalp, not much longer than the thick stubble across his chin. He had, Smith thought, nice eyes, as warm and brown as Sylvester's. And a smile that he kept sending her way. Chen wore a gold band on the third finger of his left hand. Tocek, she hadn't failed to notice, did not.

John Winters and the Chief Constable came in. "Good job, all of you," Keller said, radiating stale cigar smoke and looking pleased with the world.

"Is it over?" Chen asked.

"Everyone who isn't spending the night courtesy of the citizens of Trafalgar's gone home. Sleeping the sleep of the innocent, most of them, I'm sure."

"We'll be on our way, then." Tocek tossed his cup into the trash. Chen stood up.

"Appreciate your help," Keller said, shaking the Mounties by the hand.

Solway, Evans, and Smith mumbled thanks.

Tocek looked at Smith. "See you around." His brown eyes shone, and he winked.

"Go home," Keller said. "We'll debrief in the morning."

Evans and Solway left.

"Molly?"

"In a minute, sir. What about Harris?"

"He's resting in one of our finest cells. The doctor's seen to him. Just a broken nose. He's threatening to sue you for police brutality, but I wouldn't lose any sleep over that if I were you. Good night, Molly."

"Night, sir." She got to her feet.

"Do you need a ride home?" Winters asked.

"No thanks, I've got my mom's car."

"I saw what happened, Molly. You did good."

She tucked a loose strand of hair back into its braid. "I don't even remember. It's all a blur."

"We'll get Harris for inciting a riot and for an attempted assault on a police officer," Winters said.

"Doesn't seem like much."

"As the lad seems to have a fondness for fire, we've taken his truck to the lab and tomorrow Ron Gavin'll be going over it with a fine-toothed comb."

◇◇◇

Lucky and Andy were in the kitchen when Smith got home, but only Sylvester greeted her with any enthusiasm. The bags under Andy's eyes were heavier than ever, and Lucky's hair fell around her shoulders in lifeless strands. "Tea?" she said.

Smith ignored the offer. "What were you playing at tonight, Mom? Do you know that Jane Reynolds almost got hurt, badly?"

"I helped her into the ambulance. She broke her arm, but she'll be okay. She's a tough old bird."

"Tough? Tough! Are you crazy?" Rage stoked by the fear that had been building up inside her ever since she arrived at the park boiled over, like a pot of rice left on high heat too long. "What the hell were you playing at? You've seen Ashcroft on TV. You've seen the sort of blowhards—on both sides—that are invading our town over this. And you and your so called committee, every one of you middle-aged, or older, put yourselves right in the middle of it."

"Don't talk to your mother like that," Andy said. "Apologize right now." As if Molly were fourteen and fighting with Lucky over the clothes she wanted to wear to school.

Smith smashed her fist on the table. The salt shaker fell over. No one bothered to pick it up.

"Stay out of it, Dad. You weren't there." But childhood habits took over and she lowered her voice. "Come on, Mom. It was midnight. You didn't just happen to gather your friends and go down to the park to enjoy the night air. You knew something was up."

"That Harris character told me to stay away because they were planning a demonstration." Lucky blew her nose. "I won't let his type intimidate me."

"Planning a demonstration." Smith's voice dropped even further. "Oh, yeah, he told you to stay away like I'd toss a steak to Sylvester and tell him to stay away. But never mind the fact that it was a trap so obvious that they'd be embarrassed to write it into a movie, you knew they were planning a demonstration but didn't call the police. You didn't even tell me. If those two

Mounties hadn't been passing when they got the call, things could have been worse, a lot worse. Dawn Solway was there all by herself." Behind her eyes Smith saw Solway standing in the road, trying to be strong, and so relieved to see reinforcements arrive.

"Lucky," Andy said. "Why didn't you tell Molly what you knew?"

"Because I didn't think. I made an error of judgment, okay?" Sylvester whined and put his paws up on her knees. She shoved him away.

"You'd better not make any more errors of judgment. This thing isn't over yet, not by a long shot, and I don't need my own mother making my job any more difficult than it is."

"Your job," Lucky said. "How do you think I felt, knowing that my own daughter was the 'cop bitch' they were screaming at?" Her voice broke, and Andy reached out and took her hand. She burst into tears. He jerked his head toward the door, telling Smith to leave them.

She ignored him. "Is that what this is about? Is it, Mom? You didn't tell the police you knew trouble was brewing because you don't want to admit that I'm a cop? Well, tough. My life is not about you."

◇◇◇

The wide patio doors at Eddie's were open to the morning breeze, but a chair with a Closed sign propped on it blocked the entrance. Winters could see Eddie and Jolene moving about inside. He knocked on the glass. "It's going to be one heck of a busy day, and I need a fix fast."

"I bet you do," Eddie said. "Big trouble last night, I hear."

"And today's the official announcement." Winters climbed over the chair.

Eddie poured coffee. "It might be a mite strong yet."

"Strong is good. I had two hours' sleep last night."

"No charge, Detective."

Winters smiled, for the first time in what felt like days. "Thanks, but no thanks." He put a toonie, a two-dollar coin, on the counter.

Eliza was due back from Toronto this afternoon. Come hell or high water, he'd pick her up at the airport. Hopefully hell wouldn't be the right word.

He carried his coffee into the station. No one was at the front desk. He put his head into the dispatch office. "Morning, Ingrid."

The night dispatcher rubbed her eyes. "Morning already? Wow, you got coffee from Eddie's before opening. You must be special."

"That's what my wife tells me."

Ingrid grinned. "First coffee and then my news to make your day."

"What news?"

"Vancouver called. Charles Bassing was arrested in a punch-up outside a Gastown pub."

"Sweet." Both Ellie Montgomery and Frank Clemmins claimed to have never met Bassing, nor to have heard Montgomery talk about him. Unless something else came to light, which Winters didn't expect, Bassing had nothing to do with the Montgomery killing. But it would be nice to see him put away for what he did to Molly's friend.

"And Ron Gavin has something for you," Ingrid said.

"Even sweeter."

He went to his office and called Gavin. "Don't you ever sleep?" he said when the forensic investigator answered.

"Not when duty calls. Actually, I haven't started to examine Harris' truck yet. But the officer who brought it over found something interesting. A Rolex Oyster watch in the glove compartment. Inscribed 'To Reginald on his birthday. Love, Mother.'"

Montgomery.

"It was such an anomaly my guy called me about it right away. The back of the truck that picks the garbage up from the front of my house Monday mornings is cleaner than Harris' truck. He seems to have been living in it. It's a forensic investigator's wet dream. We've been waiting for something to compare with the hairs found on Montgomery. This guy's truck is so full of DNA we could clone him."

"Not that I'd want you to. I'll send someone round to get that watch. We need to ask the wife to identify it. Let me know what else you find, eh?"

"Will do."

Winters leaned back in his chair. If he could tie Harris to the Montgomery murder…. Early days yet, better not to get too excited. Anyone could pick a dropped watch up off the street, which is no doubt what Harris'd claim had happened. What motive could Harris have for killing Montgomery, anyway? They were, theoretically, on the same side. No point in speculating.

He picked up the phone and called the cells. "I hope Mr. Harris had a restful night."

"Slept like a baby," the custody officer said. "Better than you can say for me."

"I need to talk to him."

"He's called his lawyer. Guy'll be here at ten."

"He arranged a lawyer himself?"

"Yup."

The legal aid lawyer usually came from the coast. It could be days before he, or she, got here. Harris was from out of town, yet he already had a lawyer on tap? He must have known he'd be running into trouble.

"See you at ten."

Harris was a sullen, arrogant bastard. He sneered at Winters through his battered face and rubbed his tongue across his cracked upper lip at Smith, while his lawyer was getting paper and pen out of his shiny new briefcase. Winters informed them that the interview was being videotaped as well as recorded.

Smith hadn't slept a wink. The riot kept repeating itself in her mind, over and over: a bad movie locked into eternal repeat. Her terror at realizing that she was all that stood between groups of potentially violent demonstrators. Harris aiming a Molotov cocktail at Dave Evans and Jane Reynolds. And on top of the fear still churning in her stomach there was a layer of fury. Her own mother could have warned them. Yet chose not to. Out of nowhere she thought of Christa. Guilt joined the toxic brew of emotions.

She'd watched sunbeams caress the white wooden slats on her bedroom window, and wondered, not for the first time, if she were cut out to be a cop. She didn't ever want to be so frightened again. If she quit the department now, she could go back to Victoria. Get a job for the fall while waiting for the winter term to start. She couldn't stay in Trafalgar, not having failed at being a police officer. They'd whisper behind her back, say she was too weak, too *female*, to cut it.

The phone rang and she grabbed it before the first ring died away.

"We've a break in the Montgomery case. You want to be in on the interview?"

"You bet I do."

"Can you be ready in twenty minutes?"

"Count on it."

She flew into the shower. No time to braid her hair, so she fastened it with a butterfly clip. She put on jeans and a T-shirt and was running downstairs when she heard Sylvester barking at a car coming up the driveway.

"What's up?" she said, climbing into the SUV.

A grin touched the edges of Winters' mouth. She thought his eyes might be sparkling—but that had to be a reflection of the rising sun.

"Bassing is in custody in Vancouver, and we have Montgomery's watch."

"Great."

"I'm taking the watch to Mrs. Montgomery for a positive identification, and at ten I'm interviewing Harris. I thought you might want to be in on both those events."

Her dark night of the soul passed. "Should I go back and put on my uniform?"

"You're fine." He navigated the turning circle. The morning sun played with the green leaves of the trees. A hawk watched them from the top of a dying pine. Andy was always saying that tree had to come down, but he never quite got around to doing anything about it.

Ellie Montgomery identified the watch as belonging to her late husband. She told them that the coroner had released the body, and the funeral would be on Friday. If Sergeant Winters could attend it would be an *enormous* comfort to her. Smith hid a smile as he mumbled something about condolences and literally tripped over an untied shoelace in his rush to get out the door.

Winters sat directly across from Harris in the interview room. His lawyer, Mr. Parker, new in town, and apparently newly out of law school as well, took the chair beside Harris. The lawyer wore a grey pinstriped suit with crisp white shirt and blue silk tie shot through with threads the same shade of grey as his suit. By the time this interview, in this small un-air-conditioned room, was over, the shirt wouldn't be so crisp. Smith leaned against the wall, her arms crossed over her chest, trying to look like she belonged here.

"I was exercising my rights as a citizen to express my opinion in full view of the public and media," Harris said, once Winters had gone through the standard notifications and switched on the tape recorder, "when the lady…the officer here present, attacked me with no provocation whatsoever. I couldn't understand her actions at the time, but later I realized that she mistook me for someone throwing a gasoline bomb. Could have been real nasty. Fortunately the bomb did no damage, and on reflection I've decided not to sue her for using unnecessary force."

Smith almost swallowed her tongue. Winters had warned her that she was only to listen, not to react in any way. To say nothing.

"Your client," Winters said to Parker, "is under the impression that I want to talk to him about the events of last night."

"You don't?" Parker looked up from the yellow legal pad on which he was making notes.

"Someone else will be around later to talk about the demonstration." Winters took the plastic evidence bag containing

Reginald Montgomery's watch out of his briefcase and threw it onto the table. "Where'd you get this, Brian?"

Harris shrugged. "It's a watch. Never seen it before."

"It was found in your truck."

"It isn't mine."

"Can you explain what it was doing in your truck?"

"You planted it."

"Sergeant, what's the significance of this watch? Unless that watch relates directly…."

"I dropped into the jewelry store in town this morning," Winters said. "Asked for a quick appraisal of the value of the watch. Just an off-the-cuff estimate. What did they say it was worth, Constable Smith?"

"Ten thousand dollars, sir."

Winters whistled. "That's why I couldn't remember. That kind of dough for a watch is way outside the understanding of a simple police officer such as myself."

"The point, Sergeant," Parker said. "Get to the point."

"I'd put the value of your truck, and everything in it, at not more than three thousand. If I were being generous. Yet you have this nice watch tucked away in the glove compartment. Want to tell me how you came upon it?"

"I told you. I've never seen it before. Do something," Harris said to his lawyer. "They've got nothing else on me, so they're trying to frame me for theft."

"Theft," Winters said, "is not the least of it."

Smith studied the faces of the three men. Parker was as out of his depth as a two-year-old in the children's pool at Eagle Point Bluffs Park on a hot day. Harris was like the tough-talking thirteen-year-old trying to make a big splash in front of the prepubescent girls and impressing no one. Winters watched them like an unfriendly lifeguard.

He rubbed at the face of his own watch. "I've been looking for it since it was taken from a murder scene."

Parker blanched. His eyes slid away from his client. Smith guessed that he was wishing he'd taken up corporate law.

"I didn't take it." Harris jumped out of his seat. His left eye twitched. Smith leaned forward, ready to move. Parker laid a hand on his client's arm, and Harris sat down. Smith settled back against the wall.

"Forensic officers are going over your truck even as we speak. They'll be able to tell me how many times you jacked off in there."

Harris flushed, and Smith guessed that the number would prove to be quite high. The very thought made her stomach roll over.

"What else are they going to find, Brian?"

"This is a frame-up, pure and simple." Harris was showing early signs of panic. "I'm telling you I never saw that watch before. Do something, you're supposed to be my fucking lawyer." His eye flickered as if he were trying to send a signal in Morse code.

"I need to talk to my client," Parker said.

"Take all the time you need. It'll be a while before we get a full DNA analysis on the contents of Mr. Harris' truck."

"Okay," Harris shouted. "I met with Montgomery. Once. We talked about the park. He was worried that it would be bad for business. I told him I'd do what I could to help him out."

"Was Mr. Montgomery ever in your truck, Brian?"

"No. Never. I didn't kill him, for God's sake. And I didn't steal his watch. I heard the story on the radio about this so-called peace park. What's pacifism, eh? Let the terrorists win, that's what it is. Let them think we're soft and who knows what they'll do next. That's what happened on 9/11. They thought we were soft and they attacked. I drove down from Calgary to find out what was happening. I ran into Montgomery in the coffee shop. He was all hot and bothered about what the park'd do to his business. I couldn't give a fuck about his business, but you find friends where you can, eh? So I told him I'd help him out. Next I heard, he'd died, so I figured that was the end of that. I found out that a bunch of environment nuts were planning a protest outside of his place so I thought I'd check it out. That TV guy, Ashcroft, was there looking for a story, so I made up something, told him all about my dad being killed in Vietnam. Hell, my dad's laying roof tiles in Toronto right now. It got me on TV, didn't it, what's the harm in that? And that's it. End of story."

"A nice story," Winters said, "except for the fire at the park."

Harris' eyes shifted toward the window. "Don't know nothing 'bout a fire."

Winters stood. "We have a lighter. And now that you're in our custody we have your prints. Plus video evidence of you inciting a riot and assaulting a police officer. You're going down, Harris."

Harris was screaming at Parker as Winters and Smith headed for the stairs.

"Your impressions, Molly."

She felt a small glow of pleasure at being asked. "He seemed genuinely surprised at the watch."

"Yup. But he admitted contact with Montgomery."

"Seems thin to me."

"Very thin. But, along with the attempted fire bombing of Dave Evans, enough to hold him until we get some proper DNA evidence. All we need is a match to those hairs found in Montgomery's hand. I won't be surprised if they find his fingerprints on the lighter found at the arson site.

"I'll take you home, Molly. Get some rest. The announcement is scheduled for five, and everyone on the force has been called in."

"You think it's going to be bad?"

"Could go either way. Most every demonstration is ninety-nine percent peaceful folks, just wanting to make their point, and one percent troublemakers. If we're lucky the ninety-nine will have had their appetite for mass disturbance curbed last night. I saw your mother there. I hope she'll have enough common sense to stay away today."

"Common sense and my mother have never been on speaking terms."

As they approached the front doors of the station the Chief Constable came in. He looked like a kid who'd just jumped down from Santa's knee. "Don't be in such a rush, John, you'll want to hear this. Morning, Molly." Keller walked to the reception desk. "Anyone in the constables' room?" he asked Jim Denton.

"All out on the road."

Barb Kowalski stuck her head out of her office. "What's going on?"

"Spill, Chief," Denton said. "You're going to announce raises all around, and a doubling of vacation time?"

"Better," Keller said. "I've come from a meeting with our esteemed Deputy Mayor. And, in her wisdom, she's decided that in light of yesterday's near catastrophic events, it would be best not to make a public announcement today about the fate of the peace park."

"You think?" Barb said.

"The council's going to wait until, as Ms. Patterson put it, tempers cool."

"Hell will cool first," Denton said.

"Nevertheless, it'll give us some breathing room."

"You want me to tell the guys not to come in later if isn't their regular schedule?"

"No. I want everyone here. Anything can happen, and we have to be ready. Tell the Yellow Stripes that we don't need active officers, but ask them to keep their people on standby. Perhaps I'll buy a lottery ticket at lunch time. Anything else on the agenda, Barb?"

"The monthly meeting of Rotary," she said. "I was going to ask if you want to cancel."

"No, let's act as if everything's perfectly under control. Like that's ever happened around here." He laughed and headed for his office.

"You ever worn full riot gear, Molly?" Winters asked.

"Only in police college."

"There's something about it," he said. "Makes you think you're invincible. But you're not. Never forget that you're nothing more than a human. Get some rest. I'm not quite as optimistic as our chief."

◇◇◇

Rich Ashcroft slapped his phone shut and set loose a stream of naughty words.

Meredith looked at him from the driver's seat. "Trouble?"

"Pull over."

"What's up, boss?" Greg said from the back.

Ashcroft got out of the car and slammed the door shut behind him. Meredith and Greg exchanged a look and followed.

They were on their way to the park, for Rich to record an introduction to tonight's program. Meredith had pulled up outside a building with *Trafalgar and District Youth Centre* painted in giant blue letters across the double roll-up garage doors. A group of scruffy, baggy-panted layabouts leaned against the planters on the sidewalk, smoking and watching them. One of them detached himself from the pack and sauntered over.

"Hey," he said. "Rick, right, I seen you on TV. You got a couple bucks for my pals, and we'll give you an interview."

"I've got a fist for your face, jerk," Ashcroft said. "If you don't piss off."

"Screw you." The boy gestured with his finger and went back to his friends.

"Not a good idea, Rich," Greg said.

"Shut the fuck up, will you."

"No. What's happened?"

"I've been told to get back. They think it's not worth continuing with this story."

"What about the footage Greg took last night, at the protest?" Meredith said. "It's really powerful."

"Who the fuck cares what you think." Ashcroft spat onto the pavement.

She was wearing sunglasses that covered about half of her face. He couldn't see her eyes, but her red lips tightened in the expression of disapproval he was already sick of.

"I've edited out the details of the guy throwing the bomb," Greg said. "We can make it look like it came from anywhere."

"Too late. CBC got footage and aired it this morning. ABC stations in Washington picked it up. There, for all to see, is my goddamned war hero's son tossing a Molotov cocktail at a little old lady, of all things, and being taken down by a female cop who could be making good money as a stripper."

Meredith's mouth pinched. "I don't think…."

"I told you I don't care what you fucking think."

"Never mind him, Meredith," Greg said. "Rich cares about the integrity of his program so much that he sometimes gets overemotional. He doesn't mean to insult you."

"Yeah, I noticed."

Two young women, pushing strollers and carrying coffee cups, approached. Rich glared at them. They looked at Rich. Once they'd passed they turned to each other and laughed. He wanted to strangle the both of them. His interview with Lucky Smith's daughter had been an abject failure. It had been a mistake, a big mistake, to air even part of it. He'd hoped to get her in a mellow mood, a nice lunch with an old friend, so she'd confide on camera that her mother's group was a major headache for the forces of law and order. Then he could play up the idea that the police and people of Trafalgar needed help with these troublemakers. Instead the cop bolted and he'd insulted her mother. Irene, his assistant, called him the moment the segment finished to tell him he'd come across not only as a bully, but, worse, a bad interviewer.

"What do you suggest we do now?" Greg's tone indicated that he didn't much care one way or the other. He had nothing to worry about. All he had to do was take the pictures.

Rich said nothing. There was nothing he could do. Except go back to California with his tail between his legs.

"Take us back to the hotel, Meredith, then book us on the first flight out."

"You know what, Rich? I'm not your secretary. Make your own bookings. I'll drop you back in town. If you need a ride to the airport, the hotel runs a shuttle." She turned to Greg. "I have enough problems of my own, if I'm gonna make my boss forget that I almost sold out this town for that jackass."

Rich Ashcroft could have said a lot of things. He could make a big fuss, throw his weight around, and crush the girl reporter from the *Daily Gazette* under his heel. Instead he got back into the car. He'd screwed up here; he had bigger battles to face back at the network. Irene had told him that the young hotdog the network brought in to cover the rest of the program while Rich was away was proving to be very popular with women aged thirty to forty-five, Rich's prime demographic.

Chapter Thirty

Lucky Smith sat in the comfy armchair in the living room. Her book lay open on her lap, but she hadn't read a word for at least fifteen minutes. She could hear Moonlight moving about overhead, getting ready to go out. They'd scarcely spoken the last couple of days, and this morning, when Lucky used the family computer, she'd seen that Moonlight had been looking up apartments for rent.

She buried her nose into the book as she heard the *tap, tap* of heels coming down the stairs.

"Whatcha reading, Mom?"

Lucky looked up, as if surprised to hear a voice. "*Collapse.* It's a warning about what happens to civilizations that exceed their limits."

"Sounds like a barrel of laughs. Duncan should be here any minute." Moonlight looked stunning in low-rise jeans with a wide belt and a deeply cut, spaghetti-strapped, purple satin shirt. Her shoes were sandals with straps as thin as dental floss and skyscraper heels. A small black bag was tossed over her shoulder. Light from the reading lamp threw golden sparks into her hair, falling loose around her shoulders.

Lucky swallowed a lump in her throat, put the book down, and stood up. She walked toward her daughter and wrapped her arms around her. Moonlight smelled of vanilla hand cream and the locally made soap she loved. She rested her chin on the top of her mother's head.

"I hate it when you do that," Lucky said. "It makes me feel small and insignificant."

"Like anyone you've ever met has found you insignificant," Moonlight said.

The headlights of a car flooded the room. Sylvester ran to the door, barking. Lucky stepped back. "I can't imagine why Duncan drives that monster of a truck."

"Maybe he has a very small penis," Moonlight said with a wicked grin. It had been a long time since Lucky had seen light sparkle in her daughter's eyes.

"Ew. I do not want to know. And if you ever find out—don't tell me."

"Don't wait up."

"Moonlight. Molly. Before you go." Lucky struggled to find the words. "I haven't told you how proud I was of you the other night. You were so strong, so brave, so powerful out there. You saved us all from a disastrous situation."

Water gathered behind Moonlight's wide blue eyes. "Thanks, Mom. But as for being strong and brave—well, I wasn't."

Duncan leaned on the horn.

Lucky swiped her hand across her eyes. "In my day, a gentleman caller was expected to come to the front door. Spend fifteen minutes or so in the den with the girl's father while the girl and her mother peeked from behind the kitchen door. Only then would they be allowed to go to the boy's car. In which they would later screw their brains out."

Moonlight laughed. "I love you, Mom, do you know that?"

"I do, dear, I do."

It felt good to be out on the street, one of the crowd, a person with nothing to do but have fun. Smith threw her head back and let the music wash over her. The concert was held in a typical small-town venue, used for bingo one night, metal bands another. Tonight the place was packed for a concert by BC-DC, the hugely popular AC-DC tribute band from Nelson.

She saw a few people who might have been on one side of the street or another at the trouble on Tuesday. But no one looked at her maliciously and no one confronted her. And so she enjoyed herself enormously.

The crowd was slamming their bodies together, dancing or just hopping up and down with arms moving in the air. The hall smelled of beer and sweat, clothes pungent with smoke, tobacco and pot, and cheap perfume liberally applied. The audience cheered as the singer howled and the band broke into "Highway to Hell." Smith looked at Duncan. He was smiling at her. "This is such fun," she said. "Thanks for coming with me."

"Thanks for inviting me." She couldn't hear what he said, but she could read the words on his mouth.

She turned back toward the stage, lifted her arms high, and moved them to the beat of the music. She could feel as much as see Duncan eying the curves under her purple shirt and smiled to herself. It felt good. Both to be admired and to smile.

By the time the concert ended her heart was racing and her feet ached. The crowd spilled out into the night, laughing and telling each other how great the show had been. Duncan took her hand, and she didn't pull it away. A police cruiser was parked in the alley beside the hall, lights off. Dave Evans stood beside it, watching the place empty. He didn't see her. He'd called her at home on Wednesday and stammered out thanks for saving him and Mrs. Reynolds. As thanks went, it sounded as if someone were holding a gun to his head, but she appreciated the call nonetheless. Maybe he'd no longer be so quick to dismiss her as a product of token hiring. *Nah.*

"You bought the tickets," Duncan said. "How about something to eat?"

"I'm famished."

He pulled her hand. "We'd better hurry, the Mess Hall'll be packed." She tottered after him on her high heels. Fortunately the town's favorite wings joint was only a block from the hall. She wouldn't be able to walk much further than that. These shoes cost her three hundred bucks, and they'd sat in the closet since Graham's death.

They squeezed into a table for two in a dark corner. They ordered a large pizza and a platter of hot wings and pints of beer. Duncan told funny stories and Smith laughed. He tried to get her to talk about her job, but tonight she didn't want to go anywhere near work.

He got up to go to the washroom and she watched him push his way across the floor, where people were packed together like penguins on a shrinking ice floe. If she'd been on duty, she might have done a count of heads, to check if the place was in excess of the numbers allowed. But she wasn't on duty, and so she nibbled on the last wing. Duncan stopped to talk to someone sitting at the counter. She thought about her first date with Graham. They'd climbed the two hundred steps down to Wreck Beach in Vancouver. It had been late in November. The beach was empty, the fabled nudists all gone home, no one camping out waiting for the next big political protest. They'd held hands as they jumped over the corpses of giant trees—refugees from logging camps, scattered on the beach—and splashed barefoot in the icy surf.

The happiest day of her life. *Come back to the moment.* Duncan wasn't Graham, and she wasn't looking to hook up with anyone. Not now. Not yet. Perhaps not ever.

An obese man was sitting on a bar stool beside the person Duncan was talking to, blocking her view. He climbed down from his seat and lumbered away, and Smith had a clear look at the man talking to Duncan.

Claude Derochiers. Well known troublemaker, small time thief, all-around pest. What would a minor criminal like Derochiers have to talk about with Duncan?

Stop right there, Smith. You are not working and even if you were, who Duncan talks to in a crowded bar is not grounds for suspicion. Even a scumbag like Derochiers might have friends, family.

Duncan shoved Derochiers in the chest, hard, and walked away. Okay, maybe not friends.

Derochiers tossed a bill on the counter and left. He didn't look toward Smith, sitting quietly in the corner.

"Ready to go?" Duncan smiled down at her.

"I am. It's been a long week." She unhooked her bag from the back of the chair.

The street was quiet as they walked toward the truck. "What's happening with the peace garden business?" Duncan asked, slipping his hand into hers and giving it a squeeze.

"Once the American TV guy left town, and Brian Harris and Robyn Goodhaugh were tucked away in custody, the fuss died down. With no one to stoke them up, and the town keeping mum on their decision, a lot of the outsiders left."

"So, it's over."

"Not at all. The council delayed announcing their decision, but they have to do so someday. We're hoping they can spit it out without making too much of a fuss. If we're lucky there'll be a major news story breaking at the same time. Maybe Brad Pitt'll come after Angelina Jolie with a hatchet, and our town's troubles won't get much coverage."

"I'm sorry I missed the demonstration. I saw you on TV. You looked wonderful."

"You couldn't even tell it was me."

"I knew it was you, Molly."

She pulled her hand out of his on the pretext of straightening her hair. "Isn't it a lovely night?"

And it was. The sky was clear, but there was no moon. Stars danced on the river like diamonds tossed onto a black velvet cape. From somewhere up in the mountains a wolf howled. It might have been a dog, but she preferred to think of it as a wolf. A pinprick of white light moved across the sky, a small plane, alone in the darkness.

Duncan flicked the remote to open the doors of the truck, and Smith got in. He put the key into the ignition but didn't turn it. Silence enveloped them.

"Wanna come back to my place," he said at last, watching the slow-moving river, "for coffee or something?"

She'd been debating all night what to do if the question were asked. Should she? He seemed like a nice guy; he obviously liked her very much. He wasn't Graham. But Graham, she reminded herself, was dead. Graham would want her to be happy.

"Coffee'd be nice." She ran a finger across the mound of her left breast.

"Great." He threw the truck into gear and backed out of the parking bay with unseemly haste. Good thing a car wasn't coming.

"Can we stop off at your place first?"

"Why?"

He pushed the truck up to the speed limit and kept his foot on the gas. They hurtled toward the bridge leading out of town. A black shape against the black sky.

"I'd like you to get your gun."

"What?"

"Maybe not the gun. I bet the department frowns on that sort of thing. But if you could put on the belt, it would look super with that blouse. And the handcuffs, bring the handcuffs."

Chapter Thirty-one

A small blue Japanese compact leaned on its horn as Duncan left the bridge and turned far too widely into the turn.

"Sounds like a plan." A bucket of cold water dumped on Smith's early, hesitant stirrings of ardor. She tried to throw her voice low, sexy, interested in his suggestion. At least he was taking her home. Whereupon she'd run into the house and lock the doors and set Sylvester on him.

They drove down the dark highway, river on the right, mountain on the left. Smith looked in the passenger side mirror to see the lights of town fading into the distance.

"Get the truncheon, and the boots," Duncan was saying. "Those boots really do it for me."

And she'd thought her three-hundred-dollar heels were sexy.

The truck jerked. They flew forward and fell back. It jerked again. Duncan struggled with the steering wheel as if he were taming a stallion at the Calgary Stampede. He pulled off the highway and coasted to a stop. The engine died.

"This isn't a trick, Molly, really. I know it's like a joke or something to have the car break down on a dark road on a first date, but I didn't do anything."

Smith believed him. They hadn't got to her gun belt and boots yet. She pointed to the control panel. "See that 'E' there, Duncan, and the needle pointing below it. You're out of gas."

He hit the steering wheel.

"Go get some. I'll wait here." Her cell phone was in her bag. By the time Duncan walked to town and back, she'd have called her dad and be safely home. Like the time she'd left a high school party because they were drinking and a boy had tried to grab her breast. She'd called her dad to come and get her. Her parents had been so proud that she'd done the right thing.

"I don't have anything to carry gas in," Duncan whined.

"I bet you do. Something's rattling around in the back. Let's check." She jumped out of the truck. Damned thing was so high she almost needed a parachute.

He was there before her. "No need to look," he said. "There's nothing in there. You go get the gas. They'll have containers at the station. I'll stay here and guard the truck."

"No one's going to pinch your truck, Duncan. And if they try, well they can't get far, can they?"

The headlights were still on. Although they pointed straight ahead they shone a bit of light behind the truck, reflecting off beads of sweat that dotted Duncan's forehead and upper lip.

"Why don't we check it out anyway," she said, reaching for the cover over the truck bed. "Can't hurt."

"Don't touch that."

This was getting seriously weird. "Why not? Don't you want to see a cop in action? Let me have a peek and I'll let you watch me play with my gun."

His face slackened, and his pale tongue touched his lower lip, like a reptile taking scent of its surroundings. His grip relaxed, and she tore the cover back from the truck bed. All she could see was a jumble of bicycle wheels.

Understanding washed over her. Trips to Vancouver, the expensive truck, confrontation with Derochiers. "Duncan," she said, "what have you been doing?"

"It's none of your business, Molly. Forget you saw this. You're off duty, right?"

"You're snatching bikes when I'm about to come by. You're playing me as if I'm some kind of musical instrument. You think

I can forget this? Go to hell." She headed for the passenger seat and her bag and cell phone.

He hit her, hard. She grabbed the door handle, missed and went down.

"God," he said, "you are so hot." He dropped to his knees and stuck his hand up her shirt. Clammy hands groped for a breast. "I want you, Molly, so much."

She threw an awkward, backward punch into his stomach. He released her with a cry and she jumped to her feet. He stood. His breathing was deep.

"Give it up, Duncan. I've got you for theft. Don't add assault to the charges. I'm going to get my bag and my phone and make a call, okay?"

"I'm sorry I touched you. Let's forget about it. Look, the only reason I've hung around Trafalgar is you, Molly. I don't make squat at your parents' store, and the tips from the fat middle-aged women I take out on the river are a joke. I need extra cash, and figured if I pinched some bikes, you and I could have fun at the same time. It wasn't my fault, you know, that I got kicked off the university football team, things just got a little out of hand, but after he got the charges dropped my prick of a dad cut me right off. Why don't you call CAA, and we'll both wait here. How's that sound?"

"I'm not going to forget I saw those bikes, and I really don't care how hard done by you are. Back off, Duncan. Do it!"

He took a step backward. The road fell sharply away into a ditch clogged with dead branches and knee-high weeds. She kept one eye on him and reached onto the floor of the truck for her shoulder bag. She couldn't find it by feeling around, and had to turn her eyes away. As she touched the bag, he grabbed her ankle and pulled. She tumbled out of the truck, fingers holding nothing.

Her face slammed into the side of the truck. "You will not call the cops on me, Molly. I'm sorry I tried to kiss you. I won't do that again, promise." He held his hand on the back of her head. "I'm going to let go, okay? You can sit up and we can talk." The pressure eased. A branch broke under Duncan's foot.

Smith turned around. "Let me make the call, Duncan. You don't have a record, do you? You said your dad got charges dropped?" What those charges were for, she could guess. Football team, things getting "a little out of hand." Dad intervening to make it all right.

Duncan shook his head. The moon was rising over the tops of the forest behind him. "A few small charges, but I've never been convicted of anything."

So good old Dad had finally had enough, and cut his son adrift. "Then you're looking at a short sentence," she said, "maybe not even that. They might give you probation if my mom testifies that you have a good job. But you assault a police officer, or restrain her, and that's a whole other story."

"You're not a police officer now, Molly. You're my girlfriend."

She swallowed her indignation at the idea that he figured he could get away with beating her up because tonight she was his date. "You know I'm a cop. Makes all the difference."

A car approached, illuminating his face. Then the light was gone. How could she ever have considered sleeping with him?

She stood up, keeping her back against the warm metal of the vehicle. "I'm reaching into the truck, Duncan. I'm getting my phone and calling for help. You let me do that, and I won't tell them that you hit me and groped me." She lied without a qualm. "Bike theft's nothing. You'll probably get probation." *Not if I have anything to say about it.*

She'd seen her bag, half under the seat. She kept her eyes on Duncan while her fingers felt for it.

He fell to his haunches. "They won't find out about that guy, will they, Molly?"

"What guy?" She wrapped the strap of the bag around her hand.

"I just punched him. I didn't even know he was dead till I heard about it on the radio the next day."

"Oh, fuck. You're telling me you killed Montgomery."

Duncan straightened up with such speed she wasn't ready. He knocked her backward into the truck and threw the weight of his body onto hers. He pressed something into her throat. For a moment she thought it was a knife, but it was only the broken end of a branch in his hand.

He stepped back, the branch against her throat. With one hand he unfastened his belt. "I didn't actually kill him," he said. "He had a heart attack or something."

Duncan hadn't noticed Montgomery's brains leaking out of his skull?

"I don't want to hurt you, Molly. I'm going to leave you here and go. I can snatch a car and be across the border in half an hour. Turn around." He grabbed her arm and flipped her. Her face smashed into the hard metal of the truck.

She spat blood. Keep them talking, that's what she'd learned in police college. "Tell me about Montgomery. It was a clean killing, but we thought it was an accident."

"Jerk saw me snatching a bike. He wanted me to, like, put it back. As if." He pulled at her bag and the strap broke. "You won't be needing this." She heard it crash into the undergrowth. He pulled her arms behind her and wrapped one end of his belt around her left wrist.

Another car. It slowed down, and she could see the driver checking them out. Then he pressed the gas and drove away. They must look like nothing but a couple who couldn't wait long enough to get to a motel and were having a quickie up against the truck.

"I started to leave, but he pulled out a phone. He was gonna call the cops. I couldn't have that, so I put the bike up against the wall, said he could have it, started to walk away. Then I turned and punched him good. Too damned stupid to go down, he grabbed at my head. So I hit him again. He was dumb to keep fighting, wasn't he?"

"The dumbest. Why'd you stop him? I was the beat cop that night, I'm guessing you knew that. I'd have been the one on the scene."

"I wasn't ready to end our game, Molly. We were still having fun."

Yeah, great fun. "What'd you hit him with? We've been look-ing everywhere for the weapon."

Duncan chuckled. "I had a propane cylinder in my pack that I needed to fill. I'd just gotten off a trip."

"Clever."

"I'd like you to come with me, Molly. But I guess that's too much to ask." He looped the belt over her other wrist.

"Too fuckin' right." She drove the stiletto-sharp point of her four-inch heel into his groin.

He screamed like a vampire in the night woods, and his grip collapsed. She whirled around, shaking her arms, trying to get that belt off. He hadn't tied a knot yet, so it fell away. She grabbed one end and swung the length of leather at Duncan's head. The impact was as loud as a gunshot. A line of red burst across his face as if she'd drawn on it with a fat crayon.

"You bitch," he said. She swung the belt again, aiming for an eye. He ducked and she staggered toward the ditch.

Duncan ran.

Smith recovered her footing and took off after him, holding the belt as a weapon. But she wasn't in police boots. The thin heel of one sandal broke, almost taking her to her knees. She staggered to a halt and kicked off the shoes. She ran on, barefoot.

Pain sliced through her feet. She concentrated on taking deep, cleansing breaths, reaching inside for something to push the pain aside, to keep her moving. But she knew that she'd soon fall to her knees.

"Don't be a fool, Duncan. You can't get away. Don't make it worse." If he went into the woods, she'd not be able to follow, not without shoes.

Duncan turned but kept running backward. River to one side, mountain to the other, ahead of him the highway took a sharp turn. "Think of me, Molly," he yelled. "Because someday soon I'll be coming back for you."

Lights found the leaves and branches of the tall pines. Yellow eyes blinked in the undergrowth. A car was turning into the corner.

Smith yelled, "Look out!"

Brakes screamed. A cry. A dull thud.

An SUV heading out of town had struck Duncan full on. He crumpled to the roadway like an overcooked gingerbread man.

The driver tumbled out of her vehicle. "Oh, my god. He came out of nowhere. He was just there. I couldn't stop in time."

Smith fell to the pavement. She touched Duncan's neck. "Trafalgar City Police," she yelled. "Do you have a phone on you?"

"Yes."

"Call 911. Fast."

Chapter Thirty-two

This was one depressing book. Molly Smith tossed it on the table. Right now she did not want to be reading about the collapse of civilizations. Her mother had settled her into a chair in the family room, with a cup of fair-trade tea, oversized oatmeal cookies from Rosemary's Campfire Kitchen, a pile of political magazines, and this book. Lucky had arranged music on the CD player, and the lush, romantic vocals of Il Divo washed over the room.

Constable Smith was not in a lush, romantic mood.

Her face ached, and she hadn't dared look at herself in a mirror. Her heavily bandaged feet were propped up on the ottoman. Sylvester was curled up on the rug by her chair, snoring. His legs moved now and again, and she wondered if he were dreaming. Hopefully his dreams were better than hers had been of late. Dreams in which she'd been having sex with Duncan, locked to him, gasping with orgasm, staring up at him, as his eyes dripped blood.

Some cop she was—ready and willing to have sex with the perp in her first murder investigation. First and, probably, her last. She'd misjudged this one so badly, she didn't know if she wanted to ever make detective.

"That was Christa," Lucky said from the doorway. Smith reached for the phone on the table.

"I'm sorry, dear, but she didn't want to talk to you. She called to let me know that she's back home."

"She blames me. She thinks I should have protected her."

"She has to blame someone. Perhaps when Charlie comes to trial she'll turn her anger on him, where it belongs, and realize that you couldn't wrap her in cotton wool."

Smith turned the page of her book to avoid her mother's eyes. Christa might forgive her, but she herself didn't know if she'd ever be able to.

The doorbell rang, and Sylvester ran to answer it, barking greetings. Lucky didn't move. Anyone known to the family was welcome to ring and walk right in.

The bell again.

"I'd better see who that is," Lucky said.

"Company," she trilled a moment later, sounding as unlike Smith's mother as if her body had been taken over by aliens.

Sergeant Winters stood in the doorway. Lucky plucked a bunch of peach roses out of his arms. "I'll put these in water," she said.

"Step into my office." Smith made a wide sweep of her arms.

A smile touched the edges of his mouth. "Perhaps I will." He glanced at Andy's well-used recliner and settled for an arm-chair covered in plaid fabric.

Sylvester wandered over looking for a scratch. He was to be disappointed.

"How are the feet?" Winters said.

"Ready for replacements. I don't quite remember all the ER doc told me she found in there. Twigs, pebbles for sure. Ground glass, car oil. Animal poop, that was charming. Thanks for the flowers."

"My wife told me to bring them."

"Thanks to your wife then."

"You did good out there, Constable Smith. Very good."

"Then why do I feel like a total jackass?"

"We've all been fooled at one time or another by someone who pretends to be better than they are." A shadow crossed behind his eyes, and Smith looked away. She felt marginally better. "We located the family and they're making arrangements to receive the body. Duncan's father's a provincial court judge in New Brunswick. He told me that he hadn't spoken to his son in some time."

Lucky returned, the roses arranged in a plastic vase. "Andy had to go into the store. With Duncan—" she stopped and took a deep breath— "gone, he has to find a good tour guide fast."

"What about the investigation?" Smith asked.

"We found a propane canister in Duncan's apartment. The lab found traces of blood on it. It's been sent for comparison with Montgomery, along with a sample of Duncan's hair to be compared with the ones found in Montgomery's hand. But it's looking conclusive—Montgomery's wallet and cell phone had been wiped, but he missed a partial. The print matches Weaver."

He cleared his throat, and his glance slid past her eyes to focus on the wall. "I hate to tell you this, Molly, but there were pictures in his apartment. Of you. All over the walls, the screen saver on his computer. The ceiling over his bed."

A cold finger touched her spine. "Oh, no."

"Nothing improper, don't worry about that. You're in uniform in all of them, around town, on duty, lining up for coffee, visiting your parents in the store, in a cruiser."

Lucky said, "Duncan. Of all people. I could see that he had an inflated belief in his own importance, as well as a bit of a temper, but he kept it under control. I never would have thought it went so deep as to bludgeon someone to death." She fluffed pillows behind Smith's back, and her daughter felt the shiver running through her. Smith had no desire to be fluffed, but she let her mom help. She wasn't the only one fooled by Duncan.

"How did Montgomery's watch get into Harris' truck?" Lucky asked.

"We may never know, but I suspect Duncan planted it. Probably didn't have anything to do with his obsession with Molly. We found a picture on his computer—you, Lucky, talking to Harris in what looks like the Safeway parking lot. I think Duncan saw him threatening you and wanted to help you out. And get rid of some evidence at the same time.

"Chief told me," Winters continued, "to let you know that he'll be around for a visit later. He's at a meeting of town council."

"Meeting's over. They've decided." The Chief Constable came into the room. He carried a bouquet so large he could barely see out from behind it.

"More flowers, Paul," Lucky said, taking them from him. "You sent some already."

"These aren't from me."

"I haven't heard anything about the meeting yet," Lucky said, surprised that she wasn't ahead of the news.

"The council's decided, with the approval of the estate, that the park lands will be dedicated to the memory of Larry O'Reilly. Instead of a fountain, there will be a children's wading pool. The park will have a plaque mentioning O'Reilly's contributions to the town of Trafalgar, but nothing about his background as a draft dodger. An art gallery in San Francisco wants to continue with the commission of the statue, and the sculptor's agreed."

Smith expected her mother to puff up in anger and rush to the phones. Instead Lucky clutched the bouquet and opened the card that came with it. She glanced at it before handing it to her daughter.

Get the hell back on the job. Adam Tocek.

Smith felt the edges of her mouth turning up. They were all watching her. "From the Mounties," she said. "Nice of them."

Lucky gathered tea cups. "That situation isn't exactly what I would have liked. And not what Larry wanted. But a sensible decision, in the circumstances. Larry would have been most distressed to see violence breaking out over his simple bequest. I wouldn't have thought Linda Patterson to be capable of such a degree of common sense."

"Surprising what a whisper in the ear of an ambitious politician can achieve," Keller said. He gave Lucky a look that Molly Smith decided she would never attempt to decipher.

"Would you like a cup of tea, Paul?" Lucky said. "Or something stronger?"

"Tea will do. Thanks."

"So everyone can say they've won," Smith said, after her mother had left for the kitchen, "and not lose face."

The Chief Constable settled into Andy's chair. "We, the Trafalgar City Police, are the biggest winners of all. I need you back, Molly. Soon as you're able."

Smith wiggled her toes, wrapped in bandages. "I'm fine, sir. Except that I can't take a single step."

"I heard that." Lucky ran into the room. "You leave my daughter alone, Paul Keller."

Constable Molly Smith wanted to fall through the floor. Her mother was arguing with her boss. That would help her maintain the image of a tough, dedicated cop.

Keller smiled. "We can put her on the phones for a while. Typing reports, catching up on computer work."

"Oh," Smith said, "the fun stuff."

John Winters was watching her. She cocked her head to one side with a grimace, and, to her surprise, he winked.

To receive a free catalog of Poisoned Pen Press titles, please contact us in one of the following ways:

Phone: 1-800-421-3976
Facsimile: 1-480-949-1707
Email: info@poisonedpenpress.com
Website: www.poisonedpenpress.com

Poisoned Pen Press
6962 E. First Ave. Ste. 103
Scottsdale, AZ 85251